The Strength of Dark Love!

Karina Vega

Karina Vega

Book Cover by [*Karina Vega designs*]

Illustrations by [*Karina Vega designs*]

Blurbs

Sofia:

What they did to me? What they took from me? It's beyond words.

I hate men. All of them!

Except for my dad and Uncle Buddy. But the rest? They're all the same.

I promised myself at five years old, no man would ever hurt me again. Every one of them with a dick is a threat, and I'll destroy anyone who tries to hurt me. I won't be a victim again. No man will ever have power over me again.

What happened to me can never be erased. That's why I can't let anyone in. I won't!

I wish I could be attracted to women. It would make things so much easier. But then he walked in, this cocky, sunburnt Australian fool and everything I thought I'd buried came crashing back to the surface.

The first time I saw him? It was like someone knocked the wind out of me. I couldn't think. I couldn't breathe. In that moment, every defence I'd built around myself shattered, and I hated him for it.

How am I supposed to keep my distance when every day he's right there, breaking down my walls with that stupid grin, making me want what I swore I'd never let myself have?

Hunter:

God, I love her! I've loved her in secret like a fool for two years.

How the mighty have fallen. Look at the big, scary SASR man trembling with desire over a little woman who doesn't even spare him a glance.

Sometimes, I swear I can feel it, maybe she loves me too. Maybe I'm delusional. Maybe I've finally lost my mind. But damn it, I love her with everything I am.

When I joined Elijah's team, I didn't expect much. I just wanted to lay low for a while, to escape the mess I'd made of my life. The world is full of fucked-up people, and I've seen the worst of them. My reality was falling apart.

Then I walked into the Security room, and there she was a goddess, staring me down like I was something stuck to the bottom of her shoe. Her eyes, sharp as knives, cut right through me. She barely said two words, but the second she took my hand, I felt it. Her hand trembled, and in that moment, I knew. She felt it, too. She was as affected by me as I was by her.

I want her so much! I need her! I crave her! But there's something between us, something like an invisible wall of concrete. Every time I think I'm breaking through, she shoves me right back on my ass tenfold.

Author Note

Hello dear reader,

Welcome to my universe! I write darker romance stories in Australian English that can be upsetting and disturbing for some readers as I touch on difficult topics in each of my books.

My books and the main characters within them aren't for the faint of heart. My male main characters (MMCs) are obsessive, possessive, and deeply in love, entirely devoted to the female main characters (FMCs). There are no limits to what he would do for love, and no boundaries he would not cross to protect the women he cherishes.

Hunter Miller and Sofia Dominion are complex, dark romance characters, so please ensure you review all trigger warnings before proceeding.

This book contains intense and graphic content that may be distressing for some readers, including:

Graphic torture (detailed descriptions)

Explicit sexual content and mature language

Female genital mutilation (not committed by the MMC)

Rape (not committed by the MMC)

Physical and mental abuse (not committed by the MMC)

Body Dysmorphic Disorder (BDD)

PTSD, depression, and trauma-related themes

Please be mindful of your triggers before continuing, your mental health matters.

The book is recommended exclusively for 18+.

The Strength to Dark Love is part of a SERIES, and for the best experience, it should be read in order. For more things about **Karina Vega,** go to www.karinavega.com and sign up for my newsletter.

Contents

Prologue

Sofia

(five years old)

I'm crying, but no sound comes out. I think I've run out of tears. My body is shaking, but I can't feel it. It's like I'm not really here. My head feels all funny, like it's running away from everything around me. I keep thinking about the game I was playing outside with my neighbour, how happy we were.

And then... the blood.

It's like my brain can't decide where to stay. It jumps back and forth, one moment, I'm chasing after the ball and laughing, and the next, I see it. All the red, so much red, everywhere. My tummy feels twisty, like when I eat something bad, but worse. My hands hurt, but I don't know why. Did I fall?

It's so noisy in my head, but everything outside is quiet. My chest feels tight, like when I try to hold my breath under water for too long. I want to breathe. But I can't.

I look up at the man who took me. His face doesn't look like anything, no smile, no frown, just... nothing. I didn't even know someone could have a face like that. Maybe he's mad. My chest tightens further, and for a moment, I'm glad my cries don't make any noise. If they did, maybe he'd be upset. I don't want to upset him.

He's so big, but not scary. Not really. Even with that blank face. I notice his eyes bright blue, like the sky when there are no clouds. People with blue eyes are kind, aren't they? They have to be. It feels safer to believe it.

I look around, and there are three other men with us. One of them is African, like me. When our eyes meet, he gives me a small smile. It's not big, but it's there. He seems nice. That's good. At least someone can smile at me.

I notice his hands they have little lines all over them. Are those cuts? I have some lines like that on my knees from when I fell off my bike. Did he fall a lot? Why would he fall so much? I keep staring at his hands, and before I know it, my mind sees the blood again. The red from before flashes in my head, and a tiny squeak slips out of me.

Horrified, I peek up at the man carrying me. He's still holding me in his strong arms, wrapped in the blanket he covered me with. His face doesn't change still no smile, no frown, just that blank look. But we're moving so fast, weaving through a maze of houses. We're running. I don't know what we're running from, but one thing I do know... I don't want to *go back.*

That thought makes the tears come again, and this time, I can't hold back the little sounds that escape. The big man stops, and the others stop too, forming a circle around us. He looks down at me, tracing his fingers gently across my cheek. His face stays the same, but his eyes seem softer, somehow.

"This too shall pass, little one," he says.

***

Hunter

(six years old)

"Give me twenty more push-ups, Hunter!" Dad's booming voice feels like it's shaking the ground, maybe even the whole sky. It stings my ears like a whip.

We've been at this forever, or at least it feels like it. My whole body is burning, and my arms are shaking so much I can barely hold myself up. I don't want to cry. Crying isn't allowed.

Dad just got back from a deployment, and it feels like he's being extra hard on me this time around. He's cutting down my food, taking away my time with friends, and making these training sessions even tougher, like he's trying to turn me into a warrior instead of just letting me be a boy.

I want to ask Mum for a break, but I don't even know where she is right now. And honestly? I don't know if she'd let me. Everyone listens to Dad. We all do.

"You call that a push-up, boy?!" His voice roars in my ear, and it feels like thunder shaking my whole body.

Before I can even catch my breath, he's on me, pressing his boot into the middle of my back with so much force I collapse onto the ground, my arms giving out under me.

"Get the fuck up, boy!" he yells again, his tone sharp and filled with so much anger that it makes my chest tighten. I'm really scared now.

"In this world, there are killers and there is prey. What are you, Hunter?"

His voice is low and sharp, cutting through the pounding in my ears. For a moment, I don't say anything. I don't move. The weight of his boot pins me to the ground like I'm nothing, crushing my breath and any fight I might have left.

I know what he wants me to say. There's only one answer he'll accept. Only one way out of this.

"I'm a killer."

Chapter One

Hunter

God, I hate babysitting Dominic. I'm tired as hell, but I still make my way to the Barrow Building. I've got a few things to check on, but let's be real, I need to check on my *sugar cube*.

God, I miss her.

I haven't slept properly in 72 hours, not with everything Dominic's put me through. Got him drunk off his ass, but of course, the bastard sobered up and made a run for the door. I had to handcuff him to a support beam just to make sure he wouldn't disappear while I caught a few seconds of sleep.

I'm glad his woman took the leash off him. Now he can leave me the hell alone. He's pathetic, wearing his heart on his sleeve like that. What an idiot!

Who are you kidding? You could've stayed home, had your meetings online, but no, you came in, just to see her. Who's the pathetic one?

That thought knocks me back a bit because I know it's true. At least Dominic got his girl, made it happen. And here I am, working with Sofia for years, drooling over her like a horny teenager.

The first time I saw her... She gave me the coldest look I've ever gotten, like I didn't even exist. Like I was dirt under her shoe.

Fuck, that memory still stings. She's a goddess, all fire and ice. From her flawless skin to those ruthless, beautiful eyes. The way she talks, the way she moves, she owns every room she steps into. It doesn't matter who's in it or how big they are, she's always the alpha. The only ones above her are Elijah and Buddy, and that's it.

I walk into the Security Room, fire up all my monitoring software, and get on with it. Two hours in, and I'm still working, but there's no sign of my *sugar cube*.

Fucking hell, woman, where are you?

Another half hour passes, and now I'm beyond pissed. I log into the facial recognition software, and sure enough, I find her on the first floor, in an office in the East Wing.

What the hell are you doing there?

I watch her for what feels like hours. Damn, this woman is mesmerising. The number of times I've imagined my cock between those reality-shattering lips should be illegal. And the amount of times

I've pissed her off to get her to fight me, just to catch a hint of her intoxicating scent, is ridiculous, but it works.

It took me months to figure out how to get her to touch me, and after that, I learned her fighting moves. Every time she throws her arms around my neck, her body pressed against mine, I swear it's the only thing keeping me going. Now, I get my regular dose of her like clockwork.

Sometimes, I swear she loves me back. I can see it when she trembles during our fights. But every time I back off or even try to be decent, she goes full psycho on me, and that monster inside her comes out. I don't know what the hell is going on, and I definitely haven't figured out how to make her even notice me.

I know she's not seeing anyone. I know because I've been following her for two years. Since day two on the job with Elijah. And I don't care. I'll stalk her for the rest of my life if I have to, but let's be real, I'd much rather be buried inside her than jerking off to her image on a monitor.

It doesn't matter how much I want her. It doesn't matter that I've studied her more than any assignment I had in the SASR. I've tried so many ways to get close, but nothing works. There's something there, something I can't see that's keeping her from me. And until I find it and neutralize it, this fire burning inside me won't be satisfied.

The problem is, she's smart like hell. If people think I'm a genius with computers, they haven't met my *sugar cube*. She's the best of the best.

It's funny, really, how small and delicate she looks at first glance, totally at odds with the fire boiling under the surface. But my *sugar cube* could put any man on his ass and make any demon fall to his knees. I know she put me on my ass and knees, and I would happily be there for the rest of my life as long as she is mine.

I'm lost in yet another fantasy of fucking the living daylights out of her when I spot something out of the corner of my eye on one of the security monitors. A guy power-walking out of the main entrance. He's trying hard not to stand out, but he's moving faster than the crowd around him.

I turn to study his body language as he makes his way to a car across the street, and that's when I feel it. The ground beneath me shakes. I know I've fucked up...

"Fucking hell, Sofia!" I yell, not caring who hears me, as the sound of the bomb ripples through the building. The next second, I'm flying down the emergency stairs, my heart pounding, desperate to get to level one and find her.

"Fuck, I didn't even start the evacuation protocol." I yank my phone out and punch in the P1 Emergency Evacuation code, then shove it back in my pocket. I don't need to check if it worked the loud P1 notification on my phone confirms just how badly I've fucked up.

My phone starts ringing, and I know it's Elijah. I know he wants a full report, but I don't care. I don't give a fuck. I need to get to Sofia and get her out, no matter the cost. No matter Elijah's wrath, no matter if he kills me for this.

When I push open the doors to level one, I barge past people scrambling to get out, dust covering everything. People are terrified, in shock, disoriented, and flashbacks of my deployments paralyze me for a second. The smell of the bomb mixed with the dust registers in my mind, snapping me back. My training kicks in, and I start helping people around me. I lock the door open to help people escape the building faster.

My phone rings again, and this time, it's Buddy. I sigh, relieved. This conversation will be easier than the one with Elijah.

"There was a bomb," I say, my voice sharp and firm.

"Yeah, we figured that out from the footage. Why are you on level one?"

"I came to get Sofia. She's here, in the East Wing..."

"Hunter, the bomb was in the East Wing." Buddy cuts me off, urgency clear in his tone.

Buddy's words hit me like a punch to the gut. A deep nausea rises in me. *I can't lose her. I can't fucking lose her.*

"How do you know?" I try to keep my voice level to not give away the absolute panic that is within me at the possibility of losing Sofia.

"We've been watching the cameras. The question is, why haven't you?"

"I ran to get Sofia," I say, my words clipped as I hang up and head straight for the East Wing. I know I'll probably be killed for this, but I don't care. I have to find my *sugar cube.*

The sight before me could be lifted straight from a war zone. Part of the exterior wall is gone, with debris scattered everywhere. The thick scent of dust, bomb residue, and blood fills the air, blending with the grim sight of torn body parts strewn about. People died on my watch because I wasn't paying attention.

I keep running, pushing through the wreckage, until I reach the area where I last saw Sofia on the monitors. She's nowhere in sight.

"Sofia! Sofia!" I scream, my voice frantic as I search through the destruction. "Sofia!" My voice cracks, sounding foreign to me, like a wounded animal crying out for its mate.

"I'm here..." Her voice is faint, trailing off before I can even locate where it's coming from.

"*Cupcake*, where are you?" I spin, desperately searching for any sign of her. "Please, *cupcake*, talk to me."

"One of these days..." Her voice is so weak, it takes me a second to realise it's coming from beneath a massive piece of collapsed concrete, somehow pinned to a desk. She's buried somewhere in the debris. "...I'm going to cut your balls off, you..." She breaks into a violent coughing fit. "you stupid motherfucker," she finishes, as sharp as she can manage in her condition. "Now get me out!"

"Hang on, I think there's a huge concrete slab on top of you. Are you injured? Can you move at all?" My voice is steady, hiding the absolute panic coursing through my veins.

"I'm not hurt... I don't think I am, at least."

"Did you lose consciousness?" I keep her talking, needing to know she's still with me as I assess the situation and try to figure out how the hell to move this thing off her.

"Yeah... I think I did. Now get me out!"

I finally find her and kneel next to Sofia, my heart hammering in my chest as I scan the wreckage pinning her down. The slab of concrete looks like it weighs a ton, and I have no clue how the hell I'm going to move it. But I have to. *I fucking have to.*

"Hang tight, *cupcake*," I say, forcing my voice to stay steady. "I'm going to try and get this off you. Tell me if anything hurts when I move it."

I can barely hear my own voice over the pounding in my ears, panic clawing at my insides. She coughs, dust swirling around her, making her look even smaller under that giant piece of debris. Her beautiful three-piece suit she is wearing is now shredded and dirty, but somehow, she still looks pristine.

"Fucking move it, jackass," she snaps, trying to sound sharp, but I can hear the crack of panic in her voice. "We need to get these fuckers!"

I press my shoulder against the slab and push. Hard. My muscles scream, but the damn thing barely moves. My boots slip in the rubble beneath me. I shove harder, my teeth grinding together as I strain against it, feeling it shift. It's just enough for Sofia to wiggle her shoulders free.

"There you go... just a little more..." I mutter, breathless.

She tries to move, but her legs are still trapped. Shit. It's not enough.

"I'm still stuck," she grits out.

I step back, glancing around the room, searching for anything to use as leverage. My eyes lock on a metal rod sticking out from the debris pile. I yank it free, my hands slick with sweat and dust. I jam it under the concrete, positioning myself to try again.

"You're insane if you think that's going to work," Sofia mutters, her voice weaker this time.

"I've done crazier things, *cupcake*. Just trust me."

I throw my weight onto the rod, feeling my muscles scream in protest, but the slab starts to shift, inch by inch. Just enough. *Almost there...*

Then, without warning, the rod snaps with a sickening crack, sending debris crashing down. I barely have time to throw myself over Sofia before something jagged slams into my back. The pain is instant, like fire searing through me.

"Hunter!" Sofia screams, panic clear in her voice.

I grit my teeth, biting back a groan as I try to keep my body braced over hers. Every breath feels like knives stabbing into my ribs, but I don't care. I'm fine. I don't even have the strength to lie convincingly, but I do it anyway. "I'm fine," I manage, my voice strained.

"You're hurt," she says, her voice cracking.

Doesn't matter. Nothing else matters except getting her out. I push through the pain, using my free arm to shove the remaining debris off her legs. My vision blurs, but I force myself to keep going, ignoring the agony coursing through my body.

"Stop," Sofia pleads. "You're making it worse."

"I'm getting you out," I growl, using the last of my strength to shove the rubble off her. With a final push, it gives way, and I collapse onto the floor beside her, gasping for breath. My whole body feels like it's on fire, but I don't care. *I got her out.* That's all that matters.

Sofia slowly starts to stand, her hands trembling as she leans over me. "You idiot!" She yells straight into my face. "Why didn't you wait for help?"

I chuckle, though it hurts like hell. "Couldn't risk losing you, *cupcake*." My eyelids feel heavy, but I force them open, trying to focus on her face. "You okay?"

"I'm fine," she says, her eyes scanning me, filled with worry. "But you're not." She holds my gaze, and the look on her face, something I've never seen before, stirs something deep inside me.

I slowly stand, every movement sending sharp pain through my ribs. Definitely broken. It'll hurt like hell for a while.

But I got her out. *She's safe.*

You know what? Fuck it!

One second, I'm holding her gaze, and the next, I'm kissing the living hell out of her. The kiss is fire and ice, just like her, deep, passionate, and completely out of control. And I know, even if I kissed her every day for the rest of my life, it wouldn't be enough.

Fuck, she tastes amazing!

"That's it, Sofia," I growl against her lips. "From now on, no more games. You're mine. I'll fight you if I have to, but I'm never letting you out of my sight again."

In that moment, I make the decision. *This is it!* I'm never letting her go, and she will have to deal with it or fight me 'til death.

Chapter Two

Sofia

His words snap me back to reality.

No!

This cannot happen.

I won't allow it!

"From now on, no more games. You're mine. I'll fight you if I have to, but I'm never letting you out of my sight again."

"You're mine."

Two words.

A lifetime of pain, all smashed into those two words.

I will not allow it! I am not his, or anyone else's. I am my own woman, no man's property or right. I stand on my own two feet and don't need anyone's help to make my way through life. If this fucker thinks he has any claim on me, he's in for a rude awakening.

For the past two years, I've been trying like hell to push him away, and this stubborn bastard just won't give up. He's relentless goddamn it, so damn stubborn, there's no comparison. He's even been tracking me. The poor idiot probably thinks I don't know, but *I do*. What I haven't figured out yet, is why. He's not selling the information. He's not in contact with anyone from SASR or anyone outside of UBT. And I know he's not a threat to me or the organisation or he'd already be dead. So what the hell is he after?

The truth is, I've been keeping tabs on him, too. If he thinks his cameras and tracking are keeping an eye on me, well, I'm following him like a shadow, too. I don't get it. He's not doing it for some mission. He's not trying to hurt me. So why the hell is he stalking me?

And, I'll admit it, a part of me enjoys watching him work out in his home more than I should. If only he wouldn't be so fucking hot. Or, hell, if at least he wouldn't be funny and hot. There are so many guys in the organisation who are attractive, but I don't give a shit about them. But him? He had to be hot, funny, and smart.

Damn it!!!

I hate his guts. But the truth is, I can count on him.

Fuck, I hate him!

When he starts kissing me again, his tongue grazing my lips, demanding entry, I want to fight it, I really do. But a bigger part of me just wants to kiss the living hell out of him. I almost had a bomb explode right next to me, so, you know what? I don't care anymore! I'm going to let myself enjoy this fucking specimen of a man for once. I love him so much sometimes I feel like I'll have a panic attack if I don't see him every day. I know I shouldn't give in to these feelings. I know I should shut it all down, but today... today, I almost died. Today, I was trapped under who-knows-what, and no one came. No one except Hunter.

His arms are around me now, tight, holding me steady. He gently tilts my head back and deepens the kiss. He tastes so good... I try to muster the courage to push him away, but my body refuses to follow orders. Instead of pushing him off, I'm pulling him closer.

I'm not sure if I'm doing this right or if it even matters. All that matters is that I get more of him, even if it's just for these few seconds. Even if this is the only time I'll ever kiss anyone.

I don't care if he figures out I've never kissed anyone before. I don't give a shit. But when he groans in pure pleasure, I rub my abdomen against his cock, and yeah, he's hard as steel. Well, newbie or not, he seems to be enjoying me.

"Don't start something we can't finish right now," he whispers against my lips. "I'll fuck you raw, *cupcake*, but the police will be here soon, and if they see you naked, I'll kill them all and you know it might complicate a few things."

Hello, reality!

I pull back hard, and he looks genuinely shocked. His surprise is so real, it catches me off guard.

"You will do no such thing!" I snap, turning on my heel. But before I reach the door, he grabs my arm and spins me around, fury and desperation in his eyes.

"We're not doing this anymore, Sofia," he says, his tone sharp and commanding. "I already told you, no more games. You're mine!"

I want to tell him to fuck off. I want to tell him he can't just claim me like that. But the moment I open my mouth to protest, he lunges at me, kissing me fiercely and pinning me to the wall. This kiss is different, it's not sweet or kind like before. It's raw, fierce, and dominating. He's demanding control, and the worst part is, I'm enjoying it. My body responds to him, stroke for stroke, like it was made for this.

I don't know how long we've been kissing, locked in a battle of wills, but the sound of people coming up the stairs snaps me back to reality. *I have to run. I have to get to the Security Center.*

We pull away, still holding each other's gaze, and I give him a nod. I'm not even sure what I'm agreeing to, but I know I need to go. I need to clean up the footage and start tracking whoever did this.

"Go. I'll be up in a second. Let me handle the police, then we'll get to work," his voice turns cold, and it does something to me inside. I don't like it.

"I fucked up, Sofia," he says, his voice so small, it almost doesn't sound like him. "People died because I fucked up."

I just look at him, not saying anything, and nod again. He's a warrior, not some simple man. I'm not going to insult him by denying his guilt. If he says he fucked up, he did, and it means he's owning it.

I push past him and take off up the stairs. I work out daily, but sprinting up twenty-nine floors is a whole different level of hell. By the time I reach the Security Center, I've kicked off my shoes, my suit jacket and vest are long gone, and my shirt is half untucked, clinging to me with sweat and grime. The dust and debris from the chaos below coat my skin, the grit settling into every crease of my clothing. My lungs burn, my muscles protest, but none of that matters. I need to see what the hell is going on.

Inside, my dad and Uncle Buddy are working at lightning speed. I can tell by the speed of their work that things aren't as urgent anymore.

"Did you find anything?" I ask, trying to catch my breath.

"Yes. The bomb was a gift from Bogdan," my dad's deep voice booms through the room.

"Well, that's just great! How come the building didn't collapse?"

A simple "Hmm," is all the response my dad gives.

I glance at Uncle Buddy, silently pleading for more information. It's just the three of us in the room there's no reason for them not to tell me what's going on.

"When we built this place, we reinforced the building's structural integrity, taking extra care around the emergency exits. Everyone was out of the building and on their way home within 20 minutes of the P1 evacuation being activated."

"So, the building can't be brought down?" My voice squeaks with surprise.

"It can, but it would take a nuclear bomb," my dad says, his fingers still flying over the keyboard. "What Buddy's saying is, we didn't spare any expense when we built this place. I wanted my legacy to withstand people's stupidity. We prepared for a lot of scenarios. If anyone comes at us, they'll need one hell of a bomb to level this building."

I try to process everything they're saying as I begin tracking chatter on the dark web.

"We need to leave," Dad says suddenly, his phone in his hand. "We're heading to the panic room at City Hall," with that, they're out the door.

Three hours later, Hunter walks into the room, and for the first time since I met him, he stops behind my chair and presses a kiss to the top of my head. The gesture is so unexpectedly sweet and romantic that I freeze mid-sentence, completely paralysed.

He lowers himself, wraps his arms around me, and buries his face in the crook of my neck, breathing me in. I can feel my heart racing, my body heating up with every second that passes.

I should push him away. I know I should shut this down so fast his head would spin. But his embrace feels too damn good. I feel cocooned in his arms, protected in a way I've never let myself feel before. I just can't summon the will to push him off.

So I let it happen. For once in my life, I let a man touch me, comfort me, show me affection.

A deep sigh escapes him, but when he giggles softly into my neck and kisses the sensitive spot just below my ear, I realise with horror that the sigh wasn't his, it was mine. I'm mortified by my own reaction. This needs to stop. *I have to stop this!* It doesn't matter how much I want this or how unbelievably amazing it feels to be in his arms. I need to put an end to it.

As if he can read my mind, he loosens his hold on me, pressing soft kisses to the side of my cheek. "It's okay, *cupcake*," he murmurs. "We can take it as slow as you need. Just don't run from me. I'll chase you until the end of my days. You already used all of your freedom."

I want to tell him to fuck off, I really do. But the words refuse to leave my mouth. For once in my life, I have no words. No jokes. No sarcasm. No sharp retort. Just... silence.

Hunter pulls back and sits next to me, watching me closely for a few minutes. I think he's as surprised by my reaction as I am, but I don't have the courage to look up and confirm it.

"Take all the time you need, *cupcake*," he says, his voice gentle, wrapping me in warmth again.

A few moments pass as I try to steady my thoughts, find my voice, and summon my courage. Then, finally, I manage to deliver it: "Fuck off," I say, trying to muster as much authority as I can from the pit of my mind.

Hunter's deep, booming laughter fills the room, exactly what I need to hear right now.

"There you are, my *cupcake*."

Chapter Three

Sofia

We make our way to City Hall, and all I can think about is how much I want this to happen, but how utterly incapable I am of letting it take root. *God, I love him so much it makes my chest hurt.* How am I supposed to walk away now that I know what it feels like to be in his arms? But what choice do I have? I'm damaged beyond repair, and there's no way I could ever tell him what happened to me. I can't tell anyone, let alone him. I'm dirty, disgusting, damaged. How could I ever show him who I truly am? Who I truly have become?

The more I think about it, the more nausea and lightheadedness wash over me. I roll the window down and lean my head against the edge, taking deep breaths, trying to calm my racing heart.

I fucking loved him from the moment I laid eyes on him. And look at my life now. He loves me back, and all I can do is push him away. I can't have what I want so badly. How the hell am I supposed to find the strength to push him away?

I feel like crying! Like screaming! My skin feels itchy and too hot! *What would happen if I just let it all out? If I screamed at the top of my lungs?*

Hunter parks the car, and I see that many of our inner circle staff have already made their way to the panic room, their cars are in the parking lot as well.

We lost 20 people, 15 more were injured, and we're still confirming a few, probably another 10. When we were running the post-incident protocol, I was so impressed with my dad. Twenty minutes after Hunter activated the P1 Emergency Evacuation, people were already on the evacuation buses heading home. Part of the building was blown to pieces, but it stood tall.

I hope these people realise how much Dad cares about them, putting in the money to create such a building. Or even this panic room, it's more like a wing of City Hall. We still have to bribe politicians to keep this section for us, but it was worth it. A bomb, and only 20 dead. That's a win, by some standards.

But Hunter's body language tells me everything. He's hurting. He's trying to keep it together, but I can feel the waves of pain coming off him. And it shatters my heart. All I want to do is comfort him, take him in my arms, and love him for the rest of my days.

But what am I going to do? Stay cold beside him. Give him space. Let him sort himself out. Because if there's one thing I can control, it's my intent. I won't feed him any affection to provoke whatever this is between us. What is this, anyway? What would you call it?

Love? Passion? Need?

No! I cannot be with him! I will not allow it!

I'd call it... DESPAIR!

PAIN!

AGONY!

As we enter the main conference room, I notice people still cleaning up what looks like the remnants of a fight. *Seriously?* In the middle of a P1, and someone thought it was a good time to throw punches? *Dumbasses.*

I glance over at Hunter, and a fresh wave of nausea hits me so hard I might actually throw up right here in front of everyone.

I can't! I simply *cannot* do that. They all already see me as the coldest person in the room, and I've worked long and hard to cultivate that image. Throwing up in front of everyone would tear down everything I've built.

I turn toward the bathroom, determined to get out before I lose it, but Hunter steps in front of me, blocking my path.

"*Cupcake*, don't make a run for it," he says, his eyes locking onto mine, reading every expression. He knows me too well.

How can I explain to him that just being near him overwhelms me? That the weight of my emotions is so heavy, I can barely keep it together. If I suppress this agony any longer, I swear I'm going to throw up right in front of everyone.

"I'll hunt you down, *cupcake*. It's in the name. I'm Hunter, the hunter," he says with a laugh that makes me pause, despite myself. His smile, his eyes... God, he's too much. My knees are getting weak just looking at him, and I'm on the verge of either throwing up or collapsing at his feet. *Great options!*

"Fuck off, *Nuuro*!" I snap, managing to shove past him while trying to suppress a laugh, because damn it, he's so funny. I bump my shoulder into him for good measure, and he grunts, his gaze fixed on me as I walk away.

I take two steps before I feel it, his hand pinching my ass.

What. The. Actual. Fuck?!

I freeze. Shocked. Stunned. Unable to speak or move. No one has ever touched me like that. It's absurd, shocking... and if I'm honest with myself, *I liked it.*

But I can't turn around because I'll either burst into laughter or lose control and vomit right there in front of him. Maybe I should turn around and let him see what happens when he messes with me.

No, I can't. My mind is racing at lightning speed, and my head is pounding. I want him so badly, but there's no way I can ever let him see who I really am. I'm broken beyond repair, and I can't let anyone, especially him, see that.

With that thought, I keep walking, pretending like nothing happened, as though my ass wasn't just pinched for the first time in my life.

"*Cupcake*, don't run! I'm warning you!" he calls after me.

I flip him off and slam the bathroom door behind me.

Once inside, I splash cold water on my face, trying to get rid of the nausea. But it's not helping. If anything, leaning over the sink is making it worse. Finally, I give in. I kneel in front of the toilet and throw up everything, until there's nothing left but bile. I feel exhausted. Defeated. Ashamed. In pain. But most of all, heartbroken.

"Why did he have to like me back?" I whisper to myself, curling into a ball on the cold tile floor.

I feel dirty inside and out. Now I'm sitting here, next to a toilet in City Hall. *This is rock bottom!*

I can't hold it in any longer. The sobs come violently, pouring out of me like they could somehow cleanse me, cleanse my heart, my body, my soul. But they won't. They can't. I'm dirty, and what they did to me can never be undone. I will carry these scars and this pain with me forever. There's nothing I can do about it. And the only power I have left is to push away the man I love.

That thought triggers a fresh wave of nausea, and I start vomiting again, sobbing uncontrollably.

Fuck my life!

***

Hunter

Sofia's been quiet the entire time. This is not good. *Very fucking much not good.*

I can feel it in my bones, she's going to run. Her feet might be next to me, but her heart? It's ready to bolt. And maybe that's just my insecurity talking, because, hell, longing for a woman for two years is new territory for me. But this firecracker of a woman is definitely giving me a run for my money.

Still, I kissed her. And she let me. No, scratch that, she kissed me back. *She actually kissed me back!*

Okay, maybe I did just pull her out of the rubble, but she kissed me back! That's gotta count for something, right?

I've never been this terrified in my entire life. All those deployments, secret missions, all the intel I've worked through in my career in the army, it's all worthless when it comes to Sofia. I just ran on instinct to get to her, to save her. Hell, to save myself, because there's no world worth living in if she's not in it.

How could I possibly accept a reality where the woman made for me doesn't exist? I couldn't let her die. And there was no way in hell I'd start the P1 protocol without making sure she was safe first.

The only problem? Elijah.

I'm still dragging my feet to go to his office in City Hall. Not that I mind, because it gives me time to openly check out my *sugar cube* as she walks to the bathroom. Fuck, she's beautiful. No more discreet glances, no more sneaking looks. Now, I can ogle her as much as I want because I told her how I feel, and she didn't push me away. That means she feels the same. And that means she's mine. *Right?*

But, yeah, there's still the Elijah problem.

If he decides I can't be with Sofia, then I've got a serious issue on my hands. But honestly? I don't give a fuck. I'll work on him for the next two years if I have to, just like I did with her. He'll give in eventually.

This is happening.

She's mine.

She had the chance to push me away, and she didn't. She kissed me back. And fuck me sideways, it felt like my entire soul was floating with happiness.

The only downside? My fuck-up.

People died because of my obsession with her. Instead of keeping my eyes on everything, I was too busy tracking my *sugar cube* and staring at her like a lovesick idiot. Sure, my team could've spotted the guy too, and yes, he didn't exactly scream "suspicious." But I'm not in this position because of my brains or my experience. It's my instincts. I can read people, intuit what they're about 90% of the time. That's why Elijah chose me. I know that.

And now, I have to face the music. I messed up. And I want his daughter. *This should be fun, right?*

I sigh deeply and finally turn to make my way to Elijah's office. I needed a minute because, fuck me, every time I see Sofia's ass, I get so hard I don't know what hurts more, my blue balls or my head from all the times I've imagined pounding into her.

Somehow, I manage to get myself under control as I open Elijah's door and sit down in front of his desk. Buddy and Elijah are engaged in their silent communication, pointing at the screen in front of them. I use the moment to gather my thoughts, to figure out a strategy that goes from "*hey, I fucked up*" to "*hey, I want your daughter*". I love her. I've loved her from the moment I saw her, and fuck, she loves me back. This is going to be a nightmare.

"Tell me, Hunter, what happened?" Elijah's voice is emotionless, detached, as usual. But he stops what he's doing and gives me his full attention.

I lean back in the chair, take a deep breath, and own my fuck-up.

"I noticed the man leaving the building. Something about his body language felt off. As I started to watch him, I felt the explosion."

"Hmm." Elijah's hum holds all the displeasure he's feeling. And that's Elijah at his finest, barely speaks, as if every word costs him something.

"I ran to get Sofia and initiated the P1 protocol," I continue, keeping my voice steady as I gauge their reactions. "Sofia was trapped under some debris, and I got her out. We've confirmed 20 dead, 15 injured, and two more missing."

They both hold my gaze for what feels like an eternity. I know I screwed up, and if I try to diminish, dismiss, or outright lie right now, they might actually kill me. I can feel it.

"Anything else?" Elijah leans back, running a hand through his beard, while Buddy stands tall beside him.

Well, here we go. No turning back now. The only way forward is through fire.

"Yeah. I love your daughter, and I want to marry her."

Elijah's only reaction is a slight tilt of his head as he narrows his eyes at me. He wasn't expecting that. I wasn't sure how he'd take it, but this still feels like a curveball.

"Is that so?"

"Yes. I've loved her since the moment I saw her two years ago. Early today she wasn't in the Security Center, so I tracked her to Level 1. That's why I wasn't completely focused on my job. When the explosion happened, I ran to her first, and I initiated the protocol on the way." *There the entire truth is out.*

"I love her," I say, letting the words come out with conviction. "I told her as much when I pulled her out. No more playing around, she's mine."

I probably shouldn't talk to him like this, but he needs to understand how serious I am. This is happening, whether he likes it or not. The only person who can stop me is Sofia, and even then, I'm not giving up. I'll wear her down if I have to.

Elijah lets out a soft chuckle, and Buddy looks just as stunned as I am. That's definitely not the reaction I was expecting.

"You say it with such conviction, as if the decision is actually yours," Elijah says, his voice cool and measured.

Fuck. This is not good. This is very much not good. But I hold his gaze. I'm not backing down. He can come at me all he wants, I'm not letting Sofia go. Not now, not ever.

The door to the office opens, and Sofia walks in. She moves with an elegance that still takes my breath away. *God, she's so beautiful. My chest hurts just looking at her.*

I drop the mask of indifference and let my true feelings show. I love her. I love her so much. This is happening. Fuck them all, she's mine, and she'll know it soon enough.

"I see..." Elijah's voice is final, and for a second, even Sofia seems caught off guard by the shift in the room.

I half-expect her to tell me to fuck off, to start a fight, to kick and scream like she always does. But when I really look at her, something's off. She looks... defeated. *What the fuck?*

Her body language, her posture it's like she's collapsing in on herself. Where's the fierce woman who fought me over a wrong look? Where's the fire? She looks small, and something in me starts to crack because she's *running.* I warned her not to do this. I'm done with the push and pull. She's mine, and everyone better learn that fast, her included.

As if on cue, Buddy places a hand on my shoulder, a reassuring gesture. "This is big, Hunter. There are things to consider, discussions to have. I assume you both haven't had time to go over all of that?" He glances at Sofia, and the care in his eyes reminds me how much these two men love and protect her.

She may not be Elijah's biological daughter, but there's no doubt in my mind that both of them would do anything for her.

I'll find a way. I *have* to find a way.

But now there's a bigger problem. Sofia's shutting down, and I don't even know why. *What the fuck do I do?*

You'd think this conversation would be about the police, the bomb, the aftermath of everything. But instead, it's about my feelings for her.

Fuck, I love her. This has to happen. It *will* happen. There's no going back to just being near her, not after I've touched her, tasted her.

Okay, okay, calm the fuck down, or you'll get a boner in front of these guys and embarrass yourself.

"Sofia, let Hunter take you home. Discuss it, come to an agreement, and your dad and I will honor whatever you decide." Buddy's calm, calculated tone feels like a wake-up call to something much bigger than me, something bigger than us.

I knew it! I fucking knew there was something else going on.

It doesn't matter. Whatever it is, I'll work through it. I'll have my *sugar cube* next to me.

Sofia says nothing, just stands, turns, and walks out as if nothing happened.

Buddy's grip tightens on my shoulder, and he shoots me a warning glare. *Well, damn.* I didn't see that coming. *Why?* I didn't do anything wrong.

I stand and follow Sofia out to the car. She's walking slower than usual, favoring her left side. Is she hurt? *Fucking hell! I should have checked. I should have stripped her down and made sure she was okay.*

"Are you hurt, *cupcake*?" I ask.

"No! And for the millionth time, stop calling me that!" Her bite isn't as sharp as usual. Something is catastrophically wrong.

Oh, fuck. I think we're about to have a fight.

Chapter Four

Hunter – 12 years old

"How many times do I have to tell you, Hunter? If you're gonna put someone in their place, make it count. The first hit is what counts! Make. It. Count."

My dad's mad at me again. He got called into the principal's office because I beat up some prick. I mean, I won, but the guy managed to land a few good hits.

"Boy, are you listening?"

My dad's SASR, and *fuck*, I wish I could be like him when I'm older. He's only home for a few months before he's off again. I hate when he's gone. Every time he leaves, I go over everything he's taught me in my head, over and over again. That's why he's pissed now, he's told me repeatedly that the first hit is the most important. It's all about making it count. He's also always going on about *controlling the beast.*

Ever since I was little, I've felt this fire inside me like if I don't fight, I'll explode. My dad put me in martial arts when I was four, and it worked. By the time I was seven, I was fighting teenagers, and word got around that I've got a bit of a temper. Ever since, every little fucker has tried coming at me to prove something. They want to prove something? Prove *self-control.* See how that works out for you. Letting go of the beast? That's easy. Hell, it's satisfying. But controlling the beast, pretending the fire inside isn't consuming you? That's a whole different game.

I think my dad's angrier because I let the guy land his punches, not because I got into a fight. Truth be told, I needed the pain. I needed to feel something besides the constant urge to bash someone's head in for doing something stupid.

I glance at the principal's face and it's priceless. Most parents would be scolding their kids for fighting, but here's my dad giving me advice on technique how to beat someone faster. The principal looks stunned, but he's not saying a word. What could he say to a 6'6", fully tattooed muscle-bound army guy? Not a damn thing. So, he sits there like a coward, glancing back and forth between me and my dad, too scared to open his mouth.

You'd think someone might've asked me by now if I was getting smacked around at home or something. But nope. None of my teachers or this guy has ever asked if I'm okay. And to be fair, I am okay. My parents love me. They just don't show it like other parents. Hearing my dad talk to me like this should've raised some red flags for the principal, but instead of checking on my well-being, he sits there like a scared little chicken shit.

Maybe I should "accidentally" on purpose cut his brakes. *Fucker!*

"I needed it." I own my truth and hold my dad's gaze.

He nods his head, turns, and leaves the office.

I think there is more training coming my way.

Chapter Five

Sofia – 12 years old

"The female genitals look like this," the Relationship and Sexual Education (RSE) teacher says, pointing to an image that looks wrong. My classmates burst into laughter, and the teacher tries her best to calm them down, but I know something is off. *That's not what a vagina looks like. She's wrong!*

One of the pricks in my class sneaks a photo on his phone, hiding behind the commotion. *Moron!* Not only is this a inaccurate diagram, but he's completely falling for it. *What an idiot.*

"Settle down, everyone. This is not for your amusement. This is for your knowledge, and I'd appreciate it if you'd all be quiet and pay attention. This will impact your entire life."

If this is for our knowledge, shouldn't it at least be accurate, lady? What a fraud of a teacher. My dad's paying so much for me to study here with these preppy know-it-alls, and the staff doesn't even know what they're talking about. How pathetic.

"This is the clitoral hood, clitoris, labia majora, labia minora, urethral opening where your pee comes out, vulva vestibule, and vaginal opening. All of these parts make up the exterior parts of the female genitals. The inner parts..."

What the hell? She's wrong. How can she be so wrong? Where did she even get this information? Should I correct her?

My mind is spinning, and I've completely tuned out her lesson. Something deep in my gut twists, telling me something is seriously wrong here. I don't understand. How can she say it looks like that when mine doesn't look anything like this? Why are those "lips" separated, and why is she naming things that don't look separated on me?

Are women in this country different down there than I am? They're still women, right? Shouldn't we all look the same? What in the world is going on?

"Hey, Sofia, do you want to see the picture I took of the male penis?" Claudia, my classmate, whispers beside me. She giggles like the spoiled schoolgirl she is, and discreetly shows me a cartoonish drawing of something dangling between a man's legs. *Gross.* It's just an animation, not even a real image, but if it looks like that for all of them, I really don't see what Claudia and everyone else are laughing so hard about. It's disgusting.

"Put that away, Claudia. You're going to get us in trouble," I whisper-yell at her.

Claudia means well, and that's why I accepted sitting next to her. Out of all these spoiled kids, she's the least annoying, and I don't plan on killing her when we're older. The rest? Touch and go. Some of them are already on my list, and I'm tempted to pass it to Uncle Buddy to sort them out.

My dad and Uncle Buddy are both powerful wealthy men, and we've traveled my whole life. This year, they decided to settle down in England to give me a "normal" childhood as I head into my teen years. I don't think it's working out too well, though, because all I want to do is bash this Chris's head in for laughing like an idiot at a fake picture of a vagina. *What a moron!*

"That's all for today, class. Next week, we'll talk about how a baby is conceived and contraception."

"*Oooooo!*" the class sings in unison.

What a bunch of idiots. Most schools start RSE classes around year four, but at our school, given who our parents are, they postponed it because "*of course our kids wouldn't do that, they're perfect.*" Bullshit! Some of these idiots have probably done something by now or at least seen a real one. The way the guys are eyeing Corina, and whispering obscenities under their breath makes me think I'm right.

Sometimes, I wish we were back in Morocco or Spain. Preferably Morocco. I loved the colors, the music, and the beautiful riads. I would sit in the riad for hours reading, until my dad would came to check on me.

"*Sofia, what are you reading, little one?*" he'd ask, stopping beside me. It used to seem silly, him asking when he could easily read the title on the book's cover. But it took me a while to realise that my dad doesn't speak to most people. He talks to me, asks me questions even if he already knows the answer. It means he wants to talk to me, that I'm special to him. He's told me so, countless times since he took me, but I can see it, too, in how he treats me differently from everyone else.

He checks on me, even though I have two bodyguards with me wherever I go. In this school, most of the kids have someone shadowing them. For me, that's just life.

"Come on, Sofia, let's go to the toilet, and I'll show you the picture better," Claudia says, yanking my hand so fast I barely have time to protest. She drags me down the hallway, and once we're inside, she pulls out her phone so quickly, I think it might slip from her grip and crack on the tiles. Why do they call it *toilets* here? We used to say *bathroom*, since our time in America. It's been six months now, and all I want is to go back to Morocco. Maybe I'll ask again tonight. Maybe the millionth time will finally be the charm.

"Look at that!" Claudia's giggling snaps me back to reality.

"Gross! Put it away," I say, turning away. "I don't see what the big deal is. I wouldn't want something dangling like that between my legs."

"What do you mean? Apparently, most women fall in love with that part of a boy's body. Have you ever seen one in real life?" Her curious voice carries through the room, as I close the toilet door. I shake my head in disbelief.

"No, Claudia, I haven't. Can you imagine?" I answer, my voice dripping with sarcasm.

"I want to see for myself!" she says, her voice brimming with excitement, making me wonder how she could be so clueless.

"You'll have time to see one when we're older. I don't see the appeal..." My words fade because something is wrong. There's blood in my underwear.

Oh my God, what's happening? I stand up quickly, grabbing some tissue to dab myself, and sure enough, there's more blood. *Oh my God, I'm bleeding! My vagina is bleeding! Is it tearing apart or something?* Is that why that picture looked separated, and mine doesn't? *Am I going to bleed to death? Am I dying?*

"...look at these parts underneath," Claudia's voice chimes in from outside, oblivious. "Maybe they look different in real life. That's why I want to see for sure." She's still giggling.

I stumble out of the stall, my legs unsteady, and head straight to the nurse's office, leaving a stunned Claudia in my wake.

"Is something the matter, dear?" the nurse asks when it's finally my turn to speak with her.

"Hi, Mrs. Windebank," I whisper, barely audible. I'm terrified, about to freak out. I'm bleeding from my private parts, and I might be dying.

"Take a seat and tell me what's wrong," she says, gesturing to a chair in her office.

I don't like her. I never have. She has this way of looking down on everyone, like she's better than us. If I weren't *literally* bleeding to death, I'd have avoided coming here at all costs. *I should have called my dad.* But I can't. He's my dad, how could I tell him something like this? He can never know what's going on down there.

I glance at the old nasty nurse, trying to summon any courage I have left. Her forced smile is still plastered on her face, but she looks mean. *I don't want to be here.*

"I don't have all day, child. What's the matter?" Her voice turns more stern, the fake patience slipping.

"I'm bleeding..." My voice is so faint I almost don't recognise it.

"What do you mean, you're bleeding?" She leans forward, trying to see where the blood might be. "Where are you bleeding, child? Show me." Her tone is cold, impatient, as if I'm a misbehaving kid wasting her time. She steps closer, looming over me.

I should have called my dad...

"I don't have all day, young lady. Tell me what's going on, or off you go back to class." The finality in her voice cracks something inside me. *Why is she being cruel?*

"I'm bleeding between my legs..." My voice is so soft, I fear she didn't hear me and will send me away.

"Did someone hurt you?"

"No."

"Then how are you bleeding? How do you know?"

"I went to the toilet, and there was blood everywhere. I'm scared it's tearing open." At those words, tears spill from my eyes, unbidden, as if my body has its own will. This twisting pain inside feels like it's turning me inside out.

"It's all right, child. Take your clothes off, and let me have a look." Her voice is gentler now, and somehow, that makes it even worse. *Is there really something wrong with me?*

I do as she says, feeling unbearably vulnerable as I remove my clothes from the waist down. Once I sit back on the bed, she covers me with a sheet. Her hands are clinical as she checks, wiping and gently pressing. I'm terrified, uncomfortable, ashamed. For someone to look at me down there, *especially today.* What if she thinks I'm different? What if she realises I'm different? *I should have called my dad.*

"Everything looks as it should," she says, her voice calculated and cold, making me feel even smaller. *She's hiding something.*

"You recently transferred here, didn't you?"

"Yes."

"Where did you live before?"

"Morocco," I answer half-heartedly, trying to read her face. She's an old, mean woman. I can't tell where she's going with this. "Tangier, Morocco. We lived there a few years, my dad's business takes us all over the world." I study her every reaction as I continue. "Why?"

"You can put your clothes back on, love."

I'm not your 'love'! Tell me what's wrong and stop looking down on me!

I start to dress, fury building in my veins. All I want to do is scream at her to tell me why I'm bleeding.

"Where were you born?" Mrs. Windebank asks, her eyes still fixed on her *ancient* computer. The thing's probably as old as she is. You'd think with all the money this school rakes in, they'd give their staff better gear.

"Somalia," I say, wiping stray tears from my cheeks, then cleaning my hands on my skirt. "But I haven't been back since I was little."

I hate feeling weak. I hate it when someone thinks I'm weak. And I hate this woman for treating me like I'm too dumb to know what's happening. I hate that she touched me there. *I hate that I had to let her touch me there!*

"What's wrong with me? Why am I bleeding?" My voice sounds balanced, cool completely at odds with the fire raging inside me.

"There's nothing wrong. You've started your period, and the bleeding is from there," she says it matter-of-factly, as if she hasn't just shaken my world. "You're exactly as you should be," she picks up the phone and dials a number.

"We need to call your parents to pick you up."

She didn't even ask me. Just told me she's calling my parents. *Lady, what parents? I only have my dad.*

"It's fine. I can go back to class if I'm okay..."

"No, it's best for you to take a few days off, give yourself some time to learn about menstruation and how to take care of yourself." She's back to her full "bitch" status, dismissive and condescending.

She hands me a pad. "Here, go put this on. Yes, hello? I have Miss Dominion here. We need to call her parents."

I close the curtain, pull down my underwear, and try to attach the pad, but the damn thing won't stick. I touch the fabric and realise it's wet, probably with blood. A deep nausea, panic, and shame surge through me all over again. What the hell am I going to do? My dad is coming, I'm bleeding, and I can't even get this stupid thing to stay in place.

Tears start rolling again, the pain in my chest squeezing tighter. I feel suffocated. I want to run, to hide, especially from this nasty woman, but I know the safest place for me is next to my dad.

I should have never come to her. I should have called my dad.

The nurse finishes her call and barely looks at me as she says, once I'm done, I can wait outside until my dad arrives to pick me up.

This stupid pad just won't stick, so I finally give up and place it on top of my wet underwear, hoping this isn't the worst day of my life, for it to fall out as I walk down the hall. But I can't spend another second in this room with her. I wash my hands at her tiny sink, feeling her gaze on me, analyzing, condemning, mocking. *I should have never come to her. This is a mistake I won't make twice.*

One of the staff members brings my things, and I wait outside the nurse's office as if I'm in trouble. *Am I in trouble? What did I do?*

You know what? To hell with all of them. I know my dad loves me. He'll come for me. I know he thinks I'm special. *I know it.*

Finally, I pull myself together and reach for my phone. Eighteen missed calls from my dad and ten from Buddy.

See? You're loved. You're cared for.

Dad

Are you ok, little one?

I'm on my way.

Please text me back when you see this so I know you're ok.

Whatever it is, I will help you.

I'm on my way.

How could I ever tell him what's wrong? How could I explain that I'm not like other women... *down there?* How could I tell him I'm bleeding? *I can't.* I simply cannot have this discussion with my dad.

I hear the roar of engines speeding toward the school, and I sit up to look out the window. Six cars are racing down the long driveway toward the entrance. *Six cars? Really?*

Sofia

Six cars, dad? Is that really necessary?

Dad

Are you ok, little one?

Sofia

Yes, dad. I am okay.

I look up from my phone, feeling like I might pass out from the embarrassment. Men pour out of cars like ants ready to attack, twenty of them circling my dad as he approaches the principal waiting at the entrance. He doesn't even stop to speak, just strides into the building, out of sight. I hear them approaching because, well, an army is hard to miss.

The moment Dad steps into the hallway, a weight eases from my chest. I didn't even realise how much pain I was in until I saw him. He power-walks toward me, the principal trailing behind, barely able to keep up. Dad raises a hand to dismiss him, and the bodyguards instinctively block the principal from following.

"Are you okay, little one? What happened?" The concern is visible on his face, in his voice, and in the way he gently hugs me, as if he's afraid of hurting me.

My dad is different. I knew it from the moment he took me in. He's cold, clinical, distant to everyone else, but *not to me.*

He studies me with a deep, familiar intensity, and it takes me a moment to remember where I've seen that look before.

"Mr. Dominion, if I may..." the principal tries to get his attention, but when Dad turns, the look he gives him is so raw it sends a shiver down my spine.

He signals the guards to keep the principal back and turns his focus back on me. "What happened, little one? Are you hurt? You know you can tell me anything." That's a lot of words from him all at once, and the concern in his voice feels entirely different from the cold glare he just gave the principal. It's like two different people altogether.

"I'm fine, Dad. It's nothing. The nurse insisted I take a few days off. But really, I'm okay."

He studies me for a moment longer, leans down, and kisses the top of my head. "I love you, little one," he murmurs, then turns back to the overly eager principal.

Sam, my personal guard, takes my backpack and gestures for me to follow the four guards circling me now. We make our way down the hall, and over my shoulder, I watch as Dad walks away mid-sentence, leaving a bewildered principal in his wake.

Once in the back of the SUV, Vasile, Dad's personal bodyguard and driver is up front with Sam, while the remaining men urgently pile into the other cars.

"Twenty men, Dad? Isn't that overkill?" My voice sounds small and defeated. *I hate it.*

"You didn't answer your phone," he says, calm and unruffled. "And it's not twenty, it's fifty. The other thirty are stationed around the property in case we needed backup."

"Oh my God, Dad! Tell me you're joking." The alarm in my voice makes the corner of his mouth lift ever so slightly. All my antics over the years, all my cheeky comments, and the most I ever get is that barely-there smile.

"You didn't answer your phone, little one."

“You could have called the school.”

“And what if it was the school that discovered how special you are to me, and tried to take you from me?” His tone is challenging, and I know he’s won this argument. The discussion is over.

“Fine, but don’t do it again, okay?”

“Of course, little one. Next time, I’ll take the helicopter. Twenty minutes by car was far too long in an emergency. That time could make all the difference.”

“Oh my God, Dad.” The exasperation in my voice draws out another tiny “smile". As the convoy leaves the school grounds, I start to think I might get away with this without further humiliation.

Then Dad raises the partition, sealing us in the back with complete privacy, and that crushing mix of shame, disgust, and embarrassment hits me all over again. My chest tightens, my skin goes clammy, and I feel my body reacting, my mind spiraling as I remember what the principal must have told him.

He sits there, looking straight ahead, giving me all the time in the world to pull myself together. He must have heard everything the principal told him, and I’m certain he knows about the blood.

After a few minutes, when the pressure is so overwhelming that I’m on the verge of tears, a faint memory resurfaces of the last time I cried in front of him. I used to have nightmares, almost every night, and each time Dad would come, settle me, and take me to the theater room to watch something until I fell back asleep. Then he’d carry me back to bed. It’s been so long since then, I’d almost forgotten the crying, the pain, the memories.

“Little one...” Dad’s gentle voice breaks the silence. “You can tell me anything. I’ll always take care of you, Sofia.”

“I’m fine...” I rush to answer, but my voice betrays me, coming out thin and unsteady. I take a breath, trying to sound confident, like I can handle this conversation. But the words won’t come together. *I feel weak, and I hate it.*

"That's fine, little one. I won't push. Just know that whenever you're ready, for whatever you need, I'll always be here to help you. You only have to ask." He turns to me, and his gaze says it all.

I am loved.

I am cherished.

I am not alone.

Chapter Six

Sofia – present day

The drive to my apartment is silent. I want to bite back somehow, to say something sassy to Hunter, but the words just won't come. My mouth tastes foul from all the throwing up, my skin itches, and my hands are trembling like I'm a weak little kid all over again. *God, I hate being weak.*

The desperate need to kiss him, to feel his skin against mine, to pull him close, is an aching, pulsing core inside me, screaming at the pain of not having him. But another part of me, the part that knows I'm not like other women, that knows I'm broken beyond repair, tells me that my needs and wants mean nothing. That love, closeness, intimacy... are not for women like me. I don't get to be loved, especially not by someone I love. There's no happy ever after for me. I'm broken. I'm disgusting. I'm dirty. How could I ever tell anyone what happened to me?

How could I ever tell Hunter?

The despair fills me as I walk to my apartment like a robot. Once inside, I toss my things on the entry table. When I hear the soft click of the door closing, instead of the loud thud I'm used to, it hits me. I'm not alone. Hunter is here. *Hunter is in my apartment.*

Oh my God. A man is in my apartment.

I take a few deep breaths, trying to summon any remaining strength because, damn it, I'm seconds from losing it, and he needs to leave.

Now!

I don't even hear him approach, but then I feel his hand on my shoulder, his presence behind me, and suddenly my survival instincts kick in. Before I even think, I grab his arm, throw him over, and he lands hard on the edge of the couch, rolling off.

The look on his face says it all. He expected this.

"*Cupcake*, I told you, I'm done playing games. Cut the crap. I know you love me, and *this is happening.*" His voice is gentle, but there's an edge of frustration beneath it, like he's annoyed that I won't accept this.

He's annoyed?

"Leave." My tone is so cold, so final, that even I'm surprised. I didn't think I could sound like that right now.

"No." The finality in his voice is like the bell ringing for the first round.

I'm not even sure what we're fighting for, but I sure as hell know one thing, it won't be me who loses.

I launch at him with everything I've got, driving forward with sharp kicks and precise punches, but he's always a step ahead. Every blow I throw is met with a casual deflection, a dodge, or a redirect, only serves to push me further off balance. I grit my teeth, feeling the burn of desperation rise in my chest. *How is he reading every move?* I adjust, switching up my stance, aiming for quick, unpredictable jabs, but it's like he's already mapped out my entire playbook. His expression is maddeningly calm, his body relaxed, as though this isn't even a fight. Each block he makes is infuriatingly effortless, as if I'm not even a challenge. *How is he doing this? I used to beat him regularly!*

"Still fighting me, huh?" he mutters, irritation clear in his voice as he ducks a kick and sidesteps, letting me stumble. I bite back a scream, throwing a quick series of strikes, but he absorbs or redirects every one. My heart is pounding, the edges of my vision blurring with frustration, and I know he can see it. "You're not going to win this, *cupcake*," he says, stepping in close, catching my wrist and twisting it just enough to unbalance me. In an instant, his leg sweeps out, hooking behind mine. The ground rushes up to meet me. He lowers me to the floor, his body pressing down as his weight pins me, his gaze unyielding as he holds me there, immobilised beneath him.

"Sofia, stop it! This isn't worth it, and you're not going to win." His gaze is soft, loving, so painfully gentle that it feels like a scream is building uncontrollably inside me.

I twist and push, trying to shake him off, even just to lift my leg and kick, but I'm completely immobilised. *Fucking hell, I hate being weak!* I breathe out the words through clenched teeth, "How are you doing this?"

"I learned all your moves by our third fight." He leans down, brushing a kiss on the tip of my nose. "I loved fighting you because I got to feel your skin against mine. I needed to feel you, Sofia. Everything about you drives me insane." The raw sincerity in his voice, the vulnerability in his eyes, fans the flame of my own painful need for him. *I want you so much!* I want to scream it, to let it rip through this silence, but I can't. I know I can't. The thought of actually having him, having this, only cuts deeper, a new kind of painful hell I've never felt before.

A cry of agony breaks free from me, raw and wild, so gut-wrenching, it shakes him. For the first time, he loosens his grip, caught off guard as he tries to pull himself back together.

"*Cupcake...*"

"Alex? Lockdown!" I command.

"Certainly, Sofia," the home AI confirms smoothly. Immediately, the windows shut, the doors reinforce, and hidden compartments around the room open to reveal weapons and vials of chemicals.

"What the fuck?!" Hunter's surprise is almost comical, and I seize the moment to drive a kick to his ribs, forcing him to shift.

"Easy, *cupcake...*" He trails off, tightening his hold on me with a half-smile, clearly amused by the AI. "Alex? Fancy." He's pleased, as if the AI's sophistication is the best part of his day. He starts peppering kisses over my face, each touch unraveling my defenses. *God, I want this so much!* His lips are heaven against my skin, each kiss breaking down my walls bit by bit until my resistance is slipping dangerously.

I let out another guttural scream as his touch rips at my resolve, leaving me seconds from surrendering. *I can't! I won't let this happen!*

"Stop it, Sofia! I *know* you love me! Stop fighting it! Stop fighting us!" His voice is raw, every word steeped in pain and frustration.

"You're delusional! I don't love you! Get off me, Hunter, or I'll hurt you!"

"No."

For the love of God, have mercy. Leave me alone! He's oblivious to the torment ripping through me. He presses his lips to mine, soft and tender, each kiss stripping away the armor I cling to.

"Hunter, stop it! Get off me!" I scream, trying to make him listen.

"No," he whispers against my ear, and the kiss that follows is searing. It's a devouring need that I can feel pulling me in, and I'm right on the edge of surrender.

"So what then? Are you going to take me by force?" The words cut through the air like a slap, and he recoils, leaping back as though I physically struck him. Confusion, pain, and regret twist across his face.

"I would never do that." He stumbles back, his face haunted, and I push myself against the wall, reaching for the knife hidden in the skirting board.

"Well, I didn't say yes, did I? So if you push yourself on me, Hunter, it's by force!" I lace every word with venom, driving the point home that whatever he thinks this is, it isn't going to happen. The lockdown means my dad and a team of guards are on their way. Just stall until they're here. I can hold out that long.

"I would never do that, *cupcake*." The hurt in his voice is genuine, piercing. I've wounded him, and I can see it. *Good. Maybe he'll leave me alone now, forget everything, and we can go back to normal.*

But he isn't moving. His voice drops, ragged with emotion. "I love you, Sofia. I've loved you since the first moment I saw you, and I'll love you until the day I die."

Shut up! My mind screams. *Don't say that to me!* I can't bear to hear it, to feel the weight of those words. I look down, trying to fight the tears pressing against my eyes, refusing to let them fall. I can't show emotion. I have to kill this once and for all. But my whole body feels paralyzed, and I can't even take the knife in my hand. All I can do is sit in silence, staring at his feet.

"I know you love me. I *know* you do. I could feel it when you kissed me." The need in his voice is devastating, and I feel him clinging to the barest hint of hope that this is mutual. I want to tell him to get out, to fuck off, but the words won't come out of my lips.

"*Cupcake*, please." His voice is pleading, almost desperate. "Whatever it is holding you back, please just talk to me. We can work through anything. I promise." He kneels in front of me, lifting my gaze to meet his. I see my own pain mirrored back at me, the love and confusion tangled with longing. All I can do is hold his gaze and let out a soft, defeated sigh.

***

Hunter – present day

What the hell is going on? What am I missing? I know she loves me, I can feel it radiating off her. She's lying to herself. I know it, as sure as I know my own heartbeat. She loves me, but she won't give in. She'd rather fight me, claw and scream through this than admit what's between us. I reach out, cupping her face, pressing my forehead to hers, and a deep sigh escapes me.

God, I love this woman with everything I am.

This firecracker of a woman, with her wit, elegance, and a beauty that rivals a goddess.

I can feel her trembling in my hands, her unspoken love echoing back to me, calling to me. I can feel it! But then why is she fighting this? Why is she fighting us? I let go, dropping down and wrapping my arms and legs around her, holding her close as I bury my face in the crook of her neck. Her skin feels divine under my touch. Every sparring match we've ever had, every blow exchanged, was worth it because it gave me a quick taste of her. But now... this is different. This is like holding my own heart in my hands.

Being with her feels as natural as breathing, as vital as air, water, or food. My *sugar cube* has become part of my very existence, my survival. Without her, there's no point to any of it. She's everything, my world, my reason, my future. I've known it for a while now. This is happening, whether she wants it or not, because *she's mine.*

"*Cupcake*, please..." I whisper in her ear, my voice barely steady. "Please stop fighting this. I know you love me as much as I love you. *Please.*" My voice is so small, desperate. I hardly recognise it as my own. I didn't know I was even capable of sounding like this, but if begging is what it takes to make her mine, then I'll beg every day of my life.

She trembles so intensely it scares me. *Am I doing the right thing here?* Does she need more time? I'd give her all the time in the world if it meant staying close to her, as long as she'd let me be right by her side. I can't, I won't, go back to pretending I don't need her as much as I need air. Not when she's the very reason I'm alive.

"Hunter, step away." Elijah's voice cuts through, yanking me from my plea back to an unwelcome reality. I know there's no holding back my beast any longer. She's mine, damn it. *All mine.* And nothing not him, not anyone, is going to stop me from having her. If I have to fight them both, or even kidnap her until she comes to her senses, then, so be it.

Walking away? Going back to what we had before? That's not an option.

"Elijah, don't do this. It won't end well," I say, every word sharpened with intent as I clutch her like she's my lifeline.

"No. It won't end well. The only option is for you to step back. It's your choice where you want to die, here or at the warehouse." His voice is disturbingly calm, cold, as if he were simply discussing his plans for the day instead of threatening my life.

Sofia lifts her head, glancing over my shoulder at Elijah, and a strange, wrenching sound escapes her, a deep cry of pure agony. I lift my gaze to meet hers, and the pain on her face tells me everything I need to know. She's fighting this. *She loves me.*

"*Cupcake*, please..." I lean in, pressing a soft kiss to her cheek. "I know you love me. Stop fighting it. Stop fighting *us*."

"Dad, please." Her voice, barely above a whisper, breaks between us.

As her words leave her beautiful lips, a single tear rolls down her cheek, fierce and fast, and lands on my shirt. I stare at the spot, numb. *What the hell is the point of it all?* My entire life, I've wandered aimlessly, trying to better myself, to master my beast, to control my impulses, and for what? What was the point of it all? Of being alive, of finding my mate, of realising she loves me... only for her to fight it? *What is going on?*

I reach for the spot on my shirt where her tear landed, tracing it like it holds magic, like rubbing it might somehow change my reality. Because this reality, this version where I lose her, can't happen. *I won't let it. She's mine.*

But then, I feel myself being shoved back with surprising force, thrown a few feet away as I stagger to keep my balance. Damn, I think, half in awe. This woman gives me a run for my money. I stand, love-struck and steady, reaching out to help her up, but she ignores my hand, standing on her own. *Hell, she'll be the death of me.*

"Leave," she says, one single word with devastating force.

"No." I hold her gaze, unwavering, my resolve like steel.

Her eyes narrow, holding all the menace she can muster, but I don't flinch. I'm not letting her go.

"Leave!"

"Never!"

I can feel her fury radiating off her, her breaths coming fast and deep, like she's seconds from losing control. "I would rather die a thousand deaths than leave you, Sofia! *Are you hearing me?* I would rather die than leave you! So if you want to kill me, here I am. Do your worst because I will never let you go. *Do you hear me, woman?!*" I scream, every word raw and unrestrained, hoping to shatter whatever wall she's built to keep me out. *She's mine, damn it!*

It's like my words hit her full force. She buckles, trembling as though she's unable to hold herself up any longer. Seeing her like this, broken and shaking from my words, shatters something in me, and an excruciating pain washes over me. *All I want is to love her, to care for her, to worship her.* Yet all I'm doing is causing her more pain. *How am I doing this?* Why is she fighting so hard to keep us apart?

"I love you, goddamn it! Stop fighting me! Stop fighting *us*! I know you love me!" My voice cracks, despair echoing through every word. I don't care anymore about holding back or pretending to be strong. *They can kill me if they want,* because I'm not letting her go. She's mine, whether she wants it or not, and someday, she'll learn to love me back if that is what it'll take.

"So be it." Elijah's hand settles down on my shoulder, signaling the end of the fight.

"Stop this, Sofia!" I plead, my words barely controlled. "I know I can make you happy. I know you love me. Why are you doing this?"

She straightens to her full height, and in her gaze, I see such profound grief and pain that it feels like my chest is splitting open. *Why is she doing this?* If she didn't care for me, she wouldn't be hurting like this. *What am I missing?*

"You can't force things like this, Hunter. If Sofia said no, it's a no." Elijah's tone is chillingly calm, emotionless, a blunt reminder of how ruthless he is. I meet his gaze, and I realise that, despite everything, he came here alone. No guards. No reinforcements. Just him, as if my love and her resistance were enough of a battle on their own.

"She didn't say no, Elijah. I *know* she loves me. She just won't admit it to herself, she just won't give in, and I don't know why." I sound pathetic, small, but I don't care. *She's mine. She's always been mine.*

"No, Hunter. It's going to always be a *NO.*"

Her words numb me, like a punch to the gut that leaves me reeling. For a moment, I feel like I might collapse under the weight of it, the force of the rejection pressing down. But I steady myself, turning slowly to meet her gaze. And there it is, her beauty, so magnetic it physically hurts. I lose myself in those eyes, again. She's heartbreakingly gorgeous, and damn it, I know she loves me. I was so sure I'd finally reached her, that I'd broken through. *Maybe I'm wrong,* but they'll have to kill me before I'll ever let go of her.

I keep staring, memorising every detail... her amasing eyes that slice through me, her soft yet powerful features, her full lips that felt like heaven on mine. She's mesmerising, and she's mine. She can resist it all she wants, but that doesn't change a thing.

"So be it, then." My voice is quiet, final. "You better kill me, because there's no reality I'll accept where you're not mine, *cupcake.*"

"Stop calling me *cupcake,*" she says, her voice betraying her, desperation and pain spilling out. At least I know I'll die a loved man. *She loves me. I know it.*

I turn to Elijah, meeting his steely gaze, and then nod. He holds my stare for a long moment, then turns, and I follow. All that needed to be said and done already took place. Nothing remains but the end. If my life is what my *sugar cube* wants, then that's what she'll get. I'd rather die than live without her.

Chapter Seven

Hunter

I don't even fight it, I get into the car next to Elijah and stare out the window as if this were any other day and not the day something inside me died, just before my body's about to go do the same.

How the hell did I end up here? Why is she doing this? I know she loves me. *I fucking know it!*

My blood's boiling, my skin itching and hot, and I'm seconds away from tearing this car to shreds. *Why the hell won't she give in? Am I not enough for her? Is she ashamed of me? Ashamed of what she feels for me?*

This pain is excruciating, ripping through me with such force that I feel numb, nauseous, lightheaded, the only thing I can do is give in to the beast roaring inside me. They'd better kill me because if they don't, this will end badly for them.

As we approach the warehouse, I notice we're flanked by three other cars. *Good.* At least Elijah isn't a fool, he knows I'll put up one hell of a fight for his daughter, so he'd better be prepared to finish this, because one way or another, this is happening. The drive's silent, Elijah sitting there with his eyes closed, "meditating" or whatever the hell he does. Clearly, he thinks I'm no threat, or he wouldn't have dropped his guard like that next to me.

I'm not a fucking threat. I just want your daughter, you bastard! I love her so much I worship the ground she walks on. She's mine. She's always been mine, damn it. But it's useless. Everything I could say, everything that could have had value, was already said back at her apartment. My touch, my words, my begging... none of it was enough to make her surrender to what she feels.

Maybe this is for the best. Maybe if they kill me, I'll finally be free of this pain, because living without her is something I cannot and will not do. Living next to her, not touching her, not kissing her now after knowing how she feels, how she tastes, it would be a living hell. *Never. You hear me, Elijah? Never!*

We park at one of our warehouses, out of sight from the world, oblivious to what's happening here. The engine cuts off, and they step out, Elijah turning to me with that cold, domineering expression he wears so well.

"Everyone deserves to be loved," he says, his voice chillingly calm. He pauses, holding my gaze. "But some things cannot be forced." The words ring in my mind, a final bell tolling the end of my last match.

There's nothing left to say or do. I know I'll die a loved man, even if she refuses to admit it. Even if she doesn't love me back, my love is strong enough for both of us, and I'll carry it until my final breath.

"She said no, and we will respect her decision..."

"No!" I cut him off, my voice raw. "She is mine! She's mine, damn it! So you'd better kill me, or I'll chase her to the end of the world and to the end of time."

"SHE. IS. MINE!" The conviction, fury, and desperation in my voice is so fierce that Elijah's mouth twitches into what can only be a smirk.

This isn't funny, you bastard. She's mine!

"Ah. I know what you're feeling. I understand more than you can imagine. And yes, you do deserve to die because you're forcing something that was refused. However, you're also a valuable member of my team," he says, unruffled, "and as I said, everyone deserves to be loved."

The words cut deep, leaving me feeling awkward, pathetic, shouting my love for someone who doesn't want me. *How the mighty have fallen.*

"It's your choice, Hunter. Go back to how things were before, or you'll be kept here in the warehouse, tortured, and eventually killed if you don't let go of this foolish idea that she is yours." His tone is calm, detached, as if we're discussing the weather and not the pure sadistic pain he's promising.

I hold his gaze and, without a second thought, seal my fate. "SHE. IS. MINE!"

With that, I open the door and walk into the warehouse, heading to the area where we typically "discuss" business, and sit down in the chair like it's nothing. Because, let's face it, it *is* nothing. Nothing they do to me will matter. Nothing they can use to torture me will hurt more than this bleeding, festering wound inside me. If anything, I hope they mess me up so badly I'm unconscious for a while, at least then, I'll get some goddamn relief from this pain.

When Elijah stands in front of me, looking down, I almost hope he'll see the depth of my feelings for his daughter. If he were capable of feeling, maybe he'd understand what it means to love someone so much that they become your entire existence. That is not gravity holding you in place, *it's her*. Maybe he would understand that this is not just an obsession, this it's life itself, she is the reason I breathe and I'd face any hell and any pain, to be with her.

She doesn't want me? Fine. I want her. And I'll fight until my last breath to have her. She's mine, and sooner or later, her dad and my *sugar cube* will have to accept that or kill me.

"Do your worst," Elijah says before he turns and leaves. Ruthless, clinical, deadly, that's Elijah to a tee.

"No hard feelings, Hunter. It's nothing personal, just orders," one of the guys says, regret lacing his tone.

"It's all good, mate. The things we do for love, hey?" I wink at him, and he gives me a look full of regret before driving his fist into my face with brutal force. Blood sprays instantly, some landing on my shirt, and panic hits me hard.

The shirt.

Her tear...

I need to protect it.

I shoot to my feet, and at my abrupt movement, they all jump back as if I struck them. "Relax, guys. I'm not going to fight you. Just... let me keep my shirt clean, all right?" I say, carefully peeling it off and making my way to the corner, where I place it neatly on a chair. "That's all I have from my *cupcake*, so we can't let it get ruined."

Returning to my seat, I grin at the bewildered guys. They're probably wondering how their boss, the man they've followed into hell and back, could be enough of a fool in love to keep a shirt. *Let them wonder.* These guys looked up to me once, and now they're ordered to beat me within an inch of my life or maybe even finish me. But I don't care anymore. She's mine until my last breath.

One of them ties my arms behind the chair, probably thinking I might fight back. But he doesn't understand *I need this pain.* I need it to cut through the deadly poison running through my veins, through my mind, of wondering if she really doesn't love me. I need this fight so much it feels like I'm suffocating, as if I'm underwater, gasping for air. *So bring it, boys. Do your worst!*

The next punch slams into my jaw, snapping my head back as the sharp, metallic taste of blood fills my mouth. Pain flares up, white-hot, radiating from my face, but I grit my teeth, and hold steady, refusing to give them the satisfaction of seeing me flinch. Another blow lands, this time in my ribs, and I feel something crack, pain ripping through me like wildfire. Blood drips from my chin, splattering onto the floor as I breathe through the pounding in my skull. *Let them hit me.* I'd take this and more a hundred times over before I'd give her up.

They don't hold back, and neither do I. My gaze stays steady, even as my vision blurs with each hit. The pain in my temples pounds like a relentless drumbeat, but I embrace it. The fire in my body is fierce, but I welcome it, because as long as I can feel, I don't have to let go.

I spit out a tooth, and the sharp tang of iron coats my tongue. I grin, blood pooling between my teeth, staining the cracks in my smile. My wrists burn against the restraints, the rough fibers tearing into my skin as I strain. Blood seeps freely from my hands, soaking into the rope, but I don't care.

Every bruise. Every broken rib.

I'd take it all for her, a thousand times over, because there's nothing, *nothing*, they can do to make me let her go.

She. Is. Mine!

Chapter Eight

Sofia

The air is filled with the sweet, heady scent of lilacs, mingling with the salty tang of the ocean breeze. Here, in my secluded oasis, I've always found solace, a quiet comfort against the tumult of my thoughts. Memories of my beloved riad, fragrant with lilacs and orange blossom, have been my anchor whenever life began crumbling around me. I can recall once more the scent, the breeze, the feeling all of it. But today, even those memories aren't enough.

I collapsed to the floor as soon as they left, unable to lift myself, unable to brush myself off. *How can I possibly move on from this?*

I force my mind to Tangier, to the beautiful memories of its rich history, vibrant architecture, and winding streets. I remember the thrill of slipping away from my guards in those labyrinthine alleys, rebelling against my dad's control. How unimpressed he was when they found me eating from a local vendor like it was nothing. Because to me, it was. For one moment, I just wanted to be a simple girl, to be free.

Desperation pulls me back to memories of my riad, to the tranquil feeling of sitting with a book each day, surrounded by peace. I remember the beautiful tilework, how the home blended traditional Moroccan design with European touches, making it feel just right for Dad. He used to say he loved the place because it had "*one eye on the past and one on the future.*" At the time, I thought it was a strange thing to say, almost foolish. But now, I understand. In life's most shattering moments, when the future feels impossible to see, you keep one eye on the past to carry you through the pain and uncertainty.

I recall it as if I'm there, seated on the plush lounger, reading my book, the gentle creak of the riad's wooden beams harmonising with the rustle of leaves in the courtyard. Afternoons spent with my characters, the pages fluttering in the warm breeze as I lounged beneath the shade of orange trees. The sun kissed my skin, while the distant call to prayer echoed through the streets, grounding me in a rare peace.

Each beautiful memory of Morocco feels as vivid as the pain now consuming me, and for the first time in my life, it's not enough.

This excruciating ache in my chest won't ease, it feels like it will swallow me whole. *Why did he have to love me back?*

I reach for any memory, any refuge that might dull this reality and then it hits me, sharp as a knife... *my dad will kill Hunter.*

I have to stop him!

I have to stop him now!

Sofia

Don't kill him. He is valuable to the organisation. This, too, shall pass.

Dad

Little one, this too shall pass.

I knew he'd understand why I'm asking, how I'm begging him to let it go and not to kill him.

This too shall pass.

But I'm not really sure it will.

I manage to lift myself, the pain in my side settling into a dull ache, and I make my way to the home console to cancel the lockdown. We developed this security system years ago, installing it in every home we own around the globe. This is the first time I've activated *Alex*, so at least it wasn't a total waste of money. Though I do need to check if all the chemicals are active... for the life of me, I can't bring myself to care right now. All I care about is Hunter and how much it's breaking me to push him away.

How could I ever tell him I'm different? Show him my scars, let him see me like that, endure his disgust or, even worse, his pity.

I'd rather die than see anyone's pity. The only problem is... I want to die right there, next to him.

If Dad decides to kill him, I'll ask him to kill me too because living without Hunter isn't something I know how to do anymore.

Dad

You were right. He's valuable to the organisation, so I didn't kill him. Instead, he's being tortured until he lets go of this foolish idea that you are his.

I want to beg him to let Hunter go. I want to fall to my knees in front of my dad, to lower myself to his feet and plead as if it were my own life he's torturing. *Because that's exactly what he's doing, torturing my soul.* A deep, guttural cry escapes me, raw and unrestrained, perfectly expressing the agony clawing through me.

But he won't understand. No one will. What those monsters did to me is beyond despicable, and there's nothing anyone can do to erase the scars, to restore what's missing, what's broken.

Sofia

Yes. He will learn to let go.

I hope with everything I am that he will learn to let go.

Please Nuuro, let go.

Chapter Nine

Sofia – 13 years old

My underwear is bothering me so much and this pad is the worst. I have tried so many different brands over the past year and it is always the same. This month's period is especially painful. It feels like something is ripping at my skin down there and it hurts so much. I am too scared to tell anyone, especially that nasty nurse. I hope all the worst things in the world happen to her.

There is this deep, stabbing pain on the sides of my hips that makes me curl into a ball on my bed, clutching my knees. I do not know what to do. And to make it worse, the pain in my vagina is so sharp and deep, like it's tearing. *Can it actually tear?*

I should have researched it.

Then again, the last time I looked up anything about vaginas, it felt like my whole world was falling apart. How could it be that I am so different from everyone else? I felt trapped, robbed, damaged, broken. It took me ages, staring at those photos, to understand that this is what a vagina is supposed to look like.

That image was normal.

And mine is not.

Mine is closed up.

The nightmares came back, and all the flashbacks from when that awful woman mutilated me rushed back with a vengeance.

For the past year, I have started hating all the girls around me. Why should they be so lucky to be perfect down there, while I have to walk around with discomfort every single day because of something that was done to me? Why should they get to live normal lives while I have to suffer? You know what? It's not fair. So I decided to make them feel some of the pain I carry every day.

Pretty, rich bitches. Who do they think they are?

I beat Corina, that little whore, within an inch of her life. Because I could, and because she is a whore. Let's face it, I was doing everyone a favour.

When I smacked Claudia for being her usual annoying self, I felt her pain. She did not deserve it. I was sorry, but I could not back down. I had an image to protect, and that image said *come near me or try to hurt me in any way, and I will fuck you up.*

I remember when my dad took me as a child. All those memories came flooding back. I can still see the blood, smell the metallic tang in the air, and feel the people crowded around. I remember how I fought and kicked at that nasty old woman with her filthy blade. I remember my screams. I remember the sewing. I remember Dad.

And I remember the vow I made to myself. *Never again! I would never let anyone hurt me in any way.*

I guess I am lucky. Until now, I have had my dad protecting me so thoroughly it feels suffocating. But on the other hand, he kept the nightmares at bay. He fought my battles for me. And he won them.

Now that I know I am different, I know I will need to protect myself for the rest of my life. Yes, I will have my dad, but this side of me, this pain, this shame, this emptiness, it is mine to guard.

He has never pushed the subject all these years. He has never asked me questions about it. Even when the fighting started and I began to enjoy beating the crap out of people, he never asked me why. He never once told me off or acted embarrassed by me. That is my dad. Some people might think there is something wrong with him, but I know better. He is different. He is special.

Most of all, he took me and protected me when the very people who should have looked after me were the ones hurting me in ways I could not endure. *Why? The only thing I have ever wanted to know is why.*

How could I ever tell someone that my folds are stuck together? How could I go to anyone and say that I am mutilated? How could I admit that I am damaged? Because to me, being mutilated means being damaged.

This is what they did to me. This is what my own family did to me. *Why?*

I know my dad loves me, in his own way, but he loves me. He has always taken care of me since he took me. I know I can tell him anything and he will help me, protect me, and cherish me. But how can I tell him I am damaged? How can I tell him about something that cannot be fixed? Something that is not reversible? I cannot. I just cannot.

It is gruesome. It is shameful. It is degrading.

If what happened to me is all of those things, then what does that make me? Am I not broken? Am I not damaged? Am I not disgusting?

This past year has been absolutely awful. All the memories, all the pain of becoming a woman, all the self-loathing, all the self-degradation.

It feels strange, because sometimes it feels like two different people live in my mind. There is the little girl who keeps telling me I am worthless, damaged, broken, and unlovable. Then there is the girl who growls at everyone to stay away or she will chop their heads off, the one who is hurting for pleasure, just to make sure she is not the only one suffering.

Sometimes I wish I was not intelligent, because if I were as clueless as my colleagues, I would not overthink everything around me or understand my reality. I would live happily in a bubble of stupidity, patting myself on the back each day for how great I am.

I hate being smart. It just feeds my insecurities and my pain, adding to my complete and utter uncomfortable existence.

I wish I could bury it deep down in my mind, lock it away, and throw the key as far as I could. But I know that the girl giving the middle finger to the world is not going anywhere. She woke up when I was five, and now she is roaring at full volume in my mind.

There is no burying it for me. There is no relief, and there is no one I can talk to. It is as simple as that.

That stupid, nasty, old bitch of a nurse, telling me I am how I am supposed to be. Why didn't she think to ask my dad questions about why I am like this? Why didn't she think to actually help me?

If there is ever a nuclear bomb, I hope it lands right on her crotch and blows her into a million little pieces. Stupid, useless bitch.

Maybe I should beat her up for being such a nasty old woman.

A sharp pain explodes on the right side of my pelvis, and I squeak in pain.

"For fuck's sake!" A soft cry escapes my dry throat.

I have not been able to eat or drink since I woke up. I had to tell Buddy to call the school and let them know I am not coming in. I have been curled up in a fetal position since the morning, and the only thing I have done is go to the toilet, where I found blood on my knickers again.

"I fucking hate this! I fucking hate being a woman!" My voice is high-pitched and loud, full of pain and sorrow for my miserable existence.

I lay there as wave after wave of pain reminds me that I am a woman now, that my value is to pop out kids and serve a husband. For fuck's sake! It is a good thing I am not living in one of those countries and that my dad took me, because I would have murdered any bastard who came anywhere near me.

Another guttural scream of pain escapes me, and my entire body feels itchy. I cannot sit still anymore.

I make my way to the bathroom and turn on the tap, making sure the water is as hot as I can bear it. Once I lower myself into the tub, I close my eyes and try to relax. The sensation of the hot water on my skin dulls the itching, at least a little, and I rest there, trying to bring my mind back to the beautiful riads in full bloom. I was so happy in Morocco. I was happy anywhere but here in London.

As the painful memory of being forced to move so I could have a "normal" life takes over, the images of me leaving Morocco blur over the sunsets in the riads. My heart aches as those memories mix, and I open my eyes.

The gruesome image that takes over my reality feels like it is written in the depths of hell. The water around me is no longer clear. It has turned almost completely red. I am covered in my own blood, and in this moment, all my nightmares have come true.

The sobs that wrack my body are paralysing.
I cannot move.
The only thing I can do is cry...

Chapter Ten

Hunter – 17 years old

I make my way back into the house as quietly as I can. Today was another shit day at school, a day where yet another idiot thought it was a good idea to provoke me. I had to beat him to a pulp to remind him of his place in the world.

People can lie to themselves all they want, but in the real world, there are predators and prey. Sure, there are anomalies those so-called "normal" people, but they're the exception, not the rule.

I'm *not prey*. Never was, never will be. And I know one day I'll kill. Just not today.

Dad's been home for a few days, and as much as he's always encouraged me to "unleash the beast," I know he'll have a go at me for letting the other guy land a few punches. But that's part of the plan. I let them hit me, just enough to feel like they're getting somewhere. If I didn't, if I let loose and showed them even a glimpse of what's inside me or worse, destroyed someone without giving them a chance they'd think I'm some kind of freak.

And then what? Everyone would avoid me.

I can't let that happen. As much as I feel the urge to hurt, I refuse to become an outsider in my own story. So, I play along. I let them land a few hits, throw them a bone with a comment like, "Not bad," or "You almost had me," just to keep the facade going. No one can know what's really lurking beneath the surface.

My dad knows. He's been training me for as long as I can remember, and it's true *practice makes perfect*. If it weren't for his skills drilled into me, I'd have killed that idiot in front of everyone within the first five minutes of the fight. But again, I can't risk anyone knowing who I really am.

As I head upstairs, I catch a glimpse of my reflection in the theater room's French doors. Yep, I'm screwed. The asshole landed a solid hit, and now there's a bruise blooming on my face. I already know what's coming, an earful and probably one of Dad's "creative" punishments.

While other parents might send their kids to bed without dinner, take away their allowance, or come up with whatever clever ways normal parents punish their kids, my dad... he has his own methods.

I'll never forget the time I came home with a black eye from a fight. Dad stripped me down to my boxers and made me lie on the garage floor while he hosed me with cold water. ALL! NIGHT! LONG! It was the dead of winter.

I didn't let anyone land a punch on me for two years after that. Not at school, not in training. I knocked people out so fast I scared myself, all because I couldn't risk ending up on that floor again.

He never had to do it twice.

I learned my lesson.

As I near my door, I catch a faint, pained noise coming from down the hall. At first, I think I'm imagining it, just a trick of my overactive mind after a long day. But then something in me starts to panic, an alarm deep in my brain registering that sound as my mum.

It can't be her. She's never home this early. She always gets in long after I've finished training. This has to be in my head.

I push open the door to my room, shaking the thought off, but then I hear it again a soft, broken sound, barely more than a whisper. And that's when the panic fully sets in.

Something's wrong.

Something is very, very wrong.

My steps are feather light, my breathing steady and quiet as I make my way toward my parents' room. Each step feels heavier than the last, like I'm walking into a question I don't want to ask. *Why would my mum make a sound like that?*

I freeze in front of the door, straining to pick up any noise, any sign that this is all in my head. *Please, let it all be in my head.*

But then I hear my dad's voice, and it hits me like every punishment he's ever inflicted sharp, brutal, and inescapable.

"You like that, slut?!" His voice is cruel, dripping with venom, each word laced with dominance and rage. *"Who told you you're allowed to go to the shop?"* he snarls, the tone that always makes me feel like a small, insignificant boy cowering before a giant. *"You like men looking at you? Do you, slut?"*

What the fuck is going on?

For the first time, I understand what people mean by cold sweat. My body is burning and freezing at the same time, drenched in terror. My feet feel bolted to the floor, not by logic or reason, but by sheer terror of what I might see on the other side of the door.

I want to move. I want to act. But I can't. Some invisible force, fear, dread, maybe both holds me in place paralysing me.

"You think you can look other men in the eyes, slut, and I'd just allow it? Like it's nothing?"

That soft sound comes again, fragile and faint, cutting through the air like a knife. My whole body feels like it's on fire, my blood boiling in my veins while my skin crawls with an icy, sweat-slick chill.

What the fuck is going on?

I force my body to move, to open the door and confront whatever is waiting on the other side. But it's like I'm no longer in control, this invisible, suffocating force has me pinned. It's holding me down, drowning me in fear.

I want to move. I *need* to move.

But I can't.

Why the fuck am I not moving?!

There's silence thick and heavy for what feels like an eternity. I pour every ounce of mental strength into commanding my body to move, but the bastard just sits there, frozen, staring at the door like it's a gateway to hell itself.

"You will never go to the shop alone, ever again, slut!" My dad's voice cuts through the quiet, raw and dominating. I feel a bead of sweat trickle down my spine, cold and deliberate, landing at the waistband of my pants.

"From now on, you'll do online orders with pick-up only. Is that clear, you filthy, nasty excuse for a whore?"

No.

No, no, no. He's not talking to my mum. He can't be. My dad loves her.

They have the perfect marriage. She's always supported him, always taken care of the house, of me, of everything when he's away. *He loves her.*

He wouldn't speak to her like this. He wouldn't.

Would he?

"Just to make sure my point is clear, you nasty excuse for a wife, you'll get ten more."

The force that had been paralysing me shifts, flipping from overwhelming fear to an all-consuming rage. In an instant, I'm no longer frozen. My body moves on its own, driven by something primal, something unstoppable.

Before I can fully process what I'm doing, my boot slams into the door, sending it flying open with a crash.

And there it is.

Hell.

My mum is on the floor, crumpled on top of some torn cloths. Her clothes are ripped, her stomach covered in these shallow, neat cuts. They're not deep just enough to bleed, just enough to make it hurt. Blood drips from them, slow and thin, tracing lines down her skin and pooling around her.

I freeze again, my mind scrambling to make sense of the scene in front of me. My stomach churns, my breath catching in my throat. Then my eyes meet hers.

Terror.

Pure, unfiltered terror.

The kind of fear I could never have imagined on my mum's face. And now, it's burned into my mind forever.

If I thought I knew what pain was, one look at her taught me otherwise. This was pain. *Real pain.* The kind that shatters something inside you and leaves it broken forever.

"Hunter, my boy..."

His voice cuts through the air, but it's like my brain refuses to process the words. Complete silence takes over, an empty void where thoughts should be.

I just stand there, frozen in the doorway, staring at my bleeding mum. There's this new sound now a high-pitched white noise, faint but deafening at the same time, drowning out everything else.

I feel a hand on my shoulder. The touch is firm but not forceful, almost casual. When I turn, I see him.

If I expected him to look angry, annoyed, or even furious, I was wrong. His eyes meet mine, calm and steady, the same way they always are when he's teaching me something like this is just another day. Just another lesson.

Then I notice the knife in his hand, the blade glinting in the light. My stomach twists, a sick, heavy knot pulling me under.

And I know.

I just know.

Today is the day I will kill.

"...This is an important lesson, son," he says, his voice low and even, as if he's explaining how to fix a car or tie a knot. "You're old enough now, and this is how you train your wife to be obedient. Soon enough, you'll get married, and you'll need to know how to educate your woman. She must respect you, whether you're around or not..."

It's like someone just punched my brain, hard and square. Did he seriously just say I need to learn how to "educate" a woman? That I'll soon get married? *What the actual hell?*

"Come, son, let me teach you the death by a thousand cuts," he says.

I raise my gaze and see him moving toward Mum again, intent on teaching me something...

Before I fully realise it, I'm running. I throw all my weight into a shove, knocking him off his path. I don't stop to see how he lands or if I hit him squarely. I just need to get to Mum, to protect her.

Whatever he thinks he's going to do with that knife, he'll have to get through me first before he touches her again.

"Son, what are you doing?" My dad's voice is low, menacing, the kind that makes sweat pour down my back like I'm on command.

I don't care if I die a sweaty mess and people laugh at my funeral. He's going to have to kill me first before he touches her again.

"You're not fucking touching her, Dad. What the fuck?" My voice comes out panicked, shaky so alien to me I barely recognise it.

I know he hears it. *The fear*. The emotions I can't hide. I know he'll use it against me, twist it the way he always does. But I don't care.

"My boy," he says, his voice disturbingly calm, "as I told you, sluts need to be treated as such and taught valuable lessons like not making eye contact with men. Do you know what your mum did?"

He straightens to his full height, towering over me like he always has. For years, I wanted nothing more than to be like him. I thought his strength, his discipline, his control were what made him *a man*.

But now, as I stand here, something inside me cracks. The foundation of everything I've believed about him, about us, is splintering under the weight of what I'm seeing. It's not strength I see in him now.

"Tell him, slut!" His voice booms, authoritarian, as if he commands existence itself.

Behind me, the soft sound of Mum's cries reaches my ears. *It's heart-shattering.*

Nothing in this world could break me more than this: seeing her like this, crumpled on the floor, bleeding, humiliated, and broken into pieces.

"Tell him, slut, how you smiled at that man," he says, his tone disturbingly casual, as if this is perfectly normal. "Only sluts go to shopping centers alone, my boy. There are men there, waiting to prey on women by themselves. They rape them. And if they raped them, it wouldn't even be a problem, but they kill them too."

All the feeling drains from my body. I'm numb.

What. The. Actual. Fuck?!

"So, your dear mummy not only went to the shop by herself, right under my nose, but she had the courage to smile at someone. The fucking piece of shit slut." His voice drips with venom, each word laced with malice.

For the first time in my life, I see it... his real monster, his real beast, in its purest form.

"Did you get raped as well, slut?" he sneers. "Maybe I should cut your cunt off so no one can touch you ever again."

My mum's sobs grow louder, shaking the room, breaking through the suffocating haze that has kept me frozen. It's her cries that snap me out of my paralysis.

Nothing else matters now. All that matters is protecting her.

Fuck, my dad is big. He's a giant. But I'd rather die than let him lay another hand on her.

"Now that Hunter knows, I can cut you as much as I want, wherever I want, you dirty piece of shit. I'll make him watch. I'll teach him how to make a woman behave."

It's like everything slows down, my brain barely able to process the words before my mum's cry of despair cuts through me.

Then instinct takes over.

The pain in my knuckles registers just as I see my dad's body staggering backwards. *I made it count.* Just like he taught me.

"Make the first punch count," his voice echoes in my mind, like a sick joke now.

My body moves on autopilot, following the lessons he drilled into me for years. *"Continue with the element of surprise while your opponent is stunned or immobilised, and land another strike true."*

I see his mouth open he's saying something, but I don't care. I leap into the air, driving both boots into his chest with all my weight.

The sickening crack that follows confirms it.

I hurt him.

Maybe he's not as invincible as I thought. Maybe I can fight him off. Maybe I don't need to die today.

"Hunter, you don't want to do this," he says, his tone mocking, like he's talking to the toddler version of me.

"There's a rule in this world I taught you since you were little," he continues, his voice dripping with derision. "There are only killers in this world, and there is prey."

Before I can react, he shoves me off him with terrifying ease, like I weigh nothing.

Like *I am nothing.*

I heard the crack, right? I hurt him, didn't I?

"You need to choose, my boy. Right here, right now!"

As he rises to his full height, towering over me like the giant he's always been, I know.

I just know...

One of us will die today.

"Are you a killer, or are you prey?"

The finality in his voice sends a shiver through me, and for the first time, I truly believe it. He knows it, too.

Today is the day he'll kill his own family.

I'm only seventeen. My entire life, I've trained, studied, fought, and fucked my way through it all and for what? I've achieved nothing.

If I die today, it'll be like I never existed in the first place.

The truth sinks in, bitter and heavy. My life is empty, pathetic, even if, from the outside, I'm the strongest one in most rooms.

But despite it all, my heart is screaming at me now, screaming that none of that matters. The only thing I'm living for, the only thing that means anything, is protecting my mum.

At all costs.

"I am no son of yours, you piece of shit," I spit, holding his gaze. "You will never touch her again."

The stillness in my voice surprises even me. It takes a second to realise, yes, I do sound confident now. Maybe it's the crack I thought I heard, or maybe it's the resignation that if I die defending my mum, it'll be a good way to go. Maybe my life wasn't all for nothing after all.

Whatever it is, my entire being shifts into fight mode.

I leap onto the side chair, driving my elbow down hard on the top of his head. The impact sends him staggering back, shaking his head like he's trying to clear it. Dizzy. Stunned.

"Very well," he says, his voice calm but laced with venom. "You made your choice, Hunter."

And then it starts...

The first punch lands square in my ribs, and the air explodes from my lungs like I've been hit by a truck. I stagger back, clutching at my side, but he doesn't let up.

He's faster than I expected, his movements precise, practiced. His fist connects with my jaw, whipping my head to the side. My vision blurs, and the metallic tang of blood fills my mouth.

"Defend yourself, boy!" he growls, circling me like a predator sizing up its prey.

I raise my arms, trying to block the strike aimed at my head, but his knee drives into my stomach. I double over, gasping for air.

Behind me, my mum's broken voice cuts through the chaos. "Stop it! Please! He's just a boy!" Her cries pierce me deeper than the pain ripping through my body.

I force myself forward, launching a calculated strike at his side. My fist connects, solid and true, but he barely flinches. With a sneer, he brings his elbow down on my shoulder, sending a jolt of agony through my arm and driving me to my knees.

"Is that all you've got, Hunter?" he mocks, kicking me hard in the ribs. I roll to the side, my body screaming for mercy as I struggle to breathe.

My mum is sobbing now, her voice raw and desperate. "Don't do this! You'll kill him!"

Her words fuel me, even as I feel like my body might give out. The ache in my ribs, the burning in my lungs, the blood dripping from the corner of my mouth. All of it pales compared to the fire in my chest.

I push myself up, my arms trembling under the weight of my body and his blows. "I'm not prey," I gasp, my voice shaky but defiant. "Not yours."

He comes at me again, fists swinging with brutal precision, and I know *I'm losing this fight*. But if I can keep him away from her, if I can hold him off for even a moment longer, it'll be worth it.

My vision is blurry, my breathing shallow, and my entire body is screaming at me to run, to hide, to never look back.

Fuck that! I'll take it. I'll endure whatever he sends my way. Maybe, just maybe, I'll tire him out, and his beast will be satisfied enough for him to leave her alone.

So what if I won't be able to walk for days after this? As long as he doesn't kill me, the rest will heal. Well... my flesh will heal. My heart, the memories of my mum like this, those will be engraved in my soul for the rest of my days.

She will never be in this situation again, because even if he lets us live today, the moment I can walk, I'm taking her, and we're getting the hell out of here.

At this point, the pain is so great it feels like I'm having an out-of-body experience. It's almost as if I'm floating above my body, watching from above as my dad beats me senseless. The look in his eyes makes his intent clear.

I have minutes to live. This is it, ladies and gentlemen. This is the way I'll go – by the hand of the man who brought me into this world.

His arms swing back, gathering all the force he can muster to inflict as much pain as possible. For a moment, it's like he's more beast than man, and all he wants is to end my life, no matter the cost.

I can hear my mum's voice in the distance, as if she's somewhere far away. I hope she's happy wherever she is now. I hope she ran. I hope she finds her happiness there.

It takes me a second to realise I'm delusional. She can't be in some faraway land because she was just on the floor, bleeding a second ago. How heart warming that my first instinct was to wish her well.

I chuckle inwardly, then notice my dad's shocked expression. Maybe I even laughed out loud. Ha! That would've pissed him off, to see me laugh as he delivers deadly blows, trying to beat me into the ground.

"I love you, Mum." My voice is so small I doubt anyone could hear it over the unmistakable sound of flesh striking flesh. But it doesn't matter. What matters is that I said it. My last words were for the woman who always cared for me and loved me despite my faults.

I let go and close my eyes. My entire body pulses with pain, and I know the end is near. The ringing in my ears drowns out everything else. Note to self: if I survive this, punching someone in the ear is surprisingly effective.

A few moments pass, and I feel an overwhelming weight press down on me. I don't have the strength to open my eyes, to see what he's thrown onto me, but for fuck's sake, he could at least end it quickly. His hands around my neck would do the job faster than suffocating me under this weight. A disgusting bastard to the very end.

Muffled voices echo next to me, and I try with everything I have to open my eyes. Maybe I can catch a glimpse of my mum, make sure she's okay.

The weight lifts off me, and I gasp, my lungs burning as I cough uncontrollably. Fuck my life. Everything hurts.

One of my eyes finally obeys, opening halfway, and I see my mum hovering over me, desperately trying to stop the bleeding. If she's taking care of me, who's going to take care of her?

"Hunter, baby, can you hear me?" Her voice is frantic, full of panic, and it cuts through me like a knife. I want nothing more than to reassure her that everything will be okay. But the truth is, I don't think it will be.

I look to the side and see my dad on the floor, face down, next to me. *What the fuck?*

"Whaaa...?" My voice trails off, unable to finish the word.

"I had to!" Her voice is full of raw despair, the weight of this entire nightmare in those three words. "He would've killed you, baby. I had to! I had to defend my baby!" The words stumble out, but before she can finish, my dad lets out a low groan.

Both of us freeze.

He's not dead. He'll get up and kill us both.

I search for my mum's gaze. When she looks at me, I see it clearly in her eyes. She's lost. Her reality shattered, and she's truly gone.

I don't know how much time has passed, but somehow I manage to roll onto my side, just enough to see my dad. I need to know if he's coming to, if he's about to start attacking us again.

It's then that I notice the knife, just inches from my mum. She's shaking uncontrollably, but what really scares me is the way her head twitches, jerking as though mimicking the motion of her neck being snapped or how her head would look if she were hanged. That shit terrifies me on a whole new level, and I know I need to snap her out of wherever her mind has gone. She's truly losing it, and if she stays in that state any longer, she might not come back.

"Mum..." I try calling out to her, but nothing. I'm fairly sure the words came out of my mouth, that they weren't just in my head.

"Mum..." I try again, and this time, I know for sure the words left my lips. Still nothing.

When my dad starts moving again, I know I have just a few more minutes before all is lost. I need to end this, or he will kill us both.

I stretch my arm towards the knife, my muscles feeling like they're made of lead. The moment my fingers make contact, a wave of survival washes over me. *Maybe today isn't the day I die.*

I pull the knife towards me as my dad begins to stir, and as fast as I can, I shove his dead weight, forcing him to face me. I want to see the man I once worshipped, the one whose footsteps I followed for as long as I remember. But all I see now is the man who broke my mum. The beast that had always been there, hiding in plain sight.

I drive the knife into the only vulnerable spot I can find, under his jawline. He grabs my arm, and pure panic floods my brain.

Before I can consciously decide, my survival instinct takes over. I punch the bottom of the knife, driving it fully into his skull.

Only when his hand drops from my arm do I realise what I've done. *I've just killed my dad.*

I look at my hand, still resting on the knife handle, and can't believe I stabbed him to death.

I killed a monster. A beast who hurt my mum, who hurt me. But I did it.

I always knew that one day I'd kill. What I never imagined was that my first kill would be the man I always wanted to become.

Chapter Eleven

Hunter

Present day

My back is killing me, as I snap awake from another nightmare about my dad, the Captain, all other shit I went through. All the crap they pulled. All the crap I missed until it was too late.

What was that saying? Something about doing the same stupid thing twice meaning you are stupid? Or something like that. Who the hell knows. What I do know is that my back is bloody killing me, and the chain around my ankle is annoying as hell at this point. Let's be honest, I probably deserve it.

It has been four months in this warehouse, and after I sent my guards to the ER the first time, Elijah, in all his wisdom, decided to put chains on me as if that would help the situation.

Out of being beaten unconscious, nightmares about my demons, and the pain my *sugar cube* inflicts on me, my beautiful queen still takes the win.

Why will she not give in? What the hell is wrong with me that she is acting so badly, even though I know she loves me? *She does love me, right?*

I sit up and lean my back against the wall, sighing at the cold sensation. It feels as warm as the dead winter in Antarctica. The fact that I am shirtless does not help, but there is no way I am using my shirt. That is the only thing I have of my *sugar cube*... it needs to be cherished.

This excruciating pain in my chest is drowning me again, and I can feel my beast roaring within me. Maybe if I distract myself with my other nightmares, it would ease the hell I am in now.

My mind drags me back to when I found my Captain assaulting one of the female SASR. How he was choking her while pounding into her violently. How her hands were clawing at his arms, and her legs were flailing in every direction, trying to push him off. How there were two other soldiers in the room watching the entire horror, rubbing their filthy dicks over their pants, enjoying the scene in front of them.

I remember that bastard George approaching me when he noticed I was there, leaning in close to whisper in my ear: "Hey Hunter. Captain is just enjoying himself a bit. Then we can have the leftovers. You can join, but you will need to stay in line and wait your turn."

I remember the utter disgust that settled like a rock in the pit of my stomach at hearing his words. "Leftovers." "Wait my turn."

What. The. Actual. Fuck!

The look on my face must have said it all because he dared to put his filthy hand on my shoulder, squeezing it in what he must have thought was a reassuring way, and continued his word vomit. "It's ok, mate. The Captain always shares, and today it was Justine's turn to do her female duties."

The laugh that came out of him at his own sick joke will haunt me until the day I die.

I look over at Justine. She is thrashing her body like a wild animal, desperate to escape.

None of this is normal.

None of it!

This is as fucked up as it gets, and she is being raped right in front of me. And this idiot is telling me to wait my turn to rape her.

Is he fucking high?

I look over at Chris, and the bastard has his dick out now. He is jerking himself off like this is just another normal day where someone being raped is something to get off on.

What the fuck is going on?!

I look back at the desk, and the Captain is so violent with his movements that little shocked cries escapes Justine. Then I see the blood.

My entire beast comes to life in one go, and all the pain from my dad comes bubbling to the surface with a vengeance.

I am on autopilot now, only registering the large missing part of George's head when his body hits the ground. I aim my gun at Chris and shoot him in the hand still holding his dick. The excruciating growl of pain that explodes out of him makes my chest feel a little lighter. I know I hit my target. He will suffer until I deal with the Captain.

I turn and aim my gun at the Captain, but he is already holding a gun to Justine's chest. He is not moving anymore, but he is still buried inside her.

What sort of sick fuck do you have to be to keep raping someone during a life-and-death situation?

"Hunter, my boy!" His tone is cheerful, as if this is just a misunderstanding and all of this will sort itself out in a few seconds. "You did not need to shoot the guys to get some pussy," he says, smiling menacingly over his shoulder. "You could have just asked me to leave you some good pussy before she passes out. No need to be rude."

The conviction and detached tone in his voice stand in complete contrast to the atrocity he is committing.

"Now be a good boy, sit down, and enjoy yourself while I empty my load into this bucket hole."

Chris's screams continue to boom through the room as he writhes on the floor, clutching what remains of his dick with his good hand.

The next second, a loud gunshot explodes in the room, and I snap my gaze back to the Captain.

"What a fucking crybaby!" he says, smirking at me. "I am busy emptying myself into this slut. A bit of courtesy and patience would be much appreciated!"

It is my personal hell all over again.

It is like they looked into my brain, picked out every fucked-up thing I despise, and manufactured this twisted scene just for my benefit.

When Justine's whimpers start again, I notice the Captain pounding into her relentlessly.

Yep! We are done with this shitshow!

I take a step towards him, but before I can raise my gun, his voice halts me in my tracks.

"Not so fast, Hunter!" he says over his shoulder, still delivering merciless blows to Justine. "Make your choice, boy! What are you? Killer or prey?"

It feels as if someone has reached into my chest and squeezed the life out of me. I am back in my parents' room, all those years ago.

I am no fucking prey!

He clicks his tongue at me and motions towards the gun pressed against Justine's chest. She has stopped thrashing and fighting him off. She is either shutting down or terrified of the gun. Either way, I would rather die than let him hurt her for even one more second.

I take another step forward, raising my aim, but the bastard shoots Justine straight in the heart.

I freeze for a second.

"What a waste. I was about to release my load in her..."

The bullet flies as if it has a will of its own, and only when the Captain collapses onto Justine do I realise that I killed him.

I killed my superior. I killed another monster. I killed another bastard I once thought I wanted to become.

The memory of the betrayal burns like poison in my chest. I can feel my blood boiling in my veins and the overwhelming need to inflict pain on someone.

"Hey, fuckers!" I yell at the guards who are watching me today. "Is that all you've got?"

I glare at them with as much menace as I can while straightening to my full height.

"You fight like little schoolgirls."

Before they can even register what I have said, I launch myself at the one closest to me, driving my knee into his abdomen and sending him flying. Big mistake for them to play cards so close to me. Clearly, they did not take the time to measure the length of my chain properly.

This is a mistake they will not have the opportunity to make twice.

The second one grabs my hair, yanking me back, but I twist in his hold. The pain in my scalp is unbearable, but it is such a sweet relief from the ache in my chest.

"Hunter, don't do this!" he screams into my face, his voice shaking.

"Do what? Beat the living shit out of you two fuckers?" I reply in a calm voice, grabbing his neck and driving my fingers mercilessly into his skin. "Because that is exactly what is going to happen."

I accentuate my ruthless words with mocking tones, making it clear that this is happening and that he is about to regret ever being assigned this babysitting shift.

I move like a force of nature, every strike landing with purpose, every move designed to hurt. The first guard barely sees it coming when I twist his arm, feeling the satisfying crack of bone beneath my grip. His scream only fuels me. I toss him into the wall like he weighs nothing and turn to the second one, already driving my knee into his stomach before he has a chance to react. I can see the fear in his eyes, and it feeds the beast inside me. They try to hit back, but their punches are weak, their movements slow. I have trained harder, fought tougher opponents, and lived through more hell than they can even imagine. This is not a fight. It's an execution of pain.

I am not fighting to win. I know I will win. I am fighting to hurt them, to make them feel something close to the chaos burning in my chest. I aim for the soft spots, clawing at an eye, driving my elbow into ribs, and stomping down hard on a kneecap until I hear the sickening snap. Their groans and screams blur into the background as my vision turns red. This is not discipline or control. This is raw rage. This is me silencing the memories, drowning them in their pain. When the second guard crumples to the ground, I grab him by the throat and slam him down again, my breaths coming fast and shallow. The beast inside me demands more, and for a moment, I want to give it everything.

As my fists land with merciless force, the memories of the night I killed my dad surge through my mind like a flood I cannot hold back. I see my mum's eyes, wide with shock as they registered the blood splattered across the room. Her body shaking uncontrollably, her neck bent at a strange angle that seemed almost unnatural. That look in her eyes, that moment it's burned into my memory, etched into my soul, and no matter how hard I hit these guards, I cannot punch it away.

I had passed out from the pain that night, but waking up brought no relief. It was the same nightmare, my own personal brand of hell. The man I had spent my entire life fighting to impress was nothing more than a predator, and the woman I thought was cherished and protected had been broken, mistreated, and abused for years. It all happened right under my nose, and I had been too blind, too naive, to see the pain she carried or the horror she lived through. I had failed her then, and even as I fight now, unleashing my fury, that failure claws at me like a wound that will never heal.

For fuck's sake! I am no smarter now than I was when I finished off my dad or the Captain. There is something there, something my *sugar cube* is hiding, and I cannot see it. I cannot protect the love of my life from it. *What kind of absolute loser am I if I cannot protect the woman I breathe for?*

When I snap out of the pit of my self-loathing, I realise I am driving my boot into one of the guys' skulls. The force of it could cause permanent damage, and the sight jolts me back to reality.

What the fuck is wrong with me?

Both guys are unconscious and bleeding. The fight did not help at all, because these idiots clearly cannot fight to save their lives, and now I am left with two thoroughly bashed bodies to deal with.

The real problem is... they did not deserve this. I fucked up, big time, again.

I collapse to the ground and sigh. I can feel my pain weighing me down, as if it wants to crush me into the cement floor.

I lay flat on the cold cement, the chill against my skin reminding me of my shirt and the tear my *sugar cube* left on it. The thought tightens the ache in my chest. I wish Elijah would just kill me. I wish someone would put an end to my misery, my stupidity, and my inability to protect the people who matter most to me. Adding my *sugar cube* to the list of people I failed to see hurting right in front of me breaks something deep within me.

I really wish Elijah would finish me off.

I could end it here and now myself, but I cannot do that to Sofia. Until my last breath, I will love her. Whether she wants me or not, it does not matter. I have lived for her since the moment I saw her looking down on me two years ago.

I reach into one of the guys pocket and pull out his phone and text my boss...

Hunter

Come and collect the guys. They are unconscious and waiting to be picked up.

Elijah

I should have killed you.

Hunter

That you should have.

Chapter Twelve

Sofia

Present day

I will fuck them up! Fucking assholes thinking they can come after my family, bomb our building, and they can live to tell the tale? Like hell they will!

People say time heals all wounds. What a pile of crap! In the past four months, it has been nothing but a living, breathing hell on earth for me.

We are tracking on all of Bogdan's associates from Romania, and I am planning to narrow it down to a zone and drop a fucking bomb in their lap. The only advantage is that I can send a drone. I do not need to send the mercenaries we had sent a while back to Bucharest. I already sent the drone on its way to Romania, and it will arrive in the next hour, so by then I will zero in on all these fuckers.

And NO! I am not sending a bomb on them because I am mad about something. Or frustrated! Or breaking! Or silently crying inside!

I am fine!

I! AM! FINE!

As I carry on, I make sure to add all the known associates, families, friends, and enemies of every associate we know. The fucking list is huge, and with every passing second, I get more and more irritated by these bastards.

NO! I am not thinking about a certain idiot who should be helping me right now. He is fucking lazy, clearly! He just does not want to help me fix this mess. He is probably playing rest-up in that fucking warehouse, completely oblivious to the fact that I actually need his sorry arse to help me!

Fucker!

Why will he not just listen and come back to work?

"FUCKER!"

"MOTHERFUCKER! ASSHOLE! DIPSHIT! FUCKER!"

As all the curses fly out of me, roaring my fury into the Security Room, I stand up and start smashing the keyboard on my desk. I hit it so hard that a few keys fly into the air at top speed, but I do not stop. I keep bashing the damn thing against the desk until it breaks clean in two.

Once it is broken, I toss the piece in my hand onto the floor and look around in rage, searching for something else to break, and fast.

It is then I notice the room is empty. All the staff have left, and I am alone with my fury.

"Fucking pussies!" I scream into the empty space.

I storm over to one of the desks near the window and start smashing everything on it. Pens, papers, monitors, it all goes flying as I unleash. I need to make this count. I need to get this fury out of me because I feel like I am burning from the inside out. My skin feels itchy, my body restless, and I cannot stay still.

I need to scream. I need to break. I need to cry.

But I cannot cry. I fucking cried for a man! WHAT. THE. ACTUAL. FUCK! Me... crying for a man? I must have lost my mind when that debris fell on me, because why in the world would I let him, he *who shall not be named*, kiss me? Why would I ever let him get close to me? I do not let guys get close to me. I do not let them kiss me. And I sure as hell do not love anyone!

I. DO. NOT. LOVE. ANYONE!

By this point, I am out of breath, I toss aside the personal item I just destroyed, probably belonging to another guy who ran off like a chickenshit. *Fuckers and chickenshits. All of them!*

I stand there, studying the chaos around me as I try to catch my breath, not even realising that my dad is leaning on the edge of the door, just watching me.

Oh, fuck!

Since *he who shall not be named* decided to take off and leave me with all the cleanup, I might, or might not, have these outbursts on a daily basis. And I might, or might not, have beaten the shit out of a few people for being incompetent. I was not mad. Or triggered by anything other than their incompetence. *I was not!*

The fact that *he who shall not be named* is like a festering wound in my soul has absolutely nothing to do with my reaction. They were incompetent. They needed to be beaten into submission so that maybe next time they would take their work seriously, and I would not need to deal with this shit every day.

They cannot leave the organisation. I still think my dad should kill anyone who decides to leave us. Who are they to enjoy the benefits of both lives? To have all the money and still keep their hands clean?

Yeah, like that would ever work.

You want money and power? Real money and real power? You need to get your hands dirty. It is up to individual people, but real power comes with a lot of shit you need to do. These bastards do not even understand how good they have it under my dad.

The day my dad steps back, if I take over, because let's face it, we have never discussed this, things are going to change. And I will start with this foolish shit of hooking up at work. I will fucking shoot their cocks off if I find out any of my staff are sleeping with each other.

That shit needs to stop!

But a bullet to the head is guaranteed if someone comes to me and says they are in love with each other. Fucking hell. *What even is love? Why do we need it? And most importantly... how the fuck do I get rid of it?*

My breathing is fast and shallow, and the pain is invading my mind as I hold my dad's stare. *How do I make it stop?* I implore him with my gaze.

We stand there, rooted in place, holding each other's gaze for what feels like an eternity. I am begging him with my eyes, silently pleading for him to tell me how to make it stop. *How do I make the burning pain in my chest go away?*

When I finally look away, it is because I already know he will not bring it up. I know my dad. He will not tell me I am wrong or cruel for what I am doing. He will not say I was cruel for sending Hunter to his death. He will stay quiet, let me work it out, and wait for me to ask for help when I am good and ready.

Fuck! I just thought of his name.

FUCK!

He who shall not be named ever again can make his own stupid decisions. He was the one who refused to go back to how things were and chose to leave me clean up all this mess, rather than forget about his feelings.

He left me!

As I think through this chain of events, a sharp pain grips my chest, and I start to feel short of breath. I drop into the nearest chair and try to take deep breaths to calm my mind and heart.

He did not leave me.

All of this is my doing.

If he dies, I will ask my dad to kill me as well, because there is no world where I can live if Hunter is not in it.

Fuck! I thought his name again.

How the hell am I supposed to *live without him*?

"I like what you have done to the place," my dad's deep voice snaps me out of my thoughts.

I lift my gaze and take in the state of the room. It looks like a tornado tore through it, leaving me as the only survivor.

I do not even remember smashing the monitors on the wall. Maybe it happened with the chairs that are now scattered all over the floor.

Shit! I just remember the drone!

"I cancelled the drone, little one." His reassurance calms the panic rising in my mind. He must have seen it on my face, the moment I realised the drone should be over Romania by now.

"I needed that," I say in a small voice. If ever there was a day I wanted to appear confident in front of my dad, it is today, especially after the outburst I just had.

"Sure. For what?" he asks in that calm, detached tone of his.

Well, clearly not to wash my back!

"To send a bomb on Bogdan's associates, of course," I reply in an exasperated tone.

He holds my gaze for a second longer than necessary, and I know. I just know he is not impressed right now.

"I see," he says, as if this is just another casual conversation about the weather. "Have you considered the casualties?"

Boom!

There it is.

Regret...

"Have you at least considered the percentage of casualties?"

Silence. I have nothing to say.

"Dad..." My voice is small because, truth be told, I did not consider anything like that. I wanted them to suffer just as much as I am, and I wanted to make it hurt real bad.

"No, little one. We are better than that." His voice is short, commanding, and final. "Just because we can hurt someone does not mean we should."

The air in the room feels like it has been sucked out at lightning speed. I feel like a child again, standing in front of the largest man in the world. Embarrassed, ashamed, and, quite frankly, I feel like an idiot for making such a poor decision.

I should be better than this.

A lot of people thought I got this position because of my dad. What they do not know is that he started teaching me to code when I was ten years old. Years later, I hacked into his organisation for fun, just to prove myself to him. It took me a long time to achieve that, but I did it. By then, I had already landed my first job in IT. I worked on the service desk like every other level one entry into the IT world, it was great, but I wanted more.

The proud look in his eyes when he realised it was me was one of the most rewarding moments of my life. When I told him how I did it, it was one of the rare occasions when my dad's lips curved into a small smile.

It was beautiful.

I fought with everything in me to make sure I never let him down. To make sure he knew exactly why he chose me for this role.

There was such an immense learning curve when I started in cyber. Working my way up to Head of Cyber was excruciating, and the only thing that kept me going was my fury and determination to be strong, to be powerful, to never let anyone hurt me again.

I had been Head of Cyber for a couple of years when that fool walked into my life.

I hate him so much.

I hate how he changed the course of my life.

I hate how he changed me in so many ways.

But most of all, I hate that he taught me what love really means.

I just want these feelings to *go away*. I feel suffocated, trapped, and broken all over again.

And now, to top it all off, I have to look my dad dead in the eyes after I was about to kill innocent people just because they were around bad people.

We are around bad people every day. Walking past them on the street. Smiling at them in a supermarket. Saying hello like it is the most natural thing. When, in fact, they could be the most fucked-up people you will ever meet.

And no one would ever know, would they?

One thing is for sure *my dad is right*. Just because we can hurt people does not mean we should.

How would that make me any better than those horrible people who hurt me?

"I'm sorry." My voice is so small and weak, a perfect portrayal of the devastation tearing me apart inside.

"Little one..." My dad's voice is as warm as it ever was, and that only adds to my pain. It means he knows I am breaking apart, but I cannot put myself back together.

I do not know how. How do I put myself back together?

I lower my gaze to my knees. I always take my time dressing, savouring every moment as I slip into one of my tailored suits. There is something deeply satisfying about the sharp lines and dominating textures that hug my frame, giving me the aura of power I crave. The clean cuts and bold fabrics always feel like armour, a second skin that commands confidence and demands respect the moment I walk into a room. Every detail matters. The perfect fit of the blazer, the slight taper at the waist, the crisp edges that show I am in control.

This is not just clothing. This is a statement. A declaration that I should not be underestimated, that I own every inch of space I take up. Dressing like this is not just pleasure.

It is power...

The only problem is that not even my armour is providing me with any power at the moment. I feel completely defeated, inside and out.

"You need to make a choice, little one." My dad's words register as he approaches me. "You need to make a choice, because this needs to stop."

He places his hand on my shoulder and squeezes gently, and my insides tremble at his reassuring touch.

I lift my gaze, but as always, there is nothing to read in his expression. I could sure as hell use some comfort right about now.

"You need to go kill him, little one. I am not going to do it for you."

If I thought I knew what pain was, I was mistaken. Utterly and deeply mistaken.

It feels like something inside me is being torn apart, like my very essence is bleeding out, and I am powerless to stop it. This paralysis, this numbness, cannot be normal. My head pounds as if it is about to split open, every throb sending shockwaves of agony through me. The relentless pulse and ringing in my ears drown out everything else, their deafening roar a cruel reminder of my anguish.

But the pain in my chest eclipses it all, sharp and unforgiving, like my dad just shot straight into my soul. His words were not just spoken, they were a blade, carving through everything I thought I could bear. He is killing me from the inside out.

How can he ask something like this of me?

Moments pass as I stare at my dad, my chest tightening with every second of silence. He just holds my gaze, steady and unyielding, letting me process this pain in whatever way I can.

"Dad... I, I..." My voice breaks, the words catching in my throat. I cannot even voice my refusal. *I just cannot.*

"You can, and you will, little one." His gaze is cold, powerful, and commanding, a force I cannot fight against.

In moments like this, I wish he could be like other dads. I wish he could understand the true pain his words inflict, let alone the gravity of what he is asking of me. I wish he could feel emotions like the rest of us, so he would understand that I would rather put a bullet in my own brain than hurt Hunter.

"Dad..." My voice trembles, weak and pleading.

"It was your decision, and you need to live with the consequences of your choice," he says, his tone unwavering, unfeeling.

No!

A tear rolls down my cheek, as if trying to escape the agony within me. Then another follows, and another, until I realise I am no longer in control of my body. I am completely numb, paralysed by the shock of what he is asking of me. The only thing I can do is stare into his deep blue eyes, eyes completely devoid of warmth or compassion.

"I let things go on for long enough, and now it is time for you to clean up after yourself," he says, his voice cold and unyielding. He squeezes my shoulder again, and for a fleeting moment, something flickers in his eyes.

Then he delivers the final blow.

"Tomorrow, Sofia."

And with those words, I know... tomorrow will be my end.

Chapter Thirteen

Hunter

"Well, I kind of deserve it," I sigh, trying to make small talk with the guards on duty today.

Let's just say they are not impressed with my jokes. If they ever pitied me, that is long gone. Forgotten. The guys I beat yesterday ended up needing to be put into an induced coma.

I feel like shit because they did not deserve it. They did not deserve to have the beast unleashed on them. But at the time, my blood was boiling in my veins, my demons were suffocating me, clouding my mind, and the constant pain in my soul from my *sugar cube* made my reality snap.

And I fucked up. I sigh again.

They did not deserve it. I fucked up.

They made the chain smaller and added another one around my wrist. I look like some chained-up security dog, and it is clear no one wants to come anywhere near me.

The guards are tucked into the opposite corner, most definitely not playing any games. Both of them are studying my every move with such menace that, in another situation, I might have found it funny. But given that I am the one in the wrong here, I do not dare crack a joke or try to provoke them.

I deserve this, and I will take it. I rattle the chain around my wrist again, the cold metal biting into my skin. The pain in my back from all these nights spent on the cold floor, with nothing but bare concrete beneath me, is taking its toll.

They feed me twice a day. Bland, disgusting food, probably meant to break me, to wear me down. The joke is on them! I am terrible at cooking, my mum was average at best, and in the army, taste buds were never a priority for the mess cooks. Feeding me crap will get them nowhere, really fast.

Every other day, they hose me down in some pitiful attempt to wash me, and that in itself is an experience. I remember listening to a comedian once, Canadian I think, but who knows for sure. He cracked a joke that men would wear underwear until it disintegrates. Something about wearing it twenty times on one side, then flipping it and wearing it twenty more. If they could, they would wear it until it turns to dust and flies out the window when the wife tries to freshen up the air in the room. The image still makes me smirk, even now.

That stupid memory brings out a burst of laughter so loud and deep that, when I finally calm down and look at the guys, they are staring at me like I have completely lost it.

"It was a stand-up comedian," I say, my voice still bubbling with laughter. "Something about men's underwear."

I try to reassure them with a grin. "No fighting today, I promise."

I push my pants down slightly and glance at my underwear, the same pair I have had since being locked up here and I cannot help but laugh again at the joke.

"Yep, not far off now," I mutter under my breath. "If they leave the door open for too long, they might just fly away."

And with that, another wave of laughter takes over, loud and uncontrollable.

I jump to my feet, and the guys flinch as if I had just shot them. Their stupid reaction almost makes me smile, but I hide it. I get it. I really do. If I were in their shoes, I would not trust someone like me either, not after all the shit I have caused since I first asked to be killed.

As I move into position to start my exercises, my mind drifts back to Elijah. Fuck, if I do not wish with everything in me that he would just end it. End me. Every day is getting harder, and it has nothing to do with the conditions they have put me through. It is because I do not see her. My *sugar cube*. The light of my eyes and the sweetness of my soul.

If at any point I thought she might have loved me, I know now.

I know *she does not*.

She sent me to my death and did not look back.

I think it has been over four months now, and the only person in pure agony is me. She has well and truly forgotten me, and I have had to accept my reality.

I push myself harder and faster with my push-ups, crossing my arms and landing on one hand before switching to the other. My muscles are burning, my breath is fast and shallow, and I balance my entire weight on either hand. I move on to different exercises, targeting other muscle groups in a desperate effort to exhaust myself so completely that I drown out every other thought.

Anything to keep my demons from suffocating me. Anything to drown the pain in my soul.

I am not sure how long Elijah plans to keep me here. Perhaps my end is sooner rather than later.

The first month, they beat me every day until I was unconscious. At least, I think it was a month. After a while, everything became a blur, what day it was, what I needed to survive, it all started to feel irrelevant. The only thing keeping me going was my pain, because I could not accept that she does not love me. I felt it. Or at least, I thought I felt it.

Now... now I am not sure. Perhaps my obsession with her fed me the idea that she loved me back. Because if she did love me, why would she fight so hard to keep us apart?

As I start on my triceps, shoulders, and chest, I move from a handstand on both arms to balancing on one. It is hard as hell on the arm with the chain attached, but I just mutter a curse under my breath and push through.

I deserve it.

My muscles burn like hell, and I make a mental note that if, by some miracle, I survive this, I need to make it up to the guys from yesterday. Those two took the worst of it, and they sure as hell did not deserve it.

I switch to my other arm and try to focus on my counting, but the sound of the warehouse door opening snaps my attention away. The last person I ever expected to see strolls in like he owns the place.

"Fuck me, you stink!" Dominic's voice booms through the warehouse.

I scramble to my feet but misjudge the new restraints. I land hard on one knee, pain shooting through me like fire.

Fuck, that hurts like a motherfucker!

"What is this nonsense, fucker?" he snaps, pinning me with a glare. "Now you drop to one knee like some fucking superhero to impress me? Sorry, I'm taken. You can go off and fuck yourself!" He bursts into laughter at his own stupid joke. "You just needed to lift one arm in the air, and the pose would be perfect," he adds, still laughing like the jackass he is, unable to stop.

"Come closer, dipshit," I dare him, my voice low and dangerous. "Let's see if I can wipe that laughter off your face."

I stand slowly, my movements deliberate, never breaking his gaze.

He steps closer, stopping right in front of me. He searches my gaze for something, what I have no idea, but he studies me like I actually matter to him. Then, without a word, he extends his hand to shake mine.

As I reach out, he pulls me into a hug.

Fuck, I needed this!

"You really do stink, man!" he says as he lets go, brushing himself off theatrically. "I think I'll need to burn these clothes after this."

He starts sniffing around like a lunatic, as if searching for another source of the smell.

"Why the fuck are you sniffing, you lunatic?" I burst out laughing. "Clearly the stench is from me!"

"Oh, don't mind me. I'm just sniffing around for your dignity. Has it left the building?"

When he finally turns and meets my gaze, he bursts into laughter so deep it is hard not to join him.

The fucker! I fucking missed his stupid face!

"Well, we cannot all be pussy-whipped like you. Some of us had to murder our dignity to get somewhere."

Oh, fuck! That did not land right. It was meant to be a comeback, but it just came off as a sad remark.

Fuck, I am so off my game.

"Okay. Life is sad. Your humour has clearly died from your stench," he says, patting me on the back before bursting into laughter again. "Sad, sad day."

I cannot help but laugh too, because, damn it, his joke was funny.

He looks good, *really good.* Angela must be keeping him busy because this is the first time he has visited me in all these months, and the fucker is glowing like he is pregnant.

Maybe I should make a joke about that, see how it lands.

"Hunter, your hair is not even white anymore. You look awful, man." His tone is full of concern, his gaze searching. The longer he looks, the more worried he seems.

"So... the witch?" he concludes, then sighs heavily. "Out of all the women in the world, it had to be a witch?"

I start laughing at his antics, because if anyone hates my *sugar cube*, it is Dominic. He is a good-looking bastard, and honestly, I am glad he cannot stand her. It would be a pity to have to kill him just because he thought my woman was hot.

My woman.

Fuck!

"Yep. What can I say? I have good taste," I say with a wink before bursting into laughter again. "Where have you been, fucker? It's been a few months. Is that how little I mean to you?"

"You mean fuck all, don't get ahead of yourself!" he snaps back, landing a punch to my chest for good measure.

Fuck, yes! He came to play. Finally, someone I can actually enjoy myself with!

"Is that right?" I say, pretending to reach for his shoulder before sweeping his legs out from under him. He hits the ground with a thud, completely caught off guard.

I burst into laughter, pinning him with my gaze. "All that lovey-dovey nonsense has made you weak," I say, emphasising every word, a genuine smile playing on my face for the first time since I ended up here. "I might stink, but I can still teach you a thing or two."

The words are barely out of my mouth when the idiot headbutts me so hard that I slam into the wall with a thud.

"You think, pretty boy?" he mocks, grinning as he watches me recover. "Or should I say, pretty stinky boy?"

Before he can retreat, I land a side kick to his head, fast and hard, sending him flying across the room. I watch him as he shakes his head, trying to recover, and quickly assess whether the chains will let me land another kick or if I'll end up flat on my ass, making a fool of myself.

Yep. Not going to happen. I need to let him come to me, make sure my kicks knock him out instead of sending him flying out of reach.

I feel like a trapped animal.

Dominic starts laughing as he gets back to his feet, his grin wide and infuriating. Then, we start dancing...

Dominic moves in, his grin infuriating as always, and I meet him head-on. His jab is quick, but I sidestep, driving a kick toward his side. He blocks effortlessly, his movements smooth and natural, like he has been doing this his whole life. I counter his next strike with a punch that glances off his shoulder.

"You could've visited earlier, fucker," I spit out between breaths, humour lacing my tone.

"I got married, you selfish prick!" he fires back, his tone cutting as he dodges my next kick with ease. "And then Angela and I went travelling for a while."

I lash out with a punch that barely grazes his arm, but he deflects and lands a quick kick to my thigh. Pain radiates up my leg, but I grit my teeth and keep going. "Figures," I mutter, glaring at him.

"Don't act like you're surprised," he quips, stepping back to assess me, his smirk as annoying as ever. "Anyway, I knew you wouldn't die, so I didn't exactly rush to check on you."

I burst out laughing despite the ache in my body. Dominic is a bastard, but he's a funny bastard.

We clash again, this time with no fancy moves, just fists flying and hands grappling like we are two street kids with something to prove. Dominic gets a good hook in, and I repay him with an elbow to the ribs that makes him grunt. We stumble together, locked in a grapple, trying to throw each other off balance, until his knee collides with my thigh, sending a jolt of pain up my leg. I manage to shove him back, but he dives in again, and we both end up crashing to the floor in a tangled heap, punches still landing but weaker now, sloppier. Our breath comes in short, ragged bursts, sweat pouring down our faces as our strength gives out. Finally, we lie flat on the cold floor, limbs sprawled, too exhausted to move. Dominic is laughing softly, his chest rising and falling with each breath, and despite everything, I cannot help but join him. The fight might be over, but neither of us really won and neither of us cares, because this was not about winning. This was about giving me a break from my reality.

The moment my breathing evens out, I turn my head toward Dominic and thank him. This was exactly what I needed. It might have come later than I wanted, but it came.

We both laugh at our own ridiculous antics, the sound echoing through the empty warehouse. The door creaks open again, but I do not bother to look. It is probably just the next shift of guards coming to take over.

Then, the most divine voice cuts through the vast room, commanding and authoritative, as if she shapes existence itself.

"Leave."

My brain feels like it is short-circuiting. I could swear that was her voice... my *sugar cube*.

Slowly, I lift my gaze toward the door, and there she is, standing in all her perfection.

My sugar cube.

And in that moment, I forget how to breathe.

Chapter Fourteen

Sofia

"Leave." My voice is calm, calculated, and authoritative, so much so that even I am surprised at how well I am hiding the agony tearing me apart inside.

I came prepared. I am dressed in one of my signature three-piece suits, the colour and texture exuding power, wealth, and dominance. I did not bother taking my gun out once I was inside, because the moment the car pulled up to the warehouse door the gun was already out. I attached the silencer, opened the door, and walked straight in.

And there they are, those two idiots giggling like foolish schoolboys on the floor.

Yep, he is suffering so much because of you. That relentless inner voice mocks me.

He could not care less. Look at him.

The moment he turns and our gazes meet, I genuinely feel like the blood in my veins is itching, burning under my skin. It is as if fire is coursing through me, and all my strength is now focused on not letting my sorrow and agony spill out for all to see. All the confidence, all the power, all the wealth, and all the intelligence I possess mean absolutely nothing right now.

In front of him, I am nothing more than a wounded, broken woman so desperately in love with him that even my inner voice has stopped trying to make me feel like shit. It's now simply screaming, raw and unrelenting, in agony and pain.

I raise my gun and fire at the floor next to Dominic's head, a deliberate sign of defiance. My gaze burns into them, daring them to test me, daring them to see if I would or would not kill them all to get to my *Nuuro*.

"Fuck!" Dominic jumps like the bullet ricocheted and hit him. "Fucking witch! You almost got me!" His voice is hysterical, his body tensed as if he is ready to lunge at me.

I dare him with my gaze, silently inviting him to come at me because that is all I need to unleash my fury.

He holds my stare for several long, charged seconds. Whatever he sees in me must be enough, because he mutters another string of swear words under his breath and storms out of the warehouse.

The other guards are long gone. Now, it is just me and my *Nuuro.*

He is still lying there, staring at me upside down from the floor like a damned fool.

He does not care. Look at him. He is playing around with his mate without a single worry in the world, while I've been unable to breathe since my dad told me to come and kill him.

Damn fool. That is what you are.

That pestering voice in the back of my mind stops screaming and instead resumes its relentless self-loathing, tearing into me with all its might. *Why would he care? You are not like other women. Why would he care? Why would he ever love you?*

He moves slowly, leaning his back against the wall. His movements are deliberate, almost sluggish, as if he is in pain. Clearly, all that play with Dominic took its toll on him.

But then his eyes meet mine again, and he lets out a deep sigh.

And in that moment, he shatters my world to pieces.

"*Cupcake...*" The pain in his voice cuts through me like the rustiest, dullest knife, twisting deep to create maximum agony.

Did he miss me? Is he in pain?

We just stare at each other, the silence stretching into what feels like hours. I stand on my feet, prim and proper, my gun resting at my side, every inch the composed figure I forced myself to be. And there he is... dirty, smelly, and resigned, sitting on the filthy warehouse floor, waiting for his verdict like a condemned man.

Since my dad ordered me to execute him, I have been unable to function. I have been completely numb since that moment. I did not sleep the entire night, just sat on the floor of my bedroom, staring at the suitcases I pack every year on my birthday to confront my biological family.

I am so pathetic. Every year since I was 17, I have packed them, and every year I fail to find the courage to act on it. The farthest I have ever taken them is to my front door, on the inside, mind you and then simply froze.

Hunter coming into my life made it even worse. For the past two years, I have not even been capable of opening the suitcases, let alone taking the clothes out and putting them away. They just sit there, mocking me, reminding me that I am weak, broken, and unlovable.

I cannot kill him. I know I can't. But I am praying to everything in this universe that he will understand, that he will listen to me and let go of this idea of us being together. *He does not really love me... right?*

"H, Hunter..." I stutter, barely able to say his name. All traces of the confident, powerful woman who walked in here have completely vanished.

He does not love you, fool. Calm down and lay down the law. Tell him he needs to stop this foolishness because no one can love you the way you are.

"You better kill me, *cupcake*, because I will never let you go." The finality in his voice mirrors the pain it carries, cutting through me like a blade.

And just like that, I am back in my apartment on the day I lied, telling him I did not want him. I can still hear him, screaming at the top of his lungs that he loves me and will never let me go.

He loves me?

"Y, you don't understand..."

"Then make me understand!" he cuts me off, shouting, his voice raw and demanding. "Make me understand! Because I know you came to kill me, but you won't be able to. I can see it all over your beautiful face."

The cruel agony in his voice tears through me, breaking me apart piece by piece. He gestures toward the gun in my hand, and that is when I notice it. I am shaking so badly that I am genuinely surprised my arm and hand are even capable of this.

Maybe, finally, your mind is joining the rest of your body and breaking apart. Let's be honest, it is well overdue.

How can I possibly tell him the truth? How could I ever tell anyone the truth?

"No!" My voice booms through the vast space, sharp and sudden, like another gunshot echoing in the air.

"Then you better steady your hand, *cupcake.* Aim well at my head and press the trigger. Because even you cannot be that cruel to come here, let me see you, and then leave again."

His voice is so small, filled with pain and sorrow, and by the end of his words, it sounds as if he is fighting back tears.

I study his gaze, the glossy sheen in his eyes betraying the rawness of his pain. His expression is unguarded, stripped of all the defences he usually wears so effortlessly. He is not hiding from me anymore. For the first time, he is laying himself bare, showing me everything, his anguish, his longing, his desperation. It feels like looking into a mirror I cannot escape from, one that reflects all the pain I have caused, but cannot fix.

Something inside me breaks, sharp and deep, a wound I know will never heal. *I cannot see him like this.* This is the man I have always thought of as invincible, as unbreakable, and yet here he is, breaking in front of me, it's too much and is all my fault.

I can handle my own pain. I have learned to carry it like armour. But his pain? His pain is shattering me. It's a burden I cannot bear. *I cannot see him like this.*

Tears stream down my face in an unstoppable flow, each one carrying a piece of the anguish I can no longer contain. My chin trembles, betraying the control I am desperately clinging to, and my lips press into a thin, unsteady line as I fight against the unbearable weight of seeing him like this. The pain is suffocating, a force I cannot escape, no matter how hard I try to push it down.

"Shoot me," he commands, his voice sharp and unrelenting. "Shoot me!" he repeats, the words dripping with the kind of desperation that only sees death as the release from this hell.

"Fucking shoot me, Sofia!"

His roar is a violent eruption of pure pain, fury, agony, and despair, slamming into me like a whip cracking with full force, leaving invisible wounds I know will never heal.

"SHOOT! ME!"

I fall to my knees, as a broken woman, defeated by my emotions. I would rather die myself than hurt him.

"I can't." My voice is barely a whisper, fragile and broken, hidden beneath the weight of my sobs.

I would rather face his rejection, his pity, or even his humiliation than see him like this... shattered and drowning in despair.

I love him. I love him so much it is fucking breaking me inside. I know my life will never be the same, because this pain, this unbearable agony of seeing him suffer like this, will haunt me for the rest of my days.

I did this. This is all my fault, and I will never forgive myself for it.

"Then make me understand!" His voice breaks, trembling as though he is crying too. When I look up, his beautiful eyes are swollen and shattered, filled with anguish. Tears roll down his face, each one a silent plea that cuts through me like a blade.

I broke a warrior, and it is all my fault.

I cannot bear this.

I cannot take it anymore.

Whatever happens must be easier than this, because I feel like I cannot breathe. My chest aches as if I have been shot, my head pounds with relentless pain, and my body shakes uncontrollably. It feels completely numb, like someone else is in control of it, not me.

Telling him the truth must be easier than this, even if it means he is disgusted by me and rejects me.

I look down, lowering the gun to rest beside my leg. Pressing my palms against the cold concrete floor, I take a few deep breaths, trying to calm my mind and summon the courage to tell him.

"I am mutilated."

I do not dare look up. I do not dare say anything more. I do not even dare to breathe.

I just sit there on my knees in front of him, staring down, bracing myself for his rejection.

Minutes pass, and he says nothing. The only anchors to reality are the sound of our breathing, the awful smell hanging in the air, and the cold concrete beneath me.

"I don't understand," he finally says, his voice small and uncertain. "What do you mean you're mutilated?"

"I mean I am not like other women... down there." My voice breaks at the end, trembling with the weight of the words, because how can I outright tell him?

"I don't understand!" His voice is filled with rage, raw and uncontained, but the pain is unmistakable. "Why? How did this happen? Who do I need to hunt down and kill?"

The panic in his voice is so evident now, almost palpable.

"It does not matter," I say, trying to reassure him, though my voice is barely steady, my gaze still fixed on the floor. "What matters is that we cannot be together."

"Wait a minute! What?" If I thought I knew what a panicked Hunter sounded like before, I was wrong. His voice trembles now, a volatile mix of fury and pain. "What does one have to do with the other?"

"We cannot be together, Hunter. Please understand. I am not like other women. I'm... I'm defective."

As the words escape me, a full-body sob wracks through me, and I collapse onto the floor, crying. I scream and wail in agony.

At my life!

At the cruelty that was inflicted upon me!

At the heartbreak of finding my pair and knowing I cannot be with him!

At the relentless self-loathing that consumes me.

I stay there, my face buried in my palms, crying my heart out, drowning in the weight of it all.

As my sobs begin to subside, a noise pulls me from my anguish. I lift my head, my vision blurry, and it takes several tries to clear my eyes and comprehend what is happening before me.

Hunter is pulling at his chain with such force that the vibrations reverberate through the floor, shaking the very ground beneath us.

"What are you doing?" I ask, my voice trembling with a mix of confusion and fear.

"I am fucking getting to you. That's what I'm doing!" he replies angrily, his tone laced with raw determination. "Because if these damn chains think they can keep me away from you, they are dead wrong."

With that, he pulls so hard on the chain that I am terrified he will dislocate his shoulder.

"Stop, Hunter!" I scream, my voice desperate as I try to protect him. "You will hurt yourself!"

"Nothing in this fucking world can hurt me more than seeing you like this," he replies quickly, his voice shifting to something tender and full of love. "I would rather lose my shoulder, my arm, everything, than be away from you," he quickly adds.

"You are mine, *cupcake*!"

Chapter Fifteen

Hunter

"You are mine, *cupcake*!"

She fucking thought I would not want to be with her because someone hurt her?

What?!

Why?!

I will hunt them down and break them limb by limb. Someone hurt my *sugar cube*, and they are still living, breathing people?

Like hell they will!

I pull again at the chain, but shit man I really am about to dislocate my shoulder and my ods of her taking me to ER are very slime. Regardless I cannot stay here one more second. I need to plead, I need to beg, and I need to reassure her that whatever happened to her does not change what I feel for her. If anything I love her more for being brave and telling me what was between us.

At least now I know what it is, and I can come up with a plan to make it better for her... if she lets me.

Fuck, she will not let me.

Fucking hell!

"Damn it! Give in already, you stupid fucking piece of shit chain!" I roar, pulling and straining with every ounce of my strength. I snap and yank, over and over, but the sorry excuse for a chain refuses to budge.

A deep, guttural scream rips from my beast, fuelled by the pain she has inflicted on me, seeing her like this, broken, sobbing uncontrollably on the floor, thinking she is defective.

What does that even mean... mutilated? Whatever it is, it does not matter. What matters is getting to her! Taking her in my arms, holding her so tightly that she cannot slip away from me again. Loving her with every broken, jagged piece of my soul. Protecting her from the shadows of her past and the demons that haunt her.

And drilling it into her mind, into her very essence, that *she is mine.* That she always has been, and she always will be.

Whatever happened to her, none of it is her fault. I will find them! Every single one of the bastards who dared to hurt her, to touch her, to leave her feeling like this and I will make them pay. They will beg for mercy they will never receive.

Because she is mine.

And with that, it hits me...

Why did Elijah not kill them all?

Was it him? Was Elijah the one who hurt her?

A guttural scream escapes me, raw and primal, as the thought grips my mind. The possibility, the horrifying thought, that she has been living with her tormentor every single day of her life twists inside me like a blade. To think she has been trapped in the same space as the one who broke her fills me with a fury so violent it feels like it will rip me apart.

Pain and rage surge through me, obliterating every rational thought. If it was him, I will make him suffer in ways he could never imagine. *I will destroy him.*

A shot goes off, grazing the side of my calf. It takes me a second to register that my *sugar cube* just shot the chain.

Another shot rings out, and I do not even stop to check if I am free. I jolt into action, breaking into a full sprint, and collapse to my knees in front of her.

"Hunter, no!"

I do not care about her words. I do not care about her rejection. I do not care that I smell. I do not care that I am dirty. I do not care about the four months I have spent living in this hell.

All I care about is *my sugar cube.*

I lean over and cradle her beautiful face in my hands, gently and carefully stroking her skin with my thumb.

"I don't want you!" she screams desperately, her voice breaking as she throws the words in my face.

"I want you," I reply, my voice calm and steady.

"I don't want to be with you!" she adds quickly, her voice panicked and trembling.

"I want to be with you," I respond firmly, my voice unwavering.

"I don't love you!" she screams hysterically, her voice cracking under the weight of her words.

"I love you enough for the both of us, *sugar cube*," I say, my voice soft but resolute.

With my admission, a tear slips down my cheek and falls onto her pristine suit jacket, leaving a mark as raw and vulnerable as the moment itself.

Her inhale is so sharp, so deep, it is as though my words struck her with the force of a physical blow. She freezes, her chest rising as if the air itself has betrayed her, and I see it, the raw shock etched across her face. Her wide eyes search mine, filled with disbelief, fear, and something else I cannot place.

She does not move. She does not blink. It is as if my words have shattered her carefully constructed walls, leaving her exposed and unsure of what to do next.

I lean down and press a soft kiss to the top of her forehead, lingering as I breathe her in. She smells of sophisticated perfume, rich and elegant, but beneath it, she smells like *mine.*

She smells like *she belongs to me.*

It is time for her to learn that, to accept it once and for all.

"Y-you... cannot... love me," she chokes out, her voice barely audible through the sobs wracking her body. Each word feels like it is being torn from her, fragile and broken, as if speaking them is causing her physical pain. "I-I... I am damaged. No one can love me," she cries, the words tumbling out in a raw, anguished wail.

Her shoulders shake violently as she tries to pull away, as though distancing herself could protect me from her self-perceived flaws. Her pain is so consuming, so absolute, that it feels like the room itself has folded in on us, heavy with the weight of her despair. She clutches at her chest as if trying to hold herself together, even as her words fall apart.

Like hell she will! She will never pull away from me again! I will make sure of it! Whatever it takes, wherever it leads, from this day forward, there will not be a single moment where we are separated. I vow it to myself, to her, to the universe.

I vow it with every beat of my heart and every ounce of my soul. She is my life now, and I will protect her, hold her, love her... forever. She does not get to slip away from me. Not now! Not ever!

"You are mine," I whisper, my voice low but unyielding, as I pull her close and feel her trembling against me. My arms tighten around her, grounding us both in the moment. "You are mine to love," I murmur, brushing a tender kiss against her forehead, lingering as though I can press my devotion into her skin.

"You are mine to protect," I say softly, my lips brushing against one delicate eyelid.

"You are mine to cherish," I vow, kissing her other eyelid, tasting the salt of her pain and silently promising to ease it.

"You are mine forever, from this day onward," I declare, leaning down and pressing the lightest, most reverent kiss to her lips, a touch filled with every ounce of love and devotion I have for her. Her pain, her doubts, her walls, they are no match for what I feel for her.

She freezes in my hold, her body rigid, as if she is unable to process my words and actions. But to me, everything is crystal clear. Whatever happened to her changes nothing. It does not alter the strength of my love for her. It does not diminish my devotion or the future I want to build with her, for her.

If anything, it strengthens my resolve. I will hunt down the bastards who hurt her, every last one of them, and make them pay dearly, even if it is Elijah who is responsible.

"You are mine," I whisper against her lips, my voice soft , as if the words alone could anchor her to me.

"H-Hunter..." she stammers, her voice trembling, caught somewhere between disbelief and surrender.

I pull back slightly, studying her expression and the emotions so clearly written on her beautiful face. "No, *sugar cube*. This is happening, and you need to accept it. You are mine, just as much as I am yours," I say, my voice steady and filled with quiet determination.

I pull her into a hug again, wrapping my arms around her trembling frame. Her entire body shakes uncontrollably, and I hold her tighter, as if my embrace alone could shield her from everything that has ever hurt her.

"You love me," I whisper, the certainty in my voice unshakable. "And even if you think you don't, I love you enough for the both of us," I say it again, letting the weight of my love press into every syllable, every breath, until there's no room left for doubt. She needs to understand, crystal clear, there is no escape from this.

Gently, I lean back, never breaking our connection, and guide her onto my lap. Her body feels so fragile in my arms, as though the weight of her pain has worn her down. I cradle her against me, my hands moving instinctively to steady her, to remind her that I am here.

As I hold her, I press my lips to the top of her head, a silent promise passing between us. Whatever battles she is fighting, they are mine now. She may not believe it yet, but she is mine, completely and utterly, and I will carry us both if I have to.

The feel of her against my body is nothing short of heaven on earth. It's as though every moment of longing, every ache and hunger I have endured in this lifetime, has led to this, the moment my starving soul is finally fed.

Her warmth seeps into me, calming the storm that has raged within for so long. She is everything I have ever needed, everything I have ever dreamed of, and holding her like this feels like I am piecing together the shattered fragments of myself. She is not just in my arms... she is in my very being, filling a void I did not know how to heal.

We hold each other like that for what feels like hours, neither of us willing to let go. Then, slowly, she pulls away just slightly and begins to search my face, her eyes filled with a mix of curiosity and hesitation.

"You really smell, *Nuuro*," she says softly, her voice so small it feels like she is afraid of offending me.

"And you smell mouthwatering," I reply with a grin, my laughter breaking free as I catch the surprised expression on her face.

"Can we go now, *sugar cube*?" I ask, my voice steady and firm. "Do you understand now that there is no stopping this? You. Are. Mine." I enunciate each word deliberately, daring her to contradict me again, to even attempt to lie that she does not love me. My gaze locks onto hers, unwavering, as I wait for her to accept the inevitable truth.

She just nods her head ever so slightly, and I burst out laughing, the sound echoing around us. I never would have imagined Sofia being this small, this vulnerable inside. It is almost unbelievable, seeing the fierce, commanding woman I know reduced to this shy, hesitant gesture.

She is absolutely *adorable*.

I start attacking her with kisses, my lips landing wherever I can reach, while my fingers dance along her sides, tickling her mercilessly. Her angelic laughter fills the space, a perfect symphony that soothes my broken soul.

As I pin her beneath me, still kissing and tickling, her laughter grows louder, bright and unrestrained, and for the first time in what feels like forever, the weight in my chest begins to lift. She is my light, my salvation, and I will never tire of hearing that sound.

Only when I catch a whiff of my own smell do I freeze in my tracks. "Mate, that is feral!" I say for good measure, bursting into laughter at the absurdity of it.

I stand and extend a hand to help her up. She hesitates for a moment, then slowly places her hand in mine. I pull her up so quickly she stumbles forward, landing right in my arms. Without a second thought, I wrap her in a tight embrace, burying my face in the crook of her neck and breathing her in.

She is mine...

Chapter Sixteen

Sofia

We make our way to the car, and it is only when I see Vasile, my dad's personal bodyguard and chauffeur, standing there waiting, that it truly hits me.

I have Hunter.

I am with Hunter.

I will never be alone again.

I expect to panic, to feel the familiar rush of fear rising inside me. I expect my mind to start calculating escape routes, devising a plan to overpower him.

But it does not come...

I take my seat in the back passenger side, and Hunter slides in next to me. That god-awful smell hits me again, sharp and undeniable. What kind of conditions did my dad keep him in for him to look and smell like this?

But then I catch myself staring.

He is even more muscular now, if that is even possible. He was big before, but now... there is not an ounce of fat on his body. His pectoral muscles and abs are so well-defined it feels almost unfair. Honestly, it should be illegal for someone to look this hot.

I have to fight the ridiculous urge to reach out and touch him, to explore, to lick, and to bite at him like some kind of lunatic.

A deep sense of remorse and self-loathing crashes over me, overwhelming and relentless. That all-too-familiar feeling of doom, the excruciating pain of my own actions, floods my chest.

It weighs on me, heavy and suffocating, as if trying to crush me beneath the sheer force of my despair.

It is as if he can read my mind. He reaches for my hand, intertwining our fingers, and moves closer to me. The simple gesture cuts through the storm inside me, and I release a shaky breath I did not even realise I was holding during my panic attack.

I turn to him, and the moment our eyes connect, the way he looks at me takes my breath away. There is a sweet, unguarded adoration in his gaze, a warmth that feels impossible to deserve. He does not just look content. No... he looks happy. Truly, deeply happy.

"Where to, Sofia?" Vasile's deep voice cuts through the air from the front seat, though it feels like he is light years away from us.

I am completely lost in Hunter's gaze, utterly consumed by the vortex of emotions swirling between us. I have never seen this look on his face before, and it draws me in, holding me captive. I am completely absorbed by him, by the sheer intensity of his presence, as if nothing else in the world exists.

"Her home," Hunter's gentle voice brings me back to reality, snapping me out of the trance I had been lost in.

Vasile grunts in disapproval at Hunter answering for me, his dissatisfaction clear in the sound. I clear my throat, trying to gather whatever fragments of confidence I can muster in this moment.

"Take us home, Vasile. Thank you," I say, my voice steadier than I expected.

The entire drive to my apartment, Hunter gently strokes my hand with his thumb. I try, and fail, to keep my gaze from drifting to his hand. His powerful arm rests casually on his thigh, and his strong, long fingers are intertwined with mine.

The contrast is extraordinary. Such strength, yet such unbelievable gentleness and care. And it is all for me.

Because of me.

Because he loves me.

He loves me.

It feels surreal. Unreal.

As if my mind has finally snapped, and I am crafting a reality where I get to end up with him. The thought terrifies me, clawing at my sanity, leaving me so fucking scared that this might not be real.

Desperate to anchor myself, I jolt my gaze out the window, watching as the car glides smoothly into the building's garage.

When I feel Hunter's lips press softly against my knuckles, I turn toward him and immediately catch a fresh whiff of his horrendous body odour.

That is the reality check I needed.

I am not dreaming. I am not hallucinating. My mind has not snapped under the weight of my fears.

He is really here.

He really loves me.

The elevator ride to my apartment feels as if his body is now fused to mine. His hands rest on me with a perfect blend of fire and comfort, igniting something deep within me.

I would have expected my body to fight, to reject him, to struggle under his touch. But instead, the only thing my body does is lean into him, seeking more of his warmth, more of his presence.

An overpowering sensation takes hold of me, a primal need to cocoon myself into Hunter, to merge with him as if we were always meant to be one. The feeling rushes through me, fierce and consuming, like a burning volcano erupting from the core of my very being.

The soft click of the front door pulls me back to the reality of the moment. Hunter is in my apartment again.

But this time... this time, all I want is to *keep him.*

He comes up behind me, wrapping me in a tight hug and burying his face in the crook of my neck. His touch is impossibly gentle, yet his hold is unyieldingly strong.

I feel the tremble of his body against mine, a silent vulnerability that speaks louder than words. One thing is certain... I will not be leaving his embrace without his approval.

"I love you."

His declaration lands with the force of a thousand raging bulls, powerful and overwhelming, yet his voice carries the delicate softness of a whispered promise.

"I have loved you since the day I first saw you," he continues, completely unaware of the devastating effect his words have on me. Each syllable tears through the walls I have so carefully built, leaving me exposed and trembling.

"And I will love you until the day I die, *sugar cube*."

With those words, he presses a soft kiss to the side of my neck, and a full-body shudder courses through me, raw and uncontrollable.

Oh! That felt amazing.

"You liked that?" he asks, his voice laced with a soft chuckle.

"The things I want to do to you..." His voice softens, filled with warmth and tenderness, the words carrying a promise rather than a demand.

"But it will have to wait, *sugar cube*," he adds with a playful tone, his chuckle deepening. "I really need a shower."

"You think..." I start, but a giggle escapes me before I can finish. For a second, I wonder who's that fool giggling like a schoolgirl could be, only to realise, mortified, that the sound came from me.

"Oh my God! You giggled!" he exclaims, before bursting into laughter so hard his entire body shakes, and with it, I am shaken too.

"Stop that, you idiot!" I snap, trying to cut him off and inject as much menace into my voice as possible. "I did no such thing!"

Unfortunately, that only makes him laugh harder. One of his arms tightens around me, his hand settling just below my chest, while the other hand begins mercilessly tickling my sides.

A deep, uncontrollable laughter bursts out of me, part from his relentless attack and part from the shocking realisation. I am ticklish.

Like, what the actual hell?!

"Huunteeer!" I cry out between giggles, the sound so foreign to me, much like these unfamiliar feelings running through me. This relationship, this overwhelming happiness, feels almost too much for my soul to contain.

As I twist in a futile attempt to escape his relentless tickling, my movement causes me to brush against him. Then I feel it... his erection, hard and unyielding.

The sensation freezes me in place, as if all the air has been sucked out of the room in an instant.

"Easy, *sugar cube*," he murmurs softly into my ear, his hand gently brushing against my cheek in a soothing caress.

"Just ignore it," he continues, his voice tender and calm, wrapping around me like a safety net. "We are going to take all of this really slow. Please, don't panic."

I try my best to control my body, to project some semblance of confidence, but the traitorous thing has a mind of its own. It betrays me completely, trembling under his touch as if Hunter's very existence is electrifying, igniting something deep and uncontrollable within me.

"Easy, baby. Okay?" he whispers, placing a soft kiss on the side of my neck.

"I honestly cannot control it. Just having you in the same room drives me insane, but holding you in my arms... it is beyond madness, *sugar cube*. Touching your skin feels like my arms are on fire, like the universe itself is surging through me. The feel of you here, with me, is as if creation itself has finally completed me."

He pauses, his voice lowering into something raw and unshakable. "You are mine."

He is right. This feels so normal, so natural, that it is almost unnerving in its strangeness.

I never thought feelings like this could exist in the world. Yet here I am, wrapped tightly in Hunter's arms, and it feels nothing short of incredible. *It is as if creation itself has finally completed* ***us****, as though we were always meant to fit together like this.*

For the first time, I feel at peace. I feel untouchable, as though nothing in the world could hurt me. And, more than anything, I feel like I am no longer alone. *Truly, deeply, not alone.*

I am not sure how long we stand there in silence, completely absorbed and transfixed by the feel of each other. Time seems to blur, each second stretching endlessly in the warmth of his embrace.

Then, Hunter gently steps back, his hands steady as he turns me around to face him. His gaze locks onto mine, intense and searching, as if he is trying to uncover something hidden deep within me. I do not know what he is looking for or if he finds it, but the look in his eyes, so raw, so unguarded, disarms the last shreds of fear I have been clinging to.

God, I love him so much.

"So, we're good, *sugar cube*? Can I go have a shower without worrying you'll bolt?" he asks, a smile playing on his beautiful lips, though concern lingers in his eyes.

"Please..." he trails off, his voice softening when I do not immediately respond.

I do not respond, but it is not because I want to bolt. It is because of the look in his eyes.

If someone had told me that this towering, 6'5'' tall clown of a man could wear such a look of pure adoration, I would have called them a fool. Never in my wildest thoughts would I have believed he was capable of something so tender, so vulnerable.

It is extraordinary to see him like this. My heart melts just watching him, just seeing him happy.

"*Sugar cube*, whatever it is, we can work it out, okay?" he says softly, leaning in to press a gentle kiss to my forehead. "Please..."

"It's okay. I won't run," I reassure him, my voice small but steady. "Go have a shower."

He holds my gaze for a long moment, studying my reaction, probably trying to determine if I am lying. A smile escapes me before I can stop it, and I quickly lower my gaze to hide it.

I never imagined myself with anyone, not really... except him. And now that he is standing in front of me, all kind, docile, willing, and impossibly loving, it is overwhelming, to say the least.

But there is also this feeling in the pit of my stomach that I cannot quite pinpoint. It's a tangled mess of nerves, excitement, and overwhelming happiness. None of it feels like me, not the person I thought I was. And the way he looks at me, with that tender, unshakable affection, is not helping me process any of these unfamiliar emotions.

He slowly lifts my chin, his fingers gentle yet firm, and lets out a long sigh of relief when our eyes meet. Whatever he was searching for in my gaze, he has finally found it.

"Fucking hell, woman," he murmurs, his voice thick with emotion. He takes my hand and places it on his chest, right over the steady thrum of his heartbeat.

"You'll be the death of me," he adds, his words a mix of exasperation and raw affection.

He holds my hand firmly against his chest, as if he is afraid I might pull away. But all my instincts scream at me to stay. To explore him. To touch. To feel. To discover every inch of him.

I am startled by the intensity of these urges, how acutely they call to me, and before I can stop myself, my fingers move ever so slightly across his chest. His breath hitches sharply at my touch, his body freezing completely, as if terrified that even the smallest movement might scare me away.

It is then that I realise, I have never initiated contact with him before. It has always been him, reaching for me, loving me, even in my dreams. *Always him.*

A profound pain shoots through the middle of my chest, raw and unrelenting. All I want in this moment is to love him back. To show him, in any way I can, that I love him just as much as he loves me.

I want him to know that my heart burns with the same intensity, that I ache to love and protect him with the same fierce devotion he has shown me.

I take a small step closer, leaning the side of my head against his chest. With a trembling breath, I wrap my free arm around him in a soft, tentative hug.

The full-body shudder that courses through him is something to behold. How can a man this powerful, this unyielding, be so completely undone by my touch?

Encouraged by his response, I tighten my hold on him, pulling him closer, as if I could anchor him to me. Slowly, I lift my gaze to meet his, and the moment our eyes lock, my heart skips a beat. His beautiful blue eyes are filled with so much love, so much longing, it's as if I am not just a part of his life, but a part of his very soul.

We stand there, wrapped in each other, until I feel his erection nudge against my abdomen. The absurdity of the moment overwhelms me, and I burst out laughing, pulling back slightly.

"You have a problem," I say, trying to keep a straight face but failing miserably as a smirk tugs at my lips.

"Yep, sure do," he says, leaning down to press a gentle kiss on the top of my head. "Actually, I've got two problems," he continues, winking at me with that playful glint in his eyes.

"One, I've been walking around with a hard-on for the past two years." He pauses, smirking at my stunned expression. "And two, I really need a shower. As kind as your dad was to hose me down every other day, trust me, if you open a window, my boxers might disintegrate and fly out in sheer desperation."

The idiot bursts into laughter, clearly delighted by the confused expression on my face.

Unbelievable! My mate, my other half, had to be a 6'5" clown.

"I'm not even going to ask," I say dismissively, waving him off as the corner of my mouth twitches, fighting to join in his banter. "The master bathroom is that way," I add, pointing toward my bedroom with its private ensuite.

As I gesture, my gaze lingers on the door to my bedroom. For a moment, I can see a younger version of myself lying on the bed, a book in hand, my hair wild and untamed, with a pile of snacks cluttering the bedside table. The memory hits me with startling clarity, and along with it comes the deep loneliness I used to feel growing up.

I remember how I would lose myself in romance books, idolising the strong, passionate, and outspoken female characters. I rooted for them, cheered for their happy-ever-afters. But the moment the book ended, reality would crash back in. I knew for a long time I was different, that no one could love me as I am.

Now, staring at that familiar doorway, that same dreadful feeling begins to creep up on me, sinking its claws into my skin. I am not good enough. Not strong enough. Not pretty enough. And no matter what I want to believe, those thoughts still linger, always ready to pull me back under.

I do not even notice Hunter walking back into the living room until he steps into my line of sight, blocking the view of my bedroom.

Oh, God. He really stinks.

Get on with it, mate! Go take that shower already! I think, my pesky inner voice proving just as blunt with him as it always is with me.

Lovely. Truly lovely.

"Easy, baby," he says softly, his voice laced with concern. "Don't worry about it. We don't have to do anything you're not ready for."

He gently lifts my chin, guiding my gaze back to his, and begins that intense, unrelenting analysis of his once again, trying to read every hidden corner of my soul.

"Easy, *sugar cube*," he repeats, his tone steady and reassuring. "I told you, we're going to take this nice and slow. You don't need to worry about a thing. I love you. I adore you. And I will wait for you, for the rest of my days, if that's what it takes."

Why is he so kind?

Is this what love feels like? True love from a man? To be kind, considerate, and patient in a way that feels almost foreign to me?

I do not know what to say. My thoughts are a whirlwind, and the silence grows too heavy. So, I blurt out the first stupid thing that comes to mind.

"You really smell," I say in a small voice, my lips twitching before I burst into giggles again.

He lets out a sigh of relief, his laughter bubbling up again. "Don't run, okay?"

What an idiot. As if I could ever run from him. No, from now on, I will only ever run toward him.

I nod, a small smile playing on my lips, and gently push against his chest. Oh, God, he is so beautiful.

"Go," I say softly. "Have your shower. We can talk later."

He turns and begins walking toward the bathroom, but just before he disappears from view, he glances over his shoulder, his eyes searching mine one last time.

Yes... This is what true love from a man is... a quiet strength that holds you without restraint, a kindness that seeks nothing in return, and a consideration that sees past the surface to the soul beneath. It is devotion, unyielding and unshakable, the kind that makes you feel safe, cherished, and whole.

My gaze drifts back to the bed, and for a fleeting moment, I see her again... the little girl I used to be. She lifts her eyes to meet mine, a gentle smile gracing her face now.

Then she vanishes...

Chapter Seventeen

Hunter

The warmth of the water cascades over my skin, soothing yet igniting something primal within me. Her scent saturates the air, wrapping around me, and it's all I can think about. If I walked in here already aroused, what's happening to my body now is beyond control, unstoppable, unrelenting.

I glance down, and my cock is painfully hard, the veins along its length prominent and flushed, pulsing with a fury that feels almost alive. It's as though my own body is rebelling against me, demanding something I'm powerless to deny.

What can I say? I've been jerking off for the past two years because, since I met my *Sugar Cube*, no other woman has even made my cock twitch. And now, here I am, aroused beyond anything I've ever felt, just from her being in the other room and her scent lingering in the air.

To say I'm about to lose my mind is the understatement of the year. Let's be honest, two years of this torment is bad enough, but the last four months? I didn't even have that release. It wasn't that I didn't want to, my cock wouldn't even get hard. The pain of thinking my *Sugar Cube* might not love me was more than my body, or my mind, could take.

That is all behind us now. The only thing that matters is our future together. Her pain, her suffering, her disappointment in herself, it is all in the past. I will care for her with every breath in my lungs. I will love her so completely that she will finally see how perfect, beautiful, and unbelievably intelligent she is. She is everything, and somehow, I am lucky enough that she loves me back.

I rest my head against the shower tiles, letting the water cascade down my back, easing the tension in my muscles, my mind, and my soul all at once. I close my eyes for a moment, but the image of my *Sugar Cube* on her knees, crying, flashes through my mind. I have never felt desperation like I did when I saw her on the floor, broken like that.

I would have torn my arm and leg from my body and crawled to her if it meant comforting her, if it meant easing even a fraction of her suffering. The pain in my wrist and shoulder lingers, but it pales in comparison to the fire in my chest, the overwhelming love I carry for her. Every fibre of my being is calling out to her, and now that I know she loves me back, the final piece of me is whole.

I will do anything, become anything, to make sure she is happy for the rest of her life.

Some might call that pathetic. Some might call it stupid or weak. What would I say to people like that? Simple—*fuck off*. You have never experienced a love like this. A love so deep, so powerful, so unshakable that no broken past, no broken body, and no broken soul could ever keep us apart.

What happened to her... I feel the weight of her pain in every cell of my body. My beast is consumed by fury, raging inside me, desperate for blood. It has been screaming since I learned what happened to her, since the moment I found out what was separating us.

He is howling for us to bathe in their blood. He is howling for vengeance, for their blood to soak the ground beneath her feet. He demands their suffering. He wants it to hurt so deeply, so agonisingly, that they would beg for mercy I will never grant. He wants it to hurt. He wants it to hurt so badly that they would beg me for death, screaming in agony, and even then, I would not end them. I would make it last and I would make it truly hurt.

My body feels like it is on fire, consumed by fury and a desperate need for my *Sugar Cube*. I shake my head, trying to rein in the chaos, to tame the beast clawing at my insides.

I cannot scare her. I cannot hurt her in any way. If that means I have to bury or even kill the beast inside me to make her happy, so be it. I need to control every ounce of chaos when I am around her. I need to show her that she is perfectly safe with me, that nothing and no one will ever hurt her again as long as I breathe.

She is not just another possession. She is not just another woman. She is everything I never knew I needed. That is what she is *a need*. The way I need oxygen in my lungs to survive is the same way I NEED my *Sugar Cube* by my side to live. There is no today or tomorrow without her. There is only her, and that is all there will ever be.

I feel the beast retreating, so I open my eyes and grab her body wash, bringing it to my nose for a deep inhale. "Fuck, that smells good," I mutter, my voice thick with arousal. *Do they put some sort of aphrodisiac in body wash now?* The thought is ridiculous, so I brush it off and start lathering it over my skin.

Big mistake. Big, big mistake.

I glance down again at my painfully throbbing cock. I really, really do not want to be the guy who jerks off in her bathroom the first time I'm here, but there is no way I can hold back any longer. She is everywhere, her scent, her essence, her presence and if I don't take care of this, I might actually die from blue balls.

Can someone die from blue balls? I should probably Google that. Because if I do, that asshole Dominic would put something ridiculous on my tombstone like, "*Hunter, the Blue Ball Chaser!*" or, "*Here rests Hunter, who ran, tripped, and shattered his blue balls.*"

I start chuckling at the thought, because I know that idiot would try something like that or worse.

There are beads of precum on the tip of my cock so large, I didn't even know it was possible for a cock to weep like that for attention. Case in point, it absolutely can and does.

That's it! I'm doing this! I need to release or I'll lose my mind, and worse, I'll end up wanting to jump on her. I cannot scare her. Not in any way.

Whatever happened to her, whatever we need to face, it is *our* problem now, not just hers. And no matter how she is down there, it doesn't change how much I love her. It doesn't change how much I *need* her by my side for the rest of my life.

I grab my cock, my grip firm and unrelenting, and begin stroking with a desperation that borders on madness. The sensation is overwhelming, every nerve igniting as my hand moves in steady, powerful strokes. The water cascading down my back feels like molten pressure, grounding me in this moment even as my thoughts spiral out of control.

Her face floods my mind. Her beauty, her strength, the fierce intelligence that glows behind those fiery eyes. She is untouchable to the rest of the world, a fortress of resilience, yet she chose to show me her vulnerability. To me. That truth alone has my hips jerking into my fist, my breaths short and ragged, the tension coiling tighter in my core.

I picture her soft skin, the delicate curve of her lips, the sweetness of her scent. It is everywhere, consuming me, becoming a *need* as vital as air in my lungs. My balls tighten painfully, my body trembling with the sheer force of what is coming. As I twist my wrist over the tip, my release shatters through me like a tidal wave.

Hot streams of cum shoot against the tiles in sharp, endless bursts, and my vision blurs as my entire body seizes. For a few seconds, I lose myself completely. My mind blank, my lungs burning, my legs unsteady. I slam my free hand against the tiles, bracing myself as my other hand continues to milk every drop, pouring my very soul into this release for her.

The guttural sound I let out during the strongest orgasm of my life is raw and primal, a testament to the way she owns me. She does not have to touch me to undo me. I am hers, utterly and completely. My love for her is so consuming, so absolute, that it terrifies me. Without her, there is no me. She is my purpose, my obsession, my everything. I am scared I my lose my mind loving her so desperately.

"Fuck!"

I watch the streams of cum swirl and vanish down the drain, but when I glance down, my cock is still painfully hard, throbbing as if mocking me. The release wasn't enough. It could never be enough when all I want is her.

I cannot scare her. I have to rein in the crazy, suppress every bit of it, and be the anchor she needs. Losing her is not an option, because even with her right next to me, I feel like I am drowning in the sheer force of my love and need for her.

I'm scared. Truly scared. I have never felt anything like this before. It is all-consuming, overpowering, and if I would have died for her before, now... now there is no limit. I would do anything under the sun for her, anything to keep her safe, to see her smile, to make her happy. She is my everything, and I have never been more terrified of failing at something in my life.

I finish rinsing off and step out of the shower, the entire bathroom now thick with steam. The heat clings to my skin, but it is nothing compared to the fire still raging inside me. That was an amazing shower, even without my release. But with it, it was the most incredible shower of my life.

I grab a towel and wrap it around my waist, adjusting it carefully as I try to position my cock in a way that does not make it glaringly obvious it is still rock hard. Not that it is cooperating. It seems intent on reminding me just how far gone I am for her.

In an effort to calm it down, I glance at it and let out a deep sigh before starting to talk to it. "Do you mind? Could you please calm down? We cannot scare her. She might not have even seen one of you before, and if she gets scared and bolts, who do you think will suffer with me, mate? You! So how about you give me a break and go soft for a while?"

I take a few deep breaths, hoping my words will do the trick, but my cock decides to be a complete dick about the situation. It stays fully at attention, as if my little pep talk never even happened.

"Fucker," I mutter under my breath.

I quickly grab a toothbrush, making sure my mouth is crystal clean. I am going to kiss the living hell out of my *Sugar Cube*. Before, I did not dare to kiss her, even when every fiber of my existence screamed at me to do it. To kiss her. To taste her. To bite her.

But none of that matters now. What matters is that she loves me back. She. Loves. Me. Back.

I will love every inch of her. I will cherish every part of her that she chooses to give me, loving her with everything I have until she feels safe enough to give herself to me completely.

With one last look in the mirror, I tighten the towel securely around my waist and step out of the bathroom.

She is sitting on the edge of the bed, staring at the floor, looking all nervous and shit. My chest tightens, and for a moment, I feel like I could cry.

In all the fantasies I ever concocted about this woman, never once did I dare to imagine her vulnerable or unsettled by me. Seeing her like this is shattering my mind into tiny pieces.

Never did I think she would show me this side of herself. To be completely honest, I did not even think she had a side like this. She makes every man in the room shrink in her presence, so how could I have imagined she might have a vulnerable side?

She is so unbelievably strong and intelligent. Every room she walks into bends to her will as if it is second nature. There is no meeting or combat training where she does not dominate her opponent completely. Well, to be fair, I let her beat me because, honestly, who wouldn't want her to pull that move where she wraps her legs around my neck?

Let's face it, no man in my position would resist that. So, during every training session or any time I pushed her buttons just right, I made sure she resorted to that move sooner or later. It was my fix, my way of getting that hit of her core scent, like the desperate addict that I am.

Don't judge me! I took what I could get for two years, so to anyone who thinks I am pathetic... fuck off.

And even if I truly am, so what? For her, I would wear the crown and proudly be the king of pathetic men if it meant I could have my woman. So no, *I do not care*. Not one bit.

I stop in the threshold and lean my shoulder against the edge of the door, letting myself take her in. She is so unbelievably beautiful that it's almost hard to look at her directly. For a moment, I have to remind myself how to breathe because her beauty, combined with her vulnerable state, feels almost magical. It does something wild to my insides, twisting me up in ways I cannot describe.

I feel her pull, like a lighthouse siren calling out after a terrible storm at sea. It is so powerful that I have to physically hold myself back to keep from falling to my knees in front of her, begging her to let me love her for the rest of my life.

How did I end up like this? How did this woman burrow so deeply under my skin, into every part of me?

I shake my head, trying to steady my thoughts, reminding myself to tread carefully. The last thing I want is to come on too strong and scare the hell out of her.

"I'm not going to sleep with you!" she blurts out in a rush, the words tumbling so quickly that she is left breathing heavily by the end of it.

What?

For a second, I am at a loss for words, caught off guard by the way she said it. It was like the words exploded out of her with a force I never saw coming.

"I'm sorry, what?" I reply, keeping my voice steady, trying my best to sound calm and collected.

"I am not going to sleep with you, Hunter!" she yells, her voice sharp and defensive, she is bracing herself against me.

Once again, I am caught off guard by her reaction. But at least she did not run. That would have been something, me chasing her through the house, stark naked.

"Well..." she continues, her voice slightly calmer but still carrying a trace of panic. "What I mean is, we are not going to have sex right now, Hunter. I just did not want you to think something was going to happen, because it will not. And if you test me, I will cut you. No doubt about it."

I try to hold back a laugh, but a small chuckle escapes before I can stop it. She shoots me such a murderous look that I lose the battle completely and start laughing as I push myself off the edge of the doorframe.

"Easy, baby," I say, my tone soft and steady, as I take careful steps toward her, one after the other. "Easy, *Sugar Cube*," I continue, my voice even gentler as I stop just in front of her. "I already told you, we are taking it slow. Very slow. And even if I have to wait for you for the rest of my life, I will still be happy because I have you by my side."

I place my hands on her shoulders, my palms warm against her soft, chocolate skin, and gently stroke, letting her feel the sincerity in my touch. She is so beautiful. Her deep, soulful eyes, her exquisite features. It's still insane to me that she is letting me get this close. That she is letting me touch her and seems okay with it.

"Yes, I did hear you enjoyed yourself," she says, attempting to be sassy, but the shy smile tugging at her lips betrays her.

"You heard that?" I ask, even though my inner voice immediately responds for her. *The dead heard that, Hunter.*

"Sorry about that. Just ignore it, baby." I lean down and press a gentle kiss to the top of her head. "I cannot control it, *Sugar Cube*. Honestly..." My voice trails off, and I sigh. "I even had a chat with the bastard, but he still does not want to listen."

Her eyes drop to the very obvious erection straining against the towel. They widen slightly, and when she lifts her gaze back to mine, there is something there. It is something I have never seen in her expression before.

Hunger...

Chapter Eighteen

Sofia

I power washed in the guest bathroom, thinking he might do the same. Little did I expect to have a front-row seat to his grunts of pleasure coming from my shower.

The sounds he made were so deeply masculine, unlike anything I had ever heard before. They ignited something in my core, a heat that burned hotter than the sun with an almost unbearable need and want for him. It terrified me.

What he did, the pleasure he brought himself and the raw, uninhibited sounds he made *was beautiful.* Erotic. Exquisite. What scared me was my reaction, the way my body responded to him so fiercely, so uncontrollably.

He is already unbelievably attractive, but now, knowing that these sounds are his, that they belong to him, it's almost too much for me to handle.

Would I ever be able to bring those sounds out of him? The idea feels ludicrous. How could someone like me, with zero experience, ever draw something so raw and passionate from him? I only saw a cock back at school in the sex aid class or whatever it was called. And let me just add, it looked strange, all dangling there like that. Maybe it wasn't as strange as I thought, or maybe it was. One thing I know for sure is that I was completely petrified by my own situation at the time.

I sigh deeply as all the stupid memories come flooding back, popping into my mind like a flashback from a nightmare. Just like that, the heat and desire that had been building in me vanish completely.

What replaces it is anxiety. Pure, unrelenting panic.

I cannot sleep with him!

How would that even work?

The only time I researched female anatomy and realised I was different, I came to the horrifying conclusion that I was the problem. I was different. I was broken. I was disgusting. But that was not the worst thing I found out at the time.

I also learned what they do to women like me. How some men, on their wedding nights, take scissors and cut them open. That was the moment I broke, truly and irreparably. I never researched it again. I was too petrified. *How can this be?*

If anyone thinks I will ever let that happen to me, they are dead wrong. They would be sorry fools who would die by my hand before they ever had the chance. There is no way I will let anyone hurt me again. NEVER!

A full-blown panic attack takes hold of me, and all I can do is breathe uncontrollably and stare at the floor as the terror grips me.

Hunter loves me. He would not hurt me.

Hunter loves me. He would not hurt me.

Hunter loves me. He would not hurt me.

I repeat the words in my mind like a lifeline, clinging to them, willing myself to believe them with every fractured breath.

The words keep repeating in my mind like a broken record. I lift my gaze, and there it is again, my suitcase, mocking me with its silent arrogance. It seems to remind me how weak and pathetic I am for ever thinking I could have a normal life.

You might have got the guy, but you are still disgusting, that horrible voice in my mind sneers.

I want to cry.

I want to scream.

I want to run.

Run?

No!

I promised Hunter I would not run. A deep sigh escapes my lips, and that is when I feel his presence. I turn, and the moment I see him, the breath is stolen from my lungs. He is so beautiful.

Hunter loves me. He would not hurt me.

"I'm not going to sleep with you!" The words burst out of me so quickly and desperately that even I am surprised by the force of their release.

"I'm sorry, what?" he replies, his voice calm and steady, though the surprise on his face is unmistakable.

"I am not going to sleep with you, Hunter!" The words rush out, firm and absolute. I need to set boundaries. I am not sure how any of this will work, but one thing I know for certain is that Hunter loves me, and he will not hurt me.

"Well..." I pause, taking a few deep breaths, trying to steady both my voice and the storm in my mind. "What I mean is, we are not going to have sex right now, Hunter. I just did not want you to think something was going to happen, because it will not. And if you test me, I will cut you. No doubt about it."

The moron laughs. *I will cut him! I cannot kill him, we both know that, but I can cut him!*

"Easy, *Sugar Cube*," he says softly, taking slow, deliberate steps toward me. "I already told you, we are taking it very slow. Even if I have to wait for you for the rest of my life, I will still be happy because I have you by my side."

Damn! That is the sweetest thing anyone has ever said to me.

Hunter loves me. He will not hurt me.

HE. LOVES. ME.

My heart melts again, and I suddenly feel so small, insecure, and vulnerable. Before I can stop myself, I let the first stupid thing that comes to mind slip out.

"Yes, I did hear you enjoyed yourself." I try to make it sound sharp, like a playful bite, but the delivery falls completely flat.

"You heard that? Sorry about that. Just ignore it, baby," he says in the calmest and most reassuring voice I have ever heard from him. "I cannot control it, *Sugar Cube*. Honestly..." He pauses, trailing off for a moment before continuing. "I even had a chat with the bastard, and he still does not want to listen."

I try to resist, to keep my eyes from wandering, but I cannot. I have to look.

Slowly, my gaze travels down from his chest, over his defined abs, and finally settles on the very obvious, enlarged cock straining against the towel. I am not sure how cocks are supposed to look, but this... this is big. This looks incredible, even through the towel.

And just like that, the explosive fire in my core reignites with a vengeance. All I want is to ask him to let the towel fall.

I am so scared, excited, and completely intimidated, but he is so beautiful. Hot as hell.

He would drop the towel if I asked him, right?

Before I can do or say something utterly stupid, I lift my gaze. The moment our eyes meet, the look in his is the final spark, obliterating any remnants of sanity I might still possess.

"You have a problem," I say in a hoarse voice.

I have a problem too, but at least mine is not plastered all over the outside. So, I will just sit here and pretend to play it cool.

"I sure do, *Sugar Cube.*" His eyes seem to glow, the corner of his mouth twitching upward, and the mischievous look on his face says it all. *He knows...*

He knows exactly what he has awakened in the depths of my soul. I never knew feelings like this existed, but they clearly do, because I am burning from the inside out. It really is as simple as that.

He leans down so slowly that I can genuinely count every freckle on his beautiful face. He looks like a fallen angel, with his almost white hair and piercing blue eyes.

Well, that is, normally until he opens that stupid mouth of his.

But my train of thought is completely interrupted as his lips press softly against mine, in the most tender and gentle kiss I could have ever imagined.

He kneels completely in front of me, settling between my legs, his eyes fixed on mine with so much love that I can genuinely feel my heart melting right there in front of him.

He just stays there, looking at me, loving me with his gaze. There is no need for words. No need for actions. Nothing else is required, because we have each other. *We truly have each other.*

And when his expression shifts to one of pure longing, we both understand. Without a single word, we have had our first unspoken conversation.

We made it.

We are together.

"I love you, Hunter." The words come out so softly, so quietly, that for a moment we both just stare at each other in disbelief, as if neither of us can believe I actually said them.

"You love me?" he asks, his voice filled with disbelief, almost as though he is surprised by my words.

"I love you," I repeat, my voice barely above a whisper as I lower my gaze.

"Nope! None of that!" he says firmly, quickly grabbing my chin and tilting my face back up to meet his. He holds my gaze, studying every subtle movement I make.

"You love me?" he asks again, his voice softer this time. And if I did not know any better, I would swear his eyes are glistening, as though he is fighting hard to control his emotions.

His eyes are a perfect blue, as light and clear as the summer skies in Australia. Clean. Perfect. Blue.

The number of times I have dreamed about these eyes...

"I. Love. You." I enunciate each word carefully, letting them settle in the space between us. Then, placing my palm on his chest, I exhale deeply, as though releasing every ounce of doubt I had ever carried.

"Holy shit! I might have a heart attack, woman!" he exclaims, his voice booming with an emotion so raw it seems to fill the room. His wide eyes glisten, and now I am certain, he is fighting back tears.

"You love me?!" he repeats, his tone a mix of disbelief and overwhelming joy. "*Sugar Cube*, I have imagined a million ways you might look at me, talk to me, maybe even laugh at me. But not once, not even in my wildest daydreams or the filthiest wet dreams have you ever said those words to me. Not like this."

Before I can even react, he moves. In a heartbeat, he launches himself at me, wrapping me in a hug so tight it steals the breath from my lungs. It hurts, but it's the good type of hurt.

I can feel every part of him, the frantic pounding of his heart against my chest, the way his entire body trembles with an intensity I have never seen from him before. His emotions are so unguarded, so completely bare, that they consume the space between us. And any lingering doubt I ever had that he might not love me is now utterly and irrevocably gone.

This is real. His body is screaming its love to me. His words are shouting it. His soul is calling out to me with a love so pure and overwhelming that it takes my breath away.

I. AM. LOVED.

He buries his face in the crook of my neck, and I can feel every tremor coursing through his body, as though he cannot contain the flood of emotions running through him.

I did this.

He is like this because of me. Because I told him I love him.

Crazy. Absolutely crazy.

"I love you so much, *Sugar Cube*, it fucking hurts," he says, his voice breaking at the end. "I don't deserve you, but I will take you anyway. And I will never let you go."

The determination in his tone is undeniable. There is not a single shadow of doubt about where we stand or what our future holds.

I tighten my arms around him, pulling him even closer, and whisper softly into his ear, "I love you, *Nuuro*."

His body shudders again at my words, and I cannot ignore the way his cock presses against the side of my thigh. He is trying so hard not to move, not to let himself rub against me, but the strain is evident in every part of him.

"Baby, I need to let go," he murmurs, his voice deep and raw, like he is in physical pain. "You are driving me insane, and if I don't let go of you now, I am not sure I can control myself any longer.

There is something in his tone, a plea, almost desperate. He is begging for his life, teetering on the edge of restraint and surrender.

He rises to his full height and extends his hand to me. When I place mine in his, he lifts it to his lips, pressing a deep, lingering kiss on my knuckles before gently moving my hand to rest against his cheek.

"Let's just sleep tonight," he murmurs, his voice soft and steady. "We have a lot to discuss, but it can all wait until tomorrow."

He settles behind me, wrapping his arm and leg over me, cocooning me completely in his embrace. His body is heavy and warm, and the scent of him, mixed with me, is intoxicating.

I never thought I would love the feeling of his weight on me so much, but it is grounding, comforting in a way I never imagined.

Within seconds, I am asleep.

I am safe.

No one will ever hurt me again.

Chapter Nineteen

Hunter

I've never slept better in my entire life. Hands down, the best sleep I've ever had, and it's all because of the firecracker of a woman curled up in my arms. She's soft, beautiful, and so damn delicious I swear I could inhale her. Not love. Not adore. Not want. I could actually inhale her. That's how unbelievably obsessed, utterly dependent, and irreversibly in love with her I am.

I woke up when the first light cracked through, but I just tightened my hold on her and drifted back to sleep. She feels absolutely perfect in my arms. It's like second nature, like she was the missing piece of me out there in the world, just waiting for me to find her. And find her I did. Now... now there's no stopping this. This is as inevitable as the sun rising in the sky every day. If someone can stop the sun from coming up, then maybe, just maybe, they'd have a chance at stopping what's happening between me and my *sugar cube.*

We didn't move the entire night. Not an inch. She didn't pull away. If anything, she pressed back into me even further. Now half my chest is leaning on her back, and there is no way she isn't feeling the weight of me. She feels incredible beneath me. Absolutely perfect.

Well, that is a sentence I never thought I would say. I have said it in my mind a million times, but for it to actually come true like this? No way. I never thought she would show me a vulnerable side.

And the way she told me she loves me? I was crying inside like a bloody baby. She was so scared, so vulnerable, opening up to tell me those words. She loves me. She actually loves me.

SHE. LOVES. ME.

I got my woman.

I bloody got my woman!

"You really do have a serious problem, Hunter," her sleepy voice pulls me back from my daydreams of her.

I burst out laughing right next to her ear, and she flinches.

"Sorry, baby. Too loud?" I press a kiss just under her ear, and she moves her beautiful ass against me without meaning to. A groan escapes me before I can stop it.

"You are poking me. That's the only way I can describe it. Does that thing ever go down? Don't you feel light-headed or something?" She tries, and fails, to hold back her laughter.

"That thing is called a cock, *sugar cube*," I reply, grinning against her skin. "And it's all yours to do with as you please. So no, I sincerely don't think he's going down anytime soon."

I finish my little explanation with a trail of kisses along her neck and shoulder.

She is so sensitive to my touch it is absolutely maddening. Goosebumps erupt all over her body, and she trembles in my arms. She starts to turn, and that is when I realise my towel has fallen from around me. I am completely naked behind her.

Fuck. She is going to see me and get scared.

"Baby, no!" My panicked voice comes out so fast it freezes her in place.

"What?"

I take a deep breath, a last-ditch effort to calm the fucker down. But, as always, he is just a dick about it, standing tall and proud like this is the day he will finally get to taste her. *The idiot.*

"Sorry, baby. My towel fell, and I don't want to scare you. Just hold on, I'll cover up in one second," I say in a rushed tone, fumbling to manoeuvre the towel back into place.

Her soft hand lands on my arm, bringing me to a sudden stop. Her touch is gentle. Her fingers are small, feminine, and slim, but there is the faintest tremble running through them.

We stand there for what feels like an eternity until she breaks the silence. With her words, any connection to reality I might still possess disappears in her presence.

"What if I want to see you?" she asks, her voice small and almost scared. "Would that be okay?"

She adds the words softly, her fingers tighten around my arm. Is she afraid I might pull away? I would never pull away from her. Even if I were dying, I would crawl my way back to her.

"Of course it's okay, *sugar cube*. I just don't want to scare you."

I lean down and place another kiss on her shoulder, right on the spot I've discovered she particularly likes.

Honestly, I still cannot believe she is letting me do this. I am touching her, kissing her, learning her body, and storing every detail to bring her as much pleasure and happiness as humanly possible.

Because if anyone on this planet deserves to be loved, it is my *sugar cube.*

I move back behind her and wrap my arm around her again because if I am doing this, we need to set some ground rules from the start.

"I want to see you, *Nuuro,*" she says softly, placing a kiss on my arm. Then, just for good measure, she bites and tugs at my arm hair.

"Ouch!" I cry out, feigning offence. "Actually, I liked it. Do it again," I add with a playful nudge.

She wants to see me. Fuck my life. Yesterday, I was ready to die. The day before, I was beating those guys to death because of my grief. And today? Today, I am in heaven.

My life is insane, and it is all because of this gorgeous *sugar cube* in my arms.

"Baby, if you want to see me, I am all for it. Trust me, there are no complaints from this side," I say, then burst out laughing. *What kind of fool would I be to say no to her?*

"But we need to agree on some rules, baby."

"What rules?" she asks, freezing in my arms, completely taken by surprise.

"I don't have a problem with you doing anything to me. Honestly, I can't think of a single thing that would bother me if it came from you." I try to search my mind for something that might put me off, but either I am too intoxicated with love for her, or I truly am down for anything when it comes to her.

"But I need you to swear to me that you will tell me the moment you feel uncomfortable with something I do or say."

I lift myself onto my elbow and gently turn her beautiful face to me. The second my eyes land on hers, I am floating, completely untethered, like the damn fool I've become.

"Hi," I say, my voice cracking at the end like a sick teenage boy. "God, you're beautiful in the morning." I am completely melting next to her because she is just too much.

She rewards me with a shy look and a smile so sweet on those beautiful lips that I am drawn to them with the force of a thousand raging bulls.

I lean down and press my lips to hers in a soft, gentle kiss. I don't dare lose myself in it now, so I pull back. The discussion we are having needs to be set straight.

She needs to understand that she is safe with me, that I would never hurt her in any way. She needs to know that I would do anything for her, be anything she needs me to be, and that I would kill anyone who dared to harm her.

"Promise me, *sugar cube.*" I study her gaze, making sure she is not just saying it but truly means it. She nods her head.

"No. I already told you," I say softly, my voice gentle but firm. "None of that. We are going to be crystal clear with each other, because you are the light of my life and the air in my lungs. I cannot lose you, *sugar cube.*"

Whatever she sees in my eyes makes her smile that sweet smile at me again, and my insides turn to liquid.

"I promise," she says softly, turning her hand to gently stroke what is now a full-on beard. "I like the beard, by the way," she adds, stroking it again.

Then, with a cheeky grin, she says, "Now be a good boy and show me that cock."

She bursts out laughing so hard her face contorts, making her look absolutely ridiculous and utterly adorable.

Well, that is a sentence I never thought I would hear from her. But hey, who am I to complain?

"I want to see you, *Nuuro*," she says again, quickly repeating herself, her voice carrying a mix of determination and vulnerability.

Any remnant of sanity, clarity, or restraint vanishes as every drop of blood in my body rushes to my cock at a maddening speed. This time, I actually feel light-headed.

I hold her gaze, and there is so much love, longing, and lust in her eyes. I know with absolute certainty that she wants this as much as I do. She is not scared. I can see the curiosity, desire, and need in her gaze as clearly as they are in mine.

"You sure, baby?" I ask, making one last attempt to give her a chance to change her mind, while inwardly praying she truly wants to see me.

The smile on her face is absolute perfection. She does not say a word. Instead, she reaches over and gives me a push. It is not hard enough to make me move or cause any pain, but it is definitely clear what she wants.

I don't move. I told her I want everything crystal clear between us. If I hurt her, even by accident, I know something in me would die. She holds the key to my heart, my mind, and my soul, and nothing, not even me, will ever hurt her again.

"Let me see you!" she says, her voice exasperated. "Come on, get on with it!" She pushes at my arm again.

I rise slowly, every movement deliberate, as if I can control how much of me she takes in at once. The truth is, I am mortified. Not of being seen, but of what she might feel when she sees all of me, completely naked.

At almost 7 feet tall, I am a lot for anyone to take in. I have been training in martial arts since I was a boy, pushed to be strong, fast, and unbreakable. The years in the army and the SASR only sharpened me further, sculpting my body into something built for war. Bench pressing 200 kilograms is just another fact of my existence, but none of that strength matters here, not now. Right now, I feel like a raw nerve, every inch of me exposed to her gaze.

The tattoos that cover my skin, the scars from battles won and lost, and the heavy muscle that ripples under her scrutiny, they all feel amplified under her attention. And then there is my cock. It stands fully erect, twelve inches of unrelenting need, that has its own agenda. It's proportional to my size, sure, but that only makes it more intimidating.

For a moment, doubt claws at me. It is not just the fear of her reaction to my body, it is everything. What if she feels overwhelmed? What if she sees too much of who I am, the man behind the muscle, the man behind the jokes? *What if I am too much?*

This is her first time seeing a man like this, fully naked, fully hard, and fully hers. I know it is a lot. Too much. And yet, even as fear grips me, I cannot deny the hope that lingers, the fragile belief that she might not just accept me but want me... all of me, just as I am.

My movements are slow, deliberate, as I try to steady my breathing and muster the courage to stand to my full height. She can see my back now, every inch of it, and the gasp that escapes her lips hits me like a jolt. I do not need to see her face to know what she is reacting to my size, my tattoos, or maybe both.

I draw on every ounce of resolve I have, reminding myself why I am doing this. She asked to see me. She asked, not once, but multiple times. That thought alone anchors me. She might not know it yet, but there is nothing she could ever ask of me that I would not deliver. She will learn that in time.

What she does not yet realise is the sheer power she holds over me. It is not just about the way her words or touch undo me. It is something far deeper, far more consuming. The control she has over me goes beyond reason, beyond logic, beyond life or death. She asked to see me, and so she will. Because for her, there is no limit to what I will give.

I turn slowly, every movement deliberate, as if rushing might shatter the fragile tension in the air. Her gaze hits me like a physical force, and I let it wash over me, steadying myself against the weight of her scrutiny.

Her eyes start at the top of my head, trailing down with unhurried purpose. They pause on my broad shoulders, her breath hitching almost imperceptibly. She continues to my chest, down the hard lines of my abs, before her gaze finally lands on my erection.

Her reaction is instantaneous, raw, and unguarded. Her eyes widen, pupils blown so large they nearly eclipse her irises. Her lips part slightly, as if the very sight of me has stolen the words from her mouth. The faintest tremor passes through her, so subtle it would be easy to miss, but I catch it. I catch everything when it comes to her.

I do not move. Not an inch. I make no attempt to turn away or cover myself. This is not a moment for hiding or hesitation. It is for her, and her alone. Whatever she sees, whatever she feels, I will give her all the time she needs to take it in.

Her gaze is not just curious, it is hungry, filled with something deeper than mere desire. It is as if she is seeing me, truly seeing me, for the first time. In that moment, I am not just a man standing naked before her. I am hers, fully and irrevocably, stripped of pretense and shield.

The silence between us stretches, thick with unspoken words and emotions I cannot name. My body hums with anticipation, with burning desire, but I hold it all back. This moment is not about me. It is about her, her exploration, her understanding, her acceptance. Whatever she needs from me, I will give it, no matter how long it takes.

Her eyes continue their journey down my body, traveling slowly and deliberately. They linger on my thighs, then my calves, before beginning their ascent, taking in every inch of me as though she is committing me to memory. When her gaze finally meets mine, I am completely undone.

Her eyes, those deep and endless pools of brown, have always felt like an abyss where I could willingly lose my sanity. But now, this look is something else entirely. This is not just her seeing me. This is her stripping me bare in ways far deeper than skin, and I let her.

I am no longer just a man in her presence. I am something unmade, brought to my knees by a single glance. The rawness in her eyes holds me captive, and for a fleeting moment, I am weightless, suspended in the gravity of her. She does not need words to convey her power over me. It is in the way she looks at me, the way she owns me without ever saying a thing.

I say nothing. Words would only shatter the fragile, electric silence between us. Instead, I hold her gaze and wait, giving her the space to make the next move at her own pace. Whatever she decides, I will follow, because in this moment, I am hers completely, without condition or restraint.

"You are beautiful, Hunter," she says in a hoarse voice.

A chuckle escapes my lips, and I lower my gaze. Of course, my cock is weeping for her, like she is its master and it desperately needs her.

"And that..." she pauses for a moment, her finger pointing directly at my cock. "That is beautiful, *Nuuro*."

She adds the words with a softness that sends a shiver down my spine, and then she licks her lips, making me feel like I might lose whatever shred of control I have left.

Fuck me sideways. Come on, woman, have mercy on me. There is only so much restraint I can manage.

"Can I touch it?" she asks, her voice small and tentative, yet filled with a bold curiosity that sets me on fire.

Before I can even respond, she shifts onto her knees, leaning back on her heels, her movements fluid and unguarded. Excitement, curiosity, lust, and love radiate from her face, so vivid it takes my breath away. It's clear as the way my body is yearning for her... her touch, her love, her very existence.

If there was ever a moment in my life to feel proud of my body, it's this one. Not for the muscles, the tattoos, or the strength I have honed over years of training, but for the way it stands before her now, unguarded and hers to command. The woman of my dreams, the one who owns my heart, my soul, and whatever fragile grip I have left on my sanity, just asked if she could touch me.

Fuck yes, she can.

But I cannot say that. Not like this. I cannot throw all my joy, my longing, and all my crazy at her feet all at once. She deserves better than that. She deserves care, control, and a steady hand that proves I am more than the chaos she stirs in me. So I gather myself, pulling every fragment of restraint I have left, and slow my breathing. Every move I make, every word I speak, is deliberate. Calm. Measured.

Because this moment cannot stop here.

She may not realise it yet, but she holds a power over me that transcends anything I have ever known. This is not just about her asking to touch me. It is about the trust in her voice, the curiosity in her eyes, and the love that radiates from her every glance. This is her choosing to reach for me, and I will not take that for granted.

"You can do whatever you want to me, *sugar cube*," I say, keeping my voice steady, even as the words reverberate through my chest with undeniable truth. "I am yours."

Chapter Twenty

Sofia

Nothing could have prepared me for what I am looking at.

Holy shit!

I knew Hunter was big. I mean, I knew he was really big, muscular, broad, and all the rest of it. But this? Fuck! This is something else entirely!

In all honesty, I have no idea what came over me when I asked him to let me see his cock. Seriously, where did that even come from? But once the thought lodged itself in the pit of my being, burning like an unrelenting fire, there was no stopping it. The words spilled out before I could think twice, like a secret I did not even know I was keeping.

So I said it out loud.

You can imagine my surprise when he insisted on setting up rules before I could look at him. At first, I wanted to tease him, to make a joke of it, but the second he turned my face and our eyes met, everything shifted.

I saw it. His concern was there, clear as day in his gaze, but it was not just something I noticed. I felt it in my chest, an ache that was not my own. He was scared, Not of me, but for me. He was trying so hard, fighting to make sure I would not be afraid, yet he was the one who was terrified.

My heart softened in a way I was not prepared for. It melted completely. He stole my breath with just a few words. Every second I spend next to him, he somehow burrows deeper under my skin, and I am losing my mind over him.

He loves me.

HE. LOVES. ME.

It is not just that he loves me. He *cares* for me. He cares for me above and beyond anything I have ever known. The thought of protecting myself from him, setting rules or safewords, or whatever the hell people do, never even crossed my mind. Not once.

So you can imagine my surprise when he loved me more than the weight of my own fear and disgust. He cared enough to create boundaries I never thought to make for myself. He loved me more than the doom I have carried, the disgust that has lived under my skin for as long as I can remember. And somehow, I love him more than those fears too.

It never occurred to me to set limits with him, because with him I feel... *safe*. Absolute, unwavering safety. So this morning, when that fiery need bloomed deep inside me, I let my heart take the leap.

As my gaze roams over his body, I take in every detail, the powerful muscles, the intricate tattoos, and every defined line that I ache to explore with my tongue. My eyes travel lower, drawn by an invisible pull, and the moment they land on the sharp V-shape leading down, I freeze.

There it is. The crown of his cock, standing tall and looking painfully hard.

I forget how to breathe. Just like that. The air catches in my chest as I stare, shameless and unhurried, like a starved woman given a feast. It is big. It is beautiful. I never thought I would use the word "beautiful" to describe a cock, but either I have lost my mind, or this one deserves the title.

The crown is smooth and shiny, with a tiny bead of something glistening at the tip. Is that... cum? How is that even possible? Can guys release cum like that without any kind of stimulation? I *need to ask him about it later, because there is no bloody way I am Googling this.*

I might be utterly ignorant when it comes to things like this, but I am not stupid. I know exactly what would happen if I typed those words into a search engine. The abyss waiting on the other side. Pain, agony, and the inevitable spiral of self-loathing would swallow me whole. It would be forceful, devastating, and absolutely certain.

So, no. Not a chance.

I try to steady my thoughts and focus, studying his cock a little more. The veins stand out, purple and bulging, almost as if they are angry. There is hair at the base and on his balls, but not on the shaft itself. Is that normal? I always assumed there would be hair everywhere, but apparently not.

As I look closer, I notice a few faint hairs along the length of it, if that is even the right word for it. I think it is called a shaft, but I am not entirely sure. The hairs are so light they are almost invisible, but they are there.

I let my gaze drift lower to his balls, hanging beneath his cock like two jewels. One sits slightly lower than the other, and they look heavy, almost swollen, even with the hair covering them.

My eyes continue their descent, landing on his thighs. They are so muscular, so powerful, I cannot help but imagine the sheer force he carries in those legs. If he put his full weight into them, I swear he could crush someone's head without breaking a sweat.

Damn, that is unbelievably hot.

His calves are perfectly symmetrical with the rest of his body, thick and strong, every muscle in harmony. I feel this insatiable craving for more of him, for all of him.

I want more!

Give me more!

He looks like a warrior.

Big, angry, ferocious.

A relentless, unstoppable warrior.

His body is perfectly symmetrical. Every part of him complements the rest, each detail was crafted to bring this specimen of a man into existence and, somehow, into my world.

Slowly, I let my gaze travel over him again, starting from his toes and moving upward. I savour every inch, taking my time to memorise every detail, every line and curve. I hope with everything in me, everything in this vast universe, that he will let me do this again. That he will let me admire him like this, unrestrained and shameless, in the future.

When our eyes meet, I see the insecurity and fear hidden within them, and it feels like someone is squeezing my heart, hard. The intensity of it steals my breath for a moment.

I hold his gaze, letting myself get lost in those impossibly blue eyes of his. A small smile spreads across my lips, and I watch as the tension in his face eases. I can see it how he relaxes at the sight of my smile, as though it is enough to quiet whatever storm is raging inside him.

"You are beautiful." The words escape before I can stop them, pure and raw, desperate for more. There is no chance to think of a better way to express the burning lust surging through me. He is absolutely, undeniably, smoking hot.

"And that..." My words falter and catch in my throat as my hand slowly lifts, pointing to his cock. "That is beautiful, *Nuuro*."

I barely manage to add the words before I catch myself licking my lips. *Damn it. He caught me ogling his cock and licking my lips. Great. Just great.* As if I needed to make my admiration more obvious.

"Can I touch it?" My excitement is so obvious, spilling out in my words and reflected in my actions. Without even thinking, I lean forward slowly, anticipation humming through my veins as I wait for his answer.

Fuck. I hope he lets me. I want to touch him, explore him, enjoy every inch of him.

"You can do whatever you want to me, *sugar cube*. I am yours," he says, his voice steady, filled with a truth that sends a shiver down my spine.

I lower my gaze to my hands, which are resting on my knees, because I need a moment to process this. I feel excited, scared, hot, bothered, trembling, and so deeply in love that it's overwhelming. There are so many emotions coursing through me at once that I feel dizzy, like I might fall apart under the weight of it all.

But his words, the way he said them in that deep voice of his, filled with certainty and complete surrender, undo me completely. The way he put himself in my hands, offering me everything without hesitation, shatters every wall I thought I still had.

There is no stopping this now. Not the emotions, not the desire, not the way he looks at me like I am his entire world.

I lift my gaze to his, meeting those piercing eyes that seem to see every corner of my soul. Slowly, I take a small step toward him, then another, and another. Before I know it, I am sitting back on my heels on the bed, facing him as he stands there, naked and glorious, every inch of him laid bare before me.

My breath catches as I lean forward, my hand trembling slightly as I reach out. With the tip of my finger, I trace the thick vein running along the side of his cock, following its path slowly, deliberately, all the way to the tip.

A deep, guttural groan escapes him, vibrating through the air, and I freeze in place, panic coursing through me.

"Did I hurt you?" My shaky voice betrays the sudden worry tightening in my chest.

"Fuck no," he says, bursting into laughter, the sound so rich and unapologetic that it sends a flush of heat rushing through me.

"You fucking clown!" I spit out the words in a rush, my voice trembling with a mix of nerves and disbelief.

"You cannot hurt me, *sugar cube*," he says, his voice steady and drenched with that deep, unwavering certainty. "Do whatever you want, and if I groan at your touch, it's only because I am fucking melting in front of you."

The look in his eyes is pure, unfiltered lust and need, something raw and aching that threatens to undo me completely.

"I love you so much, *sugar cube*," he continues, his voice breaking slightly as his hand moves toward me. "My chest hurts."

A smile plays at my lips as I realise something unexpected. I thought I would feel scared, but *I am not*. Instead, I feel excited, curious, and so many other things that I cannot even name. But what stands out most, what consumes me entirely, is the need for more.

I want more.

I want to feel how he responds under my touch.

I want to hear the sounds he makes as I explore him, to memorise every groan and gasp.

I want to take in his scent when he is teetering on the edge of losing control.

But more than anything, I want to bring him pleasure.

It burns inside me like an unquenchable fire, screaming for release. I *need* to know how he will react to my touch. I *need* to see if I can bring him to the brink, if I can give him what he has already given to me. And beyond that, I *need* to know who I am in this moment. Who I am when I am with him, raw and unfiltered.

I dip my forefinger into my mouth, swirling it slowly to make it wet, then lift my gaze to his. His eyes are locked on my mouth, his stare so intense it sends a shiver through me.

I smile, a quiet confidence blooming in my chest, and place my finger at the tip of his cock, where that bead of something waits for me, glistening. Slowly, I lower my finger to the valley just beneath the crown and begin to rub it in an up-and-down motion.

It is wet, sticky, and impossibly soft.

I like it.

The texture, the warmth, the way his body responds with the slightest shift. It fascinates me, igniting a hunger to explore more, to unravel every reaction he has to me.

"Fucking hell, woman!" Hunter's deep, rough voice booms through the room as he braces one hand against the wall, his chest heaving with each breath. "*Sugar cube*, you're fucking killing me."

The look in his eyes is pure desperation, raw and unrestrained.

"You like it?" I ask, feigning innocence as I tilt my head slightly, my lips curling into a teasing smile. "Should I do it again?" I add quickly, giggling at the mix of disbelief and torment on his face.

"Baby, I need to sit down," he says, his voice strained as if even speaking is a challenge. "I don't think my legs can keep me up for this one. Scoot over."

Without waiting for a response, he lowers himself onto the bed, taking the spot I had just vacated. The sight of him sprawled out, completely at my mercy, sends a rush of satisfaction through me.

I straddle one of his massive thighs, my hands coming to rest on the sharp ridges of his v-line, but my gaze is locked on his cock.

"Baby, please don't do anything you're not comfortable with," he says, his voice gentle but firm as his eyes search mine for any hint of doubt or hesitation.

He waits a beat, studying me closely, then adds with a laugh, "Don't worry about my cock. I can handle him." His laughter deepens, rumbling through the room like a warm, familiar storm. "Total pun intended, by the way. I can go and jerk off until he's happy. It's all good, baby. You don't need to do this if you don't want to."

His words are sincere, even through the humour, and the way he looks at me with patience, love, and a hint of teasing makes my chest ache.

His cock is so hard it looks painful. If it was angry before, now it looks furious, red and purple, straining like it's demanding attention. This might be the first time I have touched a cock, but even I can tell it's reacting to me in ways that defy Hunter's calm words.

I glance up at Hunter, his face relaxed and radiating teasing warmth, and it throws me off completely. How can he look so composed, saying things like that, while his cock is clearly on the edge of exploding? The contrast between his calm words and the raw, pulsing reaction of his body surprises me. It's so evident, clear as day, he is putting my needs above everything else, even his own, even if it causes him pain.

From this angle, I take a moment to study him more closely. His balls are lifted now, drawn tighter, and there is a crease beneath them, as if his body is preparing for something I do not yet understand.

How fascinating.

I feel a spark of curiosity bubbling inside me, a desire to ask him more about this, to understand every part of him, his reactions, his body, everything that makes this side of him. I file the thought away for later, knowing there is so much I still want to learn.

I know I do not have the courage yet to show myself to him. As much as I love him, as much as I crave his touch and his acceptance, I need time. That part of me is my deepest, darkest, most shameful and disgusting secret. The thought of baring myself in that way makes my chest tighten, my breath catch.

So, no. We are definitely not at the stage for me to strip naked in front of him. Not yet. But maybe one day. Maybe if I give myself time. If he continues to show me the patience and love he already has, *I might get there*. For now, I will hold on to this moment and the way he looks at me like I am already enough.

But this urge to join him in these maddening moments is eating me alive. It claws at me, burning through my hesitation and fear. Before I can second-guess myself, I lift my shirt over my head in one swift motion.

Now, I am naked from the waist up, my skin exposed to the cool air, every nerve alight with anticipation. I am still straddling his thigh, my heart pounding in my chest as I meet his gaze. The way he looks at me, with a mix of awe and reverence, sends a shiver through me.

"Holy fuck!" The words explode out of him, raw and unrestrained, his eyes widen in disbelief at what I have just done.

He throws his arm over his face, shielding his eyes, and starts taking deep, laboured breaths. His chest rises and falls in a desperate rhythm, as though he is trying to steady himself, to regain control of something that has clearly unraveled.

I stay where I am, frozen, watching the fight for air etched into every line of his body. I did not expect this reaction. I am not sure what to do or what to say.

After a moment, he lowers his arm and lets his gaze fall to my breasts again. His eyes flicker with something wild, a mix of hunger and reverence, before he throws his arm back over his face, shielding himself once more, his breaths still ragged and uneven.

"Holy fuck, woman! I always thought I was an arse guy, and fuck if I didn't picture myself doing some nasty, filthy things to yours. But now? I think I've just been converted. Tits. Fuck me!"

I burst out laughing, the sound bubbling out of me uncontrollably, because the last thing I expected was for him to say that. I mean, they look okay to me, but apparently, they are more than okay to him.

When he lifts his arm from one eye and looks at me, his expression is pure disbelief and awe. I meet his gaze with a mischievous smile. Slowly, I slide two fingers into my mouth, wetting them thoroughly, never breaking eye contact. Once I am satisfied, I wrap my hand around the head of his cock and stroke him hard, my movements deliberate and firm.

"Fuuuuuuck!" His deep growl rumbles through the room, raw and pleading, a sound that sends heat pooling low in my stomach.

I do it a few more times, slow and deliberate, trying to learn his reactions, to understand what he likes and what he doesn't. He groans and swears constantly, his body trembling under my touch. Each sound, each shudder, fuels the fire in the pit of my being, a pleasure so raw and intense it feels like it is screaming through me.

The realisation hits me like a jolt... I am the one doing this to him. I am the one making him come undone. He is breaking apart because of me, unraveling under my touch.

But then I feel it. Without even realising it, I have been grinding against his thigh. The friction is electric, delicious in a way I never thought possible. For a moment, the thought of my pain, my scars, flickers in the back of my mind. I always believed they would stop me from ever enjoying anything like this.

I was wrong.

So very wrong.

This feels instinctive and deliberate, my movements unashamed as I work his magnificent cock with my hand while grinding against his thigh. My body moves on its own, chasing the waves of pleasure building inside me. It is uncharted, thrilling, and for the first time, it feels like I am free.

I might not know exactly what I am doing, and my movements might be amateurish at best, but none of that matters. This mighty warrior, this unshakable man, is coming undone because of me.

And I...

For once, I have decided to embrace this. To enjoy what I can have instead of letting fear and the poison of my past rob me of any more beauty in my life. For too long, I have let my pain dictate what I deserve, what I am allowed to feel. But not now.

Right now, I am claiming this moment for myself. For us...

"Baby, can I touch you?" His voice is so soft, so small, that at first, I do not even understand what he said.

"You don't have to say yes if you don't want to," he quickly adds, his words tumbling out in a rush, like he is afraid he has overstepped.

I expect to feel fear, for my chest to tighten and my mind to spiral into panic. But none of that happens. This is Hunter. Hunter loves me, he would never hurt me.

"Touch me how?" I ask, my voice steady, though my heart pounds in anticipation.

"However you would allow me," he says, his voice soft, his eyes begging for my approval. "If you're comfortable, I can play with your nipples, if you like."

His eyes are so big, his pupils so dilated, and the pleading look on his face is absolutely adorable. I never thought I would see Hunter like this, so careful, so vulnerable.

Every single step he takes is to make sure I am okay. Every gesture, every word, every look, every caress is for me.

I never thought someone could love like this.

This is more than love. This is devotion. Care. Respect. Compassion. And every single ounce of it is directed at me.

"I would like that."

There is no hesitation, no fear, no second-guessing myself. I love him so much, and I trust him completely.

I am all in.

"Yes?" he asks, lifting himself slightly, careful not to move me off his leg. "You just carry on doing whatever you want to do, and I will play with your breast, okay?"

He studies my gaze again, searching for any hesitation, before gently taking one of my breasts in his hand. His touch is careful, deliberate, and filled with so much tenderness that it almost undoes me.

"Stop me the second something doesn't feel right," he says softly, his voice a soothing promise.

His movements are slow, gentle, exploratory, as if he is learning every curve, every response. Each touch is infused with so much care that goosebumps erupt all over my body.

I love it.

I wet my other hand and place it at the base of his length, wrapping my fingers around him firmly. Without hesitation, I start stroking him in an up-and-down motion, not so gently this time.

He rewards me with another string of deep, guttural groans that reverberate through my entire body, igniting something primal inside me.

Wetting both hands again, I let go of any restraint. I surrender completely to my instincts, grinding against his thigh with no reservations. The friction is electric, and the heat between us feels like it could consume me.

He is so big in my hands, thick and pulsing under my touch. I work both hands in tandem, stroking up and down with deliberate movements. I start squeezing and twisting, experimenting with pressure, focusing on that ridge just beneath the tip of his cock. I know now how sensitive it is for him, and the way his body reacts, the way his groans deepen, only spurs me on further. Each touch there draws another guttural sound from him, raw and needy, and it drives me wild.

The more I move, the more I feel his reactions. His tremors, his groans, his desperate gasps and I cannot help but feel powerful. Every motion, every squeeze, every turn of my wrist feels like a declaration that this moment, this pleasure, is ours.

He cups my other breast, his touch sending waves of warmth through me. A tingling heat begins to build deep inside, spreading with each gentle squeeze and caress.

But more than the sensations, it is the stillness in my mind that strikes me. The constant noise, the endless thoughts, the weight of the world, they are all gone.

In this moment, there is only Hunter and me. Just us, cocooned in this bubble of intimacy where nothing else exists. The world has disappeared, and all that remains is the shared pleasure, the connection that binds us together so completely it feels like nothing else could ever matter.

His mouth lowers to my nipple, and the second his lips make contact, my body ignites. He sucks, pulls, and bites with a perfect balance of pressure, each motion deliberate and consuming. The sensation shoots through me, sharp and overwhelming, like a bolt of lightning crashing into every nerve ending I have.

And then something inside me shatters.

The pleasure comes out of nowhere, building and cresting so suddenly that it steals my breath. I cry out, the sound raw and guttural, a primal release I did not know I was capable of. The noise echoes in the quiet room, tethering me to him, to this moment, as if nothing else in the world exists.

His large hands grip my hips, strong and steady, guiding me with a tenderness that feels like an anchor in this storm of sensation. He moves me, urging me to grind against him, his fingers pressing into my skin telling me he has me that I am safe to lose myself here.

And *I do*.

The pleasure keeps building, an endless cascade that leaves me spinning, tumbling into an abyss of heat and want. I feel myself slipping, dissolving into this pit of tingling, molten pleasure that radiates from the core of my being.

But it is not just the physicality of it that takes me apart. It is the connection, the way he watches me, the way his body moves with mine, matching every rhythm, every sound, every reaction. It is not just my body that is breaking, it is my soul, unraveling in his hands as I let go of every barrier, every fear.

For the first time, I am not afraid of losing myself, because here, in this moment, with him, I feel whole.

"Fuck!" I scream, the word ripping out of me as my mind slowly returns to reality. "Fuck, Hunter!"

I hold his gaze, my chest heaving, and the surprise in my own voice mirrors the look in his eyes. But his expression, fucking hell, his expression is what undoes me all over again. It is pure love, raw lust, and unwavering devotion, all wrapped together in a way that steals the breath from my lungs.

"You are unbelievably beautiful when you come undone, *sugar cube*," he murmurs, his voice low and reverent. "Fuck me. There is nothing more beautiful I have seen in my entire life."

He leans forward, and his lips meet mine in a kiss so soft, so full of everything he feels, that it leaves me weightless. For a moment, the world stills, and all I know is the gentle press of his mouth, the way it seems to take my breath with it, leaving me utterly lost in him.

I glance down at my hands, still wrapped around his cock. In the haze of my pleasure, I had completely lost myself, stopping his in the process. He had been focused only on me, prolonging my pleasure, giving everything without asking for anything in return.

A wave of determination surges through me.

I wet my hands again, making them slick to glide effortlessly along his length. My movements become deliberate, rotating and stroking in an up-and-down rhythm. One of my thumbs circles that sensitive spot just beneath the tip, and I feel him twitch in response, his breath hitching.

I cannot hold back anymore.

I lunge forward, my lips crashing into his, devouring him with a hunger that feels endless. Our mouths collide, tongues rolling, sucking, biting, as if this kiss is a gateway to something infinite. It is a universe we created for each other, a place where only we exist, where every touch and every breath feels like a shared secret.

His groan vibrates against my lips, and the sound fuels me further. This is not just a kiss. It's a claiming, a merging, a moment that binds us in a way no words ever could.

It is delicious, maddening, and primal.

Grunts and moans pour out of both of us, merging into a symphony of pleasure we never imagined could exist. Each sound, each movement, feels like a secret language, one spoken only by the two of us in this moment.

"Baby, I'm about to come," he groans, his voice breaking against my lips, heavy with need. "Baaaaby, please..." The words dissolve into a deep, guttural sound as his body trembles, his restraint fraying at the edges.

"Baby, maybe it's too much for you," he rasps, his forehead pressing against mine, his breaths hot and ragged. "Too much for you to see me... explode."

The desperation in his voice sends another jolt through me. He is holding back for me, trying to protect me even in this moment when he is so close to losing control and showing me his most vulnerable state.

I take his bottom lip between mine and bite down hard, the pressure deliberate. I am not some fragile flower swaying in the wind, and he needs to learn that I do not want to be treated as one.

"Fucking come for me, *Nuuro*," I command, my voice low and full of conviction.

I jerk him harder, tightening my grip around his girth. His cock pulses in my hands, each throb more intense than the last, and I can feel him teetering on the edge.

"Fuuuuuuck!" The word tears out of him, raw and unrestrained, echoing through the room as his body convulses under my touch.

The primal, animalistic sounds tearing from his throat are unlike anything I have ever heard. They are raw, guttural, and completely unrestrained, vibrating through me as I keep moving my hands with precision, determined to draw out every ounce of his pleasure.

Hot streams of cum shoot out, painting my breasts, my neck, my chin, his abs, his chest, everywhere between us. It's warm, sticky, and utterly intoxicating. The sight of it, the feel of it, sets something wild free inside me.

Even as he gasps for breath, swearing and moaning through the intensity, my lips remain locked on his, devouring him even as his breath comes in heavy, ragged gasps. He swears, groans, and moans against my mouth, his body trembling beneath my touch.

I can't stop. His taste, his sounds, his very presence, have me addicted for more.

I keep working his cock, my fingers firm and deliberate, with a single-minded determination to milk every last drop from him. This is mine! All of it is mine! And he better give it all to me. I need more. I want more. Every pulse, every drop, every tremor he gives me is mine to take.

He leans forward, resting his forehead against mine, his breath coming in deep, laboured pulls as he gathers himself. One of his hands moves to cover mine, gently bringing my movements to a stop.

"It's sensitive, baby," he says in a hoarse voice, low and raw, as if the words are scraped from the back of his throat. His other hand lifts my chin, guiding my gaze to his.

"I love you so much, *sugar cube*. Thank you."

The sincerity in his words catches me off guard. For a moment, I can't move, can't speak, only stare into those blue eyes filled with love, gratitude, and something so profound it makes my chest ache.

I smile, a small, quiet curve of my lips, because the last thing I expected was for him to thank me. He's given me so much, and yet here he is, acting as though I've just handed him the world.

"Your surprised face is adorable, *sugar cube*," he says, leaning in to place a soft kiss on the tip of my nose.

"You thanked me?" I ask, narrowing my eyes at him with a suspicious look.

He bursts out laughing, wrapping his arms around me in a hug so tight it's almost painful. Again. Maybe we should have a chat about softer hugs because, damn, he's ridiculously strong.

It takes me a moment to notice the wetness between our chests. When it registers, I realise his cum is smeared all over both of us.

Damn.

I expected to feel grossed out, but instead, it's kind of... hot. The mess, the intimacy, the way it's just us tangled together, it's raw and real, and it makes my heart race all over again.

"I thanked you because that was the best orgasm of my life, *sugar cube*," he murmurs, his voice low and rough, as his lips brush the sensitive spot just below my ear. The warmth of his breath sends a shiver racing down my spine.

"I thanked you because you let me touch you," he continues, his tone soft but weighted with emotion, his lips brushing over my earlobe before placing another kiss there.

"I thanked you because you love me," he whispers, taking my earlobe into his mouth. What he does next sends a jolt through me. His teeth and tongue work together in a way that feels like he's sucking, biting, and licking all at once. It's maddening.

A deep moan escapes me, unbidden, as my body arches slightly towards him. My mind, already reeling from his words, begins to dissolve into the sensations.

Hunter has this way of making me feel like I am the centre of the universe, like nothing exists beyond us in this moment. His words, his touch, the way he looks at me with so much devotion, it all wraps around me, consuming me in a way that feels both terrifying and intoxicating.

"Oh, shit! That feels amazing, Hunter! Ahhhhh!" The moans pour out of me uncontrollably, raw and unrestrained. I have no power over them, no power over myself when he touches me like this.

"You like that, *sugar cube*?" he whispers, his voice low and teasing, a dark promise woven into his words. His breath against my ear sends shivers coursing through my body, leaving me trembling in his arms.

"You can have anything you want. Just ask, and it's yours."

The conviction in his voice leaves no room for doubt, and before I can even process his words, he's back with his lips, his teeth, his tongue, attacking my ear, my senses, and what little sanity I have left.

The heat of him, the relentless way he devours me, makes me feel like I'm coming apart in the best possible way. He isn't just touching my body, he's claiming every part of me, and I let him because it feels too good to stop, too right to resist.

When the overwhelming ticklish sensation becomes too much, I place my palms on his chest and gently push him back. My hands, however, end up coated in his cum.

I pull back slowly, and he lets me go without hesitation. My gaze drops to my fingers, wet with his release. Somehow, it feels like more than just a release. It feels like a mark of this moment, glowing with the happiness we've created together.

"Sorry, baby," he says softly, his voice filled with tenderness as he shifts further away. "Let me quickly clean this up."

I think he believes I am disgusted, when all I feel is happiness and curiosity. This overly protective thing he does, it's something we definitely need to talk about, though not right now.

Without a word, I hold his gaze. Slowly, deliberately, I bring my hand to my mouth and start licking each finger clean, one at a time.

When I finish the last finger, I let it slip out with a soft pop before smiling at him. The look on his face, wide-eyed and utterly shocked, is priceless, and it takes everything in me not to burst out laughing.

"Fuck me, woman! If you ever want me to be soft around you, you cannot do things like that. Fuck! That was hot as hell, Sofia!" His voice is deep and hoarse, thick with desire, and I cannot help but burst out laughing.

What I wanted to achieve has worked perfectly. He is flushed, bothered, and completely undone all over again.

I glance down, and sure enough, his cock is twitching between us, because it has a mind of its own.

"I didn't expect it to taste like that, *Nuuro*. It's salty," I say, my tone playful, before breaking into laughter again.

The look on his face is priceless, caught somewhere between awe and frustration, and it only fuels my amusement further.

He grabs me into a tight hug again, his arms wrapping around me like a lifeline. A full-body shudder runs through him, raw and unguarded.

I did that.

I brought this warrior to his knees. I broke him into pieces and then put him back together again. *Me.* I did that.

A deep, overwhelming satisfaction floods my mind, my heart, and my soul. It is happiness in its purest form, an ache of joy that consumes me completely.

I did that.

He shifts onto his back, manoeuvring me fully on top of him, and rests his hands firmly on my arse. I try to lift my head to study him, but he stops me with a soft shush.

"I told you I'm an arse guy," he murmurs, his voice low and teasing. "Now let's have another nap, and then we can talk some more."

One of his hands moves to my hair, his fingers threading through it as he gently strokes. He peppers soft kisses on the top of my head, each one making me feel more anchored in his embrace.

It feels surreal to be here, to feel this way, to rest so completely in his arms.

As sleep pulls me under, cocooned in his warmth, my mind circles back to the thought that keeps repeating itself over and over.

I did that.

Chapter Twenty-One

Hunter

The intoxicating smell of food pulls me in and out of sleep, teasing my senses even as I try to stay under. The air is thick with the strong fragrance of garlic and spices, sharp and mouth-watering, but there's something else too. Something sweet, rich with sugar and vanilla, cutting through the savoury notes like a quiet promise of indulgence.

I doze back to sleep, completely surrounded by the comforting aroma of homemade food from my mum's kitchen. The rich scents of tomatoes, capsicum, and spices fill the air, wrapping around me like a warm embrace, pulling me towards the kitchen.

When I make my way to her, I am overwhelmed by the beautiful sight that greets me. She is cooking and dancing, well, what she might call dancing, though most would disagree, to some upbeat tune playing on the radio.

She's wearing this stunning summer dress with bright yellow daisies scattered all over. At least, I think they're daisies. Big, round flowers with white petals, but I'm not entirely sure. What matters is how incredible she looks in it, even I know that.

She's twirling and singing as she adds ingredients to the pot, stirring with a kind of rhythm that only she could manage. She looks so beautiful in that moment, so full of life and love, that it makes my chest ache.

I love my mum so much.

The smell tickles my nose, coaxing me closer, tempting me to sneak a bite from the pot. As I approach silently, ready to swipe a taste, she turns suddenly, grabs my arm, and shoves the spatula in my face like it's a microphone.

"Come on, Hunter, sing with your mum," she says, grinning as she twirls and continues dancing in that strange, endearing way of hers.

I try, and fail, to suppress a laugh, but she doesn't let up. She insists, holding the spatula out dramatically and belting out the lyrics completely off tune, her voice loud and unapologetic.

"And you see me, somebody new.

I'm not that lonely little person,

Still in love with you," she sings, completely out of tune, holding the spatula like a microphone.

"Come on, Hunter, sing..." she urges, her eyes bright with mischief.

My heart won't let me refuse her. It never does. Even though I know I'm about to make a complete fool of myself, I can't say no to my mum. Not when she's looking at me like that.

"Go on now, go, walk out the door,

Turn around now,

You're not welcome anymore.

Weren't you the one who tried to hurt me with goodbye?

Thinkin' I'd crumble,

Did you think I'd lay down and die?"

We twirl and spin, dancing like absolute lunatics, belting out the lyrics at the top of our lungs. Spatulas become our microphones, and the kitchen our stage. The laughter bubbles up uncontrollably, and I love every second of it.

I glance at my mum, taking in the beautiful way she's enjoying herself. Her eyes shine, her smile is so bright it could light up the entire house, and her carefree laughter fills the room.

My stomach rumbles, the ache sharp and insistent, but the smell lingering in the air is so enticing it tugs at me, trying to pull me out of my dream. The memory of my mum feels so vivid, as if I'm still there, spinning and laughing with her in the kitchen.

That's one of the best memories I have of her. The way she looked in that dress. Bright, carefree, and so beautifully alive. The yellow daisies on the fabric seemed to glow against her skin, matching the warmth of her smile. Now that memory is all I have. A beautiful memory, because the woman that she was, the mum that she was, is not there any more.

I reach out, expecting to feel Sofia's soft skin beneath my hand, but there's nothing there.

My eyes snap open, and I realise the bed is empty.

I bolt upright so fast my head spins, the room tilting for a moment before my focus sharpens. My gaze darts to the closet, where I'd noticed the suitcases before, and the door to the walk-in wardrobe is closed.

"FUCKING HELL!" I roar, the sound echoing off the walls, raw and filled with rage.

"SHE FUCKING MADE A RUN FOR IT!"

I jump out of bed so fast it feels like I'm running on pure adrenaline. In two seconds, I'm at the door.

Who the fuck cares that I'm stark naked or burning with red-hot fury? This fucking woman will be the death of me.

I fucking warned her not to do this.

I. Fucking. Warned. Her.

This feeling of suffocation and despair is draining every last drop of strength and reason from me in the most excruciating way possible.

How could she fucking do this after everything we just shared?

My chest feels like it's been ripped open, as if someone has physically shot me straight through the heart. The pain is so sharp, so consuming, that I feel lightheaded. A wave of numbness washes over me, threatening to pull me under, but I push past it and sprint down the hall.

The moment I turn into the living area, it's like someone has reached into my chest and squeezed my heart with an iron grip.

Sofia is on the couch, dressed in an oversized shirt and short shorts, a plate balanced on her lap as she watches TV. The moment her eyes meet mine, a smirk plays across her lips. She shakes her head, utterly amused.

"Hahaha, you thought I made a run for it," she says, her voice dripping with playful mockery as she shakes her head again.

I try to steady my heart. I try to steady my mind. But it feels as though I'm on autopilot, driven by raw panic and despair.

All I feel is the fury of a raging bull, ready to tear apart anyone who dares to take Sofia away from me. The thought alone sends another wave of heat through my chest, feeding the fire that refuses to die down.

I am in front of her in seconds, and before I even realise what I'm doing, I'm squeezing her so tightly against my chest that my muscles ache.

What the fuck is wrong with me?

I'm trembling in her arms, shaking, my entire world has shattered into a million pieces and she's slowly putting it back together just by breathing.

I pull her closer, pushing her into me with everything I have, my beast screaming inside me to fuse her to me, to make sure she can never escape us again.

I can hear the faint sound of her voice, but for the life of me, I cannot make out what she is saying.

It feels like I am trapped in a bubble of complete despair and agony, fighting desperately for my life and clinging to the fragile hope of being with her again.

The more I run my hands over her back, pulling her closer and pushing her into me, the more I can feel air slipping into my bubble and filling my lungs. Bit by bit, I come back to reality.

Fucking hell! What's wrong with me? I completely lost my shit.

"Hunter, what the hell. Let go of me!" Her voice is sharp, tinged with irritation, and for a second, my brain struggles to process why. Then it hits me. I'm hugging her so tightly that I might actually be hurting her.

"Fuck, baby, sorry," I mutter, quickly easing my grip, but I can't bring myself to let go entirely.

"Move back, you big mountain of a man, or I'm going for your balls," she snaps, her voice low and menacing, leaving no room for debate or confusion.

I don't want to let go. Every part of me aches to keep her close, to absorb her into me completely. Maybe if I could, this desperate, all-consuming need for her closeness would finally be satisfied.

I pull back slightly, locking my eyes on hers, searching for any sign that she's lying to me or trying to manipulate the situation. But no, there's none of that. No sketchy business. Just plain, unfiltered fury.

"Move back, fucker! This is your last warning!" she snaps, her voice sharp and unwavering.

And there she is, Sofia, in all her glorious fury. This image is all too familiar, the very thing that fed my addiction to her for the past two years.

But as I take in the lines of her beautiful face, even while she's mad, something in my chest feels different. It's not the same as before. I'm not enjoying this like I used to.

Before... before she let me touch her, taste her, feel her body against mine.

Fuck, I love her. I love her so much it makes my heart ache.

"You're such an idiot clown," she snaps, her words laced with exasperation and just a hint of amusement.

I take a deep breath and let myself drop onto my arse in front of her.

Fuck!

I think I scared her.

"Sorry, *sugar cube*," I mumble, giving her a quick, uncertain glance as I try to pull myself together. "I panicked. I thought you'd made a run for it, and I fucking lost my mind."

I keep my eyes fixed on her legs, unable to meet her gaze. Not yet. Not until I can shove the beast back into the cage where he belongs.

It takes me a second to clear my vision as I focus on her beautiful, strong thighs. But then I see them... the scars.

WHAT. THE. FUCK?!

My body goes completely still. For a moment, I'm scared that my reaction will put her off even more, but she's still yelling at me. At least, I think she is.

I can hear the sound of her voice again, sharp and insistent, but her words don't fully break through the fog of despair wrapping around me like a suffocating bubble.

Why does she have scars on her legs?

Did she do this to herself?

Oh, fuck!

That thought breaks something deep inside me. The idea that this amazing, strong woman could hurt herself... it just cannot be. It's one of those things that shouldn't exist, that feels fundamentally wrong.

As I try to process it all, her shouts, the scars, her powerful presence, I remember who she is. She's free-spirited, fierce, and unapologetic, never holding back, whether it's with her words or her punches, physically or metaphorically.

No... I don't think she cuts.

But then, why does she have them?

They must be from whatever happened to her. Knowing her, she probably fought with everything she had, refusing to back down. That's who she is, strong, fierce, and unrelenting, even in the face of whatever left those marks.

I think she's noticed where I'm looking because she quickly tries to cover up.

It's only then that I fully register her voice, screaming at full force.

"Are you fucking serious right now?!"

I lift my gaze, and she is most definitely fuming with fury.

Normally, right about now, I'd brace myself for her attack. Hopefully, she'd fight me for a bit, then pull that move where her legs end up around my neck.

Mate, I love that move.

"What the fuck is wrong with you?!" she yells at full volume, her glare so fiery it feels like it's shooting bolts of heat straight at me.

I take a deep breath, grounding myself.

She'll tell me in time, when she's ready.

I'm not going anywhere.

"I love you, *sugar cube.*"

I pull myself up to my knees, leaning my head on her lap and wrapping my arms tightly around her waist. I don't care how I must look right now, probably like the idiot clown she called me earlier.

The panic that overtook me at the thought of her running, despite everything we shared, still claws at my chest. The fear that maybe she realised I'm not enough for her, that I somehow scared her into leaving, is suffocating.

That feeling... that feeling can only be described as slowly, painfully dying from the core of your being, while being forced to stay alive without the very thing that keeps you breathing.

She wraps her arms around me, and I can feel her warmth seep into me. All her anger has been forgotten, replaced by something softer, something that feels like understanding. Maybe she can sense the depth of my agony radiating from me as I fight back the hot tears stinging the back of my eyes.

But the more I fight them, the worse it gets. After a few seconds, it feels like my body is heating up, the intensity rising with each breath, I'm about to combust out of nowhere.

My body is trembling, overwhelmed by the sheer intensity of my emotions and my struggle to pull myself together. I am so careful not to tighten my arms too much around her, desperate to avoid giving her a reason to push me away again.

I just stay there, clinging to her warmth, trying to purge this feeling that's consuming my soul, even as I fight back the tears threatening to escape.

I fucking lost my mind.

But there's one thing I know with absolute certainty...

If she goes, I go.

There is no fucking way I could survive without Sofia in my life. No chance.

If something were to happen to her, or if she ever ran, my beast would tear me apart, consuming every shred of who I am until I burned in the deepest, darkest pit of hell on earth.

This is not love.

This is not obsession.

This is not lust.

This is not yearning.

This... what I'm feeling right now is absolute pain and agony.

It's the torment of being so deeply, irreversibly tied to someone that I simply know, without a doubt, that I would cease to exist without her.

She is not my everything...

She is my existence.

"Hunter, what's wrong?" Her concern is so evident in her voice that it twists something deep inside me.

I shift my head slightly on her lap and realise tears have been running down her thighs. *Shit.*

I quickly try to wipe them away, but it's no use. She's definitely noticed.

She gently pushes at me, trying to get me to move so she can look at me, but I don't budge.

I can't.

I can't move from this position until my beast calms down. I need to steady myself, to push it back into its cage. I can't risk scaring her.

"*Nuuro...*" she trails off, nudging me again gently.

There it is. That nickname.

She has a nickname for me. I love it. She loves me enough to give me a lover's name. *I am her Nuuro.*

"Baby, you're scaring me. What's wrong?" she presses, her voice tinged with worry.

"I thought you made a run for it," I manage to say, my voice cracking.

In any other situation, I'd be shocked that I could sound like this, so raw, so broken, but right now, I don't give a flying fuck.

Because now I realise the truth. She isn't just my everything. *She is my existence.*

She moves her soft hands over my back, and the sensation is so profound, so sweet, it feels like she's caressing my very soul.

"Hunter, baby," she murmurs, her voice gentle and soothing. "I told you, I'm not running anymore."

We stay there, both of us revelling in each other's touch. Her warmth grounds me, slowly pulling me back from the murderous, doom-filled thoughts that had consumed me.

"I've never felt anything like it, *sugar cube*," I confess, my voice low but steady. She needs to know where we stand, needs to understand what this is. "I felt suffocated, like my body was actually shutting down, dying at the thought of losing you."

Her touch stills, her soft palms trembling against me.

"I don't just love you, Sofia. I don't just need you. This... this isn't love, obsession, lust, or longing."

I lift my gaze to meet hers, and the moment our eyes lock, I know she understands.

She gets it.

Good.

Because I know, deep in my soul, that I wouldn't survive without her.

"You are my very existence, *sugar cube*."

I let her see me. The real me. The man beneath the jokes, the remarks, and the pretence. The raw, unhinged part of me that would destroy anyone who dared to come near her. The fucker who would torture and kill with such sadistic, unrelenting precision that it would redefine pain for any piece of shit who dared to harm her.

I let her see me and my beast. All of it.

I want her to understand that she is loved so profoundly that words like devotion, infatuation, enrapturement, or even euphoria don't come close to describing the depth of what I feel for her.

She audibly takes a breath in, and the look in her eyes is so mesmerising it feels like a vortex, pulling everything into its path and obliterating it.

Those beautiful black eyes, so deep, so consuming, are the perfect representation of the darkness I am willing to embrace for her. The depth I would plunge into without hesitation, just to keep her safe.

There is no me without her.

And from now on, she sure as fuck knows it.

"Hunter..." Her voice trails off, so small and broken, as if it were the last breath of her life.

She just looks at me, mesmerised. And I let her.

I don't hide. I don't pretend. I don't joke.

I let her see me. All of me.

The good, the bad, the wonderful, and the despicable.

Because I am all those things, and every single part of me loves her with its full strength.

When she lowers her gaze to her palms, now resting on her thighs, I can feel it, she's holding back.

And fuck me, it drives me crazy.

I want her to tell me everything. I want her to share all her pain, her suffering, every shadow she hides. I want to dive into her darkness, take it as my own, and love her fiercely in it.

Protect her in it.

Because *she's not alone*. Not anymore.

"No, *sugar cube*. None of that," I say softly, lifting her gaze to meet mine with gentle fingers.

"Please don't hide from me. I just told you... you are my very existence. Please, don't hide from me. Whatever it is, whatever that beautiful mind of yours is thinking, we'll overcome it together."

I press a kiss to the back of her hands, lingering there, letting the moment settle.

Then I look at her again, my voice steady and full of conviction. "Whatever it is, you've got me. You have me. All of me."

"I was so scared my entire life to tell anyone what happened to me," she finally says, her voice barely above a whisper.

"I can't even describe it entirely, because I don't know how to put into words the deep self-loathing that comes with knowing I'm different. No matter what I do, no matter what I achieve in life, I will always be different. What they did to me..." Her voice trails off, so small and full of emotion it strikes something deep in me, a places in my heart I didn't even know existed until now.

But I don't dare say a word. I don't dare move. I barely even breathe.

I just need her to let it out. I need her to feel safe enough, comfortable enough, to say anything to me.

"I know you love me. More importantly, I can see it, *Nuuro*," she says, her voice trembling. "But please, be patient with me. I need to find the courage to let you see me, to let you see my scars."

Her voice shakes, and I can see the tears she's fighting back.

And I can't.

I just can't.

I can't let her think I'm pressuring her, not even for a second.

"Baby..." I murmur, quickly wrapping my arms around her and pulling her into my chest.

"I love you. I adore you. You don't need to show me anything until you're absolutely sure you can and want to."

I press a gentle kiss to the top of her head, holding her closer.

"I'm not going anywhere," I continue softly. "I already told you, I'll wait for the rest of my days for you."

I pull back to search her eyes, and the relief I find there tugs hard at my heart.

A queasy feeling twists in my stomach as I think about all the pain she must have carried, believing she had to show me what happened to her. The weight of it, the burden she's been holding onto, makes my chest ache.

"*Sugar cube*, you don't owe me anything," I say softly, my hands cradling her face with care, like she's made of glass and steel all at once. "If you want to keep this to yourself, I'll understand. What I want, *what*

I need, is for you to share your pain and happiness with me, but only when you're ready. If you don't want to tell me what happened, you don't have to."

Her eyes glisten, her lips parting, she wants to respond, but the words don't come. The sight tugs painfully at my heart. I press a kiss to the tip of her nose, lingering there to let her feel how much she means to me.

And then, I gear up.

I need her to laugh, to loosen the weight crushing her, even if it's just for a moment.

"We can survive on butt stuff and blow jobs," I say quickly, keeping my face as serious as possible.

The gasp she lets out is so sharp it's almost audible. Her eyes widen, her lips part in shock, and for a moment, there's just silence.

That's it.

I burst out laughing, the sound ripping through the tension in the room as I clutch her closer.

And there it is...

3... 2... 1...

"Are you fucking serious, you clown?!" she yells, shoving at me like a wild animal.

I'm holding on for dear life, laughing so hard I can barely dodge the hits she's throwing at me. Her strikes are fast and relentless, but I'm too caught up in the moment to care.

"The day you're up my butt will never come!" she fires back, her words sharp and dripping with mock fury, punctuated by another strike.

I block her strikes as best I can, laughing uncontrollably, and tickling her every time she leaves even the smallest opening.

"Okay, okay, I hear you. No butt stuff for now," I say, still grinning like an idiot. "But where do we stand on the blow jobs?"

The second the words leave my mouth, I know I'm done for.

Her eyes narrow, and I don't wait for the explosion. I'm already running, laughing so hard my ribs ache, because I know she's really pissed now. If there are any knives nearby, I'm as good as dead.

I stop once I'm on the other side of the dining table, panting and grinning like a fool. The look on her face, pure, wide-eyed shock is absolutely priceless, and for a moment, I feel my heart come back to life.

God, she's adorable.

Her messy hair from all the tussling, the slight flush on her cheeks, and that fire in her eyes, all of it hits me like a freight train.

How did I get this lucky?

I'm in fucking trouble because she's got *Alex*, but you know what? It was worth it. Every second of this chaos, every risk I take just to see that look on her face.

I put it out there. I'd survive on butt stuff and blow jobs for the rest of my life if it meant being next to her.

Let's be honest, though. I'd survive on hand jobs if it meant staying by her side. Hell, I'd survive on nothing but being in her orbit and seeing her happy, laughing if that's all I could have. But hey, a guy can dream, right?

"Alex..." Her voice is so low, so menacing, it sends a shiver down my spine.

I know I'm in deep fucking enemy territory now. One wrong move and I'm about to dig myself into a hole so deep, I might never climb out.

"Yes, my queen?" The smooth, slightly sultry voice of Alex, her state-of-the-art home security system, chimes in. Designed to be intelligent and adaptive, Alex responds not only to commands but also to emotional cues by the looks of it, making it eerily perceptive and just self-aware enough to be unsettling.

"What the fuck?" My voice loses all trace of humour, the sharp edge cutting through the room.

Did Alex just call her "my" and fucking "queen"?

"Lockdown!" Sofia commands, her tone ice-cold and unyielding.

"Oh, for fuck's sake, woman!" I groan, throwing my hands up as I hear the unmistakable sound of bolts sliding into place and shutters descending. Alex executes the command flawlessly, trapping me in the damn house once again.

She lunges over the table, sliding on her side like a damn action hero. I catch the move from the corner of my eye just as I make a run for it in the opposite direction.

I'm laughing so hard, I can barely breathe, let alone gain any speed, but it's worth it. The sight has to be fucking hilarious. Me, stark naked, sprinting away from her, while she barrels after me like a predator locked onto her prey.

But then something catches my eye.

Hang on. Is that a knife?

Wait... what the actual fuck?

The laughter is all-consuming as I process the full picture.

She's a woman of average height, running full tilt with a murderous look in her eyes and a bloody knife in her hand, chasing me, a mountain of a man, as she likes to call me.

It's so ridiculous, so utterly insane, that I can't help but laugh harder, even as survival instincts scream at me to take this more seriously.

Fuck me!

"Fucking Alex and his trap shit all over the house!" I mutter to myself, dodging furniture and desperately trying to stay alive.

"There will be no 'up my butt,' Hunter!" she yells behind me, her voice full of fiery determination. "The day I let you up there will never rise, because I'll fucking send a nuclear bomb to the fucking sun first, you jackass!"

I stop dead in my tracks, my laughter overpowering any ability to keep running.

She can catch me all she wants, hell, she can cut me if she feels like it, but that line... fuck me, that line was absolutely hilarious!

"Okay, I heaaaaaar you, suuuuuuugar cube. Wheeeeere do we staaaaaaand on the boooooowjobs?" I manage to say, my voice cracking between fits of laughter so overwhelming I can barely breathe.

I know I'm digging myself deeper into the mud here, but honestly? It's worth it.

Sure, I might get myself cut. But I might also get myself a blowjob.

And let's be real, that's a risk worth taking. Any day.

She kicks my knee, and before I can react, I'm on the ground.

Flat on my back, with her straddling me.

Oh, fuck. She might think she has the upper hand here, but I'll gladly let her have this position any day of the week, as many times as she wants it.

Her gaze is furious, blazing with intensity, but the longer I look at her, the clearer it becomes. The slight lift at the corner of her eyes, the faint twitch at the edge of her lips, she's pretending to be mad.

Fucking jackpot!

She loves this as much as I do!

Was it the teasing?

The provocation?

The chase?

The conquest?

Whatever it was, it's electric, and I can feel it radiating between us.

I can feel myself getting harder beneath her at lightning speed.

Fuck yes!

She's a fucking goddess.

"You want a blowjob?" she asks, her voice small but menacing, dripping with mock danger.

But I know now, it's *all for show*. So, of course, I encourage her and play along.

"Well, I think you could be a good girl and do your duties. You know, lick me off," I say, my grin wide and shameless.

The words aren't even fully out of my mouth before *thwack*!

She smacks the hilt of the knife dead centre on my forehead.

"Ouch! Fuck! That hurt, woman!" I growl, rubbing the spot on my forehead because, seriously, it *really* did hurt.

And then I lose it. I burst out laughing, even though the sting is real, because fuck, this woman is too much. Too perfect.

In all my years of fights, training, combat missions, or even on real enemy territory, I've never been struck like this. Never.

And here I am, flat on the floor, taken down by a woman a third my size, who just smacked me with the hilt of a knife.

It's so absurd, so goddamn *hilarious*, I can't stop laughing.

She's *conquered* me, and somehow, I love her even more for it.

I fucking love her. I adore her.

But I can't scream it at her right now, not when we're still in the middle of this game. And, truth be told, I like it.

I like the fire in her eyes, the way her lips twitch between a smirk and a snarl. I like the way she's so effortlessly in control, even though we both know I could flip this dynamic in a heartbeat.

What else can I do to provoke her? To keep her playing?

I grin, the little devil in me waking up. *Time to find out.*

"Now, now..." The idea sparks in my mind, and I can't help myself. "Be a good girl and open wide..."

The punch to my chest lands so fast, I only register it after the impact steals the air from my lungs.

Before I can even react, she grabs a handful of my chest hair, yanking hard enough to make my eyes water.

"Fuck!" I rasp, my voice breathless. "That fucking hurt worse."

Oh, she wants *war*? She'll get her war!

Without hesitation, I flip her so fast she squeaks when her back hits the floor.

"Oh, it's on, *sugar cube*," I growl, leaning over her with a wicked grin. The fire in her eyes tells me she's ready for battle, and I'm more than happy to oblige.

Her hand is still gripping my chest hair, and every small movement sends a sharp jolt of pain through my chest, vibrating through my body and landing squarely in my cock.

If I thought I was hard before... fuck!

This new position, me on top of her, holding my weight off her with one arm while the other roams her body, tickling and teasing every inch I can reach, is maddening. Lust claws at me, overwhelming and unrelenting.

Then, in a flash, she wraps her legs around my middle. The speed of it catches me completely off guard.

But what's sending me spiralling into oblivion is the pressure of her thighs squeezing me so hard, it feels like she's trying to fuse us together. She wants to pull me into her just as much as I'm trying to absorb her into myself.

"Stop tickling me, you fool!" she yells, writhing beneath me like a wild animal, her laughter spilling out despite the venom in her words.

"There will be no 'up my arse' or blowjobs in your foreseeable future," she snaps, her tone sharp enough to cut through my amusement.

She punctuates her declaration with a brutal tug on my chest hair, sending a jolt of pain straight through me.

Oh, it's fucking on, sugar cube!

I lower my lips to her ear, letting my breath tickle her skin before giving her a soft, deliberate lick, just the way I know she likes it.

Her response is immediate, a deep inhale that sends a shiver through both of us.

And in that moment, I fucking know...

She's as aroused as I am.

"You remember, baby, what you promised me before?" I breathe the question against her beautiful neck, my lips brushing her skin as I kiss and suck gently.

She tastes like honey and damnation, a perfect mix of sweetness and danger. But most of all, she tastes like my existence... like everything I need to survive.

"Yes," she breathes out quickly, her voice breaking into a soft moan that sends fire through my veins.

That's all I needed to hear.

I know she'll stop me if something is wrong.

I take her ear into my mouth, teasing it with my tongue and teeth, starting that playful game she loves so much. Her soft, breathless moans hit my ears like a melody crafted just for me, each sound feeding the beast inside me.

It's like pure cocaine to him, igniting every primal instinct I have, clawing at my control. My beast is roaring in my mind, desperate for more, for everything, for all of her.

My hips begin to move, slow and deliberate, grinding gently against her core. The thin fabric between us does little to dull the heat radiating from her body, and every brush of my cock against her sends sparks shooting through me.

What I *want,* what every fibre of my being screams for, is to pound into her with the ferocity of a man utterly possessed, consumed by love and lust. But what I'm *going* to do is hold back. I'll let her set the pace, make the call. She needs to know she's in control, that this is her moment too, not just mine.

My love for her is a relentless, overwhelming force. It squeezes my chest so tightly I can barely breathe, a pain so exquisite it borders on pleasure.

Each slow, measured rub of my cock against her core draws me deeper into this haze of lust and love. I can feel her heat, the very essence of her, through the friction of her shorts. The rough texture brushes against the sensitive skin of my cock, creating a maddening mix of pleasure and restraint that drives me closer to the edge of reason.

She's everything... her sounds, her heat, her presence. And all I want, all I'll ever want, is to give her everything she desires.

It's a dry hump, and the pain is as much a part of it as the pleasure. The friction is maddening, raw, unrelenting, and utterly perfect.

But it's not just that. It's the added layer of her fingers tangled in my chest hair, pulling with just enough force to send jolts of sharp pain shooting through me. Her other hand grips my hair, tugging hard enough to awaken something primal, something feral, deep inside me.

The combination of pain and pleasure isn't just intoxicating, *it's consuming*. It's her. It's me. It's us, tangled in this moment of raw, unfiltered desire.

"Baby, you're fucking demolishing me," I manage to say, my voice low and strained, as I bury my face in the crook of her neck.

I can feel her heat, her pulse, her scent it's all wrapping around me, pulling me dangerously close to the edge. If I don't get a grip, I'll lose it right here, coming undone like some inexperienced, pubescent kid instead of the mountain of a man I'm supposed to be.

Well, *she* called me that, so I'm claiming it.

She starts moving her core against me in perfect, maddening harmony. Each roll of her hips matches mine so seamlessly, it feels like we've been choreographed by some divine force.

I can feel myself losing the battle... fast.

This isn't just a dry hump. This is THE dry hump. The best one in human history, I'm sure of it. And if I don't find some way to pull myself back, I'm going to lose it right here, completely at her mercy.

She tugs at my hair, her grip firm but full of purpose, trying to guide my hand so she can tilt my face toward hers.

And I let her.

Because I'm utterly useless when it comes to denying her anything.

The moment our eyes meet, the world tilts. She's so breathtaking, so devastatingly beautiful, that the last shred of my sanity slips away.

I'm mesmerised, not just by her face, but by everything. By the way her body feels pressed against mine, by the way the air between us crackles with unspoken tension, by the sheer gravity of what we're doing. She's not just in my arms, *she's everywhere.*

And then she moves. She lifts slightly, her gaze locked onto mine, filled with something raw and untamed, and before I can process it, her lips crash into mine.

The kiss is chaos and fire. It's rough, wet, and all-consuming, a battle of teeth and tongues, lips biting and sucking with a hunger that steals every breath from my lungs.

I swear I've forgotten how to breathe, but I don't care.

This isn't just a kiss. This is Sofia unleashed.

This raw, unfiltered, ferocious side of her, fuck me sideways, *it's everything.* It's more than I've ever dreamed she could be.

And *I'm hers.* Completely.

"I love you," she whispers into my mouth, her voice trembling with raw emotion.

"I love you so much, Hunter. I feel it in every cell of my body."

Her words hit me like a tidal wave, drowning me in their truth, their weight, their absolute beauty.

"Fuuuuuck!" I growl, the sound ripped from somewhere deep inside me. "You're fucking killing me, *sugar cube.*"

Our hips move in perfect, maddening harmony, rolling and rubbing together, building a friction that's both torturous and perfect. Our mouths crash and devour, loud and desperate, tasting each other as if this is the last moment we'll ever have.

Our hands roam hungrily, demanding more, more friction, more connection, more of each other. Every touch, every movement, ignites something primal and consuming between us.

It's chaos. It's beautiful. It's the kind of crazy that rewires your soul.

And it's as addictive as the most dangerous drug, because there won't be a second in my life, *not one*, when I'll want to be away from this woman.

My cock is throbbing, pulsing with unbearable pressure, demanding release. Demanding to mark her, to spill my cum all over her and claim her as mine, forever.

Unable to resist the pull, I lower my mouth to her chest, pushing her shirt to the side to expose one of her perfect, beautiful breasts.

If I'm an ass guy, then my *sugar cube* is without a doubt a nipple queen.

My hips move relentlessly, grinding, rolling, and pushing into her with everything I have. The friction is excruciatingly demanding, the kind of pain that borders on pleasure so overwhelming it drowns out everything else.

And then I take it further.

I wrap my teeth around her nipple, biting just hard enough before sucking deeply.

She screams, her pleasure raw and unrestrained, a sound so visceral, so electrifying, it freezes me in place for a second.

The sound of her cry is the most beautiful, intoxicating thing I've ever heard. It's like a promise of complete damnation wrapped in pure, unfiltered bliss.

"That's it, baby," I whisper against her breast, my voice low and full of encouragement. "Come for me. Cry your pleasure into my soul."

I lift myself slightly on my pelvis, pushing harder, rubbing against her with relentless intent. The added pressure draws out more of her heat, her scent, her everything, until I'm completely consumed by her.

Unable to hold back, I grip the fabric of her shirt and rip it open, the sound of tearing fabric filling the air. Her beautiful breasts are fully exposed now, and I don't hesitate.

I feast on them, my mouth hungry, desperate, lavishing her with every ounce of the devotion and fire she ignites in me.

Fuck me, this woman is perfect.

Absolutely, maddeningly, unapologetically perfect.

I launch a relentless assault on her breasts, kissing, licking, sucking, biting, every movement fueled by the need to claim her, to mark her as mine.

I know there will be hickeys later, dark reminders of my devotion, and she might very well kick me in the balls for it. But it's worth it.

Every mark, every faint bruise, is a stake in the ground, a declaration that she's mine.

And every time she looks at herself, every time she sees those marks, she'll remember this moment. She'll remember *us*.

Her moans vibrate through me, a symphony of pleasure that ignites every nerve in my body.

The feel of her skin against mine, warm and impossibly soft, and the intoxicating scent of her arousal lingering in the air, it's all too much.

I'm teetering on the edge, every ounce of control slipping away.

I know I'm seconds away from exploding.

"Baby, where do you want me?" I groan, my voice ragged, the strain of holding back almost unbearable. "Fuck! Baby, I'm so close."

I don't ease off. If anything, I amplify the relentless rubs against her core, desperate for more of her heat, her scent, her everything.

"Come all over my chest, *Nuuro*," she whispers, her voice low and breathless, a command wrapped in pure seduction.

Fuck me!

The words alone nearly undo me.

If I thought I could hold on any longer, I was dead wrong.

I can feel my balls tightening, coiled so tight they're seconds away from bursting, the pressure building to an unbearable peak.

Every pulse of blood in my cock feels like a desperate drumbeat, a relentless song composed for this powerful, breathtaking woman beneath me.

I lift myself onto her, straddling her with my legs on either side of her body, my chest heaving with every ragged breath.

My hand wraps around my cock, and I fist it with a furious rhythm, each stroke fuelled by the overwhelming lust coursing through me.

She's maddening, this woman beneath me, driving me to the edge of reason, consuming every shred of control I thought I had.

She wraps her hand around mine, her fingers so much smaller, softer, yet confident in their movement.

Without hesitation, she places her index finger on the sensitive opening at the tip of my cock. The sensation is instant and electrifying, a jolt of pleasure so sharp it nearly undoes me.

Her touch isn't just physical, it's commanding, intimate, and completely consuming.

"Fuck! *Sugar cube*, fuck!" I groan, my voice raw and desperate. It's like my brain is short-circuiting, scrambling to process the overwhelming sensations.

I want to call out to her, to say something, anything, but the words get stuck, trapped somewhere between my mind and my mouth.

The direct friction of her touch is delirious, every nerve in my body alight, pushing me to the brink. I feel consumed, overwhelmed, the need to come building into an unstoppable force.

"I need to come!" The words tear from my throat, raw and desperate.

"Baby... fuck! Baby, I need to come," I groan, my voice thick with need, the plea hanging in the air like a prayer I can't hold back.

Her movements grow sharper, more demanding, as if laced with anger. All the while, she keeps her thumb pressed firmly against the sensitive opening at the tip of my cock, denying me the release I'm aching for.

"You'll come when I let you come," she commands, her voice low and full of authority, sending a shiver through me.

Then she starts jerking me, her hand tightening and squeezing with just enough force to blur the line between pain and pleasure. It's maddening, exquisite torture that has me trembling.

And to drive me completely insane, she lifts her other hand to one of her breasts, playing with it in the most tantalising way, her fingers teasing and pulling at her nipple.

She holds my gaze the entire time, her eyes blazing with control and confidence, and I know... I'd give her anything.

If I thought I knew what I was walking into when I desperately fought for her, I was fucking mistaken.

Utterly, profoundly mistaken.

Because what's before me now, this unbelievable creature, this force of nature, is beyond anything I could have imagined.

She might be under me, in the so-called submissive position, but I'm not fooled. Her fire, her dominance, radiates from every inch of her, dictating every beat of my heart, every ragged breath I take.

Her heat seeps into me, her scent, her movements, all of it wraps around me, leaving me utterly consumed.

She holds my soul hostage, tethered to her in ways I'll never be able to escape.

I fought so hard to win her, only to realise I've willingly surrendered everything to her.

She might be beneath me physically, but she's the one holding my soul, my sanity, and my pleasure in the palm of her hand.

Or, more precisely, at the tip of her fingers.

The guttural moan that tears out of me is so deep, so primal, it shakes the very foundation of my reality.

She looks up at me, her eyes alight with mischief and pleasure, her lips curling into a smile that's equal parts wicked and angelic.

And then she speaks, soft, commanding, and full of fire.

"Come for me, baby."

Her words breathe life into me, igniting something unstoppable, something I can't hold back even if I wanted to.

The moment she moves her finger, the pressure shatters, and hot cum explodes out of my cock in long, fast streams.

She doesn't relent, her hand working me in powerful, relentless jerks that leave me completely undone.

I can't move. I can't think. I can't even breathe.

The pleasure is so overwhelming, so all-consuming, that it feels like the universe has collapsed into this one singular, perfect moment.

And then, as the haze starts to clear, my eyes focus on her, on the spots where my cum landed. Her breasts, her neck, her beautiful face.

Fuck me. She's radiant, painted in the evidence of what she does to me, and I can't look away.

"Holy fuck! Fuck me!" I rasp, my voice hoarse and shaky, as I try to clear the fog in my mind, chasing any remnants of clarity.

But there's nothing. No words. No thoughts. No reasoning.

There's *only her*.

And she...

She is my existence.

Even now, she's still working me, her hand relentless, determined to milk every last drop of my cum. It's like she's claiming it for herself, leaving no part of me untouched, no part unclaimed.

I've never felt so exposed, so owned, and yet so utterly complete.

"Holy fuck, *sugar cube*! That was amazing," I say, my voice still rough and unsteady. I look into her eyes, and what I see there stops me in my tracks.

Pure satisfaction.

It's written all over her face, a glimmer of pride in her eyes that I didn't expect. She's proud of herself, proud of what she's done, and the sight sends a fresh wave of awe and admiration coursing through me.

"Baby?" I smile, tilting my head inquisitively. "What's going on?"

She starts laughing, a low, throaty sound that makes my chest tighten. Without breaking eye contact, she collects the cum from her face with one finger, slowly, deliberately, and then licks it clean.

"Fucking hell, woman!" The words explode out of me before I can stop them.

The sight of her like this radiant, uninhibited, and completely owning the moment, is so hot it's borderline unreal.

This... this is the stuff erotic fantasies are made of. The kind of shit that people write about in scorching hot romance novels or dream of seeing in their wildest porn-fuelled fantasies.

But here she is. *My sugar cube.* Real. Tangible. Fucking breathtaking.

"You like that?" she asks, her voice cheerful and teasing, her satisfied, proud smile playing at the edges of her lips.

There's still cum on her face, gleaming like a trophy, but I'm not going to fucking point it out.

I want it there.

I want it all over her, claiming her, reminding her, branding her with my scent. It's not just about marking her. It's about everything she means to me, everything we've just shared.

She's mine.

And seeing her wear the proof of it so casually, so confidently, makes my chest ache with something primal and untamed.

"You're proud of yourself."

It's not a question. It's a statement, because it's written all over her face, bright and undeniable.

She just smiles, shyly this time, and nods her head.

Fuck me!

A second ago, she was a dominating little fire goddess, owning every inch of me without mercy. And now?

Now she's shy with me. Sweet. Soft. Vulnerable.

It's like she's two sides of the same impossible coin, and I'm losing my fucking mind trying to keep up with her.

I love that only I get to see this side of her.

I love that with every passing second, she feels more at ease around me, letting her guard down little by little.

But what I love most is that she's letting me in.

She's sharing pieces of herself, pieces I know she's kept hidden from the world. She's not just letting me witness her vulnerability, she's initiating moments, taking control, and now, by the look of satisfaction on her face, she's taking pleasure in *my* pleasure.

It's beautiful.

It's everything.

"I fucking love you, woman! *I exist for you.*"

The words tear out of me, raw and unfiltered, before I capture her lips in a battle that's pure chaos and fire.

It's a war of lips, tongues, and teeth, demanding, consuming, utterly intoxicating. Every kiss feels like it could devour us both, like it's too much and yet not nearly enough.

Because fuck me, I can't get enough of her.

She's insane. I'm insane.

This is more than I ever imagined love, lust, or devotion could be. It's wild, it's overwhelming, it's better than anything I thought was possible.

It's madness.

And I never want it to end.

We're a breathless, sticky mess when we finally pull apart, the air between us thick with heat and exhaustion.

And that's when it happens.

My stomach decides to make itself known with what is probably the loudest, most obnoxious growl in the history of the world.

Sofia starts laughing so hard her entire body shakes beneath me, the sound pure and unrestrained.

"Get off, *Nuuro*," she says between fits of laughter, playfully shoving at my chest. "Let's shower and eat before you starve to death."

Oh, fuck! She's showering with me?

The hopeful expression on my face must be painfully obvious because her own face falls, and I can see the realisation hit her like a brick.

"Separately," she adds quickly, her voice small and uncertain as she avoids my gaze, her cheeks flushing just enough to drive me crazy.

A man can only hope.

But she doesn't owe me an explanation, and I'm not about to push her.

I understand she needs time, time to trust, to let me in fully, to feel safe in every way. And to be honest, she's already given me more than I ever thought I'd get in years.

More of her. More of this. More of us.

"Baby," I say softly, tilting her chin until her eyes meet mine. "I told you, none of that."

I place a gentle kiss on the tip of her nose, lingering just long enough to let her feel the warmth of my affection.

She needs to know, *really* know, that she doesn't owe me anything.

I want to wipe away that flicker of doubt in her eyes, that shadow of disappointment of letting me down. She hasn't. She never could.

The only two things she owes me are to stay alive and let me be by her side. That's it. The rest? The rest will come in time.

And when she's ready, I'll be right here, waiting for her.

"I love you, *sugar cube*," I whisper, my breath brushing against her lips as I speak.

"You don't owe me an explanation. I adore you, woman, every piece of you. Take all the time you need. I'm not going anywhere," I say softly, each word meant to anchor her, to remind her she's safe with me.

Standing, I extend my hand to her, the gesture simple but full of meaning. As she looks at it, then back at me, I hope she sees it for what it is. A promise, a vow that I'll be here, always, whenever she's ready.

She takes my hand, and as she rises, our gazes lock.

She leans up, her face tilted like she's about to kiss me, her lips just inches from mine. My heart stutters, anticipation tightening every muscle in my body.

And then sharp, burning pain explodes across my chest.

"Fuck!" I hiss, realising too late what's happened. She pulled at my chest hair again.

She fucking pulled at my hair *again!*

She bolts into a run, her laughter echoing through the space, wild and carefree.

And me? I'm frozen in place, completely paralysed, watching her move.

Her beauty, her antics, they hit me like a drug, leaving me dazed and utterly intoxicated.

There she is, my sugar cube.

Unstoppable. Unpredictable. Unbelievably mine...

Chapter Twenty-Two

Sofia

I ordered so much food, you'd think I was planning to feed an army instead of just myself and the mountain of a man currently in my life.

Some people might call him my boyfriend or partner, but to me? He's still just the guy who's incredibly lucky to have me.

Okay, maybe I'm lucky to have him too.

Fine. I know I'm lucky to have him.

But admitting that, even to myself, feels like giving him the upper hand, and I'm not about to let that happen. Not yet, anyway.

But the way his touch feels on my skin... it's branding.

I never thought someone's touch could feel like this, like it's leaving an imprint on my very soul.

It's overwhelming, terrifying even, how much it affects me. How his hands provoke feelings I didn't know I was capable of, reactions I can't control.

And yet, a part of me craves it. Craves *him* with so much force.

When I woke up, I ordered food and clothes for him, because, let's be honest, as unbelievably gorgeous as he is, I'd like to be able to think straight, thank you very much.

Seriously, put some goddamn clothes on or I'm going to end up staring at your cock all day!

Obviously, I didn't say that out loud.

I might be a little crazy, but I'm not an idiot!

He's still in the shower after our little... what do I even call it? *Play party?*

The thought alone makes me laugh, a soft chuckle escaping before I can stop it.

Amateur hour at its finest over here when it comes to things like this. I don't even know the right terminology, let alone how I'm supposed to feel about what just happened.

But the laughter helps. It reminds me that I don't have to have all the answers right now. I'm safe with Hunter!

I also reprogrammed Alex to call me *my queen*, purely to mess with Hunter. And it worked like a charm. Watching him lose his mind over it was absolutely hilarious.

Oh, and that whole protocol to alert my dad? Yeah, I cancelled that too. The theatrics were just for show, another little game to see how far I could push him.

What I didn't expect was where it would lead. Or, more importantly, how my body, my mind, and my soul would react to him.

He's not just under my skin, he's in my blood, in my thoughts, in every corner of my being.

Fuck that was hot! Like really hot!

With every passing second, I feel more at ease with him. It's not just his touch or his words, it's the way he exists in my space, seamlessly, like he's always belonged there.

I never thought I could experience intimacy like this, the kind that leaves me feeling safe, seen, and utterly consumed.

Honestly, I never thought I could orgasm at all.

And now? Now I'm convinced that all it would take is one look from him in my direction, and all hell would break loose inside me.

The first time he brought me to the edge, it was like stepping into an entirely new world. The sensations were so foreign, like nothing I'd ever known, yet my body, my senses, and my instincts were all screaming at me to keep going.

It wasn't just pleasure, it was so much more...

It was *beautiful*. That's the only word that comes close to describing it. But even beautiful feels inadequate.

It was overwhelming, a flood of emotions and sensations crashing over me all at once. It was soul-shattering, breaking apart every wall I had ever built and leaving me bare in the best way possible.

No words could truly capture it. Nothing could ever do it justice. It wasn't just a moment, it was a transformation, a claiming of something I didn't know I *needed* until I *felt* it.

When he let himself go, when he placed his pleasure entirely in my hands, the weight of that devotion, that surrender to me, it was indescribable.

No words could capture what it did to me, how it reshaped something deep inside, something I didn't even realise was waiting to be awakened.

I felt it in every cell of my body. The trust, the vulnerability, the way he gave himself to me without hesitation. It was powerful, intoxicating, and grounding all at once.

I know now—without question—that nothing could ever come between us.

Nothing.

My scars, my pain, my self-loathing, all the things I thought defined me, all the things I believed I had to carry alone, now feel lighter.

With him, it's different. He has reached into the darkest corners of me and said, "*Let me hold this with you.*"

It's no longer just my pain, *it's ours*. Shared. And somehow, that makes it less suffocating, less all-consuming.

He sees me, every piece of me, even the parts I've hated for so long I forgot what it was like to feel anything else. He sees it all, and instead of recoiling, he stays.

He calls me beautiful. Not in spite of my scars, but because of everything I am.

And for the first time, *I'm starting to believe it.*

Even if I don't think I'm beautiful. Even if the mirror only reflects that broken little girl, bruised, scarred, and shattered in ways I can't seem to forget. Even if what I see is someone disgusting...

Hunter doesn't see any of that.

What he sees is strength. What he sees is the most powerful woman he's ever met.

And it's not about his words, because fuck that. I'm not one of those gullible women who fall for pretty words strung together like a cheap disguise.

It's *his actions*. Every single one of them. They are so loud, so undeniable, that they're like a shout in a silent room, impossible to ignore.

Every touch, every move, every breath he takes around me, each one feels like a declaration. A promise.

And slowly, despite the brokenness I see in myself, I'm starting to believe him.

This is not fake.

This is not weak.

This is fucking powerful. It's consuming, relentless, and so strong it feels like it could move mountains.

And I know, with absolute certainty, that he will never let go of me.

I'm not alone.

For the first time in my life, I feel it in my bones. I'm not standing on the edge of this world by myself anymore.

I have him.

And that changes everything.

A profound feeling of peace and contentment settles deep in my chest, warm and unshakable.

As it takes root, I know, *truly know*, that the day will come when I tell him everything. When I show him everything.

It won't be today, and it might not be tomorrow, but the certainty is there, steady and unrelenting.

Because with him, I feel safe. With him, I can be *me*.

Strong arms wrap around me from behind, and I melt into his touch without a second thought. Hell, I love how big he is, how strong he is, and yet, how beautifully gentle he is with me.

His scent wraps around me, a mix of my body wash and something darker, pure sin, raw and intoxicating. The thought pulls a giggle from my lips before I can stop it.

I reach behind, my fingers expecting to find fabric. Surely, he'd put on the clothes I left for him on the bed.

But of course not.

My hand lands on warm, bare skin.

Fuck no, he's still naked!

Of course he is.

"Are you allergic to clothes?" I ask, my tone dripping with mischief as I tilt my head slightly to give him a sideways glance.

His response is a deep, rumbling laugh that vibrates through me in the most delicious way.

Without saying a word, he tightens his hold on me, pulling me closer, and buries his face in the crook of my neck. His breath is hot against my skin, and the feel of him so close sends a shiver down my spine.

"Are you planning to flash me the entire day?" I ask, my voice teasing as my hands roam behind me, exploring the expanse of his body.

My fingers trace along his v-line, and the sound he makes a low, deep moan, sends a ripple of heat through me.

"Round three?" he breathes into my neck, his words dripping with hope and raw arousal.

His lips graze my skin as he speaks, and it's impossible to miss the way his body responds to even the lightest touch.

"I don't know what you're talking about," I say, playing the innocent card while my hands continue their exploration. They find their way to his hard abs, tracing the lines of muscle that feel like they've been carved from stone.

He doesn't respond with words. Instead, he kisses my neck, soft and teasing at first, before sucking on the sensitive skin so hard I know I'll have another bruise.

Fucker!

I noticed the marks on my chest and neck earlier when I showered. I didn't say anything then, but now? Oh, he's going to pay for this. I'm going to fuck him up!

"Hunter..."

My words catch in my throat, the rest dissolving into nothing. As much as I hate the hickey, well, hate is a strong word, as much as I dislike them, he's making it impossible to stay mad.

Every lick, every kiss, and the way his arms wrap around me so tightly make me feel like nothing in the world could ever harm me.

"Yes, baby?"

His voice is laced with mischief, the kind that makes my pulse race and my resolve weaken.

He knows exactly what he's doing to me. He's playing me like a violin, and damn it. *He is not getting away with this.*

I clear my throat, doing my best to sound menacing, though the way his lips brush against my skin makes it almost impossible.

"If you value your life, you will not leave hickeys all over me. Understood?"

Hunter doesn't even hesitate.

"Do you mean like this?" he asks, his voice dripping with humour before his teeth graze my skin.

He bites and sucks just on top of my shoulder, in a spot I didn't even know could be arousing, sending a shiver through me that betrays my tough facade.

The deep moan of pleasure erupting from me is absolutely filthy and shameless, a raw sound that feels like it comes from somewhere deep and primal.

And then my body betrays me completely. My arse pushes back into him on its own, and in that moment, I realise I'm a complete goner.

There's no stopping this. No stopping us.

"Fuck!"

His guttural voice rumbles through the room, low and thunderous, vibrating against my skin. I can feel him getting harder again, pressing into me with undeniable need, and the sheer intensity of it makes my head spin.

The unmistakable sound of the front door slamming shut echoes through the room, loud and jarring.

It snaps us back to reality so abruptly it feels like someone just threw a bucket of ice-cold water over us.

Every nerve in my body freezes, the warmth of the moment replaced with a sudden, sharp edge of awareness.

"Who the fuck has keys to your apartment?" Hunter's voice is sharp, laced with urgency as his eyes dart toward the door.

"My dad," I manage to squeak, panic thick in my voice as the reality of the situation slams into me.

I'm half-flashed, my shirt barely covering me right now, and Hunter? Hunter is standing butt naked in my kitchen.

If my dad walks in right now, he's going to have a full view of... everything.

"Fuck, Hunter, go put some clothes on!" I say, my voice breaking with panic as I glance nervously toward the door.

"Baby, wait."

Before I can even take a step, he spins me around so fast the room tilts for a second, leaving me dizzy and breathless.

His hands grip my shoulders, steadying me, and when I meet his eyes, the raw determination there hits me like a punch to the chest.

"Promise me," he says, his voice low but teetering on the edge of desperation. "Promise me you'll tell me the truth."

He's holding my gaze so intensely it feels like the whole world has stopped, as though he's borderline about to lose his shit if I don't give him the answer he's looking for.

"Is Elijah the one that hurt you? Because, baby, I am telling you right now, I will kill him. Right here, right now."

The cold, relentless conviction in his voice, paired with the unflinching determination in his eyes, stops me in my tracks.

I stare at him, the weight of his words crashing over me like a tidal wave. He isn't bluffing. He means every syllable, every threat.

And I love him for it.

I love him so much it hurts.

"No," I say, my voice soft but final. The word feels small in the face of his overwhelming presence, but it's the truth.

I didn't expect this, didn't expect Hunter to say he would take on someone as powerful as my father for me. But here he is, ready to do exactly that without hesitation.

He narrows his eyes at me, scepticism etched into every line of his face. It's clear he isn't convinced by my words, and I know I need to say more. I need to open up, even just a little, to make him understand.

And, honestly, to get him to leave the damn kitchen and put some clothes on.

"My dad saved me, Hunter. It wasn't him, it was my family that did this to me."

His features remain tense, but I can see the flicker of understanding starting to form in his eyes. I reach up, placing my hand on his cheek, my thumb stroking the softness of his bottom lip.

"I love you so much, *Nuuro*," I whisper, pouring every ounce of feeling into the words.

At my touch, his expression softens, the storm in his gaze calming just enough for me to know I'm getting through to him.

"Now please, go," I add gently, a small smile tugging at my lips. "I really don't want my dad to see you like this."

He turns without another word and bolts toward the master bedroom.

And me? I can't help myself. I ogle him from behind, my eyes shamelessly trailing over every inch of him as he moves.

He is so fucking beautiful.

Every line, every muscle, every effortless movement is like poetry in motion, and it takes everything in me not to laugh at how ridiculous it is to admire someone this much when they're sprinting away.

But damn it, he's mine, and he's perfect.

Chapter Twenty-Three

Sofia

"Everyone decent?" My dad's voice carries through the apartment, cutting through the silence just moments before he turns the corner into the kitchen.

I can't help it, I burst out laughing.

The sound must be his cue, because he steps into the room with a raised brow and a knowing smirk, clearly picking up on the fact that something's gone down.

"Well, good to know I still have impeccable timing," he says dryly, his eyes sweeping the room like he's assessing the situation.

It might just be me, or the love-induced coma I seem to be floating in, but as my dad walks into the kitchen and settles at the bar across from me, something else catches my attention.

Through the window, the city stretches out before us, bathed in the soft light of the setting sun. Shades of yellow, orange, and blue spill across the sky, blending and clashing in a fight for dominance, each one more breathtaking than the last.

I can't help it.

I stop and stare, completely mesmerised by the beauty of it all.

In this moment, everything feels still. Peaceful. Like the world is pausing just long enough for me to take it all in.

"You're in love." His voice is detached, completely void of emotion. It isn't a question, it's a statement. Simple. Matter-of-fact.

"That I am," I reply, keeping my answer short and quick, just the way he likes it.

My dad has never been a big talker. To be honest, I think the only people he bothers speaking to at all are me and Buddy. For everyone else, his words are like rare currency, valuable, scarce, and not something most people can afford.

It's just who he is. No unnecessary chatter, no wasted syllables. To some, it might seem cold, and right they would be.

He looks at me with that clinical stare of his, the one that feels like it could dissect a person down to their very soul.

He's taking me in, all of me, and I know, without a doubt, that his mind is already at work.

Knowing him, he's probably calculated every possibility of what might have happened between me and Hunter. Every scenario. Every risk.

And, because he's my dad, I'm sure he's also meticulously mapped out every way he could dispose of Hunter in the most inhumane and barbaric way possible if it came to that.

"I'm happy for you," he finally says, his voice steady and controlled.

But when I meet his eyes, I see it... *warmth*.

It's subtle, almost imperceptible, but it's there. As much warmth as he's capable of showing, and for him, it feels monumental.

I never thought I'd see that look from him, not directed at me.

"Thanks," I reply, the word slipping out before I can think of anything better. It sounds juvenile, almost awkward, but his unexpected sincerity completely threw me off guard.

"Everyone deserves to be loved. Truly loved."

His voice is steady, his tone firm, but the way he holds my gaze is what roots me in place. He doesn't blink, doesn't move, just looks at me with an intensity that makes the air feel thinner.

Being near him is like sharing space with a force of nature. The room itself bends to make space for him, his presence so commanding it demands attention.

"And I think Hunter truly loves you. Otherwise, he would have been long gone by now."

The corner of his mouth twitches, a faint shadow of a smile that feels more powerful than a full grin coming from anyone else.

"Yes," I reply softly, the weight of the moment settling over me. "I know that now."

"I'm glad you found the strength to let him in," he continues, his tone unwavering, as if my response hadn't even registered. "But I will forever be your dad, and my daughter forever you'll be."

I take a deep breath, steadying myself, because I know exactly what he's saying.

He's telling me that no matter what, no matter who I choose to stand beside, I'll always be his. He's telling me that I'm still a part of him, and he'll always be there for me. No conditions. No limits.

The weight of his words settles over me, and I can feel the sting of tears building in my eyes.

My gaze softens as I look at the man who saved me. The man who pulled me from the depths of hell and made sure I survived, even when I thought I couldn't.

Without him, I wouldn't be here. I'd be just another broken, destroyed woman, a ghost of what I could have been.

But because of him, *I'm not.*

And as much as I fight it, a single tear escapes, sliding down my cheek like a quiet acknowledgment of the gratitude and love I feel for him.

"Hi, boss."

Hunter walks in with that effortless confidence of his, calm and composed, and thank heavens, dressed this time.

I quickly turn away, focusing on the plates in front of me, piling food onto them like it's the most urgent task in the world. It's not that I'm scared or embarrassed, it's just... him and my dad in the same room? I need a second to find my composure.

Hunter steps closer, and I feel his presence like a warm current before his hand rests reassuringly on my shoulder.

The gesture is so simple, yet it feels like an anchor, grounding me amidst the storm of emotions swirling in my chest.

I glance up, just briefly, and see him facing my dad head-on, his posture straight and unflinching. There's no hesitation in his stance, no fear. Just calm, quiet strength.

And for a moment, I let myself breathe.

"What brings you in? Can we help with anything?"

Hunter's voice is professional, polished, slipping seamlessly into his work mode treating this were just another meeting. But he doesn't realise, of course he doesn't, that my dad isn't here for anything work-related.

No, my dad is probably just here to make sure we haven't either ended up at each other's throats and in fact we completely given into this madness.

"Oh, I just wanted to make sure Sofia was all right," my dad replies, his voice steady but carrying that weight it always does. "She's had a few difficult months recently."

His words settle in the room like a quiet storm, filled with unspoken meaning, and I swear I can feel Hunter tense slightly beside me.

"You don't say?" He shifts his gaze to me, his eyes narrowing slightly as if trying to see right through me.

I don't look up. Instead, I focus on the plates in front of me, piling on more food with an air of practiced innocence.

"I was completely fine," I say, keeping my response short and clipped, like it's the most obvious thing in the world.

"She trashed the office more times than I care to count."

My dad delivers the line so nonchalantly, you'd think he was talking about the weather.

"I might have tripped on a chair and broken a keyboard," I reply, my voice laced with mock innocence. "People love to exaggerate."

"She beat Stefan and Liam and called them incompetent," Dad insists, his voice carrying that dry, matter-of-fact tone that only makes it worse.

Hunter takes an audible gasp, his eyes widening as if he's picturing the scene, before he bursts into laughter.

The sound fills the room, deep and rumbling, and I glare at him.

"They were in the way when I tripped, and I accidentally stepped on their toes. Again, people exaggerate," I say, my voice light and innocent, the most reasonable explanation in the world.

But when I glance down at the plate in front of me, my stomach drops.

It's a disaster.

Sweet piled on top of savoury, savoury drowning in sweet, and the whole thing looks like a culinary crime scene.

Fuck!

Panic flares as I try to fix it, nudging things off one another with quick, clumsy movements, but it only makes it worse.

Fuck, fuck, fuck!

"She was about to send the drone to bomb Bogdan's associates. You know, just in case," my dad adds casually, like he's discussing mundane things.

That's it! I've fucking had enough!

What is this? Truth day? Fuck that shit!

"Are you done?" I snap, spinning around so fast my hair whips over my shoulder. Fury and menace radiate from me, and I make sure every ounce of it is directed at my dad.

But when I glance at Hunter, my intimidation tactic falters.

He's laughing. Hard...

So hard, in fact, he's clutching his sides, barely breathing, his face red from the effort.

"Why are you laughing?" I snap, my stare drilling into Hunter. "What's so funny?"

He doesn't answer, his laughter only growing louder, his shoulders shaking with the effort to contain it.

I shift my gaze to my dad, and of course, the corner of his mouth is slightly up, betraying the smug satisfaction he's clearly feeling.

He's enjoying himself.

The chaos, the mayhem, it's his handiwork, and he's sitting there like the puppet master pulling all the strings.

I've had enough of both of them.

Without a second thought, I grab the spoon I was using and smack Hunter over the head with it.

"Ouch!" He rubs the spot, his laughter momentarily faltering, only to come back stronger than before.

"What's so fucking funny?" I growl, my voice low and deadly, the kind of tone that could make anyone think twice.

"You better stop that shit, you clown, or I'll activate Alex for real. Then you'll really need to run."

That does the trick. He sobers up instantly, his laughter cutting off as he straightens, standing at attention like I've just barked an order at him.

But then he looks at me.

Dead in the eyes.

And his gaze isn't fearful or apologetic, it's sparkling. Glittering, even.

With love.

Heart eyes, pure and unfiltered.

WHAT. THE. FUCK?!

"You are sooooooo into me, *sugar cube*, you've lost your shit!"

He's beaming like a damn fool, radiating happiness that's so infectious it should be illegal.

I stare at him, completely speechless.

And of course, he knows it.

Because the moment he sees my surprised, wide-eyed expression, he bursts into laughter again, his whole body shaking with it.

Utter dread grips my mind like a vice. This tiny, traitorous piece of information, that *I am*, in fact, utterly into him, is now out in the open.

And worse? He knows it.

I would have gladly taken this secret to my grave.

Oh, I feel so exposed, like a nerve stripped bare at its most vulnerable moment.

And it's all thanks to my dad blabbing his mouth.

I shift my gaze to him, ready to throw daggers with my eyes, but then I see it, the glint of calculation in his expression.

This wasn't about exposing me.

This was about exposing Hunter.

And, knowing my dad, probably creating a little chaos while he's at it, just for fun.

He's watching Hunter closely, quietly studying him with that razor-sharp focus he reserves for moments like this. He's enjoying himself, savouring every move Hunter makes like it's all part of some intricate chess game.

Then, with the precision of a Machiavellian genius, my dad delivers Hunter's shame on a platter, leaving it right there in the open for me to take.

"This one put twenty of our best men in the hospital during his raging episodes."

My dad's voice is calm, calculated, delivered with the same energy as if he were commenting on political news.

But the words land like a bomb.

Hunter freezes, the laughter draining from his face as if he'd been smacked... hard. The shift is so sudden, the air in the room seems to thicken, tension pressing down on all of us.

I glance at Hunter, his jaw tightening, his whole body going still. He doesn't say a word, but I can see the storm brewing in his eyes, the battle between panic and control.

"Oh, actually..."

Hunter's words are abruptly cut short as my dad continues, his tone unyielding and matter-of-fact.

"Yes, actually, the last two are still in induced comas. The swelling on their brains hasn't gone down yet."

The air in the room turns even more heavy, oppressive.

Hunter's face shifts, whatever attempt at deflecting or explaining he was about to make dies on his lips. His jaw clenches, his shoulders stiffen, and I can almost feel the weight of my dad's words pressing down on him.

I take in a deep breath, trying to steady myself, then spin toward Hunter and shove a finger into his chest.

"Who lost their shit? Hmm? Who lost their shit, I wonder?!"

I can't hold it in any longer, I burst out laughing, the sound echoing through the room as I clutch my stomach.

Hunter just stands there, letting me mock him, his lips twitching in that way that tells me he's taking it all in stride.

And honestly? Fuck if it doesn't feel amazing for the shoe to finally be on the other foot.

"I might have tripped a few times on the chain around my ankle and accidentally landed on some of the guards," Hunter says, his voice so casual, like he's explaining an honest mistake.

His excuse is so small, so utterly pathetic, it's almost endearing.

Almost.

It only fuels my laughter because I know, *oh, I know,* he's so full of shit.

This is too good. Too damn good.

I'm going to mock him for *years* about this. That he lost his shit so epically, so magnificently, that even his attempts to explain it sound like the ramblings of someone who knows they're caught.

"The best part..."

"Elijah, no!"

Hunter cuts my dad off so fast and so sharply it makes me freeze mid-movement.

Wait. *What?*

Hunter just interrupted my dad. *Hunter!* That never happens. Ever.

This is too good. Whatever this is, I have to know!

I glance over at my dad, and of course, he's as detached and passive as always, like he didn't just drop the most tantalising breadcrumb.

But then I look at Hunter.

He's practically begging with his eyes, a million silent prayers aimed at my dad, pleading for something I can't yet understand.

What is it?

What is it?

My gaze bounces between the two of them, hopping back and forth, anticipation burning through me like fire. My mind races, imagining all the possibilities, the secrets.

I *need* to know!

"He was guarding the shirt you touched the entire time, like it was his lifeline."

My dad's words hit me like a punch to the chest, knocking the air clean out of my lungs.

For a second, I don't know how to react.

Part of me wants to laugh, confused by the sheer absurdity of it. Why would he do that? It seems ridiculous, almost comical.

But the other part of me, the deeper part, finds it so unbelievably sweet, so heartwarming in its raw intensity, that I can't help but stop and let the moment sink in.

I stand there, caught in the overwhelming wave of emotions crashing over me.

Because this isn't just about a shirt. This is about *him*.

And the way he feels about *me*.

I look at Hunter, and he lowers his gaze, his confidence stripped away, leaving him raw and exposed, probably as raw as I felt just moments ago.

I can feel his vulnerability radiating off him in waves, crashing over me, suffocating and heavy.

And I can't take it. I can't take *his* pain. It's too much.

Fuck it.

I don't care that my dad is sitting right here, watching this unfold.

I adore this man with everything in me. Every fractured piece, every jagged edge, every beautiful imperfection, *he's mine*. And I won't let him sit there, drowning in whatever storm is raging inside him.

I cup Hunter's face, feeling the roughness of his jaw beneath my palms, and lift myself onto my toes. Without a second thought, I crash my lips into his, kissing the living hell out of him.

I pour everything into that kiss every ounce of lust, vulnerability, and the desperate, all-consuming love I have for this man.

I fucking adore him.

He kept a shirt because of me? Guarded it like it was the most precious thing in the world?

Fucking hell, that's the most romantic, humbling, and impossibly sweet thing I've ever heard.

"And that's my cue to leave," my dad's voice cuts through the fog of the moment.

But I don't care.

Because right now, it's just Hunter and me, and this kiss that feels like it could hold the universe together.

The kiss is sweet and profound, a silent exchange of everything we felt in those moments apart.

It's more than just a kiss, it's raw vulnerability, a mutual unveiling of the pain, longing, and love that consumed us.

His lips move against mine with a tenderness that steals my breath, and I pour every ounce of my devotion into him, letting him feel the depth of what he means to me.

It's deep. Sweet. All-consuming.

By the time we finally pull apart, our foreheads resting together, we're utterly breathless, as though the world itself has gone still to give us this moment.

"I can explain," he says, his voice small, uncertain in a way that pulls at something deep inside me.

"Okay," I reply softly, pausing just long enough to meet his gaze. "But you don't need to."

I make sure my words are steady, reassuring, because the last thing I want is for him to feel like he owes me anything or that he's standing here exposed, *needing* to justify something so deeply personal.

"It was the shirt your tear landed on when I was fighting for you," he says, his voice barely above a whisper, each word dripping with raw emotion. "I couldn't bring myself to wear it. So I just placed it on a chair next to me and kept guarding it."

He wraps his arms around me, pulling me close, and I feel the frantic, unsteady rhythm of his heartbeat, the drumbeat of a chasing animal, relentless and wild.

"Wait," I say, pulling back just enough to meet his gaze. "You're telling me you were shirtless for four months?"

I blink, struggling to wrap my head around it.

The image is so absurd, yet so heartbreakingly sweet, that I don't know whether to laugh or cry.

"Did you... Did you sleep on the floor without a shirt?" I ask, my voice tinged with disbelief.

"Yep."

His reply is so short, that I just blink at him, completely stunned.

"They hosed me down one day, and some water splashed on it, that was the first time I snapped and beat the living shit out of the guards," he says, his tone disturbingly casual, like he's recounting a minor inconvenience.

It's the ease with which he speaks, as if this happened to someone else and not *him*, that sends a strange chill through me.

"They chained me after that," he adds, almost shrugging. "Well, my ankle. They probably figured they'd have a head start if I made a run for them."

He pauses, a faint smirk playing at the corner of his lips.

"Didn't really work in their favour, though."

"And the wrist chain?" I ask, my voice barely above a whisper, afraid of the answer.

"Oh, that one came after my mind snapped," he says, his tone unsettlingly calm. "I couldn't shake the nightmares that came sometimes. I needed the pain because even the nightmares couldn't drown out the agony I felt from not being next to you."

He pauses, his gaze distant, as if he's reliving every moment he's describing.

"So I fought. I lost my mind. And the guards ended up in ICU."

A full-body shudder courses through me, sharp and involuntary, at his admission.

The weight of his words presses down on me, suffocating and raw. This man, this beautiful, broken man, had been through hell. *For me.*

Fuck!

His pain was so deep, so raw, it resonated like a dark chord, vibrating through every part of me.

I thought I was suffocating, drowning in anguish, shattered beyond repair.

But looking at him now, hearing his words, I realise my agony was a mere ripple compared to the tidal wave that consumed him.

"You're not laughing," he says, pulling back slightly to study my features, his eyes searching mine.

How the fuck could I laugh?

"It's not funny, *Nuuro*," I say softly, pouring every ounce of love into my gaze.

For a moment, I let him see me, the small, vulnerable side of me that I don't allow anyone to witness.

"I think it's the most endearing, sweet thing I've ever heard in my entire life."

I place my palms on his chest, and the powerful rhythm of his heartbeat mirrors my own, thundering under my fingers.

"I'm so touched and humbled that you would do something like that," I whisper, my voice trembling as I fight to steady it.

Because this... this is something I never thought possible.

I never imagined that someone like Hunter could cherish something as insignificant as a shirt, simply because it reminded him of me.

And if he guarded that shirt with all his might, how much more would he guard *me*?

The realisation crashes over me in waves, both overwhelming and freeing.

I am not alone.

I am not alone.

I am not alone anymore.

As my mind repeats the words over and over, a steady mantra of reassurance, my hands remain glued to his chest, grounding me in the moment.

It's here, pressed against him, feeling the strength of his heartbeat beneath my fingers, that I realise something monumental. There's no limit to how much I can love this man.

He doesn't just speak his love, he *shows* it.

In actions that are bold, unyielding, and powerful. Actions that scream his devotion, his care, and the depth of his love for me.

So what's holding me back?

What's stopping me from surrendering completely to this love, from letting it consume every part of me?

Nothing.

There's nothing left standing in the way.

I take a deep breath, searching for the right words to explain what happened to me, but before I can even begin, he moves.

As if on cue, sensing the shift in my posture, he places his hands under my bum and lifts me effortlessly onto the bar counter.

He settles between my thighs, his presence grounding me in an instant.

In this position, we're nearly at the same height, and I can't tell if he did it on purpose to make me more comfortable, or if it was just an excuse to get closer to me.

Either way, I'm grateful.

Now I can look into his eyes, really look, without the strain of craning my neck. I can ogle his beautiful face as much as I want, and for once, I don't need an excuse.

I remember the first time when he teased me, asking how I managed to look down on him when I was so much smaller than him. I told him to fuck off, naturally, and from that day forward, I wore the highest heels I could find just to make my point.

But the truth is, I am smaller than him, inside and out, he is just larger then life.

And yet, even so, this mountain of a man loves me with a fierceness and depth I didn't think possible.

If he can love me like this, without limits or hesitation...

I can do the same.

"Baby, you don't need to tell me anything if you don't want to."

His voice is thick with concern, every word weighted with genuine care for me. It's so raw, so real, that it takes me aback.

I haven't even said anything yet, but somehow, he's already assessed me, understood me, and anticipated what's about to happen.

Fuck, he's smart.

I adore him and his beautiful mind, his unwavering patience, his way of seeing me even when I'm trying to hide.

"It's okay," I say softly, steadying my voice. "I want you to know."

I study his expression as I try to gather every ounce of courage I have. My hands are clammy, my pulse racing like I were training for combat. My mind screams at me to stop, to bury the secret I've guarded my entire life.

But I don't.

"You guarded a shirt for me," I whisper, my voice trembling. "I can share my scars with you."

The moment our eyes meet after those words, his gaze is so soft, so achingly full of love, that I find the last bit of courage I need.

He gives me the strength to open up, to finally let out the secret I've held for so long.

"When I was five, we had some sort of party," I begin, my voice soft and measured. "I loved parties because it meant we'd have sweets. And, let's be honest, what kid doesn't love sweets?"

Hunter doesn't say a word.

He just stays there, perfectly still, his entire focus on me, absorbing every word like it's his last lifeline.

It's so intense, so utterly him, that it borders on comical.

A small smile tugs at my lips, but I don't say anything.

Because he's too cute, and I don't want to break this moment.

"My neighbour across the street was so excited, laughing and playing with us, even though she wasn't invited to the party. We were out on the street playing before things officially started. Inside, my aunties and my mum were busy cooking and preparing everything, telling us to stay outside until they called us in."

I pause, taking a steadying breath, my fingers gripping the edge of the counter as I gather my thoughts.

"I didn't think anything of it. It was just another party to me, and I was happy because... sweets. Who wouldn't be happy about sweets at that age?"

I force a small, humourless smile, but it quickly fades as I continue.

"Then my neighbour asked me and my cousin if we were excited about the ceremony. I had no idea what she was talking about, so I just nodded and smiled, thinking it was about the sweets. I mean, of course, I was happy."

Hunter's gaze doesn't waver, his presence a grounding force as I let the memory unfold.

"Then she asked us which one of us would go first. Something in me shifted in that moment, even at that young age. It was fear, sharp and instinctual, bubbling up before I even understood why. And because I was a little tomboy back then, always pushing boundaries, I quickly shoved my cousin forward and told her she was going first. I didn't even think, I just acted. Self-preservation kicked in."

I take a deep breath, my chest tightening as I look into Hunter's eyes. There's no reproach in his gaze, no judgment for what I did.

For so long, I hated myself for that moment. For being weak. For sending my cousin into that situation instead of myself.

"But I was so small," I whisper, my voice trembling with the weight of the admission. "I was so scared. I didn't even know what I was doing, it was just instinct."

I search his eyes, silently pleading with him to understand. He must know it wasn't ill intent. It wasn't malice.

It was survival.

I try to study him, searching for any flicker of shame or reproach in his eyes, but his demeanour doesn't change.

He doesn't flinch.

He just sits there in silence, letting me speak. Not asking questions, not moving, just *loving me.*

His calm presence chips away at the wall I've built around this memory, and before I can stop myself, the words burst out of me like a dam breaking.

"I did the wrong thing!"

The scream rips from my chest, raw and jagged, echoing in the quiet room.

"I sent my own cousin to go through that... because I was scared. I was weak. I was pathetic! I saved myself until I couldn't even do that anymore."

Tears roll down my face, stubborn and relentless, defying every ounce of my will to hold them back.

"I did the wrong thing, Hunter!" I choke out, my voice breaking under the weight of my anguish. "I know I did, and I hate myself for it. I hate myself so much."

He doesn't speak.

He doesn't try to console me with empty words or platitudes.

Instead, he moves closer, his warm, steady hand running over my back in a reassuring rhythm. It's quiet, deliberate, and grounding like an anchor pulling me back from the storm inside my head.

And for that, I'm grateful.

Because there's nothing he can say to erase the years of guilt and pain.

But his silence, his presence, *him*... that's what I need.

Before I lose my nerve and make a run for it like the coward I once was, I force myself to keep going. This cancer has eaten away at me for years, and I refuse to let it consume me any longer.

"When my aunties and mum called us in, I shoved my cousin so fast in front of me she didn't even have a chance to complain."

My voice trembles, and I can feel my chest tightening as I relive the moment.

"They took her into one of the rooms and told me to wait outside. And then it started... the screaming."

I squeeze my eyes shut, but it doesn't block out the memory.

"The unimaginable screaming." I gasp for air, tears already streaming down my face.

"Hunter, I was five. Five! I swear, in my entire life, I've never been as scared as I was in that moment." I pause, my hands trembling against my lap, before the next words come tumbling out like jagged stones.

"And I fucking ran."

The admission cuts through me, sharp and unrelenting.

"I bolted from the house, and even now, I can't remember how I ended up on the street. All I know is that I ran. But the problem was... the men who came to this so-called party started running after me. To catch me. To bring me back."

The words catch in my throat, my sobs growing heavier, breaking me apart as I try to speak.

"And I was so small, Hunter. I fucking ran as fast as I could. I gave it everything I had."

The tears pour freely now, my face trembling uncontrollably as I force out the rest.

"I hid. I hid, thinking I'd finally escaped. But I was so tired, so breathless... and they fucking found me."

The sobs wrack my body, so profound that I can barely speak. My words come out in broken gasps, trembling with the weight of years of pain I've carried alone.

And through it all, Hunter doesn't say a word.

His presence, warm and steady, feels like the only thing tethering me to the ground as the storm of my emotions threatens to tear me apart.

He just pulls me into his chest, holding me close, and that's when I notice it, his muscles are so tight, his body so wound up, that he's trembling.

And yet, despite the storm raging within him, his hands remain gentle as they soothe my back, offering me the quiet strength he knows I need.

He just holds me there, loving me in silence, caring for me in the way he understands best.

I don't know how much time passes before I finally pull back, more in control of myself.

I look into his eyes, searching, terrified of what I might find.

Has his view of me changed? Does he see me differently now? Does he see *us* differently?

But all I find in his gaze is love. Compassion. Care.

And that's when I know it's okay to keep going.

"They brought me back," I whisper, my voice steadying as I continue. "By the time we reached the house, my cousin was curled into a ball on the sofa, crying silently."

I pause, my chest tightening as the memory floods my mind.

"I was slung over one of the men's shoulders, and the closer we got to the house, the more I knew... something was really, really wrong."

Hunter's jaw tightens, his lips pressing into a thin line, but he doesn't speak. He just listens.

"They put me in the same room as my cousin," I continue, my voice barely above a whisper. "And there they were my aunties, my mum, and this old woman I'd never seen before."

I swallow hard, forcing myself to push through the lump in my throat.

"When I saw my mum, I thought to myself, *For sure, nothing will happen to me now. It's my mum, she'll protect me, right?*"

The words hang heavy in the air, my voice trembling as I add, "But I couldn't shake the feeling in my gut, this screaming voice inside me that kept saying something was really, really wrong."

I close my eyes, the memory washing over me like a tidal wave.

I see her, my mum, standing there, and for a fleeting moment, I was filled with hope. Hope that she would save me. That she would put an end to all of it.

But that hope was ripped from me in the most sinister way possible.

Hunter cups my face gently, his hands steady despite the fury and anguish radiating from his body.

He starts peppering soft kisses on my forehead, trying to kiss away the pain etched into my soul.

And God, *I love him for it.*

I turn slightly, placing a soft kiss on his hand in gratitude, but then I pull back.

I have to push through this.

I have to let it all out.

"The moment they put me on the bed," I whisper, my voice trembling, "they jumped on me." I squeeze my eyes shut, the memory so vivid it's as if I'm there again.

"I screamed, Hunter. I screamed and I fought with everything I had. I gave it my all, but then..." My voice cracks, and I feel the tremor run through Hunter's hands as they tighten ever so slightly against my skin.

"Then I saw her."

I force my eyes open, meeting Hunter's unyielding gaze.

"My mum. She was one of the women holding me down." The words barely make it out of my throat, choked and raw.

"And I froze, Hunter. I froze for a second, just staring at her. I couldn't understand how she could do this to me. How she could betray me like that."

The tears are falling freely again, but I don't try to stop them.

"And that's when they took my clothes off. That's when they started cutting."

Hunter inhales sharply, his jaw tightening as he struggles to keep his emotions in check, to stay strong for me.

"I screamed, Hunter. I screamed as loud as I could, but by the time they were stitching me up, there was nothing left. Only these deep, animalistic growls coming out of me, like I wasn't even human anymore."

I pause, trembling, barely able to speak as the weight of the memory crashes over me.

"And that's when my dad, Elijah, barged into the room. He came in with Buddy and three guards, all of them fully armed."

I take an audible breath, my chest rising sharply as I realise I haven't been breathing properly while recounting the memory.

I glance at Hunter again, and I could swear he's fighting back tears. His body is so rigid, his jaw clenched so tight, it looks like he's waging a silent war within himself just to maintain control.

"He took me," I whisper, my voice trembling. "It was as simple as that."

My gaze falls to my hands, which are shaking uncontrollably, and for some reason, a faint, bittersweet taste fills my mouth.

"He pushed past my aunties and my mum and threw a comforter over me. He wrapped me in it, like I was something fragile he had to shield from the world."

The memory sharpens, the details painfully vivid.

"And he took me out of there."

"He didn't ask for permission."

"He didn't ask what they were doing to me."

"He didn't care."

"He just... *saved me.*"

The words hang heavy in the air, and when I finally gather the courage to look up at Hunter, my chest tightens.

The rims of his eyes are red, glistening with unshed tears. His face is raw, unguarded, every line etched with the effort of holding back the emotions threatening to overwhelm him.

Does he pity me now?

Does he see how broken I truly am?

Does he want to leave?

The questions whirl in my mind, each one cutting deeper than the last.

"No!"

His voice cuts through the fog of my thoughts, pulling me back into the present. Whatever he saw in my gaze just now, it forced him to speak for the first time since I started opening up.

"None of that, *sugar cube.*" His voice is low, raw, and trembling with emotion. "I adore you, woman. Don't lock up again."

He leans forward and places a gentle kiss on my forehead, grounding me in the warmth of his touch.

When he pulls back, I see them, the tears, slow and steady, rolling down his cheeks.

He does pity me.

"I don't pity you, *sugar cube*," he says, his voice thick with emotion, trying and failing to steady himself.

More tears follow, his composure slipping with every word as he leans into me, wrapping his arms around me tighter as if he could shield me from the weight of my own past.

"I don't pity you, *sugar cube*," he repeats trying to anchor me with his conviction.

"My heart breaks for the five-year-old Sofia," he whispers, his words Shaking with the depth of his anguish, "and for the fact that *I wasn't there to protect her*."

His voice cracks at the end, and before I can say anything, he's sobbing, his whole body shaking as he clutches me tighter, like I'm the only thing keeping him together.

I freeze at his words, at his reaction, at the way his body and mind are breaking down right in front of me, for *the little girl* I once was, the one who was broken in ways no child should ever endure.

I thought I understood what love was.

But now I realise I only understood it on an intellectual level, a concept shaped by logic and reason.

Because what's in front of me now is love in its purest, most unfiltered form.

A man so big, so strong, stronger than anyone I've ever known, is crumbling into pieces, not because of something that happened to him, but because he couldn't save the small, vulnerable version of me that was shattered so long ago.

He's breaking *for me*.

For a child he never knew, for a moment he wasn't there to stop, and the weight of it has consumed him entirely.

And in this moment, I understand.

This isn't the kind of love you see in books or hear about in movies.

This is real. Raw. Unstoppable.

This is the kind of love that tears through everything and leaves no doubt in its wake.

And *it's mine.*

My body feels numb, like every nerve has been dulled.

And yet, my insides somehow feel lighter, the weight of everything I've carried is finally beginning to lift.

My head pounds, and there's a strange, sweet taste lingering in my mouth.

I don't cry. I don't move.

I'm not even sure how well I'm breathing, but none of that matters right now.

What stops my reality, what anchors me to this moment, is the sight in front of me.

This mountain of a man, the strongest person I have ever known, sits with his gaze cast down to my lap. His massive arms are wrapped around my back, his hands moving in soothing motions, trying to mend the pieces of me he thinks are still broken.

And he's sobbing.

Not for himself, but for me. For something he could never have prevented or protect me from.

But even so, the pain he feels for what I went through is so acute, so acidic and rotten, that his body cannot contain it.

I never thought Hunter was capable of crying.

Not him. Not this indomitable force of strength and will.

But what he's doing now... this isn't just crying or even sobbing.

This is breaking.

He is breaking, splintering under the unbearable weight of the pain I endured.

"*Nuuro...*"

I cup his face gently, lifting his gaze to meet mine.

"None of that. Remember?"

I throw his own words back at him, my voice soft and full of the gentleness I know he needs right now.

His eyes, still glistening with unshed tears, hold a rawness that tugs at something deep inside me.

"Thank you for not pitying me," I whisper. "I wouldn't have been able to handle that, especially not from you."

His gaze sharpens, sobering as determination settles over his features.

"You are not that little girl anymore, Sofia," he says, his voice low and resolute, every word laced with conviction.

"You took their fucking actions and turned them into a weapon. That's what you are, *sugar cube*. You're not just a woman, *you're a warrior*, inside and out."

Before I can process the weight of his words, he starts kissing me, fiercely and reverently, everywhere he can reach. Each kiss feels like a declaration, a vow etched into my skin.

"You are strong," he whispers against my shoulder.

"Powerful," he murmurs into the curve of my neck.

"And unbelievably intelligent, Sofia."

His lips press against my temple as his hands tighten around me, grounding me in his presence.

"You took a broken girl and transformed her into this mighty woman that men tremble before," his tone is strong, determined full of conviction.

Each sentence is punctuated by a kiss, on my jaw, my forehead, my hands. It's as if he's trying to erase every ounce of pain I've ever carried with the strength of his love.

"I adore you," he continues, his voice thick with emotion.

"I adore what you've become. But most of all, I adore you for protecting that little broken girl. For taking care of her when no one else did. And for turning her into the extraordinary woman you are today."

His words seep into me, filling spaces I didn't even know were empty, and my chest tightens with an overwhelming mix of emotions.

This isn't just love... it's reverence.

Fuck me!

The tears come, spilling freely down my face, and for once, I don't fight them.

I give in to him completely, letting him kiss and hold me as much as he wants. I cling to his touch, his warmth, his strength, as I process his words, words laced with so much care, love, and respect that they wrap around me like a protective cocoon.

I don't just feel numb anymore.

I feel like I'm floating, weightless in the expanse of his love, and the only thing anchoring me to the ground are his strong arms and the beautiful, reverent words that continue to flow from his lips.

His presence doesn't just hold me, it rebuilds me, piece by piece, until I feel like I might not just survive but thrive next to him.

I never thought of it the way he explained it.

I've never had anyone to talk to about my pain.

No encouragement, no support, no one to tell me it wasn't my fault.

I just suffered in silence, carrying my trauma like a shadow that refused to fade.

And now, as I try to process everything, the raw emotions of what happened, his words, his actions, his pain, his care, his unwavering respect—I realise something profound.

There was never anyone better to share my pain with than my *Nuuro*.

With him, I feel safe.

With him, my suffering isn't a burden but a truth he holds with me, without judgment or pity, only love.

For the first time in my life, I am not carrying it alone.

"I love you so much, my *Nuuro*," I whisper into his skin, pulling him closer, wanting to melt into him and never let go.

"I love you, *sugar cube*," he says, his voice low and filled with raw emotion. He presses the softest, most reverent kiss onto my lips, a kiss that feels like both a promise and a prayer.

"Thank you for confiding in me, for sharing your pain with me," he continues, his voice trembling slightly as he buries his face in the curve of my neck, his arms tightening around me like he's afraid I might disappear.

We sit there in silence for a moment, the weight of everything hanging between us like a fragile thread.

Then, in a voice laced with quiet fury, he murmurs against my skin, "I will kill every last one of them."

His words are chilling and resolute, a vow spoken with the kind of conviction I know he means every word.

I burst out laughing, the sound bubbling out of me before I can stop it. Honestly, what did you expect? An ex-SASR warrior taking someone's shit lying down? I would have been seriously disappointed if he hadn't reacted like this.

The only problem is... I never had the courage to go back, not even after all these years.

"Is my big boy going to go and fuck them up?" I say in the cutest voice I can muster, trying to lighten the moment.

That was intense, really intense, but somehow, I feel lighter now. There's this strange sense of floating, like my senses are slightly off, but in a good way. Maybe it's the relief of finally letting it out, of finally not carrying it all on my own. Whatever it is, one thing is clear: I feel like I'm exactly where I'm meant to be.

"I. WILL. FUCK. THEM. UP."

He joins in the play, enunciating every word with exaggerated precision, his voice vibrating with both mischief and the deadly seriousness I know he's capable of.

"Just point me in the right direction, *sugar cube*, and they're all fucked."

Before I can respond, he leans in and kisses me, his lips soft, as if he's vowing everything into me with that single touch.

I start laughing softly because, yep, I definitely know where this was going.

"They're still my family," I say gently, trying to temper the fire I know is already blazing inside him. "We can't kill them."

His eyes narrow slightly, and I see the flicker of dangerous determination before he replies.

"It doesn't need to be a 'we.' It can be an 'I.' And maybe a 'we' if I take a team with me, but you don't need to do anything."

He pulls back just enough to hold my gaze, studying me intently to gauge if I'm still playing or if I'm serious. His features shift slightly when he realises I'm not joking.

"Oh, fuck, baby, please let me kill them," he says, his voice laced with desperation and pain, the words pouring out as though they've been bottled up too long.

I don't answer, and that's when it hits him.

"Fuck!" he yells, the sound echoing through the room like thunder. His fists clench at his sides, his entire body taut as if he's trying to purge the fury surging through him. It's not just anger, it's a visceral need to protect me, to right every wrong ever done to me, no matter what it takes.

"I tried for years to build the courage to go back and face them, Hunter," I confess, my voice quieter than I intended, as if saying it too loudly would make it even more real.

"The farthest I ever got was my front door. On the inside, may I add," I continue, laughing awkwardly to cover the wave of shame creeping in. "I can't. I know I can't."

He's silent for a moment, his jaw tightening as his eyes darken with something I can't quite name, but I can feel it, raw, seething, and unrelenting.

"But I can," he finally says, his voice low and drenched in menace, like a beast that's just caught the scent of its prey.

"I can, and I will. Fuck them up, as you said."

His words are laced with a ferocity so sharp it sends a shiver through me. It's not a threat. It's a vow.

I burst out laughing, this time a genuine laugh. He's so cute, going all intense and overprotective on my behalf, like a big, grumpy guardian.

"We can talk about it later," I say lightly, waving it off. *And by later, I mean never, but he doesn't need to know that little detail.*

"Is that what the suitcase in your walk-in is about?" he asks, his tone shifting slightly, and I can see the wheels turning in his head.

I just nod, unable to trust my voice. It's pathetic, really. The mighty woman he thinks I am, the warrior he sees in me, can't even bring herself to face her demons.

His hands trace my back again in that comforting, reassuring way of his, grounding me in the present, pulling me out of the shame spiraling in my mind.

And then his words... his words tilt my entire world off its axis once more.

"I want to go with you and face your family," he says, his tone steady but laced with an edge of unshakable resolve.

"If you want me to kill them all, consider it done. But if you want to go and face them, to demand answers or confront them on your terms, I will sit beside you as your weapon, your shield. And when you're ready, if you ask me to, I will annihilate every last one of them."

His words are so calm, so calculated, so profound. Yet beneath that calm, they carried a deadly edge, powerful, devoted, and unwavering. I knew, the day I go back to face my demons is coming sooner than I ever thought possible.

"Okay..." My voice is small, fragile, trailing off like a whisper lost to the wind.

"Okay," he repeats, his voice deep and steady, a rock against the storm swirling inside me. Strong. Strong enough for the both of us.

Chapter Twenty-Four

Hunter

It took everything in me not to scream, to release the rage clawing at my chest from her revelation. *What the actual fuck?* Who would do such a thing to their own daughter? My hands clenched involuntarily, shaking with the need to destroy. I will hunt them all down and end them, every last one of them!

My blood burns like fire in my veins, poisoned by the betrayal she suffered. The very people meant to protect, cherish, and love her were the ones who shattered her, breaking her in ways no one should ever endure. They fucking cut her! The thought alone is enough to make bile rise in my throat. Her words replay in my mind, each one carving into me like a blade.

How could they?

I fucking shattered into small, insignificant pieces at the image of a young Sofia, broken, screaming, with no one there to save her. That pain is unbearable to picture, suffocating me with its weight. And then to know it took a complete stranger to come and take her, like a thief in the night?

Why didn't those fuckers fight for her? Why didn't they stop him and keep her safe? She deserved more. She deserved for them to fight, to protect her with every ounce of their strength, not stand by and let her leave with someone she did not knew. The betrayal cuts deeper than I thought possible. How could anyone, let alone her own blood, fail her so catastrophically?

I crack my neck, taking a few deep breaths in a futile attempt to calm the storm raging in my mind. But it's no use. Every breath fuels the fire, every thought sharpens the blade of my fury. Fuck, I want to kill them all.

I *need* to kill them all.

How the fuck could they do something like that?! You don't want kids?! Fine! There are countless ways not to have them. But don't bring them into this world only to break them, to destroy them. The thought churns in my stomach like poison, my fists clenching tight enough to bruise.

"Fuck my life!!!!!" I scream in the room.

All night, I tossed and turned, tormented by the vivid images my mind conjured of little Sofia. Every version of her suffering shredded me further, each one more brutal than the last. But in every twisted scenario, there was one constant... I was there, hunting them down, making them pay.

I killed them slowly, so sadistically that their screams of pain devolved into raw, animalistic growls of agony. The satisfaction was fleeting, though. No amount of imagined vengeance could undo the damage they inflicted on her. *FUCKERS!*

I push back from the desk, the weight of my tasks forgotten. I'm supposed to be working, digging for leads on the bombing, catching up on everything that happened while I was locked away. But it's impossible. Every time I try to focus, Sofia's words come rushing back, crashing into me like a tidal wave.

That suffocating feeling grips my chest, like a powerful claw tightening with every breath, dragging me into a pit of fury and despair. My beast roars within me, demanding vengeance, demanding their blood flow in rivers of pain. Not just for Sofia, but for every little girl they might have hurt, every life they could have destroyed. The thought of it sickens me, ignites something feral and unrelenting in me. *They need to pay. All of them.*

"Fuck!" I roar again, the sound echoing through the room as I start jumping up and down, desperate to expel this relentless energy coursing through me. My beast is raging, roaring, slamming against the walls of my control, demanding release. Demanding they all die.

I can feel it clawing its way to the surface, a dark force urging me to unleash every ounce of fury on them, to execute them all in the most sinister, brutal ways imaginable. But even as the fire threatens to consume me, fear grips me tighter. I can't lose control, not like this. Not with Sofia near. The last thing I want is for her to see the shadows of the beast I keep locked away.

"Again?" Sofia's sweet voice rings out from behind me, cutting through my turmoil like a lifeline. Sweet. Adorable. If she knew I was thinking that, though, she'd probably kick me square in the balls, out of sheer principle, no less.

"I really want to kill them," I say, pulling out the best puppy dog eyes I can muster. I take the coffee from her hand like it's some sort of peace offering and try again. "At least one or two? Come on, *sugar cube*. I don't think anyone would even notice."

I've been begging her all night, half-joking, half-serious until she finally snapped and told me to shut up or face the consequences. Naturally, my filthy mind went there, and I laughed. She kicked me. Hard.

"They would notice," she replies, deadpan, her sharp tone making it clear she's not about to indulge me.

"Okay, so not your mum and dad. But how about one of your aunties? Just one. Or maybe two, if you really love me," I say, grinning as if her firm dismissal meant absolutely nothing.

"Nope," she replies flatly, her tone as sharp and final as a gavel.

"Baby... please!" The words come out raw, almost feral. It feels like there are bugs crawling under my skin, poison coursing through my veins, eating me alive from the inside out. I can't sit still. I can't breathe properly. My beast is fully unleashed, prowling just beneath the surface, visible for anyone to see. There's nowhere to hide him, no way to shove him back into his cage.

I'm losing control. I know it. Any second now, she'll see him for what he truly is.

She turns to face me, standing toe-to-toe, unflinching despite the storm raging inside me. Even as she looks up, her gaze holds that unshakable authority she commands so effortlessly, making it feel like she's the one towering over me.

I try to hide my beast. I really do. I force myself to pretend that I'm fine, that this isn't eating away at me like a corrosive poison in my soul. But it's a lie. It's all I can do to keep the growl from escaping my throat.

They dared to touch her when she was at her most vulnerable.

Those shitheads need to die.

They need to die.

I force my body to stay still, battling the raging inferno coursing through my veins. Every muscle is coiled, fighting the urge to explode. But I can feel it slipping, the heat rising to my face, my skin practically burning, and the faint tremble in my hands betraying the control I'm desperately clinging to.

"What's going on, Hunter?" Her voice is calm, calculated, and laced with unshakable confidence.

She knows.

Damn it, she knows.

She's onto me, peeling back the thin veil of control I'm trying so hard to maintain.

I could lie. I could pretend everything is fine. I could say nothing now, bide my time, and then hunt them down and annihilate every last one of them. Slowly. Very, very slowly, in ways that would leave even my darkest instincts satisfied. I want it so badly I can taste it, but no. I can't do that to my *sugar cube*. She is my existence, my light in the shadows. If I give in to the beast clawing inside me, I'll destroy the most important thing in my life... her trust, her love, our bond.

She is more important than my beast. More important than my thirst for blood.

"Hunter, what's going on?" Her voice is sharp, laced with calm authority. "You're shaking, and the rims of your eyes are red, it's not from tears." She narrows her gaze, studying me like she's trying to dissect my very soul. "You look like you're about to explode. Spill!"

That last word is a command, firm and unwavering, and it's a stark reminder of the kind of woman I've ended up with. A force of nature who won't back down, not even when faced with the beast raging inside me.

I let out a heavy sigh, my chest rising and falling as if trying to expel the weight pressing down on me. Slowly, I lower myself into the chair and pull her onto my lap, her presence the only thing keeping the inferno inside me from completely consuming my sanity.

Fucking hell! The last thing I wanted was to tell her about my beast, my dad, or the skeletons that still rattle in the shadows of my mind, the ones left behind from the army and all the blood-soaked nightmares that came with it.

"You are not allowed to leave me!" The words burst from my lips, raw and uncontrolled. The sheer force of them surprises even me. She cannot leave! She *cannot!* If I tell her, if she sees this part of me, she might get scared. She might run, and I wouldn't survive that.

"What?" Her brow furrows, confusion clouding her face. "Why would I leave you?"

She studies me, her sharp eyes narrowing, peeling back layers I thought I'd hidden. All traces of amusement drain from her features, replaced with something far more serious.

"Hunter." Her voice is firm, steady, yet gentle, like a command wrapped in a plea. "What's going on? Why are you like this?"

My hand tightens around her waist, instinctively grounding me, and maybe her too. If she jumps from my arms, I tell myself, I can hold her. I *will* hold her.

"I have moments of something... beyond fury. Fury feels too small, too... human for what this is. When I was little, it felt random. Maybe back then you could have called it anger or frustration, but now? Now I've learned to live with it, to keep it caged. Most of the time, it's quiet, dormant even. But when something triggers me, it's like a fire ignites in my veins, clawing at my skin, screaming for release, demanding blood. It's not just anger, it's a primal force inside me, a need to scream, to chase, to conquer, and to utterly break whoever or whatever triggered it."

I study her expression, searching for any flicker of fear or hesitation, anything that says knowing what's inside me has changed the way she sees me. My chest tightens, bracing for the rejection I feel I deserve, even though I can't bear the thought of it.

"I joke a lot, not just to make others laugh, but to keep myself steady, to stay in what I call the green zone. The truth is, most of the time, the jokes are more for me than anyone else."

"Is that what happened in the army?"

"You know about that?" My tone comes out sharp with surprise, the words snapping out before I can stop them. Fuck. How does she know? I cleaned my tracks. After I sent that building straight to hell in burning flames, wiping it and everyone in it, including that goddamn captain off the map, I made sure no trace of it would follow me.

If I could bring that bastard back, I'd kill him again. Slowly this time. Painfully. But I didn't have the luxury then. After I shot him, I had to move fast, burn everything, and destroy those fucking records. I know I covered my tracks. So how the hell does she know?

A soft smile plays on Sofia's lips, and they look so irresistibly adorable, full, inviting, and utterly captivating. I know they're made for me to lose myself in them, to claim them. My chest tightens with the thought, and I lean in, half-expecting her to pull away, to hesitate. But to my surprise, she leans in too, meeting me halfway. Her kiss is a tender answer, sweet and soothing, pouring calm into the chaos inside me. With every second, her touch quiets the raging beast within me, coaxing it into submission with her unspoken promise of love.

"I've been stalking you for the past two years," she whispers against my lips, her voice soft yet teasing.

I freeze for a split second, taking an audible inhale, her words hitting me like a curveball. Then, it happens, I burst out laughing, the sound deep and uncontrollable, echoing through the room.

"Are you serious, *sugar cube*?" I manage to say between bouts of laughter, my chest vibrating with joy.

She doesn't respond, just raises an eyebrow with that smug little smile of hers that says everything.

Fuck me, she's so into me! This moment, this revelation, only makes me fall harder.

"Hold your horses, big boy," she tries to cut me off, but she just called me 'big boy'. She should count herself lucky I don't jump on her and devour her whole. "I already know you were stalking me as well." That dampens some of the laughter bubbling inside me, but I still can't resist taking the piss a little.

"You are sooooooo into me," I laugh, the sound vibrating between us as I lean in to kiss her jawline, letting my teeth graze her skin in a playful bite. "I adore you, *sugar cube*," I add, my voice dipping into a mix of amusement and reverence, as if the words themselves could barely contain the depth of my feelings.

"I'm not *so* into you," she says, her tone light but teasing, though the smirk on her lips betrays her amusement. "I normally stalk anyone who crosses paths with us for a few months, sometimes longer." She trails off, pointing her finger squarely at my chest with a dramatic flourish. "You," she emphasises, her eyes narrowing playfully, "you I caught stalking me back. So I had to keep a close eye on you to figure out why."

"I had no idea," I say, bursting out into uncontrollable laughter, the irony of it hitting me hard.

"Head of Cyber," she declares, pointing at herself with pride. "Head of Security," she adds, pointing at me with exaggerated flourish. "I outrank you." The satisfied smile on her face sparkles like diamonds catching the light, radiating her triumph.

I can't resist. I have to mess with her just a little. "Yep, but it depends on how you look at things," I say, grinning as I lean in closer. "I'm still bigger than you. And stronger." I chuckle at her adorable reaction, right up until she, accidentally I'm *sure,* steps very not-gently on my little toe.

"Ow!" I yelp, hopping back slightly, while her grin widens with unmistakable mischief. "That was uncalled for!"

"Oops," she says, her expression the picture of feigned innocence, though the glint in her eyes tells me she's anything but sorry.

"Sorry, was that your foot? I was just getting more comfortable on your lap," she adds, her voice dripping with mock sweetness, while the corner of her mouth betrays her amusement.

I narrow my eyes at her, about to retort, but she cuts me off. "I don't know all the details," she says, her tone shifting, suddenly calm and calculated. "But I know there was a fire, I know there were bodies, and I know you, Hunter." Her eyes lock onto mine, searching for answers in my face. "Who did you kill?"

The shift in her demeanour stops me cold, her question hitting like a bullet, direct and unrelenting. She's not just curious, she's demanding the truth.

All humour vanishes from my mind, replaced by a flood of dark, twisted memories that grip me like a vice. The laughter and teasing are gone, swallowed whole by the weight of everything I've been hiding.

Oh, fuck. I need to tell her.

The images flash like lightning in my mind bodies, flames, the chaos of that night. My throat tightens as I try to push them away, but they're relentless.

But she deserves the truth. My *sugar cube* deserves everything, even the darkest corners of who I am.

"So, you know how I told you I have this thing inside me? The need for action, for fights, sometimes even for pain?" I pause, watching her as she shifts slightly, her full attention now locked on me. She nods silently, her gaze steady, waiting for me to go on.

"My dad was in the SASR," I continue, my voice carrying the weight of memories. "And he was pretty much the way I am now. A big guy, bigger than life, really. There wasn't a single person who wasn't intimidated by him, myself included. But despite that, I wanted to be just like him. He trained me from the time I was small, almost as soon as I could stand. Even when he was deployed all the time, every moment he was home was dedicated to me and my training. He pushed me hard, but it was because he believed I could take it."

I pause, exhaling deeply, the memories vivid and raw. "He was my hero, and I wanted to be everything he was. But sometimes, what you want comes at a cost you don't see."

I stop, drawing in a deep breath, and lower my gaze. My chest tightens as the weight of what I'm about to say presses down on me. *What if she sees me as a monster now?*

"I didn't see it, *sugar cube*," I manage to whisper, my voice barely audible. It feels so weak, so defeated, like I've been stripped of every defence. "You have to believe me."

Her hand gently lifts my chin, bringing my gaze back to hers. I brace myself for rejection, for fear, but instead, her eyes radiate warmth and compassion. It's so unexpected, so tender, it almost undoes me.

"What didn't you see, *Nuuro*?" she asks softly, her voice steady yet filled with care. Her question lingers in the air, wrapping around me, heavy and unyielding. I steady myself, grounding every fragmented piece of me in her warmth, in the unwavering patience she offers.

"He was abusing her," I finally force the words out, though they feel like shards slicing my throat on the way out. "And I didn't even fucking see it." My voice cracks at the end, the weight of my admission crushing down on me. "I thought they had a good marriage. You have to believe me, *sugar cube*. I didn't see it coming."

Her hand stays firm on my cheek, her thumb brushing against my skin in a soothing gesture. The compassion in her eyes doesn't waver, even as my confession hangs between us, raw and exposed. I let out a shaky breath, hating myself for missing it, hating him for doing it, and hating the world for letting it happen.

Her expression softens even further, her gaze tender and unwavering. She leans her forehead against mine, the gentle touch grounding me in the moment. It's beautiful and sweet, and yet it feels like I don't deserve it. But I need to tell her. She deserves to know the whole truth.

I take a deep breath, steadying myself, and pull back just enough to look her in the eyes.

“When I found him abusing her,” I begin, my voice raw and heavy with the weight of the memory, “there was a fight, and I killed him.”

The words fall between us, thick and unforgiving, like a stone dropped into the stillest of waters. The air feels charged, heavy, but she doesn’t flinch. She doesn’t look away. We just stay there, locked in silence, holding each other’s gaze as the truth settles between us.

"The person I looked up to most in life, the person I wanted to become... was a monster." My voice doesn’t even sound like my own. It’s hollow, empty, as though the words themselves have drained me.

Sofia places a palm on my cheek, her touch gentle and grounding, her thumb stroking in soothing motions.

"I killed him," I continue, my voice quieter now but no less weighted, "and I would do it again, Sofia. Because he broke my mum. Even now, after I killed him and we buried him under the avocado tree in the garden, she’s never recovered from that night. Her mind broke, and she’s forever a prisoner to her own reality."

I don’t mean to raise my voice, but the last words explode out of me like a dam breaking. "I would kill him again, Sofia!" The intensity of my admission hangs in the air, raw and unapologetic, but her touch never wavers.

She leans over and wraps me in an embrace so soft, so sweet, so utterly devoted that it knocks the air from my lungs. Her warmth envelops me, and in that moment, I realise my body is trembling. I didn’t even notice, but she did.

She holds me tighter, her hand stroking the back of my head in soothing circles. Her voice, gentle but resolute, whispers in my ear, "It’s okay, *Nuuro*. He fucking deserved it."

"Yes, he did," I say, my voice trembling. "But that's not what’s breaking me. I looked up to him, Sofia. I wanted to be like him." The words taste bitter, like poison spilling from my lips. I tighten my hold on her, burying my face in her chest as this unbearable, primal need to scream rises from deep within me. It claws at my throat.

"And then..." My voice cracks, barely a whisper. "To make matters worse, when I was in the army, it fucking happened all over again."

Her arms don't loosen their grip on me, not even for a second, but the pressure building inside me doesn't relent. "How fucked up can I be inside to keep picking the worst monsters in this world as my role models? What the fuck is wrong with my insides?"

The words spill out, raw and unfiltered, exposing the fractured parts of me I've tried to ignore.

She doesn't say anything. She doesn't move, doesn't flinch, doesn't complain, or pull back. She just stays there, her arms around me, steady and unwavering, letting me take what I need. Letting me lose myself in the solace of her presence.

"Every time I think I'm in control of my beast," I whisper, the words cracking under the weight of my confession. "Every time I think I've got a handle on my pain, something happens, and it all shatters again. I break inside all over again." My voice is raw, barely audible, the truth gnawing at my insides.

She doesn't respond with words, doesn't try to fill the silence with platitudes or empty reassurances. She just holds me. Her arms are like an anchor, keeping me tethered when everything else inside me feels like it's falling apart.

When I finally pull back, bracing myself for the rejection and disappointment I'm sure will be written across her face, I find none of it. There's no judgment, no disgust, no fear. Only compassion. *Only Sofia.* Her beautiful, steadfast gaze sees every part of me, the beast, the brokenness and still, *she stays.*

"Okay, I will tell you something, but you need to swear to me you'll keep the secret." Her tone is soft but carries a weight that immediately pulls me from my spiral.

I narrow my eyes at her, the abrupt shift in our conversation throwing me off balance. How did we go from me baring my soul, exposing the ugliest parts of myself, to her offering to share something hidden?

"What?" I ask, my voice sharper than I intend. Not out of anger, but confusion. My mind is still trying to process her unwavering support, and now she's giving me this?

She smiles, her expression so tender it feels like a balm on the raw parts of my soul. Both her palms settle on my chest, warm and steady, grounding me as she looks up into my eyes.

"For real, Hunter, if I tell you this, everything will make so much more sense to you," she says, her voice gentle but sure.

I frown, confused, my mind still swirling with self-loathing and doubt. "Why aren't you scared of what I just said? Shouldn't you be, like, '*Oh, he's so fucked up*' or something?"

Her laughter erupts, bright and melodic, filling the room with a warmth that dissolves the tension like the sun burning away a heavy fog. She nods her head between giggles, wiping away a tear from the corner of her eye.

"I think that every day. What are you talking about?" she manages between bursts of laughter, her expression so open, so beautifully carefree. The sound of her amusement is so infectious that I can't help but laugh along with her, the weight on my chest momentarily lifting.

"Okay," I say, still chuckling, "tell me."

She studies me for a moment, her eyes scanning mine, as if measuring my readiness to hear what she's about to share. Then she smiles softly and nods, seemingly reassured by whatever she finds in my expression.

"You know how my dad is very cold? Calculated? And doesn't speak a lot?" she begins, her tone lighter but carrying a certain weight beneath it.

"Okay..." My voice trails off as I narrow my eyes slightly, trying to piece together where she's going with this. "And?" I prompt.

"He's actually a diagnosed psychopath," she says with startling calm, "exhibiting narcissistic and Machiavellian tendencies, alongside a diagnosis of Asperger's syndrome, which falls within the Autism Spectrum Disorder (ASD)."

"Holy shit!" The words tumble out of me before I can stop them. My mind races, piecing together everything I know about Elijah in light of what Sofia just dropped on me. Sure, I always knew he was... different. Everyone knows he's a genius, but *Machiavellian? Narcissistic? Psychopath?*

I blink rapidly, trying to process it all. "Breathe..." Sofia's voice is calm, a steadying force as she studies me with those piercing eyes, her gaze so intent it feels like she's reading every thought racing through my head.

"Well, I'm okay. But you... are you okay? He raised you," I say cautiously, unsure how much weight Elijah's nature might have placed on her shoulders.

She tilts her head slightly, her expression soft but firm, as though she's considered this question a thousand times before. "He doesn't process emotions like the rest of us," she begins, her voice even but thoughtful. "After he took me, he never pushed me to open up or forced me to do anything. Especially in the beginning, when I was having nightmares every night, he stayed up with me watching movies. It was his way of being there without overstepping."

Her gaze flickers to the floor for a moment before returning to mine, steady and unflinching. "After a while, he told me I was always safe with him. He said that even if he came across as cold, he wasn't, it's just that he doesn't know how to show emotions the way other people do. He told me he understands emotions, even recognises them in others, but they don't manifest in him the same way."

"When I was older, Uncle Buddy told me the rest of his condition," Sofia continues, her tone calm but introspective. "To the outside world, he's seen as the most notorious, ruthless businessman, all wrapped up in expensive suits and extreme diplomacy. But he's not the type of person to move a single finger without considering all potential outcomes and ensuring he benefits from every interaction."

She looks at me, her expression a mix of understanding and resignation, as if she's recounting a story and not true life events.

Fuck me! Seriously? I mean, I always knew Elijah was a sharp, no-nonsense businessman, but from being savvy to... this? That's a hell of a leap.

"Take, for example, his little visit yesterday," Sofia says, her tone so light and conversational it feels surreal considering the weight of her words. "He claimed he came here to check on us, to make sure we didn't kill each other. That was a pile of shit, though. His true motive was to expose us, more specifically, to lay bare just how unbelievably broken we both are without the other."

"He probably calculated every variable, every possible outcome, and realised it was in *my* best interest for us to confront the truth how we are when we're apart."

I want to say he's a fuckhead, plain and simple. But the truth is, him forcing us to confront the truth about ourselves, about each other, has brought us so much closer. As much as I'd like to hold onto my irritation, I can't ignore the way it's strengthened the bond between Sofia and me.

He was right.

"The only exception to that rule is me and Buddy. Since he took me, he's never tried to manipulate or push me in any direction. If anything, he shifted his entire business to accommodate me, and that's how we ended up settling here."

I take her hands in mine and press a soft kiss to the back of them. I want to do more. I want to say more. But the truth is, I don't know what to say. Relief floods me, a heavy wave that I hadn't even realised I was holding back. *She wasn't alone after all.* And Elijah, for all his twisted, messed-up ways, has always looked out for her. Thank fuck for that.

"I see it in a different way, Hunter. I think you and your beast as you call it are more stronger then you think, because the moment you saw this monsters for what they truly were you pushed back. And not a little, you pushed back all the way, took their lives and relieved the world of their filth. You are so fucking strong, you blow my mind."

I'm speechless. What just happened?

Her words carry so much weight, heavy and solid with every syllable. But instead of pulling me down, they make me feel lighter, as if they've untangled something inside of me that's been knotted for years.

"You had the choice to become like them, to become a monster, and you didn't. What you did, Hunter, is you killed them. You destroyed them. So whatever pain still lingers inside you, please know this. Men like them would compliment you, gift you, pamper you with whatever your heart desires, all to make you trust them, so in the end, they could profit of you. You didn't really stand a chance. But then, when you discovered their true nature, you killed them. You stood against them no matter what."

"So no, I'm not scared, ashamed, or whatever else your mind might think I feel. The only thing I am is *proud.* Proud because you know who you are. Proud because, despite everything, you've kept true to what you want to be."

I am utterly speechless. Her words hit me with a force I never could have prepared for, tearing apart every dark thread I had woven around my self-perception. She's not just shifting my view, she's obliterating it, dismantling the image of my life I've carried for years and showing me something extraordinary in its place, like I was looking at the wrong thing all this time. How does she see this version of me? How does she take all my broken pieces and craft them into something strong, something *worthy*?

And in this moment, I know, I am in so much trouble...

If I thought I loved her before, it was nothing compared to this. Now, I am deeply, dangerously, and irrevocably in love. Every cell in my body gravitates toward her. It's no longer air that keeps me alive, *it's her*. Her warmth, her strength, her unparalleled ability to understand me like no one else.

"I adore you, Sofia," I say, my voice thick with the weight of everything I can't put into words. I need her to know, to feel, to understand just how much she means to me.

My words feel so small in the magnitude of this moment, inadequate to truly convey the awe I feel for this woman. How could I ever articulate the depth of what's coursing through me? She's not just remarkable, she's otherworldly in her strength, her compassion, and her ability to see me, the real *me*, and still choose to stay.

Her features soften, and she leans in, placing a gentle kiss on my lips. It's a soft, unhurried touch, but it carries the weight of everything unspoken between us. In that kiss, I feel her understanding, her acceptance, and her quiet reassurance that *I am enough*.

I don't know how to tell her just how much she completes every broken piece of me. Words fail me, leaving a void where I need them most. So, I do what I do best... *I crack a joke*. Well, half a joke. Anything to lighten the mood and start my usual routine of begging for blood again.

"Does this mean you'll let me kill at least that neighbour of yours?" I ask, amusement lacing my tone, though the plea in my eyes reveals just how serious I am.

She bursts out laughing, her laughter warm and unrestrained, filling every corner of the space. I can't help but bask in it, in her radiance. *God, she's magnificent.*

"Fine! Next week!" she declares, her eyes sparkling with mischief. "You and your beast, as you call him, are mine to play with now." Her features shift into something dangerous, a promise of all the delicious chaos that's about to unfold.

"Speaking of... what's going on with that lady from the shop? The one we looked into, the civilian. Did Elijah lose interest in her?"

Sofia bursts out laughing, her whole body shaking with the force of it, her joy so infectious it pulls a smile to my lips despite the topic.

"What?"

"Oh, nothing. It's just funny that you'd think he lost interest when, a few months ago, he sent a billion dollars to her charity just to get her attention."

"What?!"

"Fuck, yes, he did," she says, still laughing, her body shaking with amusement.

"You know how I look after people around me?" she begins, a mischievous smile playing on her lips. "Well, when I noticed something was off, I hacked into the cameras around the shop to see what was happening. And, I might or might not have connected to the cameras inside the shop too. Anyway, my dad went to visit that woman every single day the shop was open. And get this... he has three cars of guards assigned to her. I kid you not!" She bursts into laughter again, her shoulders shaking with the effort.

"He figured me out, though," she continues, her laughter subsiding slightly. "Told me to cut it out in that no-negotiation voice of his, so I disconnected everything. But I just know in the pit of my stomach that something's going on. And by that, I mean that woman is truly fucked. If my dad put his eyes on her, there's no escaping him."

"Fuck!" I mutter under my breath, letting the tension ease slightly. I feel better, but I know it'll take time to fully process Sofia's perspective on my life and let go of what I thought for years would be my future.

"So," I say, steering the conversation back to the issue at hand, "are you going to let me kill them all after you get your answers?" I widen the net, trying to nudge her toward my preferred resolution.

"Are you serious?" she laughs, her voice light but teasing, as she tugs at my hair again.

"Ouch! Also, pretty please?" I add, feigning a pout.

She takes a deep breath, her gaze steady but distant, and then sighs softly. "We can go next week and deal with it. Whatever will be, will be."

"Fuck yes!" The words explode out of me as I scoop her up, spinning her around in pure happiness.

Her laughter rings out, mingling with my excitement, but all I can think about is the satisfaction of finally putting an end to them.

Those fuckers don’t know what’s coming for them!

Chapter Twenty-Five

Hunter

A week of blissful pleasure with my *sugar cube* has passed, a week where she let me touch her more, give her more of myself, and take more of her in return. Each day she surrenders a little more to me, to us, and it drives me wilder for her. I never imagined something like this could exist. I thought I understood women. I thought I knew lust, knew what could make me lose my mind. But all of that pales in comparison to what Sofia stirs in me.

It's not just the way she challenges me at every turn, pushing back to prove her strength. It's not just the fire in her spirit when she fights for control. It's the way she yields when I pleasure her, the way she surrenders so completely, as if she trusts me with every fibre of her being. For someone like her, someone with her past, to trust me like this is more than I ever dared to hope for. It's not something I take lightly, and it's something I will never, ever betray.

Every time my mind spiralled out of control with fury this week, she was there, caging my beast with her bare hands, as if he weren't a killer dressed up in a funny and handsome package. At the end of the day, that's what I am, *a killer*, and that's what I will always be. But I think she's started to learn my tells. Every time I seemed close to losing it, she'd just appear, settle on my lap like it was the most natural thing in the world, and get to work on her computer.

The first time it happened, I was too stunned to do anything except stare at her beautiful ass perched on my lap. The way she acted like nothing had happened, like sitting on the lap of a raging killer was the most normal thing in the world, completely threw me off. I sat there, mesmerised, until she told me she'd poke me in the eyes with her stylus if I didn't stop staring. I didn't stop, of course. So she poked me. Did I care? No. It was worth it. That ass is the death of me.

And maybe, just maybe, I let my hands wander a little, accidentally on purpose, until they landed on her nipples. A little teasing, a little nipple play, and she was moaning softly, proving just how much she liked it. But then she turned, poked me again, and this time I didn't like it. Worth it? Fuck yes!

Good times.

Finally, we make our way to our flight, and I wasn't sure what to expect when Sofia mentioned a private jet, but this was beyond anything I could have imagined. Instead of the usual chaos of an airport, we pulled up to a private terminal, a sleek, glass-walled building that looked more like a luxury hotel than anything remotely connected to planes. Inside, there were no lines, no metal detectors, no barking announcements about delayed flights. Just a quiet lounge where someone handed Sofia and me drinks while our documents were cleared.

It all happened so fast, I barely had time to process it before we were stepping into a car that took us straight to the jet. No one rifled through my bag. No standing around awkwardly while security officers eyed me like I was a walking threat. Instead, the pilot greeted us at the base of the stairs, his demeanour as polished as the jet's glossy exterior. For a moment, it almost felt like we were royalty, stepping into a world that operated entirely on its own rules.

The jet itself was impressive enough, sleek and polished like something out of a billionaire's dream. But what struck me most wasn't just the luxury, it was the efficiency of it all, how seamlessly the world seemed to shift to accommodate us. I knew Elijah had money, and I'd already guessed that Sofia had grown up surrounded by her fair share of privilege. But this? This wasn't just rich. This was the kind of wealth that bent the rules, reshaped them entirely. It was as if Elijah lived in a reality crafted by his own design, where the normal constraints of life simply didn't apply.

The sleek exterior of the jet shimmered under the tarmac lights, its polished silver finish radiating an air of quiet power and refinement. As the cabin door swung open, it revealed an opulent interior crafted for indulgence and ease. Deep cream leather seats, buttery to the touch, were arranged with generous spacing, their elegance accentuated by fine mahogany accents framing the armrests and tabletops. The air carried a subtle hint of cedarwood, mingling with the soft hum of hidden air vents, wrapping the space in an understated yet undeniable elegance.

Crystal glasses sparkled on the built-in bar, stocked with an exquisite array of fine spirits, while warm ambient lighting cast a soft, golden glow over every bespoke detail. The ceiling arched gracefully overhead, adorned with hand-stitched leather panels that created a seamless canopy of understated elegance. A luxurious chaise lounge rested near the far end, positioned beside a private suite partitioned by frosted glass. Every detail, from the silk throw pillows embroidered with a discreet monogram to the touchscreen panels elegantly embedded in the armrests, reflected Elijah's unyielding pursuit of refinement and perfection. This wasn't merely a mode of transport, it was a declaration of unparalleled wealth and impeccable taste.

The carpet muffled my steps as I moved through the jet, every detail quietly screaming Elijah's name in that infuriatingly understated way of his. His initials, *ED*, were everywhere, woven into the patterns on the seat cushions, etched discreetly into the glossy wood, even stamped onto the crystal glasses. Subtle, elegant, calculated. It was all too much like him for my taste.

When I reached the frosted glass door at the back, I pushed it open and stepped into a suite that could've belonged to royalty. The bed commanded the room, its pristine white linens arranged with such precision it felt like an insult to touch them. The headboard gleamed, upholstered in leather so smooth it seemed to dare me to run my fingers across it. Warm, golden lighting bathed the space, casting soft, shifting shadows that made the room feel both intimate and untouchable. The faint scent of cedarwood lingered in the air, a trace of Elijah's cologne, no doubt, but I ignored it. That wasn't why I was here.

My attention locks onto the bed, and just like that, my thoughts aren't about this damn jet or its perfection anymore. *Sofia.* I can see her there, tangled in those sheets, her skin flushed and warm beneath my hands, her breath catching as I pull her closer. Heat curls low in my stomach, spreading through me as I let the image take root. Her laughter fills this space in my mind, her body, her presence, erasing every trace of Elijah's calculated perfection. This room might be his now, but I'm already making it ours in ways that will sear into my memory, leaving nothing but her in its wake.

"Don't get any funny ideas, Hunter. We need to work the whole way there." She's interrupted by the pilot's voice coming through the speakers, crisp and clear, announcing the details of the flight. Once again, I'm caught off guard by how smooth and seamless everything about this jet is, even the sound system feels like it's on another level.

"Good afternoon, ladies and gentlemen. This is your captain speaking. Welcome aboard the Gulfstream G650, bound for Somalia. Our flight time today is approximately seven hours and thirty minutes, cruising at an altitude of 41,000 feet. The weather along our route is clear, so we're expecting a smooth journey. Please make yourselves comfortable, and if there's anything you need, our cabin crew will be delighted to assist. Thank you for flying with us, and we'll be underway shortly."

"Fancy," I trail off, pulling her into my chest. I notice she's not wearing her usual high heels anymore, and now she's noticeably shorter than me and I love it. Not because she's shorter, but because she no longer feels the need to appear bigger or stronger around me. With each passing day, she softens in my embrace, giving more of herself to us, uniting us in a way that blurs the lines. I don't know where she ends, and I begin anymore.

"Cut that shit out, Hunter!" she yells into my chest. "Seriously, does your cock ever stay soft? What the fuck is wrong with you?"

I burst into laughter, the sound echoing through the cabin. Who even talks like that, especially to a man like me? God, I adore her!

"*Sugar cube*, come on. I already told you to ignore it, I'll handle it. Also, if I remember correctly, I told you I can't control it, woman. The moment I feel you in my arms, I lose my mind." I place a kiss on the top of her head and breathe her in.

The past week has been absolutely incredible. Every single day, I've made her come, and every single day, I've found a new way to blow her mind. I am completely addicted to the sound of her moans, the intoxicating scent of her skin, and the way her touch ignites every part of me. She's not just under my skin, she's the very blood running through my veins, the force keeping me alive.

I grind my cock against her discreetly, just enough to provoke her, and then tighten my hold on her.

I know what's coming... 3, 2, 1...

"You fucking pig. Get off me!" she snaps, thrashing in my hold like a wild animal. I know she enjoyed it, but today is not a good day for sure.

She's been on edge since we woke up, and the moment we rolled those suitcases out of her apartment, everything about her shifted. Her breathing changed, quicker and more shallow. Her muscles are tense, her movements stiffer. Even the pitch of her voice has climbed, a sure sign she's teetering on the edge of losing her shit.

Her calling me a pig? Not exactly nice, but fair. If she had direct access to my thoughts, she'd probably call me a pig every five minutes. But that's beside the point.

I can feel her pain radiating off her, so sharp and overwhelming that it cuts through the air between us. I've spent the entire morning trying to make her laugh, to ease the weight pressing down on her, taking everything she's thrown at me, both metaphorically and literally.

Case in point: the shoe she hurled at my head in the car. I caught it at the last second, but the message was clear. She's drowning in anxiety, *my sugar cube*, and it's spilling out in every possible way.

This isn't just a journey across continents, it's a journey back to the root of her pain, to confront the family who had stolen so much from her. She didn't need to say the name of the place aloud to feel its weight pressing down on her.

Honestly, I'd do anything to take this pressure off her, to lighten the load she's carrying, or at least convince her to share it with me. But I don't even know how.

So, I do what I do best. I wrap her tightly in my arms, holding her against me, and pour as much love into this embrace as I possibly can.

"Easy, *sugar cube*," I whisper in her ear, my voice low and soothing. "I adore you. My body adores you. Easy."

After a few more seconds, her resistance melts away, and she stops thrashing in my arms. I take the opportunity to pepper soft kisses along her neck, slow and deliberate, letting her feel the depth of my care.

She lets out a shaky breath and, to my relief, she wraps her arms around me, pulling me closer. It's not just surrender, it's trust. It's everything.

"I love you, *Nuuro*," she finally says into my chest, her voice soft.

I tighten my hold on her, letting those words settle deep in my bones, but before I can respond, she shifts slightly, already moving her focus to what's next.

"Now let's get back to work. There's so much to do. I think your hunch about Maramureș might be something. I've already found a few of Bogdan's colleagues from Uni working there, but I couldn't find them through the facial scan. We still need to set all of that up."

That's Sofia to a T. Whenever she's stressed, instead of slowing down, she doubles her pace, throwing herself into the work as if solving a puzzle could keep the world at bay. It's infuriating, impressive, and so completely her.

I let go of her, and she gets herself set up on one of the loungers. Within seconds, she pulls out monitors as if by magic, arranging them with the precision of someone ready to conquer the world. My face must betray my disbelief because she notices immediately.

"What?" she calls out from behind a screen, peeking just enough to catch my expression.

I raise an eyebrow, gesturing at the tech she's somehow produced mid-flight.

"We always do a lot of work on the plane," she says, her tone matter-of-fact, like this was the most normal thing in the world.

I wanted to play it cool, and up until now, I think I managed it. But this? This just blew my mind! She's sitting there with *three* 34-inch monitors seemingly floating in front of her, all connected and running in mere seconds like it's the most normal thing in the world. Meanwhile, I'm trying not to let my jaw hit the floor.

I've been doing my best to keep things classy, not pointing out that I've never even seen a private jet up close, let alone flown in one. Hell, I've always flown economy. This entire experience is a glaring reminder of the worlds we come from, the stark difference in our upbringings. But you know what? Watching her behind those monitors, her fingers flying over the keyboard with purpose, she's so effortlessly beautiful that I can't help but point it out, she's absolute perfection in her element.

"Fucking hell, woman! You are absolutely stunning, sitting there working like that."

She stops typing, raising her gaze to meet mine. For a moment, the look on her face is so sweet, so soft, with a hint of something sad lingering in her eyes. It's the first time today she's truly let me in, and my chest tightens at the sight of her vulnerability.

But before I can savor the moment, she snaps her defenses back into place. Her mouth curves into a sly smile, and she fires back, "Are you planning to ogle me all day, or are you actually going to do some work?"

There she is, my *sugar cube*.

I sit on the lounge opposite her, mimicking her movements as I set up my laptop. The screens flicker to life, a pretense of productivity in place. I'm supposed to be chasing leads on Bogdan, combing through his network and cross-referencing every friend of a friend to uncover where he's hiding.

Instead, I lean back slightly, my eyes drifting over to Sofia as she focuses on her work. The intensity in her gaze, the way her fingers fly over the keyboard, it's mesmerising. I know I should get to it, but watching her like this, completely in her element, feels like the only thing worth doing right now.

Last night, Sofia opened up about the moment she first realised something was wrong with her body, a revelation so traumatic it reshaped her entire sense of self. She described the horrifying discovery that her most private parts didn't look like other women's and then said, with a haunting quietness, that they had sewn her together. Her words struck me like a physical blow, leaving me frozen and utterly mute. Each time she peels back another layer of her past, I am consumed by disbelief and fury that such a barbaric act could be inflicted on a little girl in this day and age.

She told me about the day she googled it after some sort of a sex class in school, desperate for answers, only for the fear and stark reality to crush her completely. That paralysing terror has stayed with her, so much so that she has never mustered the courage to look further, not even once. Her pain is like a ghost, lingering and unseen but so palpably present that it echoes in every word she speaks.

To an ordinary person, I could understand the hesitation, but for someone as technical as Sofia to admit she couldn't bring herself to research her condition, it was like a gardener confessing they couldn't touch soil anymore but still wanting to grow plants. The contradiction hit me hard. Once the initial shock of her words passed and I delved into the deeper meaning, the raw undercurrent of her pain, agony, and brokenness became unmistakably clear. It shattered me, piece by piece.

I couldn't bring myself to leap out of bed last night and start digging into the depths of what she described. Even this morning, the weight of it held me still. But now... now, it feels like the floodgates are open. It's time to dive in and face the truth, both for her and for me.

Sitting opposite her, with my monitors angled completely out of her line of sight, I dive into my work, mirroring her relentless focus and speed as I chase down every lead. My fingers fly over the keyboard, scouring articles and resources, piecing together a picture of the unimaginable cruelty that others, like Sofia, have endured.

I uncover stories of other women who've bravely come forward, shedding light on the brutal reality of female genital mutilation. Each article I read feels like a blow, but it also fuels the fire in me to understand, to help, and to fight for her in any way I can.

I come across the stories of extraordinary women who've turned their pain into purpose, fighting to end female genital mutilation and support survivors. Jahan Dukureha, endured FGM as an infant before moving to the United States. She went on to found Safy Hands for Girls, an organisation devoted to eradicating FGM and providing a voice for survivors.

Nimca Aly, a British-Somali survivor, co-founded The Fives Foundation, an organisation focused on ending FGM on a global scale. Her efforts have been instrumental in raising awareness and driving policy changes in the UK and beyond. Then there's Susane Maslingy, a Senior Trial Attorney at the U.S. Department of Justice, recognised for her relentless work combating FGM in the United States.

Each story is a testament to resilience, and with every word, my determination grows to stand by Sofia and fight this darkness, however I can.

The more I read about these incredible women and the horrific reality they're working to change, I realise this is so much more than Sofia's pain, it's a global issue, a relentless problem that persists even in countries where it's been banned. Article after article reveals stories of women coming forward, begging for help, shedding light on the unspeakable acts still being inflicted on little girls. Each account is a dagger to the heart, a reminder that this isn't just history, it's happening now, and it's horrifyingly *real.*

I feel sick to my stomach. My hands hover over the keyboard as I lower my gaze, trying to steady my breath. I can't let Sofia pick up on how drastically my mood is shifting. The anger bubbling beneath my skin is overwhelming, and it takes everything in me not to let it consume me right here and now.

This has to stop! ***This fucking has to stop!***

I look over at Sofia, her fingers flying across the keyboard with a speed and precision that never fails to amaze me. She's so strong, so beautiful, so intelligent. And yet, someone dared to break her. The thought ignites a fire in my chest, my fury simmering just beneath the surface.

I can feel my body heating, my fists clenching as the rage starts to take over. But this isn't the time or the place to lose control. Still, the thoughts won't stop. How could they? The explanations, the excuses, the misinformation fed to justify something so vile, it's all fucking disgusting. Worse, making it illegal but still secretly paying to have your daughter mutilated?

What the actual fuck is wrong with people? My fists clench on reflex, my knuckles white against the rage threatening to erupt.

I get it, bad guys, go after them. Torture them, mutilate them, kill them in the most sadistic, fucked-up ways imaginable. Grey-area people, the ones who pretend to be good but are rotten to the core? Yeah, they deserve it too.

But the small, hopeless ones? The ones who prey on children, on the most vulnerable? Because apparently, in this disgusting research I discovered it's not just girls, it's worse than I could have ever imagined. That's a whole different level of fucked up. These are the people who absolutely need to go.

No excuses.

No mercy.

You want to prove you're strong? Then measure your strength against someone strong. Not against the weakest of the weak and call yourself powerful. That's not strength, that's cowardice.

I swear, by the end of this, I'll drop a fucking bomb on these bastards.

Fuck!

I should've brought some guards with us! I fucking knew it! My gut told me, screamed at me to get some men to come with us. But Sofia? No, she was all calm and rational with her, *"Stop being ridiculous. They're my parents. We're going in peace. I just want answers. How bad can it be?"*

I'll tell you how bad it can fucking be. Bad enough that I'm standing here ready to kill them all. Bad enough that I'll probably end up chasing my *sugar cube* across the globe to make her forgive me for what I'm about to do. That's how fucking bad it's going to get!

"Did you find anything?" Her voice cuts through my spiraling thoughts, pulling me back from the storm of rage brewing inside. She sounds calmer now, her tone steady, and I know better than to risk triggering her again.

"No. Not yet," I reply, keeping my voice as neutral as possible. I glance up briefly to meet her gaze, offering a small, reassuring smile before turning back to my screen. Whatever answers we're looking for, I'll find them without letting her sense the chaos raging within me.

I start typing again, focusing on one of the stories from a survivor who mentioned reconstructive surgery, an option to undo some of the damage caused by FGM. Sofia hadn't said anything about that, so I assume she never got that far in her research. If I think back to what she told me, the only thing she managed to look into was images of vaginas, trying to confirm what she saw in class. That search alone shattered her because the article she stumbled across boldly claimed that all women looked the same down there.

It's no wonder she shut down. The idea of finding answers only to have them reinforce her worst fears must've been unbearable.

I feel my chest tighten painfully at the thought of Sofia as a child, stumbling upon the realisation that she was different. The confusion, the fear, and the crushing weight of that discovery, fuck, it must have hurt like hell. No wonder it traumatised her all over again, burying her under a fresh layer of agony so deep she never dared to look into it further. It's no wonder she locked that part of herself away, trying to protect what little peace she could find.

Much to my surprise, I discover that France offers *free reconstructive surgery* for FGM survivors. Apparently, since 2004, this service has been available, benefiting nearly 3,000 women. I look at the number again, and to me, it feels like a drop in the ocean. Yes, they're leading the world in this area, but when you consider that over 3,000 little girls are subjected to this barbaric practice every single day, it seems painfully inadequate.

The Netherlands appear to be making progress as well, *good on them*, but it's still nothing compared to the sheer scale of the issue. In the United States, there's some work being done, but again, it barely scratches the surface. And then there's the UK... fuck me! If Sofia had done this research, she would've flipped. They're dragging their feet like it's someone else's problem. Out of sight, out of mind, *it's infuriating.*

As I read more, a few things hit me like a ton of bricks. First, I realise how ignorant I've been to it all. I can't recall anyone ever talking to me about female genital mutilation not in school, not in the military, not anywhere. It's as though the world decided to turn a blind eye to this horror.

Second, I see how insidiously clever it is to call it "FGM," reducing something so horrific to a cold, sterile acronym. Call it what it is mutilation, barbarism and add that it's disgusting and must stop.

Third, the more I read, the clearer it becomes that I can't keep this up for much longer. My fury is bubbling too close to the surface, and my beast is roaring in my ears, demanding action, screaming at me to organise boots on the ground and end this nightmare for good.

For now, I need to step back, or I might lose control entirely.

I shift my focus back to work, configuring TrackMate with the details of Bogdan's university colleagues. Frustration tugs at me as I think about Romania's lack of street cameras. If we were in the UK, we could locate someone in a matter of hours. Then an idea strikes me, deploy the drones we have stationed in Poland. They're equipped with long-range and advanced capabilities, so flying them to Romania wouldn't be an issue.

The real problem is recharging them once they arrive.

Think, out of the box, Hunter!

Got it!

I can send the guards we have stationed in Bucharest to Maramureș. I'll have them secure a warehouse there to set up a charging station for the drones, ensuring they can be deployed daily for consistent surveillance. It's not the perfect solution, but it's a solid plan. Time to set it in motion.

"I got it, *sugar cube*," I say, excitement bubbling in my tone. This plan feels solid, and I can already picture her being impressed. "Why don't we send the drones from Poland to Maramureș to scan for these guys?"

Sofia peeks at me from behind one of her monitors, her expression unreadable as she studies me for a few long seconds. Then, finally, she smiles a soft, knowing curve of her lips that makes my chest tighten in the best way.

"See, I knew you were more than a sexy piece of arse," she says, then bursts out laughing.

"Fuck, *sugar cube*. Sexy piece of arse?!" I clutch my chest dramatically, pretending to faint as I collapse back into my seat, all to coax more of that beautiful laughter out of her. Her laugh is medicine, it's light, warmth, and everything I want to keep hearing, especially with what we're walking into soon.

"Does this mean you're up for anal?" I shoot her a mischievous grin, raising an eyebrow for good measure.

"What the fuck is with you and anal? Seriously?!" she yells, striding toward me with that fiery determination I love so much.

"A guy can try, right?" I flash her my most innocent grin, though the mischief is all too evident in my eyes.

Her glare narrows as she crosses her arms over her chest, but the faint twitch at the corner of her mouth gives her away. "You're impossible," she mutters, though there's no real heat behind her words.

"You okay?" she asks, her voice softening as she steps closer, concern flickering in her dark eyes. Damn it. She's picking up on my beast still clawing just beneath the surface.

"I'm all good, *sugar cube*," I reply, trying to sound light, but the edge in my tone betrays me. I glance away for a moment, attempting to steady myself. "I just... I would have liked to have more people with us. You know, just in case."

"I will defend you," she declares confidently, settling herself on my lap like she belongs there. Which, let's face it, she absolutely does. This feeling will never get old, the weight of her in my arms, the warmth of her body against mine, and, yeah, the unmistakable effect she has on me as my cock hardens rapidly beneath her.

"Something is seriously wrong with you, Hunter," she quips, though her words lose their sting as she wiggles her arse deliberately against me. The little minx. She complains, but then she provokes me more, testing my self-control like it's some kind of game she always plans to win.

"There's nothing wrong with me!" I feign mock offence, my tone playful. "If anything, it'd be a problem if I didn't get hard around you." I lean forward, brushing my lips against her shoulder, and then suck gently on her skin, leaving a mark. A reminder for both of us, she's mine, and I'm hers.

"I keep forgetting to ask you," she says, her voice laced with curiosity, "but why *sugar cube*? You annoyed me for two years with cupcake, and then you just changed it? What's that all about?"

Her question catches me off guard, so random given everything going on. I can't help it, I burst out laughing. Of all the things to ask, this is what she chooses to bring up? But then again, that's Sofia. Always surprising me.

"Seriously?" I manage between chuckles, wiping at my face. "That's what you're thinking about right now?" But I get it. I really did take every chance to annoy the hell out of her back then, just to get her to pay attention to me. And let's be real, it worked, didn't it?

I glance down at her, warmth spreading through my chest as I tighten my hold around her. "Well, I got my girl, *sugar cube,*" I say with a smirk. "That's all that matters."

"I always called you *sugar cube* in my mind," I confess, my voice low as I press another kiss to her shoulder. "Because you're all prickly and strong on the outside, but I could always see this amazing, sweet woman underneath."

Her gaze locks onto mine, and the intensity in her eyes makes me pause. She just holds my stare for what feels like an eternity, her expression unreadable. My heartbeat picks up, not out of fear of rejection but because I can see the wheels turning in her mind. At this point, I'm pretty sure she's calculating all the ways she'll make me suffer for daring to call her *sweet.*

She shifts slightly on my lap, and my body tenses. Instinctively, my hands fly to cover my cock, a self-preservation reflex kicking in. "Hey, hey!" I say quickly, trying to appease her with a grin. "I meant sweet in the badass kind of way, okay? Don't take vengeance on the goods!"

A slow smirk creeps onto her face, and for a split second, I'm not sure if I'm safe or doomed.

"What...?" she trails off, her voice distant and filled with surprise as she watches me, her expression softening in a way I rarely see.

"That was the most amazing thing anyone has ever said to me." Her voice trembles slightly, and her glossy eyes glint with emotion, as though she's fighting back tears. Those big, dark eyes always fierce and guarded seem impossibly vulnerable now, like they hold the entire universe within them. It feels like looking into infinity, a depth I can't quite comprehend but never want to look away from.

My chest tightens, and the instinct to protect, to cherish, wells up so powerfully it threatens to take over entirely. This is my *sugar cube*, stripped of her walls, her sharp edges softened, and I am so utterly, irreversibly hers.

"I love you, Sofia." I place a kiss on her shoulder and then pull her more into me. "I love you so much, my *sugar cube*."

She leans over and kisses me, and this kiss is different. It's not rough or savage like some of the others that leave us both breathless and wild. This kiss is deep, sweet, and tender as she's revealing the woman I've always known was beneath her armour. The woman I've loved from the moment I saw her, even before I fully understood what that meant. I love her so much it's almost unbearable, my chest tightening to the point of aching.

When she pulls back, her forehead rests against mine for a second before she shifts, laying her head on my shoulder, her arms wrapping around me like she's afraid I might disappear. "Can we just sit like this for a bit?" she asks softly, her voice carrying a vulnerability that punches through every last wall I have. She tilts her head up, her dark eyes searching mine, pleading, as if I'd ever be stupid enough to push her away.

"Of course, *sugar cube*," I say softly, leaning back and adjusting myself to make sure she's comfortable. I shift her more fully onto my lap, cradling her as if I could somehow shield her from everything in the world. I don't want her to move, not until I've had my fill of her warmth and this quiet closeness.

"As long as you need," I add, my voice barely above a whisper. I place a kiss on her forehead and linger there, breathing in her scent. It's grounding, intoxicating. In this moment, I'm overwhelmed by gratitude, grateful for her trust, for the rare glimpse of vulnerability she's sharing, for her. This side of Sofia, the one no one else gets to see, *is mine*. She's letting me have it. I'm one lucky man.

As the jet descended, the rugged beauty of her homeland came into view, a breathtaking contrast to the scars she carried from her past. The sprawling landscapes below seemed untouched by the pain that had marked her so deeply. This was the place where it all began, the source of her agony, but it was also where she hoped to find the answers she so desperately needed. God, I hope she finds what she's looking for. Even if she won't let me take justice into my own hands, I hope with everything in me that she finds the peace she deserves.

"It's beautiful," she whispers, her voice soft, almost reverent, as we both gaze out of the plane's window. "I didn't remember it being like this. But it's truly beautiful."

"A beautiful place created a beautiful woman," I say, my eyes shifting from the view to her. The sunlight streams through the window, casting a soft glow on her skin, highlighting every perfect feature. She's stunning. *My sugar cube. My existence.*

"Let's get you some answers," I add, my voice firm with quiet resolve. If this place holds what she needs, I'll make sure she finds it.

Chapter Twenty-Six

Sofia

I did not sleep last night.

I wish I could have tossed and turned, but sleeping next to Hunter is like lying beside a furnace. The man radiates heat like an open flame. If that was not enough, he is such a light sleeper that the second I move, even the slightest shift, his hand automatically reaches for me. I could not even turn over, let alone get comfortable. I just lay there, trapped with my tormenting thoughts.

I want to say it is pure paranoia, the trauma from years of service that turned him into a soldier even in sleep, but I cannot. This is simply who he is. And to me, it is one of the most endearing things about him.

London with its *beautiful sunny days*, not, and its *peaceful easy nights*, even more not, has taught me that sleeping next to the man you breathe for has its benefits.

I do not know how he does it. I woke up in the middle of the night to the softest brush of movement, only to realise he was lifting the blanket over my back to make sure I was warm. I was not even cold. I did not stir, did not shift, did not make a sound. But he still woke up because a blanket had slipped off me. Who sleeps like that?

It is sweet.

It is kind.

It's Hunter.

And if I was not silently screaming inside at the fact that I am back in the country where my biological family still exists, I would be wrapped around him, losing myself in his quiet, instinctive gestures of love.

Instead, I barely moved all night. Afraid to bother him. Afraid to let myself have this. Afraid of everything.

I love him so much. I breathe him in.

This past week has been wonderful. Every morning I wake up, and his presence was everywhere around me, even if I cannot see or hear him. There has not been a single morning when I have doubted that he is somewhere in the house, waiting for me.

The mornings when I found him in the kitchen, shirtless, will be imprinted, no, *tattooed* in my brain forever. He is mouthwatering hot.

I had to physically stop myself from going over and licking his body like a crazy person. Again, I might be crazy, but I am not an idiot. As I said the week was fabulous.

I want to blame his extreme body heat for last night, and of course, the temperature here is so different from England. But the truth is, everything in me is screaming to leave, to not face my past, to run into the sunset with Hunter and never look back.

But that is not the person I have become, and more importantly, that is not the person *I want to be.*

My instincts are telling me we should have brought more men with us, that I should have scoped out the location more thoroughly, that I should have come up with an emergency evacuation plan. My father gave us the location, and he insisted on taking guards as it's not safe, fact that I completely disregarded.

The other part of me, the broken little girl buried deep inside, is screaming that I am being paranoid. This is my family. And even if they did what they did, maybe, in some messed-up, personal way, they love me. Maybe I just do not understand it.

The rational part of me sees the facts. It understands the lack of logic in my decisions. But the emotional part of me has taken full control, shutting down all reason.

I can sense the real risk we are in. I know it. But somehow, logic has left the building, and I am driving us purely on emotion. I am putting us in danger, especially with active rebels in the area.

The only positive, no one knows who we are.

We came with false documents, checked into a hotel under fake names, and rented the most average-looking car I have ever seen.

Hunter struggled to get in it, and when I saw him, I almost cracked a joke about how ridiculously big he looked. He reminded me of a stuffed chicken or something.

Maybe I should have told him that.

But in that moment, there was only a very small, insignificant part of me still willing to laugh.

"You did not sleep, *sugar cube*," Hunter says with a sigh.

Nothing.

I have absolutely no reply because if I was a mess yesterday, today I feel like someone else is driving my body while my conscious mind is only a guest. The closer we get to my parents, the more I feel myself slipping. It is as if I am unraveling, shifting, becoming that little girl again.

I am scared. Petrified of her.

At the same time, I realise that she is me. And I realise that the only thing she ever wanted was to be loved. To be safe.

And the truth is... she had neither.

"*Sugar cube...*"

Hunter's voice trails off as he turns me to face him.

We are sitting in bed in a cheap hotel, the kind they probably consider clean and fancy, but in reality, it is anything but. The walls are dull, the air stale, and everything about this place feels temporary.

The moment my eyes meet Hunter's, I feel like I am going to break. I can already feel the tears pushing forward, threatening to spill in front of the strongest man I have ever known.

He thinks I am strong. But the truth is, I am falling apart.

His gaze shifts, soft and loving, but haunted, and it does terrible things to my insides. I shut my eyes and take a deep breath, trying like hell to steady myself.

"Baby, please."

His voice is so broken, as if he is carrying this burden with me, as if he feels the same pain I do.

"Tell me how I can make it better, please..."

The last word is a whisper against my skin as he presses a kiss to my forehead.

"Please tell me how to make it better. Ask me for anything, and I will do it. I just cannot see you like this."

He wraps his arm and leg around me, shielding me from the outside world.

What a beautiful thing he just said to me.

Ask of me anything, and I will do it.

How extraordinary.

The only problem is, I cannot think of a single thing I want.

The little girl inside me is taking over, creeping in with every passing second. I can feel myself losing control. The only thing left is that terrible scream of pain echoing in my mind.

There is nothing Hunter can do.

There is nothing *I* can do.

And the saddest part, the part that makes me ache for myself, is that all she ever wanted was to be loved.

How messed up is that?

Hunter wipes at my eyes, but the tears keep falling, as if they, too, are in agony, desperate to leave my body.

There is no stopping this.

I am sobbing in front of him, breaking apart right before his eyes.

He rolls us over, shifting me effortlessly until I am lying on top of him, my body flat against his, my face buried in his chest. His strong, steady heartbeat is the only thing anchoring me, but even that feels too far away.

My tears spill over his skin, washing across his beautiful muscles. My pain wipes away his happiness.

Maybe he will see me as small after this. Maybe he will look at me differently.

But to be honest, I do not even have the strength to care. The thought of losing him barely registers.

The only thing I feel is the agony.

The pain of it all.

And the profound, aching need to *know why*.

I look up at Hunter when I feel his body shivering against me, his arms holding me tightly to his chest.

Tears roll down his beautiful face, and for a split second, I question how my tears ended up in his eyes.

How absurd is that?

They are not my tears. They are his.

He is in pain *with* me.

Is this what real love looks like? I am not sure. But what I do know is that Hunter is crying a silent cry with me.

I place my hand on his cheek, wiping the tears from beneath his eyes. He leans into my touch, as if it is the most natural, normal thing in the world.

"If the only thing I can do with you right now is cry, *sugar cube*, then that is exactly what I am going to do. Because this pain of seeing you like this needs to come out somehow, or I might actually explode. I might combust if I do not let it out."

I smile at his silliness and wipe his tears again.

I am not alone.

I *can* do this.

Even if I am breaking apart, Hunter is with me. He will keep me safe. And if I shatter completely, he will pick up the pieces and put me back together.

"Don't let me fall, okay?" I finally say.

"Never!"

His response is so fast that in any other situation, it would have been comical.

But here, in this moment, it feels powerful. It feels strong. It feels *true*.

We start getting ready, and once breakfast is delivered, I turn on the TV in an effort to distract myself.

The only thing playing on most channels is news about rebel activity spreading across the country. But what sends a chill through me is the coverage of their presence *right* here, all around the city we are in.

We should have brought guards with us, I think to myself.

"We should have taken some guards with us," Hunter comments as he lifts the lids from different dishes. "Do you want me to make some calls?"

"No, *Nuuro*. It is my family. They would not hurt us."

Right?

Doubt creeps into my mind the moment the words leave my mouth.

"We will be fine. You promised you would not let me fall, so we will be fine."

"Never!"

His reply comes fast, without a trace of hesitation or doubt.

A small smile is all I can manage, but it seems to be enough for him. Without a second thought, he moves closer and wraps his arms around me.

Twenty minutes later, we are in the car, driving to the place that once was my home, my life, and the foundation of my future.

Over the years, it transformed into something else entirely. The place that held the most horrific thing I have ever lived through and witnessed.

Yes, we are part of a modern mafia, where real power lies behind a keyboard, knowing you hold the information everyone needs and wants. But my father insisted we all learn how to get our hands dirty.

I have tortured and killed grown men without hesitation. I never second-guessed it.

But this...

This was preying on the smallest, most vulnerable thing there is.

When I carried out those acts before, I knew those men could defend themselves. More importantly, I knew they deserved what I was delivering.

But small little girls...

How the fuck would they ever be able to defend themselves?!

I lower my eyes to my hands, watching them tremble.

This is the first time I have ever seen them do that.

All of this feels like an out-of-body experience, like it is happening to someone else.

Because there is no way this could possibly be happening to *me*.

Strong fingers intertwine with mine, steadying me.

And once more, I am reminded that I am not alone.

Hunter is with me.

Hunter will protect me.

Even if I break down, he will pick me up. He will carry me to safety.

We make our way through the villa-style houses, and I almost laugh to myself when a memory surfaces.

When I was little, my biggest dream was to live in a house like this.

They looked so beautiful, so unreachable to little Sofia. Back then, nothing seemed more magical than owning a villa, eating sweets whenever I wanted, and having as much meat as I could possibly eat.

A soft smile spreads across my face at the absurdity of that dream compared to the life I grew up with next to my father.

"You good?" Hunter asks, his thumb gently caressing my hand.

"I wanted to live in one of these houses when I grew up. Eat sweets whenever I wanted. Salami as much as I wanted."

I let out a small breath, almost a laugh.

"Isn't that funny?"

"Oh! You wanted to be a chubby woman," Hunter says, and I burst out laughing.

Because, of course, a clown is a clown. He just *had* to turn the tables on me.

"That is funny," he adds, lifting my hand to his lips and pressing a soft kiss to the back of it.

"For the record, I would have loved you even if you were a little rounder. Actually, I *would* love it. More of you to love."

Then he winks at me.

I laugh again because he is so silly, but in the best way.

"You're such a clown."

"Anything to make you laugh, *sugar cube*."

He lowers my hand to his chest, and I feel it the rapid, relentless pounding of his heart, racing a million miles a minute.

I do not feel alone anymore, trapped in my pain.

It feels lighter now. Halved. Shared with the man I breath for.

I open the car window and take in the beauty of the city the stunning villa-style houses, the rich colours, the almost indescribable atmosphere lingering in the air.

But as we cross into the middle-class neighbourhoods, where flat, shoebox-style buildings replace the grand villas, a familiar dread surges through me.

Pain floods my veins with a vengeance.

The air smells different here. Familiar. Comforting in a way that makes my chest tighten.

But that same familiarity forces little Sofia to rise to the surface, taking over completely this time.

As we turn the corner, a modest concrete house stands tucked among others just like it, their flat roofs stretching in a monotonous line beneath the harsh sun.

The walls are dull and worn, painted in muted shades of ochre and grey, their surfaces cracked and weathered by years of relentless exposure. The scent of sun-scorched cement mingles with the tang of rust and faint traces of burning wood from nearby cooking fires.

At first glance, every house appears the same, simple, functional structures pressed close together, their narrow alleys winding between them like veins through stone. Windows are barred with iron, curtains drawn tight, shadows stretching long across the shared spaces. The air hums with an unspoken tension.

The street we are driving through is the street I once played on.

The memories crash into me all at once, slamming through my chest with the force of a tidal wave.

Panic. Agony. Dread.

The narrow spaces between buildings feel too tight, too close, as if they are closing in, trapping me in the past.

The informal housing surrounding the concrete cluster is a stark contrast, its makeshift structures leaning into one another like weary bodies braced against the wind.

Corrugated iron sheets clatter softly in the dry breeze, their thin walls patched with whatever materials could be scavenged, old wood, plastic tarps, scraps of cloth. Smoke rises in thin tendrils from scattered fires, carrying the scent of cooking meat and burnt trash.

The air feels heavy with desperation and survival.

Here, life is raw and exposed, caught between the cold permanence of concrete and the fragile impermanence of patched metal and cloth. The narrow alleyways twist into a maze, a place where it is easy to get lost and even easier to disappear entirely.

As kids, my mother never let us play there, afraid something might happen to us.

I remember looking at those alleys, at the people who lived there, and I can still recall the feeling.

That quiet relief.

That selfish comfort in knowing I was not the lowest of the low.

As we get closer to the house I once called home, my body is no longer numb. It is paralysed with fear.

The closer we get, the more unbearable it becomes.

When we are just three houses away, something inside me snaps. Without thinking, I reach over to Hunter and press my arm against his chest in a clear sign for him to stop.

"You okay?" The panic in his voice is obvious as he brings the car to an abrupt stop.

I feel like throwing up again. I feel like screaming. I feel like crying. I feel like my skin is crawling. I feel like my blood is boiling in my veins.

But more than anything, I feel the desperate need to run.

I stay frozen, my arm still stretched across to Hunter, my gaze fixed on my knees. I take deep, measured breaths, fighting the urge to scream.

"You can scream, *sugar cube*," Hunter says, as if he can read my mind. "You can do whatever you need to. You can even bite me if it helps take some of the pressure off."

I turn my head, startled by what he just said.

Bite him?

Why would I do that?

But as I look at him and try to process everything my body is putting me through, the more I realise it might not be such a bad idea.

"Are you for real?"

The voice that comes out of me does not feel like my own. The person speaking, the one controlling my body, is the grown-up version of little Sofia, and my heart breaks for her all over again.

"Baby, bite away," Hunter says, placing one palm over my hand on his chest while extending his other arm in front of me like an offering. "Just tell me how to make it better and I will. Biting is nothing compared to what I am willing to do for you."

I look down at his forearm, the muscles so strong, the veins standing out, engorged, angry.

I think I am going to bite him.

I study his gaze for a moment, weighing my options, weighing the consequences of everything happening right now.

And there is a very real possibility that I *am* going to bite him.

"I know you, Sofia. I know you want to walk into that house like the warrior queen you are. And if biting me will bring you any comfort or release even a little of the pressure inside you, then go for it, my *sugar cube*."

I look back at his arm, and before I even register my own actions, my teeth are already sinking into his skin.

My jaw locks onto his forearm with such ferocity that anyone watching would think I was trying to tear a chunk out of him. The pressure is so intense that within seconds, the metallic taste of blood hits my tongue.

Through it all, Hunter does not pull away. He does not cry out. He does not flinch.

Instead, he relaxes into my touch, his grip steady as he holds my hand against his chest.

When I finally pull back, the mark I leave behind is brutal. The skin is raw and deep, more like an animal attack than a bite from a person.

I yank my hand from his grasp and cover my mouth in shock.

I actually bit him.

I *actually* bit him.

But... I *do* feel a little better.

"I'm so sorry, Hunter," I say quickly, turning to face him. "Oh my god, I really bit you."

"It's all good," he reassures me without hesitation.

But how the hell can it be all good?

He leans over to grab the first aid kit, and I watch in horror as blood drips onto the car. He works quickly, dressing the wound with steady hands, as if this is nothing more than a scratch.

Once he is done, he takes my cheeks in his hands and presses a soft kiss to my lips.

"Feeling better?"

"A bit, yes."

"That's all I needed to know," he says with a smile.

And that smile, his actions, *everything* about him is what settles little Sofia. She is not alone. She is safe with Hunter.

"Tell me when you are ready to keep going."

"No, are we keeping going?" I ask in a small voice.

"Nope," he answers without hesitation. "I know you, *sugar cube*. Even if you have to crawl to that house, you will fight for your answers."

He is not wrong.

I came for answers, and I will leave with them.

"Let's go."

He drives the car the last few houses and parks directly at the entrance, blocking everyone in.

Once SASR, always SASR, I suppose.

He is just as nervous about this as I am, probably minimising risks with every move or at least trying to buy us more time in case we need to make a quick exit.

Now that we are here, I understand.

He was right. We *should* have brought men with us. And we *definitely* should have brought guns.

I open the car door, and it swings directly into the narrow space between the house door.

Before I can process anything, I glance over and see Hunter moving.

He slides effortlessly over the car bonnet and lands beside my door in one swift motion.

"Everything is okay, *sugar cube*. We are only here to talk, nothing more. Deep breaths, my love. Everything is going to be okay. I am right here, and I will not let anything happen to you."

His words register, but I am on autopilot. I cannot even nod in response.

I turn and step into the house.

The moment I do, my eyes drop to the floor. Shoes and random belongings are scattered everywhere, a mess of things left carelessly behind.

As I move further inside, my gaze drifts to the first room.

A man is sleeping with his back to us—in an open crib.

What the fuck?

I look across into the next room. Another man is lying on a bed, his phone in one hand while the other is shoved down his pants.

Well, that is disgusting.

I keep moving down the hall, Hunter close beside me. My eyes flick into different rooms as we pass, each one more disturbing than the last, yet all carrying that unmistakable scent of home and dread.

As we near the kitchen, voices filter through the air.

I freeze.

One of them, I think, is my mum.

Hunter stops too, his instincts sharp as ever. Without hesitation, he wraps an arm around me, holding me in the most reassuring embrace, one I desperately need right now.

I look up at him, drawn to the quiet strength in his stance, the solid presence that grounds me.

For a moment, I feel like I might cry.

"You can do this, sugar cube. You are a warrior. Strong men tremble in front of you. You *can* do this."

He is probably right.

But what he does not realise is that Sofia is only a guest now.

Little Sofia is in the driver's seat, and she is screaming two songs at once.

One tells me to run. To get as far away from here as I can.

The other cries out for something else entirely *the acceptance and love of my family.*

As difficult as this is, I *will* get my answers.

I take a deep breath, steady myself, and step into the kitchen.

The room is full of people, men and women, conversations buzzing around me. But my focus narrows in on one figure.

A woman stands at the kitchen counter, her back to us, busying herself with something.

My breath catches.

I *think* she is my mum.

Then she turns.

The moment our eyes meet, there is no doubt in my mind.

She is an older version of me.

She *is* my mum.

Her hands fly to her mouth, a sharp gasp escaping her lips as the plate she was holding crashes to the floor.

I do not move. I do not speak.

I just stand there, taking her in, frozen in the moment as voices swirl around me, blending into nothing.

There might be a lot of people in this room, but right now, only two feel real.

Hunter.

And her.

"Hi, Mum."

Chapter Twenty-Seven

Sofia

"Hi, Mum."
The room falls silent.

All eyes turn to me, their gazes burning into my skin, demanding my desperation, my pain, my surrender.

Hunter moves beside me, wrapping his arm around my waist, his hand resting firmly against my middle. A silent claim. A quiet warning.

To me, it is something else entirely.

It is his way of telling me I am not alone.

I am not alone in this.

I have Hunter.

And he will not let me fall.

"Who the fuck are you?"

A man stands, his posture aggressive as he moves towards me, probably intending to get in my face.

I glance around the room.

All the women have shrunk into themselves, their bodies folding in, as if trying to make themselves smaller. Invisible.

Something inside me roars to life.

Fury. Indignation. A rage so sharp it feels like a blade against my skin.

Because I know—*I know*—that every single one of these women has endured what I have. They wear their scars as if they are just another part of life.

But they *should not* be.

This *should not* be life.

Yes, the warrior in me is screaming in indignation.

I turn my gaze back to the man now standing in front of me, his expression twisted with anger, as if he is ready to tear into me for daring to speak.

I look him over, sizing him up.

I know I could put him on his arse in a few hits.

If I wanted to, I could probably kill him in two.

Decisions, decisions.

"I came to speak to my mum. I do not want any trouble." My voice is calm but strong.

For a moment, I silently pat little Sofia on the back for managing to sound so confident.

"You do not speak until spoken to, Fadhi-ku-dirir."

Hunter grunts beside me, a low, deliberate sound.

The man finally registers the giant standing next to me.

He was probably so used to women shrinking in front of him that he had not even noticed Hunter... until now.

"Naag laan-gaab, you think you can run away for years and just walk back in here, speaking as if it is your right?"

The menacing laughter that escapes him is a clear act of intimidation, but his eyes never leave Hunter.

He is holding his gaze, challenging him.

And now, without a doubt, I know, *we should* have brought men with us.

This piece of shit, whoever he is, must have guns nearby to be this confident in front of a man twice his size.

I look up at Hunter, and he is smirking at the guy. Knowing him, he has already come to the same conclusion as me.

"Please..."

I freeze.

My mum's soft voice breathes into me, her plea cutting deep.

Memories crash over me, hugging my mum, cooking together, playing, laughing. They overwhelm me, flooding every part of my mind, every part of me.

All I can do is stand there, paralysed, as if the weight of the entire world has settled on my shoulders.

"What do you want, Naag laan-gaab? You want to speak to the girl who ran away?"

His voice drips with venom, each word laced with spite.

"I thought she was dead. Or at the very least, that man would have kept her as a slave or a whore. But look at her."

I am speechless.

That's right. He is not seeing little Sofia. He is seeing *me*. The calm, calculated version of Sofia. An elegant, strong woman who demands respect and inflicts fear in the hearts of men.

I look him over again, sizing him up.

He is a dead man.

A breathing corpse, living out his last few moments.

Because if I know Hunter and *I do* know him, there is no way this man walks away from this conversation alive.

But I want my answers.

So I am going to get them.

"I told you, I just want to talk to my mum. I do not want any trouble."

He throws his head back and laughs so hard that saliva sprays from his mouth, some of it landing on my clothes.

Disgust curls in my stomach.

I glance at Hunter.

His gaze is locked onto me, begging me to let him loose.

I shake my head, small, discreet, but firm.

I cannot scare these women more than they already are.

Most of all, I cannot scare my mum.

I just want to know *why*. Why did she do this to me?

I look past the man's shoulder and see my mum shrinking in fear.

One hand grips the counter for support, as if she does not trust her legs to hold her up.

"You do not talk to her," the man says. "You talk to *me*."

His voice is thick with arrogance.

"And better yet, you need to *pay me* for permission to speak to me."

I need to pay for permission to speak.

I need to pay for permission to speak.

I need to pay for permission to *speak*.

The words loop in my mind, over and over, until their weight settles deep in my chest.

It does not matter that I look like a warrior. It does not matter that I appear wealthy and powerful.

To this man, I am just Naag laan-gaab—*insignificant.*

I have two choices.

I can kill him.

Or I can pay up.

Without hesitation, I reach into my pocket and hand him everything I have on me.

To me, money is no longer a currency. It holds no meaning.

So his pathetic display of power means nothing.

He just does not realise it yet.

"Look at that! The insignificant, useless whore is paying to speak to us," he sneers, waving the money like a trophy as he glances over his shoulder at the other men.

Then he turns back to us, laughing.

Something cuts through the air, too fast for me to register—until the knife is buried deep in his mouth.

Not until his body drops flat on his back, hitting the floor with a dull, lifeless thud from the sheer force of Hunter's throw.

I look up at him.

And *yep*.

His beast, as he calls this side of himself, is out in full force. That is for damn sure.

"I tried, *sugar cube*. I really did," Hunter whispers to me.

I glance at the men.

Their stunned, furious faces say it all.

They never thought we were a real threat.

"Easy," I say, my voice calm, measured.

"I just want to talk to my mum, that is all. There is no need for more bodies to pile up today."

"There is no need for more bodies to pile up today, the whore says," another man repeats mockingly as he pushes himself up from the table.

His gaze locks onto me, filled with contempt.

"Do you know who that was?" He pauses for a few seconds, letting the weight of his words settle.

"That was one of the rebel leaders. And your brother, Naag laan-gaab."

"Call her insignificant or a whore one more time, and you will be joining your friend in the afterlife," Hunter says.

When I turn to look at him, he is standing there, calm and steady two guns aimed directly at the man.

Well.

I might have thought this would be an easy conversation, but clearly, Hunter came packing for war.

Everything moves in slow motion.

The man steps towards me.

Hunter's guns go off.

I sprint towards my mum just as another man jumps from the table, guns in hand.

I throw myself over her, landing hard on the floor as bullets rip through the air, flying in every direction.

I do not look over my shoulder.

I do not need to.

I know with *absolute certainty* that these men, or even fifty of them, do not stand a chance against someone like Hunter.

"You good, *sugar cube*?" Hunter asks once silence descends over the room, the only sound his boots striking the floor as he walks towards me.

"I'm perfectly fine. I got to her in time."

"That's good. We need to go."

As the words leave his mouth, another shot rings out, the bullet flying past Hunter's head.

My eyes snap in the direction it came from.

One of the women at the table is holding a gun.

Another shot fires.

This time, the woman slumps to the side, a clear hole in her head.

"Seriously?" Hunter's agitated voice booms through the room. "Do I need to kill *you all* as well?"

His gaze sweeps over the remaining women, assessing them for any other threats.

I pull myself up, dragging my mum with me.

Up close, it is like looking into a mirror, one that reflects a version of my future.

And as much as I want to hate the woman standing in front of me, as much as I want to scream and throw punches, the only real feeling in my heart *is sadness.*

"We need to go, *sugar cube.*"

Hunter's reassuring hand on my shoulder pulls me back to the present.

"Was he right? Was that man part of the rebels?" Hunter directs the question at my mum, and she just nods.

His grip on my shoulder tightens instinctively.

Then he looks down at me, his gaze softening probably realising that I am running on autopilot, completely paralysed, my hands still clutching my mum.

"We are taking her with us."

It is not a question. It is an order.

The next second, he is on the phone, speaking to who I assume is either my dad or Buddy.

"We need an extraction. Yes, I know. But I also know that I need to make her happy, and to do that, I need to listen. Now, where do we go? Send me the coordinates once you have them."

Before I can even process what is happening, I am hauled over his shoulder, and my mum is secured under his arm like she weighs nothing.

He is carrying us both like sacks of potatoes, as if we are nothing more than dead weight.

And by the looks of it, it takes him zero effort.

"I can walk," I say, but my voice is so small that I am not even sure he hears me.

Gunfire erupts again as we make our way to the car.

Hunter literally throws my mum into the back seat and slams the door shut.

Then, with so much care it almost feels out of place, he gently sets me down.

He studies me for a moment, his eyes searching mine.

Then he presses a soft kiss to my forehead.

"I got you, *sugar cube*. You are not falling. I got you."

We are speeding down the road, and Hunter is on the phone with someone.

But all I can think about is the danger I put us in because I actually believed these people *cared* for me.

I try to process everything that has happened, but all I feel is fear.

I glance at my mum again.

Yes.

I went home, and I took my mum away.

And that is when it hits me.

All those years I tried and *failed miserably* to come back, I could not do it.

I just could not do it.

Because I did not have Hunter with me.

I did not have someone I could rely on so blindly, someone who could anticipate my needs so accurately it was as if they were his own.

Someone so in tune with me that a simple look could scream a thousand words.

I have been waiting for him all these years.

And now that I have him, I finally feel like *I could heal someday.*

The cracks that have split me apart for so long those jagged, broken pieces are slowly being held together *by him.*

Not with words.

Not with promises.

He just *is.*

"I love you, *Nuuro,*" I whisper.

His hand on my thigh tightens, a silent confirmation that he heard me.

"Will be there in two minutes," he barks into the phone. Then, as if it is the simplest question in the world, he asks...

"Your dad is mad. Can we kill them all now?"

Can we kill them all now?

I repeat the words in my mind, letting them settle.

They had their *chance* to take care of me.

They had their *chance* to speak now.

And on both counts, they chose to be the most inhumane pieces of shit.

I am done.

"Yes."

A sob comes from the back.

I turn to look at my mum.

Is she crying for *them*?

Is she crying for *me*?

Or is she crying for *herself*?

"Everything is going to be okay, *sugar cube,*" Hunter murmurs, his voice steady, anchoring me.

"Your dad called the CIA director. He lent us one of their safehouses. We will stay there until we have some men, then we will head to the airplane. Everything is going to be okay."

A shaky breath.

Then...

"Ayaan..."

It feels like someone has hit my brain with a sledgehammer at the sound of the name my mum gave me.

That *is not* my name.

My name is the one I chose.

I still remember when my dad asked me if I could change my name, what would it be?

There were so many children's books in the house, and one of them told the story of a little girl named Sofia.

She was happy.

Smiling.

Dancing on every page.

I wanted that.

I wanted to be happy so desperately that I claimed the name as my own, believing with my whole heart that as long as I was Sofia, I *would* be happy.

I feel the blood drain from my face as I turn to face the woman who *could have* and *should have* protected me.

"My name is Sofia! You killed Ayaan the day you pinned me to that bed and mutilated me!"

I scream the words with everything in me, even as my voice trembles under their weight.

Hunter parks the car next to a house, his movements precise. He checks the area, scanning every direction, making sure no one is around.

I do not move.

I do not look away.

I just keep glaring at the woman who holds all the answers I need.

"Listen here," Hunter's voice booms with authority.

"You are here for answers. It is up to you whether I have to extract them in the most sinister way imaginable or if you are willing to speak and keep your body exactly as it is now. But make no mistake, lady, if you insult, lie, or even so much as look at Sofia the wrong way, you will die in the most horrific way that comes to my mind in that moment. Is that clear enough for you?"

My mum freezes, her entire body rigid, eyes wide with fear at Hunter's words.

"Nod if you understand me."

She nods slowly.

The next second, Hunter is out the door, yanking me over the console, his body shielding mine the moment we step outside. My mum is completely left behind having to fend for herself.

The moment we step inside, I take it all in.

Hunter is already on the phone, his voice low and controlled as he moves through the house, checking every corner to ensure we are safe.

I glance at my mum.

She is frozen in the hallway, completely still, not making a sound.

She has shrunk into herself, as if trying to disappear.

It feels like this is normal for women here.

To be silent. To shrink. To exist without taking up space.

In all honesty, Hunter's words even scared me.

I take a slow step towards her and gently guide her to the couch.

She does not resist.

She shakes as she sits down, her skin damp with sweat. Her breathing is so fast and shallow that, for a moment, I think she is about to have a panic attack.

"I just want to talk," I say softly, trying to reassure her.

"I do not want to hurt you. *We*..." I glance over at Hunter. "We do not want to hurt you. I just want answers."

She finally speaks, her voice quiet.

"Who is he to you?" she asks. "You called him your light."

"He *is* my light," I say without hesitation. "And my heart."

"And her future husband," Hunter yells over his shoulder, still on the phone.

In a different situation, it would have been comical, him shouting something like that, the forever clown, cracking jokes no matter the circumstance.

Chapter Twenty-Eight

Hunter

Oh, I fucking hate them!

It is on, motherfuckers!

Sofia said yes, and Elijah is mad, *really mad*. Rebels or not, there is no saving this town now.

When I called Elijah, he went off.

He. Yelled. At. Me.

And called me every name under the sun for being so irresponsible with his daughter, for putting her in so much danger.

Only after I told him I had killed everyone in that house did he finally calm down.

I did hear a woman's voice in the background too.

Maybe that helped.

A little.

I got Sofia and her mum something to eat, but they are both frozen on the couch, staring into dead space.

The food sits cold on the table, completely forgotten.

In all honesty, I do not know how to help Sofia beyond organising manpower and getting her the hell out of here before Elijah rains hellfire down on this place.

I tried holding her, comforting her, but she just pushed me away.

I do not know if it is because her mum is here, or if she is mad as hell at me for killing everyone before she gave the okay.

But fuck that.

Brother or not, that fucker called her insignificant.

Sofia

Insignificant?

How could he ever be allowed to live after saying something like that?

I could not hold back.

Even I was surprised at how fast my beast threw the knife into his mouth, erasing his words forever.

But how did Sofia not recognise her own brother?

Why would they speak to her like that?

Sofia *insignificant*?

Sofia *a whore*?

Oh, just the memory of it makes my blood boil.

I should have killed the fucker slower.

He got off far too easy.

I hear a cracking noise outside.

The blood drains from my face.

Elijah's mercenaries have not arrived yet, and the last thing I need is a bloodbath while Sofia is in this state.

Another sound.

I glance at Sofia.

The moment our eyes meet, something in her shifts and just like that, *my warrior* is back.

This morning, I knew.

Before we even left the hotel, I felt it.

Something screamed inside me that everything would go to shit, that we would end up trapped.

So I might, or might not have packed a few guns, knives, and other toys.

Just in case.

In two long strides, I am in front of Sofia, handing her two of my guns.

The small gasp her mum lets out is yet another reminder of how little this woman knows about my *sugar cube*, how deeply she underestimates her own daughter.

But I know her.

And the mischievous glint in Sofia's eyes is all the reassurance I need.

She is ready to play with me.

And even in this state, whoever is outside has no idea what is about to hit them.

"Get behind the couch and do not make a sound. Whatever you do, do not make a sound," Sofia whispers to her mum, guiding her into place.

Then it is on.

She looks at me and smiles, a smile that does terrible, nasty things to my insides.

And when she winks?

It is really on.

My body reacts to her like she is a magnet, and I am helpless steel drawn to her.

Well... this is just great.

I am about to kill some fuckers with the beginnings of a hard-on.

And if I call her out on it, she will absolutely call me a pig. In front of her mum.

This fucking sucks.

I press a quick kiss to her forehead, then signal that I will take the right while she covers the left.

Moving through the house, I measure every step, keeping my movements precise.

Once in the kitchen, I spot two figures lurking outside the first window.

I glance at the other window.

Three more.

Well, at least these boneheads killed my erection.

I am not sure if I should be relieved or disappointed, but one thing is for sure thoughts about my cock are not productive right now.

So I park that thought and focus on the task at hand.

Two on the right. Three on the left.

Simple numbers.

I steady my breathing, every instinct sharpening as years of training kick in.

Eliminate the immediate threat first.

Do not give them a chance to regroup.

My eyes track the two shadows by the first window, their movements careless, untrained.

I crouch low, moving toward them like a ghost, silent, deliberate.

My fingers flex around the grip of my Glock smooth, familiar, almost comforting.

I fire once.

The crack of the suppressed shot cuts through the still air.

A soft thud follows as the first man collapses.

His partner does not even have time to react before I send him to the floor to meet the same fate.

Two down.

I glance at Sofia.

She is already moving, fast and controlled deadly grace in motion.

Her silhouette flickers through the dim light as she closes in on the other window, not even hesitating.

My heart should be pounding from the adrenaline.

But all I feel is calm.

Watching her like this is a strange kind of poetry, something dark, raw, and impossible to explain.

If I was not already in love with her, I would be fucked for sure.

The remaining three hesitate, thrown off by the sudden silence from their friends.

It is a fatal mistake.

Sofia locks eyes with me.

In that second, I know exactly what she wants.

We move together.

Fast. Precise. Ruthless.

The way only we can.

The men drop like flies, collapsing to the ground before they even know what hit them.

As their bodies thud against the floor, I know we have minutes before more come.

I pick up my phone and dial the number of the onsite CIA agent Elijah gave me.

"Fucker, your men better be close because we just had company."

"Do not fuck with me, you psycho," the CIA operative yells into the phone.

"Who the hell walks into enemy territory with their fucking hands in their back pockets?!

You should consider yourself lucky I found any manpower on the ground, given the shitshow you have put yourself in."

"I will be sure to take all your complaints, wipe my arse with them, and then report them back to Elijah just to make sure one of the bombs lands right on your fucking head."

"Bombs?!"

The fucker yells again, his accent thick with panic.

It does not help that he is Serbian and has a smart-arse comment for everything.

"This was not part of the deal, Hunter!"

"It is Elijah's daughter, mate. What the fuck did you expect? For him to lay low and just take it?"

"Hunter, we need to evacuate if that is the case. We have safehouses and people all over the city."

"Oh. Is that right?"

I lean into the phone, my voice calm, deadly.

"Now tell me, Joseph, which one is the true version?

Do you not have enough people to send for our evacuation?

Or do you have too many and need time to get them the fuck out?"

Silence.

Then it hits him.

He fucked up.

"Measure your words very carefully," I warn, my voice like steel.

"Because there is no fucking place on Earth you can hide from us. And trust me if anything happens to Elijah's daughter, he *will* find you."

"We do not have mercenaries, Hunter. We have civilians.

Informants we have relied on this entire time to gather intelligence on the rebels.

As advanced as your tech is, and as much as the director benefits from his relationship with you lot, in countries like this, it is legwork, not tech work, that keeps us ahead.

I want to evacuate them because if war is about to break out, they will not survive it."

"Fair. Where are my men?!"

"About that..."

His voice trails off, just as I hear the rumble of approaching cars outside the building.

"As I said, I could not get the number of mercenaries you needed in such a short timeframe, so I reached out to the local drug lord."

"YOU. DID. WHAT?!"

Sofia quickly stands, moving to the window for a closer look at the approaching cars.

She assesses the men, her sharp gaze scanning every detail.

Then, as our eyes meet, we both know...

This is as fucked up as a situation can get.

"What the fuck did you expect me to do? It was drug lord men or no men!"

"If I ever see you in person," I say, my voice calm, calculated, "I am going to take my pound of flesh from you for this."

The menace in my tone is undeniable.

This is, without a doubt, one of the stupidest things that has ever happened to us.

"They owe us a lot of favours, so nothing will happen to you. Get in the car and drive to the airport."

"Do they know who we are?"

"No. I made sure not to mention you."

A beat of silence.

"Are you lying to us again?"

My voice drops, quieter now deadly quiet. My blood boils with rage.

"Because if you did not run your fucking mouth, then how the fuck did they know to come straight for this house just now?"

My grip tightens on the phone.

"Why did we have company, fucker?"

Silence.

For a few seconds, nothing.

This CIA motherfucker is dumb as shit.

Where the fuck did they recruit him from?

Or is he one of those pretty boys they parade around for campaigns and promotions someone who looks good in a suit but cannot think two steps ahead?

"I might have mentioned it to the second drug lord... and promised him some protection from Elijah."

"Oh."

I let the word sit, calm, deadly.

"I hope you enjoy your last few days on Earth, fucker because if Elijah does not come after you, I sure as fuck will."

"It was drug lord's men or NO men! What the fuck did you want me to do?!"

"Call me, you stupid fuck!"

I am roaring now, barely holding back the urge to smash something.

"You should have called me! Not made a decision with your stupid fucking brain and put us in even more danger!"

"What happened?"

Sofia's calm voice pulls me back to her.

I look down into her beautiful eyes, and in that moment, I know...

Even if I die today, I will die a loved man.

Loved by the woman I exist for.

"This imbecile recruited the drug lord's men to escort us out of the city."

"Oh, he's dumb!"

Sofia does not miss a beat.

She grabs the phone, voice sharp, unwavering.

"Oh, mate, if we catch you, you will learn what true pain looks like!" she yells into the receiver.

"It was those men or NO men! How many fucking times do I need to repeat myself?!"

Sofia hangs up, and moves back to the window.

Men are spilling out of the cars like ants scrambling for food.

Six cars.

Around twenty men, all armed.

Some in tactical gear, others not, clear distinction between the way they look and carry themselves.

They are glaring at each other, tension thick in the air.

We both know exactly what this is.

A disaster about to become a monumental fuck-up of a disaster.

"Guns?" Sofia asks.

There she is... my *sugar cube*.

No fear. No hesitation.

Instead of cowering, she locks in, hyper-focused on the task at hand.

She is not panicking.

She is working with me, thinking fast, ready to come up with a strategy to get us the hell out of here.

"God, I love you, woman!"

My heart feels like it is about to explode with pride, love, and something deeper I cannot even name.

I have seen grown men cry in battle.

I have seen soldiers throw up in enemy territory.

I have seen men piss and shit themselves when captured.

And my *sugar cube*?

All hell is about to break loose, and her mind does not freeze.

It hyperfocuses.

"Cut it out, Hunter! Or do you need me to kick you in the balls to get you to focus?!"

I want to jump on her.

Or at the very least, laugh, because fuck that was funny.

But I know better.

She will only get more pissed.

So I do as she says.

And bury my laughter deep inside.

I move over to where my bag of goodies sits, exactly where I left it when we came in heavy with the weight of preparation and the promise of doom.

I unzip it, fingers brushing over the cold metal inside loaded mags, extra Glock rounds, a couple of smoke grenades for cover if shit goes south, and some fragmentation grenades to ensure we really do have fun.

Nestled at the bottom is my suppressed MP5 compact, reliable, perfect for close-quarters work.

I tap the side of the bag and glance at Sofia.

"Got extra 9mm, 7.62s, and two frags if we need to make a statement. Grab what you need. Let's see what these dead idiots outside brought for us."

I crouch beside the bodies, stripping them for anything useful. My voice stays low but firm as I toss a spare mag towards Sofia.

"AK-47s. Standard shit. Cheap, mass-produced. But they'll tear through a body like paper if you let them."

I hold up a battered Makarov pistol from one of the dead men, ejecting the mag and checking the chamber.

"Russian-made. Old. Probably jams if you breathe on it wrong."

I toss it aside, useless weight.

Digging into the webbing of a tactical vest, I pull free a couple of extra 7.62 mags. Holding one up so she can see.

"Steel-core rounds. These'll punch through walls, so don't rely on cover if they start shooting back."

I shove the mags into my vest, moving to the next guy.

"Hand grenades are missing. Means either they're dumb enough to leave them behind or they've got friends carrying them."

I glance up at Sofia just as she checks a mag before pocketing it like she's been doing this her whole life.

"Reload now. Drop the mag before it's empty, keep a full one ready. You don't want to hear that click in the middle of a firefight."

I slide a fresh mag into my Glock, snapping the slide forward.

"They came heavy, but not smart. We finish this and we get to our plane."

"Agreed. We move together, my mum in the middle."

I want to fucking scream.

Her mum in the middle?

Like fuck she is!

"Baby, please."

I step closer, my voice low but firm.

"Your mum is not the most precious cargo here. You are."

I lean in, pressing a soft kiss to her forehead, taking way too much pleasure in the fact that she does not pull away.

Instead, she wraps her arms around me, her cheek resting against my chest.

"She will take a bullet for you if she has to," I murmur, my grip tightening around her.

"Same as I would any day of the week.

She is not the most important thing here, *sugar cube*.

You are."

"I want my answers, *Nuuro*. Otherwise, all of this was a big, utter fuck-up and I still do not know *why*."

I exhale, my jaw tightening.

"I'm sorry, baby, but your safety is the most important thing to me right now."

I cup her face, forcing her to look at me.

"I adore you. And if she gets shot, I fucking swear I will give her my own blood if I have to, to save her.

But you go in the middle.

And that's final."

Sofia nods against my chest.

She knows I am right.

She knows this is the best option right now.

And she knows that if her dad finds out she put someone else before herself, he will lose his shit even more.

She moves to get her mum while I grab the bag of ammunition, and we make our way outside.

A full-on pissing contest is happening between the gangs, and honestly?

I'm glad.

If they are too busy fighting each other, they will not have time to get any bright ideas about kidnapping us for ransom.

So, good on them for being absolute idiots.

"Are we going, or do you still need a minute to fight it out?"

I throw the words out with mock humour, just to fuck with them.

"We are heading to airport hangar 4. We need to be there in ten minutes."

I have already spoken with the pilot to arranged our papers, make sure we can clear customs, and told him to have the plane ready for immediate takeoff.

Ten minutes since that phone call is more than enough time for him to have everything set.

I grab Sofia's mum, toss her into the back seat, and drop the bag next to her.

And just for good measure, I slam the door shut, hard.

She flinches.

Let her be a little more scared.

"Is that really necessary?"

"Yep," I respond, no hesitation whatsoever.

As far as I am concerned, she should consider herself lucky I have not killed her already.

But mark my words after she gives Sofia her answers, she is mine.

And trust me, I will take my time.

Because her death will be as painful as what she inflicted on Sofia.

The cars around us move like frantic ants, completely disorganised, no strategy, no structure just pure inexperience and stupidity.

I take control, positioning our car in the middle of the convoy, my entire focus on Sofia and her safety.

I love her so much that there is no version of reality where I could survive without her by my side.

My attention is laser-sharp, tracking these morons, and as much as I try to hold position, they keep overtaking each other like reckless idiots thinking the front is the safer spot.

Fucking amateurs.

We are almost at the airport, the GPS counting down the final stretch.

Then, in an instant, the last car in the convoy explodes, blown to smithereens.

Fucking rebels.

They are after my *sugar cube*.

My beast awakens so fast it feels like he was never truly caged, raring to protect her, to tear through anything in our way.

This is not the moment to lose control.

I know that.

But the fear of losing her is so overwhelming, it chokes me, burns through my veins like fire.

A soft hand lands on my leg, pulling me from the storm in my head.

I glance over at Sofia.

The smile she gives me is all the peace I need in this moment.

"We are going to be okay, *Nuuro*," she says, her voice steady, unwavering.

"Remember, I am not a delicate flower in the wind."

Then she winks at me.

"You keep the car steady, and I will take care of them."

No hesitation. No fear.

Before I can even respond, she lowers the window, pushes halfway out, her gorgeous arse perched on the car door.

And then she starts shooting.

Like it is nothing.

Like it is just another day.

"Sofia Dominion, get your sweet arse back in this car right now!" I yell, reaching out to grab her leg, ready to haul her back in.

The kick to my chest is so fast, it knocks the breath out of me.

"Stop that, Hunter!" she snaps.

"Or I will shoot you as well, you idiot!

Now keep the car steady!"

All hell breaks loose around us as the gang members open fire.

I am so fucking terrified that one of these idiots might accidentally hit Sofia.

I slam my foot down, pushing the car to the front of the convoy as fast as I can.

In the rear-view mirror, I see the enemy cars hot on our trail, gaining fast.

Sofia *is* a warrior queen.

From the way she holds herself, poised and deadly, to the way she fires with precision, already taking out two enemy cars.

It is a thing of beauty.

The kind of sight that wet dreams are made of.

"Fucking hell!" she yells at full blast.

"These guys are fucking useless!"

My heart stops.

"Are you shot?!"

The words rip out of me, raw and panicked, a cry of pure despair.

"No," she says, breathless but steady.

"Well... it was a near miss, so we need to hurry things along."

She kicks the roof of the car, her voice sharp.

"Mum?"

Nothing.

"Could you please be a dear and hand me the grenades?"

I glance over my shoulder.

The woman is crouched down, wedged between the seats, arms over her head—thinking of no one but herself.

Selfish bitch.

I swear, I will kill her myself.

Sofia kicks the roof again, frustration bleeding through her movements.

And then I snap.

"Oi! Get your sorry arse up, look in the bag, and hand her the grenades!"

Still nothing.

I reach over, grab her, and shove her back onto the seat.

"Get the fucking grenades!"

"I... I... don't know what I'm looking for," she stammers, her voice shaking so hard, pure fear lacing every word.

Sofia does not even flinch.

"The one that looks like a funny pineapple, Mum. Just pick it up from its bum and hand it over."

She reaches out, waiting.

The woman fumbles, then hands her the grenade.

Sofia does not hesitate for a second she pulls the pin and sends it flying towards the enemy cars.

We wait.

Five seconds.

Nothing.

Fuck.

I already know she handed Sofia a smoke grenade, not a fragmentation grenade.

Oh, I would punch her so fucking hard right now if I could.

And if Sofia wouldn't kill me for it afterward.

"The other type of pineapple!"

I roar, letting her see the beast inside me, the real danger of being next to me.

She scrambles, reaching into the bag, and hands Sofia another grenade.

This time, I check it fast as Sofia takes it, making sure it is the right one.

She pulls the pin, throws it, and in two seconds, two cars explode into fire and shrapnel, torn apart by my *sugar cube*'s might.

A sharp, audible gasp escapes her mum, her breath catching as tears spill down her face.

She never believed Sofia was capable of this.

They called her insignificant.

But she is a mighty warrior queen among mortals.

"More! Hand me a few more!"

Her mum hesitates, frozen for a few crucial seconds.

But we are almost at the hangar, and I know, these last few throws will be the difference between making it into the air or not.

"Now!" I roar, my voice sharp and unyielding.

She jolts, fumbling into the bag.

No more hesitation.

Not now.

She hands Sofia two more grenades, and she throws them like a pro.

One hits its mark, a perfect explosion tearing through the enemy.

The other?

Smoke. Again.

I just shake my head, grinding my teeth.

This.

This right here is the perfect example of a fuck-up that could get people killed in enemy territory.

"Hand her one more!" I yell, slamming the car into park right next to the hangar door.

Sofia throws the last grenade just as the car slams to a halt.

The explosion erupts behind us, the perfect camouflage for our sprint to the plane.

We run up the stairs, every second counting.

Then Sofia hesitates.

Her eyes lock onto the approaching cars.

She freezes, recognition etched across her face.

We do not have time for this.

I grab her, lifting her up and hauling her inside before slamming the cabin door shut.

"Go! Now!" I yell at the captain, my voice leaving no room for argument.

The plane lurches forward, wheels lifting off the ground.

The moment we are in the air, I exhale, a long, ragged breath.

Fuck me, that was close.

Next time we go out to play, I am bringing men with us, even if they stay in the shadows.

"Was that Humda?"

Sofia's voice is ghostly, so small I barely hear it.

"It might have been," her mum answers, her voice shaky, uncertain.

"I did not see. A lot has changed."

"Yes," I cut in before Sofia can speak.

"A lot *has* changed."

Sofia needs space, I see it all over her face.

And I will make damn sure this woman understands, she is not here for us to answer questions.

She is not here for favours.

She is here at our pleasure and when that runs out?

She will be disposed of.

"We are going home," I say, my voice calm but unyielding.

"You are going to learn who Sofia *really is.*"

I see it then, the fear in her eyes, the way she shrinks away from me.

Good.

As it should be.

But if she thinks I am the big bad wolf...

Oh, I cannot wait for her to face Elijah now that Sofia has let us kill them all.

Chapter Twenty-Nine

Sofia

We got back to England a day ago, and I really, really want to interrogate my mum.

But this fucked-up part of me, this scared little girl, just will not fuck off.

I want to scream.

I feel like a coward.

I feel small.

I feel weak.

How can I have my mum here, after all these years, and still not have the courage to go and talk to her?

We locked her in one of the guest rooms in my apartment.

And Hunter? Well, he might or might not have exploded a little after that mess on the ground.

Now we have four guards stationed around the clock, guarding our apartment even though we have *Alex*.

In all fairness, I get it.

It was my mistake.

I let my feelings take control instead of my rational mind, and it almost got us killed.

That moment when Hunter threw the knife straight into my brother's mouth after he called me insignificant and a whore still plays in my mind.

Even now.

That was a work of art.

I know people have their limits, kinks, and whatever else, but fuck me, seeing Hunter's power and reflexes move so poetically in my defence was something else.

That was *beautiful.*

The fool hit the ground, his face frozen in stupid shock.

He really thought he had the upper hand.

Coming back to the problem at hand, I can waste more time hiding in my room or burying myself in work, but I know that sooner or later, I need to face my past.

Right now, all I have done is drag it closer, letting it torment and terrify me all over again.

Now it is not just a shadow in my mind.

It is standing right in front of me, up close and personal.

I expected her to fight.

I expected her to rage, to resist, to refuse to accept what was happening.

She is most definitely scared shitless of Hunter, and the prick is enjoying it.

But I think she might be scared of me too.

I do not think she ever believed I was capable of combat or that I would stand up for myself in her kitchen.

One thing is certain.

I am terrified *of her* and the answers she holds.

"Hi, *sugar cube*," Hunter purrs like a fool from the doorway.

I look over at him, and the beautiful smile playing on his lips makes it painfully obvious what he is up to.

He came to tease me, probably thinking he can steal some touchy-touchy time while he is at it.

I should roll my eyes.

But if I am being honest...

I do miss him.

"Fine," I say with a sigh, rising to my feet.

Before I can blink, he bolts towards me, dropping into my chair so fast it spins from the momentum.

When he steadies it, I sink onto his lap, resting my head against his chest.

One thing I have noticed about Hunter, he is so in tune with my needs that most of the time, all it takes is a single look, and he moves into action.

Case in point.

"Is today the day you let me kill her?"

There is hope laced in his voice, like he truly means it.

He does not outright ask me if today is the day I will face my past.

He does not push, does not probe or pick at my feelings.

Instead, he asks if he can end her, making it easier for me.

So I do not have to admit that I am too much of a coward to go near her door.

Hunter has been leaving trays of food outside her door since we got home.

Because I cannot.

Not yet.

"I am not sure," I respond after a while.

Hunter does not push.

"Do you need me to do anything?"

His voice is gentle, steady.

"Tell me how I can make it better for you. Ask me for anything, and it will be yours."

His words hit deep, touching something so raw inside me that I fear I might break.

I am scared I might cry in front of him, scared that he will see just how small and weak I feel.

Why am I so afraid to face her?

I do not know the answer to his question.

So I say nothing.

"*Sugar cube*," Hunter says softly after a few moments pass.

"If I may... I am not a psychologist, of course, but it seems to me that you are scared.

Maybe a small part of you is scared.

Or maybe it is the shock of finally standing face to face with something you have wanted for so many years."

His arms tighten around me, his warmth enveloping me.

He brings my hand to his lips and kisses it gently, and I inhale his musky scent, grounding myself in his love, his presence, his strength.

"Take all the time you need, *sugar cube.*

These are your feelings, and no one, not me, not anyone, should tell you how to process them."

He pauses, his voice steady.

"But I want to remind you of something.

The answers you are seeking are for the little version of yourself.

And that little girl?

You took her and turned her into the mighty woman you are today."

He tilts my chin up slightly, forcing me to meet his gaze.

"So whatever you feel, however you process this, it is all good.

Just remember...

You make grown men piss themselves in front of you."

We sit there for a while.

The gravity of the situation, the weight of Hunter's words, the comfort of his embrace, the feel of his touch, and the familiar scent of him all press down on me.

It is overwhelming.

After a while, my body gives in, and I drift off.

When I wake, I am still wrapped in Hunter's arms, the room now dark, the world outside quiet.

I have no idea how long I was out.

I can only imagine how numb Hunter must feel after holding me for so long.

But for some strange reason, I feel better.

It is true that I have not slept in days, and Hunter's safe embrace must have cradled me into rest.

But still, the weight of everything has been too much, robbing me of my words and my strength to keep going, until my body finally shut down.

"What time is it?"

"No idea," he says casually, then smirks.

"But I think I just found my new favourite kink."

I pull a face, and he bursts out laughing, clearly enjoying himself.

"You're an idiot," I say, but as the words leave my mouth, I burst into laughter along with him.

Especially when I feel his hard cock beneath me.

He is so silly, with all his jokes, comments, and most of all, the way his body reacts to me.

Even in my daydreams of him, I never imagined he would be like this with me.

Not like this.

"You feel any better?"

I take a moment.

That suffocating weight on my chest has somehow eased.

I am going to confront her.

There is only one way through pain.

And that is through it.

No *shortcuts.*

No *avoidance.*

The only way is *through*.

"I am going to go and talk to her. It is time to get this over with.

Enough is enough.

Today, I am taking my power back from her."

With that, I stand and walk towards the door.

"*Sugar cube*, can I come, please?"

I just shake my head, my focus locked onto one thing, my mum.

"Okay, I respect that," Hunter says, but then his voice turns mischievous.

"But can I stay outside the door? You know... just in case she pulls a kung-fu move on you, so I can jump in and fuck her up?"

He bursts into laughter, clearly pleased with himself.

He is such an idiot, but I adore him for it.

Always cracking a joke when the tension is about to choke the air out of the room.

He is the most easy-going person I have ever met.

And I am definitely not.

But for some reason, he loves me.

And I most definitely love him.

"Sure," I say, a small smile tugging at my lips as I make my way to the room my mum is in.

I stop right in front of the door and just stare at it.

I can feel it all...

These feelings, crawling over my skin, making it itch, burn, tighten.

The self-loathing.

The self-doubt.

The self-pity.

The disgust.

The desperation to be normal.

The pain I felt when I thought I could never have Hunter.

My body starts to burn, the heat rising in my chest as a familiar panic creeps in, wrapping around me like a suffocating fog.

Numbness follows, creeping into my fingers, threatening to pull me under.

I place my hand on the doorframe, gripping it for support, and force myself to take slow, deep breaths.

I need to steady my mind.

I need to control my body.

I cannot let myself spiral.

Not now.

"Baby..."

Hunter's voice comes from behind me, low and steady, as his arm wraps around my waist, grounding me instantly.

"You don't have to do this today. Take all the time you need."

I place my hand over his, gripping it, and lean back into him, trying to absorb his strength.

I am not alone.

Hunter loves me.

I am not alone.

Hunter loves me.

I am not alone.

Hunter loves me.

The words loop through my mind, over and over, until they are the only thing anchoring me to this moment.

"I am doing this," I say suddenly, my voice steady.

"If it is the last thing I do, I am getting my answers."

Hunter's grip on me tightens.

"If anyone is going to die, it's her, *sugar cube*."

His voice is calm but firm, leaving no room for argument.

"That's not funny, so please do not joke about things like that."

I open the door and step inside, leaving Hunter behind.

But as I take my next step, a wave of unmeasurable panic crashes over me.

I feel alone.

Alone with myself, my demons, and her.

My chest tightens, my breath shortens, and without thinking, I reach back and grab a fistful of Hunter's shirt, yanking him inside with me.

Our eyes meet, and in that single moment, he knows.

He knows I need him here.

Nothing else.

Just him.

My mum is sitting on a chair by the floor-to-ceiling window, staring out at the city.

The moment she notices us, she stands abruptly, her movements sharp, panicked.

Fear is written all over her face.

She is a beautiful woman.

I do not know if others would see her that way, but to me, she has always been beautiful.

There was always something about her, this unmistakable elegance that made even the simplest clothes look refined.

I loved my mum so much.

I looked up to her.

I longed to be loved by her.

But over the years, I had to make peace with the truth.

She did not love me the way I needed her to.

As I look at her, taking in her beautiful features, I feel confused.

Why is she scared of me?

I may not have all the answers, but in this moment, I know one thing for certain...

I will not let my dad or Hunter hurt her.

I just can't.

Even if the answers she gives me are lies or meaningless, I know I do not have it in me to cause her pain.

Because for the first time in many, many years, both little Sofia and I agree on something.

We just want to be loved by this woman.

I take a step towards her.

Then another.

And another.

With every step, my emotions twist tighter, leaving me more confused than before.

Part of me is screaming in agony.

Part of me is crying in despair.

And part of me is desperately seeking her love and acceptance.

The only thing that is crystal clear is that I want answers.

Even if it kills me today.

I take a seat in the chair next to her and gesture for her to do the same.

She hesitates for a moment before lowering herself into the chair.

I glance over at Hunter.

He is still by the door, shoulder resting against the frame, watching.

I am not alone.

Hunter loves me.

The silence in the room is thick, pressing in from all sides.

The tension is suffocating.

But the only thing I can bring myself to do is stare out the window.

To see the city from her eyes.

For the first time.

"Why?"

My voice breaks the silence, shattering the heavy stillness that has settled over us.

It feels like I have been waiting an eternity for this moment.

The only response I get is a small, broken sob.

When I look over, I see her crying, her chin trembling like a child.

My chest tightens, but before I can process her reaction, a knife flies past her head, slicing through the air.

It buries itself deep into the frame of a hidden cabinet, the impact sharp and final.

"Hunter..."

My voice is low and menacing, because I thought the fucker understood what I told him just *now*.

He shrugs, unapologetic.

"Sorry, *sugar cube*, but she does not get to cry like she is the victim here," he says, justifying himself instantly.

His eyes lock onto her, his tone turning even sharper.

"Oi! Stop that right now!"

His voice cuts through the room, thick with contempt.

"Your tears mean fuck all here, so keep your theatrics to yourself and answer her questions."

His words are so ruthless, so sharp, that I am the one who feels irritated by him now.

I rise to my feet, my movements slow and deliberate.

Without breaking eye contact, I pull the knife from the cabinet, grip firm, and throw it at him.

It lands just beside his hip, the blade embedded deep, the message unmistakable.

Be grateful it was not your cock you just lost, I say with my gaze.

I stare him down, daring him to say another word or make another foolish move.

His face drops, his usual smugness replaced by something else.

Then he nods once.

And says nothing.

"Why?"

I repeat the question, my voice kind and calm, because the truth is, I just want to know.

I want to understand why I am the way I am.

Why she took part in it.

Why I had to suffer.

When I turn to look at her, her eyes are wide with fear, so wide they almost look unnatural.

In all the years I have seen people on the brink of death, I have never seen a look like this.

Not on anyone.

And seeing it on her...

It does terrible things to my insides.

Because despite everything, all I want to do is protect her.

"He will not hurt you. Please sit. That matter is settled now."

I glance at Hunter. His face is fuming with fury, but he nods again, holding himself back.

I turn back to my mum.

"Don't mind him, Mum."

My voice is steady, but inside, I feel like I am standing on the edge of something crushing, something too vast and suffocating to be contained in a single word... *why*.

"I just want to know.

Why?

Why did you do this to me?"

As the words leave my mouth, I feel a weight shift inside me.

Like some deep pressure has finally lifted from my soul.

At last, I have asked her.

At last, I will get my answers.

"Ayaa—"

The word is cut short by my glare, slicing through the air like a warning.

She stops abruptly, her body giving up on her, and drops into the chair as if the weight of this moment is too much to bear.

"Sofia, you need to understand..."

Her voice is small, but the words still land like a blow.

"Women are itch there. If they are not cut, their hands will be down there all the time."

As the words penetrate my ears and mind, I take a few seconds to process what she just said.

I must have misunderstood.

Did she really just say that I was mutilated because it might be itchy, and this was meant to fix it?

A wave of cold disbelief crashes over me.

I shake my head, trying to force those words out of my mind.

Trying to reject them.

"And not only that, Sofia.

We, as women, have stronger sexual needs than men. If we were not cut, we would be jumping on them all the time.

So they removed those things from us, so we would not chase men for sex."

The conviction in her tone is like a slap to my reality.

She actually believes it.

Wholeheartedly.

She thinks this is the truth.

Hunter suddenly bursts into laughter, the sound sharp and unfiltered, before quickly covering it with a cough when I glare at him.

That moment is my reality check.

Yes.

She most definitely just said that I was mutilated so I would not throw myself at men.

A wave of excruciating pain crashes through my mind.

Not just from her words, but from the weight of their significance.

The absurdity of it.

The devastating consequences of what complete ignorance can do to a person.

"Listen, Sofia.

Now that you have a husband, when he opens you up, like the gift you are to him, you will deliver his baby so much more easily because you have been cut.

Precious daughter, I made it better for you."

I want to scream.

My body tenses, instincts roaring at me to attack, to lash out.

But the conviction in her voice, the pure naivety in her words, and the absolute ignorance written all over her body language and face stop me in my tracks.

She truly believes this shit.

There is no doubt in my mind.

"Opens me up?"

The words barely escape me, strangled by the scream trapped in my throat.

"Yes, open you up with scissors on your wedding night."

I jump up so fast she flinches back.

A wave of cold sweat washes over me, my body shaking at the sheer atrocity of her words.

WHAT. THE. ACTUAL. FUCK.

Open me up with scissors?!

Is this what these fuckers do to women?!

This is beyond fucked!

I am going to drop a nuclear bomb on them.

WHAT. THE. ACTUAL. FUCK.

I stand frozen in panic, trapped in front of the woman who brought me into this world.

Hearing the abomination of a life she has accepted as her own.

Hearing the future I might have had if I had stayed by her side.

A sharp sound breaks through the chaos in my mind.

Something lands by my shoe.

I look down.

Hunter has slid a knife across the floor, stopping at my feet.

A silent message.

A reminder.

I am not alone.

Hunter loves me.

I am not alone.

Hunter loves me.

I am not alone.

Hunter loves me.

The words keep repeating in my mind, looping over and over until I can finally breathe again.

When I look up, Hunter's beautiful face is calm, almost at peace.

Then he shakes his head, and in that small gesture, an unspoken conversation passes between us.

I love you, sugar cube.

I would never hurt you.

I would never do such a thing to you.

Please, let me kill her.

And just like that, something inside me shifts.

All of her reasoning, all of her explanations, all of her logic...

Flawed.

Incorrect.

Ignorant.

Dangerous.

I feel for her.

I feel for all the women who have endured what I have.

I feel for all the girls who will still go through this, because the world keeps turning a blind eye to these atrocities.

I am not sure what I was expecting to be the reason behind my agony.

But ignorance was not it.

Ignorance.

Such a small word compared to the unimaginable pain and suffering I have endured because of my mutilation.

It feels so... sterile.

So insignificant in comparison.

And yet...

It is the most powerful proof of how dangerous a lack of knowledge can be.

How ignorance, in the wrong hands, becomes a weapon.

A weapon with *devastating consequences* for those who are forced to bear its weight.

One thing is certain.

I will not keep their secrets any longer.

I will not be part of their misguided lies.

I will not stand in silence while others suffer.

I will stand with anyone willing to stand with me.

Anyone willing to *hear me.*

Anyone willing to *join me.*

Anyone willing to fight with me to *put an end* to this.

I lean down, pick up the knife, and hear my mum take in a sharp, audible breath.

She is scared.

I know she is.

But I also know she has suffered enough.

No harm will come to her.

Not while I live.

I straighten, meeting her eyes.

"You are safe by my side, Mum.

No harm will come to you as long as I live."

A sob escapes her, raw and uncontrolled, as my words sink in.

I take a slow breath, my voice steady.

"I will do for you what you were incapable of doing for me.

I will keep you safe.

And I will get you all the help you need."

With that, I turn and walk away, leaving behind the sound of my mum's sobs.

Leaving behind the burden of not knowing why this was done to me.

The reason for my mutilation no longer holds power over me.

"Are you okay, *sugar cube*?"

Hunter's arms wrap around me the moment we step into our room, his hold strong and grounding.

I do not move.

I just stop, letting myself sink into his embrace, leaning back into his touch, his warmth, his presence.

My heart is racing.

My breath is shallow and quick.

A strange lightness fills my head, while my entire body feels numb.

"I feel... numb," I finally whisper, my voice fading into nothing.

"You can feel whatever you need to feel, *sugar cube*."

His voice is gentle, his touch soft as he guides me to the bed. He leans back against the headboard, pulling me between his legs, my back resting against his chest, cocooning me in his warmth.

"Just try, next time, not to go after the family jewels."

He finally says it, then bursts into laughter.

The forever clown.

I cannot help it.

I laugh with him.

At how sweet he is.

At how in tune he is with me.

At how protective he is.

At how he just *is*.

"I made you laugh! No way! I actually made you laugh!"

He yells in my ear, his excitement uncontained, then starts peppering kisses everywhere he can reach.

"Thank you," he murmurs, pressing a kiss to my jawline.

"You're an idiot," I say, my voice flat.

"But the funny thing is... you already know you're an idiot and still do nothing about it."

I continue the tease, then pinch his leg for good measure.

I know he is in pain with me.

If the roles were reversed, I would be heartbroken for him, desperate to find a way to make it better.

So I have to play along, even if it is just for a moment.

I love him too much not to.

"Can we stay like this for a while? I feel sleepy again."

"Anything you want, *sugar cube*."

"Please tell your cock not to wake me up."

"I apologise on his behalf in advance... but I don't think that will be possible."

"See? Promises, promises. *Ask and it's yours*, yet you can't even control a simple cock."

"There is nothing simple about my cock or his reaction to you, *sugar cube*.

So please, a bit of understanding would go a long way."

I laugh again at the absurdity of our conversation, the sound light against the weight of everything else.

But my eyelids grow heavy, my body sinking deeper into exhaustion.

Maybe it is the gravity of my emotions.

Maybe it is my mind's way of escaping reality.

Either way, I cannot fight it.

Sleep pulls me under, and for once...

There is nothing waiting for me.

No demons.

No screaming.

No disgust.

No weight of pain pressing down on me.

Just nothing.

So, for the first time in a very, very long time...

I simply sleep.

When I come to, Hunter is still beneath me.

Somehow, during the night, I must have shifted because now I am sprawled across his chest, facing him.

I know he is already awake, even though his beautiful eyes remain closed.

He is too much of a light sleeper for me to believe otherwise.

But, as always, I pretend ignorance.

A slow, deliberate wiggle against him.

Just enough to provoke a reaction.

"Hmm... you do that and then ask me to be soft," he murmurs, his voice thick with sleep.

I smirk, shifting just slightly.

"I still don't understand how you can be such a light sleeper."

"It's my job to protect you, *sugar cube*.

I will sleep light for the rest of my days."

"I have *Alex*. He's better."

"Ouch!" He pretends to be wounded, clutching his chest dramatically.

"What did I do to deserve such cruelty first thing in the morning?"

I smile, shaking my head.

"I love you."

The words feel so small compared to everything he has done for me.

Compared to the unwavering support he has given me through the worst thing that has ever happened to me.

He opens his eyes, looking down at me, and then he smiles.

It is so beautiful, like the sky has opened, revealing something pure and peaceful, something blissful.

"I adore you, *sugar cube*."

His voice is soft but certain, full of something deeper than words can hold.

I burst out laughing at the tone he uses.

"It's not a competition, you know," I tease, my lips curving into a smirk.

Because if there is one thing I know about Hunter, he always has a joke ready to launch.

He wraps his arms and legs around me, completely cocooning me in his embrace.

His laughter shakes his body, the vibrations spilling into me as he rocks us gently.

"No, it's not a competition," he murmurs, his voice warm with amusement.

"You already know, you are my very existence."

I let him love me the way he needs to.

All kisses, all touching, all closeness.

Well, calling them hugs feels like an understatement.

Because sometimes, he squeezes me so tight, his body shivering, that I think he forgets his own strength.

"I need to tell you something," he says, once he has had his fill of feeling me up.

We need boundaries.

Yes.

Boundaries are healthy for any relationship.

"Okay..."

"Don't be mad, okay?"

I do not like the sound of that at all.

So I lift myself up, my eyes locking onto his, searching his face.

"You know how you said you never googled anything else about what happened to you after that first time?"

Well, hello, bucket of reality.

I really don't like where this is going.

"I did some research into it..."

His voice is careful, measured.

"Please don't get mad."

He did research?

My stomach drops.

"You know how I look down there?"

The words barely make it out of my mouth, my throat tight with something ugly and suffocating.

If I thought I knew what self-loathing felt like before, I was wrong.

So fucking wrong.

Because there is no feeling to describe what it's like to be on top of the most gorgeous man in the world, only to hear him say he knows how disgustingly mutilated I am.

"No!"

His response is immediate, sharp enough to halt the spiral of disgust clawing at my insides.

"I did research about female genital mutilation, the practice, the history, the impact around the world.

But I swear to anything you want, I never looked at photos.

I would never do that to you.

And if you choose to never show me, I will respect that."

His eyes hold mine, steady, unwavering.

"It's your body, Sofia.

You own it.

You can do whatever you want with it."

I blink, his words settling over me like something foreign.

I have never thought of my body as a thing I own.

I have always felt like a passenger inside it.

Because I did not choose this for myself.

And yet...

I am the one living with the consequences of other people's decisions.

"Don't get mad, okay?"

His voice is careful, but there is a weight behind it.

"So... what I discovered is horrendous, and I genuinely applaud you for not looking into it more.

Because, *sugar cube*, I know you would lose your shit."

He pauses, watching me, letting the words settle.

"This is a global problem.

It is still happening today.

Right now."

His jaw tightens, his frustration clear.

"But what surprised me, in the best way, is that there are countries that offer reparative surgery for female genital mutilation."

As his words sink in, my head falls back onto his chest.

The erratic drum of his heart pounds beneath my ear, a shiver running through him.

Could it be possible?

Could it really be possible to repair what they have done to me?

Could I truly have a normal life?

Could I one day have actual sex with Hunter?

I stay there, listening to his heartbeat, lost in my own mind for what feels like an eternity.

All the while, he just holds me, his hands tracing gentle patterns across my back.

I can see his love.

Not just feel it.

I can *see it* in everything he does.

In this silent gesture, in his unwavering strength, in his willingness to not just fight beside me, but to carry this burden with me.

He does not just stand by me.

He searches for solutions, for a way to undo what they have done.

It is a testament to a love so strong, so unbreakable, that there is no limit.

No battle too great that we could not fight together.

And if there is a way to fix what they have broken.

If there is a way to take back what was stolen from me.

Then I will take it.

With both hands, both legs, my entire being.

I will fight for a normal life with Hunter.

I lift my head, my voice steady, my decision clear.

"I want the surgery."

Chapter Thirty

Sofia

Two weeks have passed, and we are in Paris, the night before the surgery.

I feel a storm of emotions.

Excitement.

Fear.

Happiness.

Dread.

But the one thing I am absolutely certain of—without a shadow of a doubt—is that I want this.

For myself.

I want to take back what was stolen from me.

I know the scar tissue is significant.

I have seen it in the mirror, studied the damage, understood the extent of the reconstruction they will need to do.

I also know that there will still be scarring on and around my vagina, even after the surgery.

A fact I have drilled into Hunter's head, until he gave me a look of pure fury.

He got mad.

Because I insinuated that he might not like me, might not love me, might not want me.

So he got mad.

Fair.

My mum is still scared of us.

Of me.

And I understand why.

If you have spent your entire life fearing men, and then you see someone like me, someone who would throw a knife at my own partner just to shut him up, then yes, I understand.

I would be shocked too.

But she has started opening up more.

She has told me about my dad and how he passed away.

She has shared more about our culture and the beauty of our country.

And then she told me something else.

The night before my mutilation, she tried to convince my dad to only cut me partially.

He became so angry that he beat her like an animal.

Her exact words were, "*He punched me from the top of my head to the heels of my feet, to get all the bad out of me. No daughter of his would ever not be pure for her husband.*"

I wanted to throw up right then and there.

What is even worse is that I have ten sisters somewhere out there in the world.

From all the wives my dad had over the years.

Then came the final blow.

She told me how she bribed the old woman who cut me to leave some parts untouched.

I could not listen to another word.

I excused myself and threw up.

Because how could this be reality?

How could a mother be forced to bribe someone just to lessen her child's suffering?

I am lost in my thoughts once more, reliving my mum's words, so disconnected from reality that I do not even hear Hunter enter the bedroom.

My senses have changed since being with him every day.

I know I can trust him blindly.

And I have to admit it, well, I really do not want to, and I never will say it out loud, but he is more of a killing machine than me.

He has lived and breathed combat his entire life.

His instincts are sharper, his senses more refined.

I will never say it out loud, but I know he has noticed me lowering my guard around him.

It does not matter.

I will still not admit it.

"Nervous, *sugar cube*?"

He kneels in front of me, resting his hands gently on my knees.

"There is a lot going on," I admit, my voice quieter than I expected.

"I did not think things would move this fast... I did not expect to be having surgery tomorrow."

"How can I make it better for you, *sugar cube*? Ask me anything."

The eternal question with him.

And every time he asks it, a part of me melts under the weight of his love.

As always, I do not have an answer.

I lean in and press a kiss to his forehead, lingering for a moment, breathing him in.

Bergamot. Musk. *Him.*

His scent wraps around me like a personal blanket of comfort, grounding me in everything that is safe and familiar.

"Come," I finally say, rising to my feet.

"Let's go to bed. Tomorrow is a big day."

Chapter Thirty-One

Hunter

I am freaking out.

Actually, scratch that.

I am not freaking out.

I am coming apart at the seams with fear for Sofia.

What if she does not wake up after the surgery?

What if she wakes up in pain?

What if she wakes up and realises she can do so much better than me?

What if the surgery is not successful?

What if it is successful and she leaves me?

What if she leaves me?

The thoughts swarm my mind, dark and relentless, tearing through me with so much viciousness and power that saying I have a headache and feel lightheaded would be the understatement of the year.

The surgeon explained every step of the procedure in detail, making sure to protect Sofia's privacy as much as possible.

To be honest, I was shocked she even let me into the appointment sessions with her.

But the moment she did, I jumped on the chance, knowing full well she might change her mind and kick me out.

I am sitting in an office they have transformed into a waiting area for us.

And by us, of course, I mean Elijah, Buddy, and myself.

Well, and two guards, but they do not really count.

Both Elijah and Buddy are working away on their laptops, their focus unshaken, as if nothing life-altering is happening right now.

I am so on edge, I cannot sit still.

The fear is crawling under my skin, relentless and suffocating.

I pace up and down, my body wound tight, moving like a caged animal.

"Do you mind?"

Elijah's commanding tone cuts through my tormenting thoughts.

Rudely, may I add.

"You look a bit weak, pacing up and down."

"I'm scared," I finally admit out loud.

Like hell am I going to confess that I am terrified she will wise up and leave me.

But that is neither here nor there.

"I really love her."

"Yes, we are aware of that," Buddy adds, throwing in his two cents.

"There is nothing to be scared about.

The surgeon will do a good job.

I already spoke with him, and he knows I have his family.

When Sofia's surgery is successful, he gets his family back along with ten million.

If the surgery is unsuccessful, they all die, and he gets to watch it happen.

He agreed very fast."

Oh! I wonder why he accepted so fast? Delightful!

There you have it—Elijah at his finest, threatening people with a scalpel in hand.

"Well, that was not very diplomatic," I say, my tone laced with teasing amusement.

"Diplomatic?" Elijah scoffs.

"You should be grateful if I do not execute you as well if something happens to my daughter."

Ouch.

I feel like I should throw out another joke, but the look on his face mirrors my own feelings.

I think he is scared too.

He just hides it better.

After all, he has looked after Sofia her entire life.

Four excruciating hours later, the surgeon finally walks in.

He is sweaty, shaken, and heads straight for Elijah, completely ignoring me as if I do not even exist.

"Mr. Dominion, the surgery was one hundred percent successful.

We were able to remove the scar tissue necessary for her to have..."

"I will stop you right there," Elijah cuts in, his tone firm and final.

"That is my little girl you worked on, and as much as I appreciate your efforts, I do not need all the granular details.

You can keep those for Sofia and him."

He jerks his chin in my direction, pointing at me like I am some intruder in my own story.

Great.

"I understand. I apologise for the misunderstanding, Mr. Dominion."

The surgeon stands there, waiting patiently, like an obedient child before a disapproving parent.

Elijah does not even acknowledge him.

He is already on his phone, his focus elsewhere, while the man in front of him fidgets under the weight of his silence.

It looks almost funny.

I make a mental note to joke about it to Sofia later.

Then Elijah speaks.

"Your family has just been returned to your house, and the money is already in your bank account.

If there are complications, you will not be warned.

You will all be executed."

His voice is calm.

Flat.

Chilling.

The words alone are terrifying, but the way he delivers them—measured, deliberate, absolute— that is what makes him truly terrifying.

The guy bolts from the room so fast that this time, I actually laugh out loud.

"It's funny," I say, my amusement still lingering as everyone turns to look at me in wonder.

Another note for later—make my *sugar cube* laugh with this one as well.

"But the idiot did not even say if we can see her," I add as the laughter fades.

"We can see her," Elijah responds, his voice as flat and deadpan as ever.

"But I think you need to stay with her until she wakes up."

He does not need to tell me twice.

I make my way down the corridor, stopping a passing nurse to ask where I can find Sofia.

She leads us to the recovery room, where patients wake from anaesthesia.

The moment my eyes land on Sofia, something inside me breaks.

For the first time since I have known her, she looks completely tamed.

And for the first time, I catch a glimpse of what Elijah sees.

That small, quiet girl, stripped of her fire, of her fight.

Seeing her like this unravels something deep inside me, something raw and aching, as if a part of me is breaking open just to hold the weight of her fragility in this moment.

One thing I know with certainty, I would do anything for her.

Elijah steps around me, leans down, and presses a kiss to her forehead.

I stare, completely caught off guard.

I never would have thought he was capable of such affection, not after everything Sofia has told me about him.

I glance at Buddy, and for once, his reaction is easy to read.

He is just as shocked as I am.

But, as always, he masks it quickly, slipping back behind that unreadable expression.

Elijah straightens, says nothing, and walks away.

No explanation.

No lingering moment.

No acknowledgment of what just happened.

And just like that, I know, whatever that was, whatever brief glimpse of humanity he just allowed us to see, it is over.

I take a seat in the chair beside Sofia's bed and gently take her hand in mine, absorbing the warmth of her skin.

She feels so small.

So soft.

So fragile.

It is a side of her I have never known, and it does something to me.

Part of me is in awe of her.

Part of me likes it.

But part of me breaks to see a woman like Sofia tamed.

I only know Sofia as *Sofia*.

The woman who can dismantle you with a look or piece you back together with a smile.

But this version of her?

This quiet, weakened version?

It is soul-shattering.

This is not who she is.

Seeing her reduced to this feels like a crime against her strength.

I lean my head against her abdomen, listening to the rise and fall of her breath, and the realisation hits me like a punch to the gut.

I don't like it.

It is breaking me inside to see her like this.

Even in her sleep, her movements are sharp, as if she is still ready to fight.

She thinks I am a light sleeper, and I am.

But the way she moves in her sleep?

An elephant might be more graceful.

In all fairness, I will never tell her that.

I value my life, and some truths are just not worth dying over.

Fifteen minutes pass before she begins to wake, and the moment her clouded eyes meet mine, something inside me shifts.

The look on her face reaches into the deepest part of my soul and claims it as her own.

I could have never imagined Sofia looking like this.

But what hits me even harder is the way she needs me here.

The relief in her eyes, the silent gratitude that I am by her side.

It is written all over her face.

"How are you feeling, *sugar cube*?"

I pepper her face with kisses, unable to help myself.

A giggle comes from the nurse fumbling with the equipment.

Well, I get it.

She has probably never seen a man like me.

Big, covered in tattoos, and scary as fuck.

Speaking so gently, kissing someone like they are my entire world.

Yes, I see the irony.

But she can fuck right off if she thinks I care.

And if she does not want a bullet in her head, she better wipe that smirk off her face.

I make that abundantly clear with the glare I send her way.

She is the one intruding on my moment, and she better get the fuck out.

"Stop glaring at people, you idiot," Sofia murmurs, her voice weak.

My gaze snaps back to her.

"Baby, are you okay?"

Her soft tone catches me off guard, and for a moment, panic floods through me at full speed.

"I'm okay," she reassures me, blinking slowly.

"Just really drowsy."

I take her hand and place it over my chest, letting her feel the erratic rhythm of my heart.

Beating for her.

The moment she registers it, a soft smile tugs at her lips.

And just like that...

All is right in the world.

Because Sofia smiled.

Two weeks later, we are back in the surgeon's office for Sofia's check-up.

He examines her progress, checks for infections or discomfort, and the entire time, the man is sweating like a pig.

It is absolutely hilarious.

And when he nervously asks about Elijah, I burst out laughing.

Damn!

I completely forgot to make my joke to Sofia about how her dad scared the living shit out of the poor bastard.

"Miss Dominion, as I see it, the surgery has been a success.

The clitoris has been fully reconstructed, restored to its full function and sensitivity.

Over time, that sensitivity will only improve, so be patient with it.

The labia suffered significant damage, but we have corrected as much as possible by removing scar tissue and performing reconstructive surgery.

Your vagina itself was not affected, with the exception of the hymen not being present.

My assumption, based on the scarring around the area and your groin, is that during the struggle, the hymen was torn.

Unfortunately, this is quite common for FGM survivors.

And for that, I offer you my sincere regrets.

The..."

"It's not FGM, doctor!"

Sofia's voice explodes at full volume, shattering the tension in the room.

"Call it what it is!

It is female genital mutilation!

You just performed surgery on me to correct such mutilation, so fucking call it what it is!"

The pure fear on the surgeon's face says it all.

Like father, like daughter.

He probably never expected to see this kind of fire in her.

But it is there, burning bright.

Unapologetic. Unbreakable.

I take her hand in mine and caress the back of it, not saying a word, but offering whatever support and comfort I can in this moment.

She doesn't need me to fight her battles, but she sure as hell knows that I will be here to support her whenever she calls on me.

"My sincere apologies, Miss Dominion," the doctor says quickly, recovering fast.

"I meant no disrespect."

He is not at fault.

Most women who have endured what Sofia has are so broken by their past, they can barely speak up, if they ever do at all.

For him to be standing face to face with a warrior, at the receiving end of her fury, of course, it would be confronting.

"I need to see you again in three weeks to monitor your progress," the doctor continues.

"As for sexual intercourse, you should wait at least six to eight weeks before resuming any activity. This will allow for proper healing and minimise the risk of complications."

The moment I feel Sofia's fingers tighten around mine, I know, she is just as nervous about this as I am.

She has never shown herself to me.

Not once.

I never asked, never pushed, because her scars are hers to bear, and I have no right to them.

But knowing my *sugar cube*, she is probably crushed all over again, realising that even her virginity was taken from her back then.

It sucks.

I get it.

But to me, it makes no difference.

I inhale deeply, drawing in the very air she exhales, as if my existence depends on it—*on her.* On the breath that leaves her lips, the space she occupies, the life she gives me just by being.

Hymen or no hymen.

Sex or no sex.

It is still her that I want.

With every fibre of my being.

Her! In all her might.

Chapter Thirty-Two

Sofia – four months later

I am fucking livid.

Hunter is holding back, and I have had enough of it.

It has been over a month since we could have actual sex—not just rub-a-dub-dub—and he is still holding back.

I will fuck him up!

"Hey, fucker!"

I slam a punch square into his chest, putting everything I have into it.

"What the fuck is your problem?"

He staggers back, caught completely off guard.

Good!

If he thinks I am going to beg him for it, he has another thing coming.

I do not beg.

Ever.

The very idea of it is ridiculous, degrading, small.

And if he thinks for even a second that this is some power play, then it is fucking on.

Enough is enough!

"What?!" he calls out, rubbing the spot where my fist landed.

"What did I do?"

I glare at him.

Is he for real?

What the fuck is going on?

Or...

Is this one of those things?

One of those moments where now that he knows everything, knows all the disturbing, horrific things that happened to me, he doesn't want me anymore?

The thought hits like a blade to the chest.

I run through the past few months, every moment, every touch, every whisper.

He has been nothing but sweet, nothing but supportive.

So why the hell is he holding back now?

I am so confused, so fucking lost, and the uncertainty is twisting something ugly inside me.

I size him up, my glare sharp enough to cut.

Then, I bite the bullet and ask the question that has been burning a hole in my chest.

"Why haven't you tried to have sex with me?"

The words hit harder than my punch.

Hunter drops back against the couch, his broad frame sinking into it like the weight of my question just knocked the air out of him.

His gaze falls to the floor, avoiding mine.

"Oh, *sugar cube*," he says, his voice small, almost defeated.

"I'm scared."

A bitter laugh escapes him, but there is no humour in it.

"Actually, scared is an understatement."

He pauses, like the words are too big, too heavy to say out loud.

"I am fucking petrified that I might hurt you."

His voice trembles at the end, a sound I have never heard from him before.

And just like that, my heart breaks.

"Why are you scared?" I ask, my voice small but steady.

"Is it the scars?"

"NO!"

His response is instant, almost desperate, and before I can blink, he launches off the couch.

In a single step, he is in front of me, his strong arms wrapping around me, holding me like he's afraid I might disappear.

"Absolutely not!"

His voice is fierce, raw with conviction.

"Don't ever say something like that to me."

He grips me tighter, his breath ragged, his body shaking with emotion.

"Scars or no scars..."

His lips press to my temple, my cheek, my jaw.

"I live for you, *sugar cube*."

A full-body shiver runs through him, and I can feel the depth of his love, his fear, his everything in the way he holds me.

"I'm scared I might hurt you in some way."

His voice is low, thick with hesitation.

"That I'll touch you the wrong way, do something wrong."

He exhales sharply, his grip on me tightening as if the very thought is too much.

"Not to mention, I am not a small guy, and I know it will hurt the first few times when my cock sinks into you."

His voice breaks, his forehead pressing against mine.

"And that terrifies me. I am so scared that it might actually hurt you, that after everything you've been through, I could add to that pain. I don't want the surgery or your progress to go backwards. Because of me."

He cups my face, his thumb brushing over my cheek so softly, as if I am the most fragile thing in the world.

"So yes, I am petrified, *sugar cube*."

His lips barely ghost over mine, his breath warm and unsteady.

"I am giving you all the time in the world to heal. I need you to understand that. I adore you."

His voice is thick with emotion, the weight of his love pressing into my bones.

"My body adores you. And there is nothing I want more than to be inside you, to make you mine in every way."

He pulls back just enough for our eyes to meet, his gaze achingly raw.

"I'm just... scared."

He buries his face in the crook of my neck, his breath warm and unsteady against my skin.

The way he holds me, the shudder that runs through him, the unspoken storm in his mind.

It is beyond anything I could have imagined.

For weeks, a small, ugly voice in the back of my head whispered that maybe, just maybe, he was disgusted by what he had learned.

That knowing the full truth about me had changed something in him.

But here he is, his entire body trembling, his mind spiraling, not because he sees me differently.

But because he is terrified of hurting me in any way.

"We are all good, *Nuuro*," I murmur, pressing a soft kiss to his shoulder.

"I've... checked down there, and I'm sure I'm ready to have sex. Plus, the surgeon..."

Hunter pulls back, his face suddenly lighting up with pure mischief.

"You touchy-touchy down there?"

His laughter erupts, deep and full of warmth, and I can feel the tension in the air finally crack and break.

"Hey! Hey! My pussy, my rights! Understood?" I declare, my mock-serious glare melting into laughter.

Hunter smirks, mischief dancing in his eyes.

"Well, by the looks of it... I might be claiming her soon. And then—she'll be my pussy, my rights."

I gasp, playing along, my lips curving into a smirk.

"Okay, I'm open to negotiations," I say, my voice dripping with mock professionalism. "Co-ownership. Final offer."

"I'll take it!"

His answer is instant, his mouth crashing into mine before I can react.

A kiss that is possessive, demanding, intoxicating.

Sealing the deal.

Just like every other time he has kissed me, claimed me, Hunter makes it clear, every part of me belongs to him.

And to be honest?

I love it.

The way he loves me, the way he takes me as his own.

For him, I would give it all.

I jump, wrapping my legs around him, my body pressing flush against his as I grind against him.

A low, guttural groan rumbles from his chest, his hands gripping me tighter as if he's barely holding on.

"*Sugar cube...*" His voice is strained, almost pleading. "Please, have mercy on me. I want to do this right by you."

I narrow my eyes, studying him with suspicion.

He bursts out laughing, his entire body shaking beneath me.

The clown.

"Don't look at me like that." His voice is soft, but there's an edge of conviction beneath it.

"It's your first time, *sugar cube.* I want to make it special."

The tenderness in his ocean-blue eyes melts something deep inside me.

Because this—this moment, this night, this first time—means something to him.

To both of us.

"Okay," I finally say, exhaling as I jump off him.

"What do you have in mind?"

A slow, devilish smirk tugs at his lips.

"Tomorrow, I'll cook, set everything up, make it perfect for you."

"Today."

My answer is short, sharp, absolute.

"Tomorrow. I have a lot to prepare," he says, exasperated, like he's holding onto his last thread of control.

"Today." I repeat, my gaze locked onto his, unwavering.

What exactly does he need to prepare so much?

He exhales sharply, raking a frustrated hand through his hair.

"You know what?" He gives me a pointed look, his jaw clenching.

"You and my cock are in perfect fucking harmony right now, both demanding I give in."

A wicked smirk tugs at my lips, but before I can gloat, he throws his hands up in defeat.

"Fine! Today."

He grabs me, pulling me into a deep, possessive kiss, his lips demanding, claiming, worshipping.

The moment his mouth meets mine, it's not just a kiss—it's a promise, a surrender, a battle won and lost all at once.

Then, with zero warning, he actually turns and sprints for the door.

I blink.

...Well, this should be interesting.

Chapter Thirty-Three

Sofia

I am so restless it's not even funny.

Excited. Nervous. In love and just a little scared of what's about to happen.

I wasn't lying when I told Hunter I'd touched myself down there.

I didn't just touch, *I looked.*

I explored.

I caressed.

And for the first time in my life, I felt it. *I felt.*

Not just outside. Inside.

I can feel.

For someone like me, someone who has endured unimaginable pain, to feel anything at all... might mean nothing to other women.

But to me?

It is everything.

It is a promise—*of a normal life with Hunter.*

A promise that his touch will bring me immeasurable pleasure.

A promise that one day... maybe one day...

I could carry his child.

The thought is so overwhelming, so pure, so terrifyingly beautiful, I feel something inside me break open with happiness I never even knew was possible.

A child with Hunter.

So many women take this for granted.

Not me.

I had nothing.

Absolutely nothing.

And now...

Now I am here, standing tall, dreaming of a future with the man I adore.

The road I have walked to get to this moment has been unbearable.

But I am still standing.

And not just standing...

Thriving.

Next to a man who loves me more than existence itself.

In thirty minutes, I need to head home.

Hunter's orders.

He kicked me out hours ago—a fact I was not impressed with—but apparently, he's going to make it up to me.

His words, not mine.

So, we'll see.

When the time finally comes and the driver's text pings on my phone, a sudden wave of anxiety crashes into me so fast, I have to pause—just for a moment—to gather myself.

A deep breath.

A steadying hand on my chest.

Then, I move.

I don't say goodbye.

I don't make small talk.

I just walk, as if some invisible force is pulling me forward, a giant magnet dragging me home.

Straight to the source of my existence.

And I have no say in it.

The car ride home is a battlefield of clashing emotions, a constant push and pull between pure, unfiltered excitement and a gnawing edge of panic at the unknown.

Pain.

Pleasure.

I looked it up. Some women crave both, *need both*.

Maybe I'm one of them.

The thoughts clash, collide, and wage war inside my head, fighting for dominance until the sheer weight of them pounds against my skull, leaving me with a full-blown migraine by the time we arrive.

But the second the elevator doors slide open, the chaos evaporates.

Because Hunter is waiting for me.

And I am pulled to a stop, not by fear, not by doubt, but by something far greater.

Him.

He leans casually against the doorframe, one broad shoulder bracing against it, a mischievous smile playing at his lips like he already owns me, like he knows exactly how this night is going to end.

And maybe he does.

Because right now? I am his.

He stands tall, unshaken, dressed in sharp, tailored suit pants and a crisp business shirt, the top few buttons undone, just enough to tease at the strong, sculpted expanse of his chest.

His sleeves are rolled back, exposing his powerful forearms, the veins bulging, prominent, begging to be traced.

His hair is slicked back, the color a perfect fusion of sunlight and moonlight, gold and silver woven together in a masterpiece of its own.

But none of it, not the suit, not the body, not the raw dominance radiating off him, is what truly unravels me.

It's the adoration in his gaze.

The way he looks at me.

Like I am gold, something precious, untouchable, worshiped.

Like I am his reason for breathing.

His very existence.

I want to be strong, want to hold onto every bit of control I have left.

But a girl can only do so much.

And standing here, before this man, this force of nature, this unshakable love that grounds me.

I know.

Even if I am weak.

He will be strong for both of us.

"I adore you, woman," he murmurs, his voice rich, deep, and dripping with certainty as he pulls me into his arms.

I melt into him, still speechless, still utterly captivated by how stunningly perfect he looks, how he feels, how he exists so completely in my world.

His embrace is solid, unyielding, wrapping around me like a fortress, like a silent vow that no matter what, he will always hold me together.

The scent of bergamot, musk, and pure Hunter crashes into me, overwhelming, intoxicating a scent I would know anywhere, a scent that has become my home.

I close my eyes, breathing him in, searing this moment into my soul, commemorating it once more, knowing I will return to it again and again.

Because in his arms, in this moment...

I am safe.

I am wanted.

I am his.

"I have big plans for tonight," he murmurs, his voice laced with anticipation and certainty, his eyes never leaving mine. "And I hope you see just how much I want to make you happy."

His fingers entwine with mine, warm, steady, a silent promise in the way he holds me, guiding me, leading me into the living area.

And that's when I see it.

A feast laid out before me, a spread so thoughtful, so intentional, it takes a second for my mind to catch up with my heart.

But that's not all.

The air is thick with the delicate scent of fresh flowers, an entire garden brought to life within our space.

Lilies.

Roses.

Chrysanthemums.

And countless others, each one arranged with care, with purpose, with a love I never expected Hunter to express this way.

It's... breathtaking.

I glance at him, shocked, speechless, because who the hell knew he had this in him?

He laughs, the sound rich and teasing. "I know, right?" He winks, reading my thoughts like an open book. "You didn't think I had it in me."

He leans in, his breath warm against my temple. "But just wait," his voice drops, thick with promise, with mischief. "It gets better."

And then he really laughs, full and unapologetic, at the expression on my face.

"I— I want to take a shower," I blurt out, the words tumbling from my lips faster than I can catch them.

Shit.

Could I have phrased that a little more delicately? Probably.

The thought of Hunter pushing everything aside on the table, in a desperate need to have me, his hands on my skin, his mouth claiming every inch, sends a shiver through me. But the realisation that I haven't even showered yet yanks me from the haze of desire, twisting that anticipation into a sudden ripple of panic.

He laughs, the sound low, warm, utterly amused, shaking his head like he just read my mind and found my internal spiral hilarious.

"Not a problem at all, *sugar cube*," he teases, that signature smirk tugging at his lips.

But then he steps closer, so close that the heat of him licks at my skin, his breath brushing against my ear, sending a full-body shiver straight down my spine.

"And just so you know," his voice drops, deep, deliberate, a promise wrapped in sin, "I will be eating you instead of food one day."

A pause.

A smirk I can feel more than see.

His lips graze my jaw, just enough to tease, just enough to wreck me.

"Tonight is going to be magical."

I make my way to our room and take the world's quickest shower, my skin flushed, my thoughts tangled in everything that's about to happen.

The anticipation is thrumming through me, hot, electric, all-consuming.

And then, a wicked idea forms.

I slip into nothing but a silk robe, tying it loosely at my waist, just enough to tease, to tempt, to destroy.

And then, I walk back out.

Hunter is on the couch, sprawled out like he owns the world, like he owns me. One arm slung lazily over the backrest, the other resting on his wide-spread thighs.

Commanding.

Possessive.

Unbothered.

Except he's not.

Because the second his gaze lands on me, on the way the silk clings to my skin, on the subtle way it parts at my thigh with every step I take, his entire body locks up.

Fuck, he's hot.

I know people say their men are hot, but Hunter? He doesn't just make me burn, he turns me to ash and remakes me in his fire.

It's not just the way he looks, absurdly handsome, ridiculously perfect. It's his presence, his dominance, the sheer power radiating off him. It's the way he makes me feel, the way he sees me, claims me, owns me without a single touch.

I take my time walking toward him, letting the fabric of my robe shift, parting just enough to reveal the bare, heated skin of my inner thigh.

He lets out a low, guttural grunt.

And re-adjusts in his seat.

When I finally stop in front of him, I see it—the tightness in his jaw, the flush creeping up his neck, the strain against the fabric of his pants.

He's holding on by a thread.

Good.

I move slowly, deliberately, straddling him, pressing my naked core against him.

His body stiffens, sharpens, reacts.

Heat radiates from me, seeping into him, and the second he registers it—registers the fact that there's nothing between us—his breath hitches.

His control? Gone.

A string of filthy curses leaves his lips, his hands gripping my waist, his restraint snapping like a live wire.

"Something wrong?" I ask, tilting my head, all innocence and sin wrapped in silk.

Hunter exhales sharply, his fingers twitching against my hips. "Please tell me you have at least three pairs of knickers under this robe—triple-knotted and secured with a deadbolt."

I bite my lip, lean in, let my breath skim the shell of his ear, knowing exactly what it does to him.

"I most definitely don't."

His grip on me tightens.

"Why would I," I murmur, voice dripping with heat, "when I could grind my bare pussy on you instead?"

And then, I do exactly that.

I roll my hips, dragging myself against the hard, unrelenting length of him, and the shudder that tears through him is violent, visceral.

A curse falls from his lips dark, filthy, desperate. Something about me killing him, wrecking him, ruining him.

Rubbish.

Because I need him inside me just as much as I need air in my lungs.

I laugh, a wicked, knowing sound that has his jaw locking, his body coiled so tightly it might snap.

And then, I do it again, a slow, deliberate roll of my hips, dragging every inch of heat over him.

And for the final blow?

I bite his neck, hard.

His response?

A ragged, broken groan, his fingers digging into my skin, his control hanging by a thread.

Perfect.

"So, you're planning to kill me, *sugar cube*? That it?"

His voice is low, teasing, but there's a strain beneath it, control slipping, unraveling.

Then, in one fluid movement, he stands, lifting me effortlessly with him, his hands anchoring me in place, gripping my arse like he owns it.

Because, let's be honest, he does.

My man is most definitely an arse guy.

The number of mornings I've woken up to the soft drag of his lips, the sting of his teeth, or the slow, greedy suck of his mouth on my arse cheeks should be absurd.

But Hunter?

He's obsessed.

And honestly?

I love every second of it.

I grin up at him, my fingers threading into his hair, tugging just enough to feel him shudder.

"Just give it up and give me your cock."

Then, I burst into laughter, because I know exactly what those words just did to him.

"Well... pum pum!" he says, then bursts into laughter, shaking his head like a man on the edge.

"Oh, if I make it through tonight without losing my mind, I swear I deserve a damn medal. Because, fuck, *sugar cube*, you are making it excruciatingly hard to keep it together."

Still grinning, he sits me down in a chair, then takes the seat opposite me, like he thinks that will put some kind of distance between us.

Yeah. Not happening.

I stand immediately, move the chair closing the space between us, my body humming with power. Then, still facing him, I lift one foot and press it straight against his cock, teasing him with the slow, deliberate brush of my toes.

The way he jerks against the touch, his muscles going rigid, sends a dark thrill through me.

The robe parts along my leg, baring soft skin, long lines putting on a show just for him.

My pussy is still covered. I think.

Maybe.

Sort of.

Hunter groans, his head tipping back against the chair, hands gripping the armrests like he's holding himself together by a thread.

"Sofia. Fuck me. Seriously, woman. Goddamn!"

I just burst into laughter, my lips curling in pure delight as I place something on my tongue, the picture of calm, unbothered, and completely in control.

"What is it? Did something happen?" I murmur, my voice soft, almost innocent except for the way I press down harder against his cock, rolling my foot ever so slightly to feel the heat of him through his pants.

His entire body tenses. "Woman, please!"

His voice is wrecked. Raw. Defeated.

The sound of it, the way he groans through the words, sends a dark thrill through me, a rush of satisfaction curling in my belly.

His fingers trace slow patterns along the inside of my thighs, a barely-there touch that makes me shiver.

He doesn't avoid the scars. Doesn't flinch.

He moves over them with reverence, like they are stories written in my skin, proof of the battles I have conquered, not something grotesque to be ignored.

"You have all the power, *sugar cube*." His breath is shaky as his hands squeeze, his control slipping further. "Please, I just want to do the right thing by you."

"Then pull out your cock and get it in me."

I say it flatly, like it's just a simple fact. No hesitation, no buildup, just a demand wrapped in absolute certainty.

Then I laugh, because fuck, if younger me could hear me now.

Never in a million years did I think I would talk to a man like this. Never in a million years did I think I would feel this bold. This powerful.

Hunter groans like I've just punched the air right out of his lungs.

"Sofiaaaa." His voice breaks apart on my name, dragged out like a man in agony.

I smirk.

Good!

"How about this?" He inhales sharply, gripping the edges of the chair like his life depends on it. "I tell you what I have planned for you, and then you can decide if it's a yes or a no. I need you to know that I want to do every single thing on my list, but" he exhales roughly, shaking his head. "I'm willing to compromise right now, because my balls are about to fucking burst."

I tilt my head, pretending to consider, but I don't stop teasing him.

"Fair. Continue."

"We can have a little snack now," Hunter begins, his voice low and deliberate, "then I've set up a massage table for you in the guest room where I'm going to pamper and worship every inch of your body. After that, I have a scented bath waiting, something to relax you completely, body and mind."

He pauses, his blue eyes searching mine.

"And then, when you're soft, loose, and feeling nothing but pleasure, I'll make you mine. No tension, no resistance. I don't want it to hurt, *sugar cube*. So this is my plan to take care of you the way you deserve, to make sure your body welcomes me rather than fights me."

I take a few moments, letting his words settle over me, letting the weight of his thoughtfulness sink in.

Hunter.

Of course he would think of everything. He might joke like a fool, but when it comes to loving me, he's in a league of his own.

And I...

I am torn.

Do I climb onto his lap right now, push him down, and take what I want? Do I let the heat, the longing, the craving for him inside me finally win?

Or do I let him lead?

Because fuck, this man...

This man has thought of everything. Every detail, every touch, every breath, designed to make me feel safe and worshipped and desired all at once.

I can feel it.

He wants me aching for him. He wants me melting, desperate, needing. He wants my body so open and relaxed that when he finally takes me, it's not just sex.

It's a moment in time.

And even though the hunger inside me is screaming for more.

I trust him.

"Fine," I say, reluctant but intrigued, "but you have to lose the pants and open the shirt up. At the very least, I need something yummy for my eyes."

Hunter exhales, shaking his head like I've just put him through hell, but he grins anyway.

"Fair."

He stands, unbuttoning his shirt slowly, teasing me with every inch of golden skin revealed. The hard planes of his chest, the sculpted ridges of his abs, the sheer power in every carved muscle.

Something primal inside me claws to the surface.

Then, he pops open the clasp of his suit pants.

And the moment his thick, hard cock springs free, straining through his boxers, my mouth waters.

Like, actually waters.

I let my gaze drag over him, taking in every magnificent inch.

"*Sugar cube*," he groans, his voice so raw it's practically sinful. "You cannot look at me like that or I might come in my boxers like a fucking teenager. Come on, *sugar cube,* have some mercy."

Mercy?

I say nothing.

Instead, I part my lips and drag my tongue slowly along the curve of my bottom lip, wetting it with deliberate, unhurried strokes.

His breath catches.

The muscles in his jaw tighten.

And then...

"Fuuuuuuuuuuuuuuuuuuuuuck, *sugar cube*! Please have mercy!"

The roar that rips through him shakes the fucking room.

"I'm full," I say, standing abruptly, dismissing the food without a second thought. Even if he cooked it, which, judging by the effort, he probably did, I can't sit here another second.

Not when my body is humming, my skin prickling with anticipation, my mind already ten steps ahead to what comes next.

Hunter doesn't argue.

Instead, he stands with me, placing a hand on the small of my back, his touch warm, grounding, yet electric all at once. He leads me down the hall, his movements unhurried, controlled. But I can feel the tension rolling off him in waves, the restraint in every step he takes.

The moment the guest room door swings open, I stop breathing.

Chapter Thirty-Four

Sofia

It doesn't look like a guest room anymore.

The soft glow of dimmed lights bathes the space in warmth, the air thick with the scent of expensive florals, something delicate yet intoxicating. A cabinet lined with sleek bottles catches my eye oils, lotions, things meant to be poured, smoothed, worshipped into skin.

And in the center of it all, where a bed once stood, there's a massage table. Luxurious, plush, inviting.

Oh, fuck!

I blink, my pulse thrumming beneath my skin, and glance over my shoulder at Hunter.

He's waiting just behind me, hope woven into every line of his face. He doesn't say anything just watches, just waits, like my reaction is the only thing in the world that matters.

I let a smile curl at my lips.

"It's beautiful."

Two words.

The only ones I can manage.

His exhale is barely audible, but then he's stepping closer, pressing his lips to my shoulder in a kiss so soft, so reverent, it steals the very breath from my lungs.

"I didn't know which massage oil to buy, so I bought forty. Please pick one you like," he finally says.

I stare at the rows of carefully chosen bottles, my vision blurring for just a moment, not from the sheer selection, but from what it means.

He bought forty massage oils. For me.

I had nothing as a child. Then I had everything. But in my entire life, no gift has touched me quite like this one. It's not the oils themselves, it's the thought behind them. The love. The care.

I know, with absolute certainty, *I'm going to be fine*. No matter what, no matter where life takes me. Because I have Hunter now.

I reach for a bottle, honestly not even registering the scent, because my entire being, body, soul, heart is singing with the sheer happiness of this moment.

Then, I move toward the massage table, turn, and let my robe slip from my shoulders.

It pools at my feet in a whisper of silk, leaving me bare, completely open to him.

It's the first time he's seen me fully naked.

And for the first time in my life, I am happy to be seen.

Because it's not just anyone looking at me.

It's him.

The man who loves me more than existence itself.

Hunter leans against the cabinet for support, his fingers gripping the edge like he physically needs to brace himself. His gaze travels over my body in slow, reverent motion, taking me in the same way I once did to him.

Like I am something to be treasured.

Like I am his.

His throat works as he swallows, his voice rough and thick with emotion.

"Sofia... goddamn."

His breath catches. His chest rises and falls too fast.

"You are so beautiful, *sugar cube*. My chest—fuck—my chest seriously hurts looking at you like this. I might have a fucking heart attack."

I smile...

"Hold your horses, big boy. First, fucking then you can have your heart attack," I tease, climbing onto the table with what I hope is sultry grace.

But as I shift, I feel it.

The unmistakable wobble of my ass.

Oh, for fuck's sake. So much for being seductive.

"Fuuuuuuuuck. Fucking—fuck! I just got my first view of your arse wobble."

I snap my gaze to him just in time to see both hands flying to the cabinet for support.

His head shakes, his breath ragged, as if he's physically trying to recover from something life-altering.

I freeze for a beat, watching him, trying to process. Is he actually struggling to breathe right now?!

A slow, satisfied grin stretches across my lips.

I've seen men break. I've broken men. Physically. Intellectually. Emotionally.

But this? This is different.

I never imagined I could do this to a man.

I never imagined that the simple, unapologetic movement of my body could make someone, a mountain of a man, a fucking warrior like Hunter, come undone.

And yet, here he is.

Clutching the cabinet like the world just shifted beneath his feet.

His face is twisted in something that is half agony, half worship.

"Are you okay?" I ask, mock innocence dripping from my tone.

"No. No, I am fucking not." His voice is raw, wrecked. His gaze flicks to me, blown wide with hunger. "*Sugar cube*, you have no fucking clue what you just did to me."

"Hey! Hey! Stop slacking off and get to work," I tease, my voice thick with mischief. "You promised me a massage."

Hunter groans, running a hand through his already disheveled hair. His entire body looks wound tight, coiled, ready to snap.

"Sofia, I'm being honest. I might not be able to do this. I am fucking dying over here."

And he means it. The pleading in his stormy blue eyes is as raw as I've ever seen it.

I could be merciful.

But where's the fun in that?

I tilt my head, tapping a finger against my lips like I'm deep in thought.

"How about this?" I say, biting back a smirk. "Lose the shirt. And the boxers. Give yourself a little... breathing room."

His throat bobs as he swallows hard.

I can practically see his internal battle, his self-control hanging by a thread.

Truth be told? I just want to see him.

See his cock.

I laugh quietly to myself at the thought.

We've played every single day in one way or another. But each time I see him, something primal in me stirs, deep and uncontrollable, this fire at my core that burns hotter than I ever imagined possible.

Hunter exhales sharply, his hands balling into fists like he's wrestling with something brutal. His entire body is a masterpiece of restraint and ruin.

"Sofia," he warns, his voice guttural.

I grin, deliberately stretching out on the table, baring myself further to him. "You're the one who said I should be relaxed, baby. And I think this might just be the perfect start."

The muscle in his jaw jumps.

He doesn't hesitate.

Not for a second.

His hands move to his waistband, and in one fluid motion, he strips away the last barrier between us.

And fuck.

The moment his cock is freed, I understand—truly understand—why he's been holding back.

He is so hard it looks almost painful, his cock thick, veins pulsing, standing in rigid defiance. His balls are drawn tight, full, aching, his entire body wound like a live wire, ready to snap.

And it hits me then, this isn't just lust.

This is Hunter holding himself back for me.

For us.

I swallow, my gaze tracing over him like he's something sacred. Because to me, he is.

"You are so beautiful, *Nuuro*."

My voice is soft but sure, filled with love so deep it feels like a vow.

"It's okay. You'll be okay."

His breath is uneven, ragged, his entire body coiled so tightly I can feel the tension vibrating off him in waves.

I reach for him, offering not just my body, but everything... my trust, my surrender, my love.

"Come give me what you wanted to give me."

The words break something in him.

He takes several deep, audible breaths, chest rising and falling in an attempt to steady himself. But I know, he's fighting a losing battle.

Then, finally, he touches me.

His hands are large, strong, yet impossibly gentle as they move over my skin.

A featherlight stroke at first tracing the curve of my shoulders, down my arms, brushing over my wrists.

But then, his fingers press, knead, claim.

His palms slide down my back in long, slow strokes, the heat of his touch sinking into my bones, unraveling every last thread of tension in my body.

And then...

The pleasure is instant, blinding.

A moan rips from my throat, loud, uninhibited, raw.

I surprise even myself with the depth of it, with how much I feel.

Hunter groans in response, his grip tightening, his body pressing closer as if he needs to feel me just as much as I need to feel him.

This isn't just touch.

This is worship.

This is love, overwhelming and all-consuming.

And I know, without a doubt, *I am his.*

"Good?"

His voice is low, rough, a whisper of desire that sends a shiver straight down my spine.

"By the way, I hope it's good," he murmurs, his tone teasing but laced with something darker, something raw.

"I'm not really sure what I'm doing here, but I do know one thing. I want to explore every inch of you before you come to your senses."

My lips part, but the only sound that escapes is a soft, muffled sigh, because his hands are on me, and fuck, *his touch is divine.*

His fingers glide, press, claim tracing the curves of my body like they were made to worship me.

"Explore away," I finally manage, my voice breathless, needy, wrecked.

He moves deliberately, purposefully avoiding my arse, and I know it's on purpose. I know that touching me there would push him over the edge, and for once, I don't tease him for it.

Instead, I surrender to the slow, deliberate way he explores me.

His hands glide over my legs, starting at my feet, taking his time, pressing deep into every muscle. He massages each toe with such exquisite care that I feel my body soften under his touch, melt into his hands.

This is... incredible.

Nothing I've ever felt before even comes close to this, the way his hands worship my skin, the way my body responds to his every touch, the slow-burning anticipation curling low in my stomach.

As he moves higher, closer, teasing the insides of my thighs, something inside me shifts.

A quiet thrill of anticipation runs through me sharp, electric, delicious.

And as if my body knows exactly what it wants, my legs part for him, opening without thought, without hesitation.

For the first time, he sees me, *truly sees me.*

I thought I would be scared.

I thought I would feel exposed.

But I don't.

The only thing I feel is love. Desire. Absolute trust.

I want this.

I want him.

His breath catches, his fingers flex, and when he finally speaks, his voice is shaking, rough with emotion.

"Are you sure?"

I meet his gaze, and in his eyes, I see everything.

The depth of what this moment means for both of us. The restraint. The reverence. The love.

I push myself further up, turning my head just enough to glance over my shoulder. The way he looks at me steals the breath from my lungs.

His gaze is heavy, ravenous, mesmerised locked onto the most intimate part of me, as if he's just been transported into a world of pure, unfiltered pleasure.

I swallow hard, my heartbeat hammering against my ribs.

"I am yours, *Nuuro*. All of me."

His breath shudders. His fingers, steady yet reverent, trace the softest, most delicate path over my core. The moment his touch brushes against me, a sharp gasp rips from my throat.

The sensation is too much.

Too new.

Too intoxicating.

Too perfect.

I didn't know my body could feel this way.

I didn't know it was possible for one touch to unravel me completely.

But I do now.

A slow, insistent heat builds deep inside me, liquid and molten, spreading outward until every nerve in my body is attuned to him—his hands, his breath, his presence.

And then it happens.

I feel it. I feel myself growing wet for him.

I feel the ache, the burning, the desperate need coiling in my core, demanding more.

A low, desperate moan spills from my lips, impossible to hold back.

"You are so beautiful, Sofia."

Hunter's voice is so deep, so raw, it's almost unrecognisable. A tremor runs through him as his fingers trail over my skin, his touch both reverent and possessive.

"I love you so fucking much," he murmurs, his breath ragged. "I need to move now because I can't touch you like this and still control myself."

Before I can respond, he shifts, moving in front of me, his hands sliding into my hair as he begins to massage my scalp. The sensation is blissful, intoxicating, but it's not the only thing I can focus on.

Because now, his cock is right there.

So close to my mouth.

And the need to taste him? It's like a core, primal hunger like the need for air, for survival.

The woman I was before? She would have never wanted this.

She once hated all men.

She once built her entire existence on outsmarting them, overpowering them... fearing them.

But Hunter? He is not just a man.

He is the other part of me.

The part that was once shattered, broken now glued back together, thread by thread, by him.

With him, I am whole.

With him, I want to experience everything.

I want to give everything.

I want to take everything.

I shift slightly, lifting myself just enough for him to feel it, and he lets me.

His cock is so close now, inches away, heavy and throbbing with restraint.

I lean forward, slow and deliberate, my lips barely parting as I flick my tongue out tracing the tip of his cock, tasting him.

Right there.

The spot I know drives him insane.

"Fuuuuuuuuuuuuuck!"

His entire body jerks, his head snapping back, his fingers digging into his thighs like he's trying to ground himself. The sound that rips from his throat is somewhere between a growl and a plea.

He pulls back, eyes wild, dark, disbelieving.

"Baby," his voice is wrecked. "Are you sure?"

I don't answer, just smile, slow, knowing.

His chest heaves, his fingers flex.

"I'm being serious, *sugar cube*," he murmurs, his voice raw with both devotion and desperation. "You don't have to do this. I'm already losing control of my reality around you. Trust me, I don't need more teasing."

I tilt my head, widen my smile, then nod again.

And just like that, something inside him snaps.

"I want it all with you, Hunter," I say, my voice steady, soft, but full of certainty.

His chest rises sharply, a deep, audible inhale pulling into him like he's trying to hold onto something, something already slipping.

"Come to me," I whisper, watching the way his pupils dilate. "Let me play with you, *Nuuro*."

He steps closer, and now he's right in front of me, bare, vulnerable, entirely mine.

I start slow, tracing my tongue around the crown of his cock, teasing him, tasting him. The deep groan that rumbles from his chest is so guttural, so raw, that for a moment, I wonder if I've hurt him.

But then I glance up.

And he's gone.

Completely lost in the sight of me, wrapped around his cock, claiming him.

I smile against his skin and trail my lips down his length, exploring him, memorising him. The feel of him beneath my tongue, the heat, the ridges, the way his veins pulse, *it's intoxicating.*

By the time I reach his balls, his hands are fists at his sides, his breathing uneven, his body shaking with restraint.

I lick, suck, explore, every reaction from him a revelation, every curse and groan a reward. Because of me, he's unraveling.

Because of me, he's losing control.

I make my way back up, slowly, torturously, until I take him into my mouth, sucking him deep, swirling my tongue around him.

The shiver I love so much runs through him again, his entire body tensing, surrendering. He leans back just enough, giving me the space, the power, the control.

And I take it!

I let instinct take over, bobbing my head, hollowing my cheeks, taking him in with slow, deep sucks, the way I know he needs.

I thought I might not enjoy this.

But I was so fucking wrong.

I am loving this!

I love that I'm the one making him come undone.

That I'm the reason he's trembling, breathless, broken in the best way.

I am doing this to him.

"Fuuuuck! Baby! Baby!" he groans, his voice raw, urgent. He pulls back quickly, chest heaving, hands gripping his thighs like he's barely holding himself together. "Oh, that was incredible, but we need to stop. I'm seconds away from coming, and I need to stop."

The sincerity in his voice is undeniable, his restraint admirable, and I know I need to follow his lead. I give him a small, knowing smile, still tasting the salt of him on my lips.

His gaze flickers with something darker, something deeper. "Do you think, perhaps, I can taste you?" His voice is softer now, almost hesitant, but the intensity in his eyes—pleading, desperate—is anything but.

"I already told you, *Nuuro*." My voice is soft. "I want it all with you."

He starts bouncing on his feet, excitement radiating off him like a live wire. His cock sways wildly with the movement, and I burst into uncontrollable laughter.

"You really are a clown, you know that, right?" I manage between giggles.

"I don't care! I don't care!" he fires back instantly, eyes gleaming with pure, unfiltered joy. "I'm about to taste you. Fuck, I'm so happy!"

I keep laughing, because honestly I never expected this. But here we are, and here he is, positioning himself between my legs from behind.

The first thing he does is take a long, deliberate inhale, drinking me in like I'm the only thing in existence. Then, a deep, guttural groan rumbles from his chest—pure, primal, unrestrained.

And that's when it truly hits me.

When all the fights have been fought and the scars are healing, when every last piece of armor has been stripped away, this is what remains. Not fear. Not hesitation. Not pain. Just this—a raw, instinctive, all-consuming need for each other.

Because just as I couldn't hold myself back from tasting him, he's right there behind me, burying himself in my scent like a man starved. Like I'm his first breath of air after drowning. Like I'm the only thing that has ever mattered.

"You smell mouthwatering, *sugar cube*," he rasps, his voice vibrating straight through me, raw and possessive.

Before I can even take a breath, his lips make contact with my core, and—holy fuck—it's like being struck by lightning, in the best possible way. My body jolts, a sharp gasp escaping me, but he doesn't move away.

He lingers, breathing me in like I'm the very air he needs to survive. The moment stretches, tightens, coils deep inside me like a tether about to snap—and then it's on.

The first slow, deliberate drag of his tongue starts at the very heart of me, a featherlight tease, before he licks up, up, up—one long, torturously slow stroke, tracing all the way to the small of my back.

Reality ceases to exist.

I understand now.

I understand what he meant when he said he completely loses himself when he's with me.

Because in this moment, I do too.

"Oh my! Hunter! Fuck!"

He freezes.

Then, like a man possessed, he yanks himself away, bolting upright so fast it's disorienting.

For a second, I blink in confusion, stunned by the sudden loss of contact, by the fact that I can now actually see his face.

And then I register the sheer panic in his eyes.

"Fuck, baby, did I hurt you?!" His voice is wild, frantic, wrecked as if the very thought of causing me pain has physically shattered him.

I stare at him for half a second, then burst into uncontrollable laughter.

"What? No!" I manage between breaths, still gasping from the pleasure and the absurdity of this man. "Get back down there, that felt amazing!"

Hunter exhales so hard it's almost a growl, then shoves a frustrated hand through his hair.

"Fucking hell, woman! You scared the shit out of me!"

"More playing, less complaining," I tease, laughter spilling from my lips.

Hunter narrows his eyes. "Okay, that's it!"

Before I can even register what's happening, I'm on my back, the massage table shifting slightly as he positions me exactly how he wants.

With zero hesitation, he reaches over, grabs a cushion, and tucks it behind my head.

"There." His voice is pure dominance, rough and full of intent. "Now I can see your reaction as I eat you out. And you? You can't give me a fucking heart attack this time."

I burst into another fit of laughter, because—holy fuck—he's dead serious.

Even his cock, always raging hard, has started to soften slightly.

And that? That alone tells me exactly how much I just scared him.

"Baby," I whisper, pulling him to me. "Stop being scared. I'm fine. The doctor told us I'm fine. I'm ready. I want this."

I press my lips to his, intending to reassure him, but the moment our mouths meet, a shock of awareness runs through me.

I taste something different.

It takes me a second to realise, I'm tasting myself on his lips.

Oh, fuck!

Something primal awakens inside me, heat coiling deep and low, twisting into something filthy, something raw.

I moan into the kiss, my tongue sweeping into his mouth, savoring the evidence of what he just did to me.

It's our first time sharing my taste on his lips.

It's intimate. It's electric.

And I fucking love it.

When we pull apart, he smiles down at me before trailing a path of slow, reverent kisses down my body.

Anticipation coils in my stomach, a slow-burning ache.

By the time he reaches the inside of my thigh, I'm trembling, my breath coming in shallow pants.

Then he pauses, so close to where I need him, and exhales a slow, deliberate breath over my pussy.

A whimper escapes me.

His eyes lift, locking onto mine, dark with adoration, with possession.

"I love you so much, *sugar cube.*"

And then... his mouth claims me.

The first lick is not gentle.

It's a deep, filthy French kiss, his tongue moving in long, deliberate strokes, licking, tasting, devouring me like he's starving.

I arch, gasping, shuddering, the pleasure searing through me so intensely that I don't know where he begins and where I end.

Holy fuck!

I can see him. Right there. Between my legs, worshipping me with his mouth, with his hands, with the sheer force of his hunger.

It's sloppy, raw, desperate! His tongue flicking, rolling, swirling, creating pressure so unbearable I can't do anything but take it, let it consume me.

The sounds of it... the wet, lewd suction, the low, satisfied moans he hums into me as he sucks my clit into his mouth—it's obscene, it's dirty and it's perfect.

Something builds, deep and low, a tingling pressure unlike anything I've ever felt before.

It's not just pleasure—it's an ache, a demand to my sanity.

I can feel something coming, something massive, but I don't understand it, don't know how to grasp it.

But my body does.

Instinct takes over.

I grab his hair, yank him closer, shove his face even deeper into me.

Wider. I spread my legs wider, opening myself fully to him, to his tongue, to the way he's breaking me apart and putting me back together in the same breath.

He groans, a deep, animalistic sound, and then—he gives me more. I want more! Give me more!

A finger presses inside, teasing, stroking, finding a spot that makes me writhe, makes my entire body ignite in flames.

More!

Give me MORE!

I want MORE!

I don't recognise the sound that rips from my throat when it happens—when I fall over the edge, when pleasure detonates through me with blinding intensity.

Everything pulses, clenches, contracts.

Lights burst behind my eyes.

My pussy spasms around his tongue, his fingers, everything, as I drown in the kind of pleasure I never thought I'd have.

Never thought I'd feel.

Never thought I'd survive.

"Fucking hell, Hunter!" I gasp, my voice raw, my body still shaking from the aftershocks.

My mind is spinning, barely able to process what just happened, what he just did to me.

"Is that how it feels?"

My voice is breathless, disbelieving, the words tumbling out between the waves of pleasure still rolling through me.

Holy! Fucking! Shit!

He's still there, between my legs, his tongue working me gently now, coaxing out every last tremor, like he's savoring me, like he's drawing out every ounce of pleasure until there's nothing left to take.

"That was..." I trail off, lost, wrecked, overwhelmed.

His hands caress my thighs, his grip firm yet soothing, and it only makes this pulsing, aching need inside me worse.

So much worse.

Because now, I feel it.

That something more. That something bigger.

That primal, desperate, soul-consuming need for him.

For his cock.

For him to fill me. Stretch me. Claim me.

Nothing else matters. Nothing...

I sit up so fast I nearly knock him back, my fingers already grabbing at his arms, his shoulders, anything to pull him over me, into me, inside me.

"I need your cock."

The words rip from me, demanding, uncontrollable.

"Now!"

His eyes darken, his jaw clenches, his entire body tenses like he's barely holding himself together.

"NOW!" I roar, my voice vibrating with pure, unfiltered desperation.

Hunter jerks back slightly, his eyes widening, like he wasn't expecting me to snap like this.

"We can do all the sweet things you want after," I grind out, my fingers digging into his shoulders, my entire body trembling with need. "But right now, I need your cock inside me. I need you to be mine, *Nuuro*. I need more!"

His chest rises sharply, his entire body tightening, like a man at his breaking point.

"Fuuuuuck, *sugar cube*."

And then, he moves.

With one swift, powerful motion, he lifts me like I weigh nothing, and I instantly wrap my legs around his waist, trying to grind against him, aching for him.

But he's teasing me. Holding me just above the tip of his cock.

Hovering.

"Hunter!" I snarl, frustrated beyond belief.

He groans, his grip tightening on my arse, his breathing heavy and uneven.

"You are going to fucking kill me, woman."

And then—he runs.

Full speed. Through the hall, through the door, straight to our bedroom.

By the time we crash onto the bed, I'm panting, writhing, ready to explode, but the second he lowers me onto the mattress, he starts moving downward.

No. Fucking. Way.

"*Nuuro,* don't you fucking dare!"

But he's already parting my thighs again, mouth open, eyes dark with hunger.

He's about to eat me out. Again.

And I might just lose my goddamn mind.

"Like fuck you are, Hunter!" My voice is raw, demanding, wrecked with need.

"I want more! I need more! I want you inside me!"

I don't care that I sound needy, that I'm practically begging.

This feeling—this unbelievable, aching hunger—isn't just desire. It's something deeper, something primal, something that feels like it's etched into my very soul.

It's him.

It's my body screaming for him.

It's my heart calling for him.

It's the heat inside me demanding that he claim me, wreck me, fills me, loves me.

That he fill me up so completely, until there's nothing left of me that isn't his.

And I need it now!

"Fuck, baby." His voice is wrecked, strained with need and restraint, his body shaking with the effort to hold back. "You can't talk like that, I might last seconds inside you. Please... have mercy."

The desperation in his eyes, the way he looks at me like I'm his whole world, is almost as intoxicating as the heat coiling in my belly.

Maybe I'm the one beneath him.

Maybe I'm the one begging.

But in this moment—I know I am the one in control.

"Are you sure, *sugar cube*?"

I don't just nod.

I offer myself.

With my body, with my eyes, with the way I open for him completely.

And he understands.

He doesn't ask again.

He doesn't hesitate.

He simply gives.

And fuck, it's exquisite.

The thick, velvet heat of his cock slides against my entrance, teasing me with slow, torturous drags, the anticipation burning me alive.

And then, gently, reverently, he pushes in.

A stretch—full, deep, claiming.

A pause—his jaw tight, his breath ragged.

There's resistance. He stills.

His fingers—gentle, patient, worshipping—find my clit and begin to trace slow, devastating circles.

Pleasure pulses through me, spreading like fire, coiling tight, sending me spiraling toward the edge faster than I can control.

And then he moves.

Rolling his hips.

Each retreat is a loss, each return is a deeper possession.

His moans—low, guttural, wrecked—are the most sinful thing I've ever heard.

And when he finally buries himself to the hilt inside me, filling me, stretching me with all of him.

His growl rips through me like a storm, and I—I break.

Pleasure explodes.

It doesn't just hit me—it consumes me.

My pussy tightens, pulses, clenches down on him, drawing him in, demanding more, more, more.

His strokes turn longer, deeper, relentless, hitting something devastating inside me and I shatter again, harder, wilder.

My fingers dig into his skin.

I cling to him—to this moment, to us, to everything we are.

And he's with me.

His arms cage me in, his mouth is on mine, his voice rasping my name like a prayer, like I am the only thing that has ever mattered.

And in this moment, stripped of everything else...

We are only us.

Completely.

Unbreakable.

Forever.

"Baby, I'm about to come," he rasps, his voice wrecked, desperate, trembling with the effort to hold back. His body shakes, muscles taut, as though he's barely hanging on. Barely restraining himself.

His forehead presses against mine, our breath mingling, our bodies melding into one, and the need in his eyes—the need for me—it's devastating.

"Please, *sugar cube*. Let me fill you up. Let me claim you. Let me make you mine—forever."

Forever.

The word sinks deep into my soul, tangling with my heart, my body, my very existence.

And I know.

I already am his.

Just as he is mine.

I pull him down, sealing my lips to his, tasting him, breathing him in, savoring this moment.

"I want it all with you, *Nuuro*," I whisper against his mouth, my words a promise, a plea, a demand all at once.

His breath hitches.

"Give me your cum," I murmur, tracing his lips with my tongue, my nails digging into his back as my body tightens, clenches, pulls him deeper.

"It's all mine now."

And with a shattered groan, he gives in.

A sound rips from his throat, something raw, something I've never heard before. It's not just pleasure—it's surrender. A breaking, a coming completely undone.

His hips jerk deep inside me, shuddering, as I feel the rush of warmth, his release, his claim. It pulses, filling me, bonding me to him in a way words will never touch.

And as I watch him, watch the way his face twists with pleasure so pure it's almost painful, watch him fall apart in my arms, something inside me shifts.

This is mine.

He is mine.

Every part of him, his love, his devotion, his body, his soul all of it belongs to me just as I belong to him.

When he finally collapses on top of me, his body still trembling, his breath ragged against my skin, I know.

Without a doubt, without hesitation.

This moment—this man—was always meant for me.

All the pain, the suffering, the broken pieces of my past...

Every scar, every battle, every fight for survival...

It was all leading me here.

To this man.

To the man who loves me more than his own breath.

"Marry me."

The words fall from his lips, still buried deep inside me, still holding me, still keeping every part of him locked within me.

At first, I think I've imagined it, my mind too blissed out, too overwhelmed, too full of him.

But then he moves nuzzling closer, tightening his grip, grounding himself deeper into me like he's afraid I might disappear.

"*Sugar cube*, for the love of God... Marry me." His voice is rough, desperate, aching.

"Because I know now—I would fucking lose my mind if I ever lost you."

It's not a question.

It's not even a plea.

It's a vow.

A declaration.

A man who has already made up his mind, who has already decided I am his existence.

And as I lie there, wrapped in his love, his devotion, his body, his soul, I know...

I want it all.

I want him.

I want this man, this life, this love.

I want his name, his future, his children growing inside me.

I want it all with him.

The only answer I could ever give him...

"Yes."

Epilogue

Hunter – six months later

I am not impressed it took us this long to plan a wedding. What the fuck is the big deal? Buy a suit. Buy a dress. Get a cake, some food, and boom—married. But no. Elijah and his new missus had to shove their big fucking noses into my business, stretching this shit out for six whole months. Six months where I could have called my sugar cube my wife. But no—I had to wait and wait and fucking wait.

I am mad. Fuming. And the only thought keeping me from ripping someone's throat out is the plan brewing in my head *to storm into her wedding room and fuck her senseless.*

I am owed at least that.

And I'm going to take what's mine.

Especially after they stole her away from me for a whole fucking week. A week! An abomination.

And no one, not even that fucker Dominic, would tell me where she was. He'll pay for that. Said it was payback for me missing his wedding. As if I had a say in it.

Fucker. He'll pay.

I move past the guards with ease. They could try to stop me, but they wouldn't be breathing much longer if they did.

When I reach the door, I turn the knob softly, slipping inside without a sound.

I thought I was prepared to see Sofia in a wedding dress.

I was fucking wrong.

Because the sight of her is like a punch to my entire being.

I freeze.

Completely.

My body? Useless. My mind? Fucked.

She stands with her back to me, and thank fuck for that, because if she saw my face right now, she'd know. She'd see just how completely she's wrecked me.

I am reduced to nothing in front of this woman.

And I don't even fight it.

I give it to her. All of it. All the control over me. As long as she's mine.

She's wearing something glowing, like the fabric is woven with light itself. Delicate, intricate, but somehow powerful, just like *her*. The dress hugs her curves, tight around her waist, rounding over that perfect fucking arse. Her shoulders are bare. Tempting. Taunting. Her hair is pinned up, cascading down one side like some goddamn fantasy I don't deserve.

And then... she turns.

And I know.

I just know.

It's not gravity holding me down.

It's her.

She is stunning.

Breathtaking.

And the only thing running through my mind?

Mine!

"You shouldn't be in here," she teases, mischief dancing in her voice. "It's bad luck and all that."

I just stare.

Completely fucking wrecked.

Taking her in, memorising every detail, burning it into me.

Because this?

This is mine.

I probably look ridiculous, standing here like some dumbstruck fool. But I can't stop. No words come. No thoughts make sense.

Fuck, she's too good for me.

I need my ring on her finger. Now. Before she smartens up and leaves.

"I'm not going to leave you."

Her voice pulls me back.

Soft. Teasing. Knowing.

Of course, she reads my fucking mind.

She always does.

"Stop freaking out," she adds, that mischievous little smile tugging at her lips.

And just like that, I'm gone for her all over again.

"You are stunning, sugar cube." My voice comes out rough, wrecked, too full of everything I feel for her. "Fuck me, it's good I came to see you. I might've lost it in front of everyone."

I exhale, shaking my head.

"You are unbelievably beautiful."

She completely catches me off guard.

Because, fuck me, is that a shy smile?

Sofia?

My Sofia?

The woman who can command a room without a word? Who walks like she owns the ground beneath her feet? Who's never once been anything less than fierce, untouchable, larger than life?

And yet, right now...

Right now, she's soft.

Delicate.

So unbelievably beautiful that I don't think any man could ever deserve her.

Certainly not me.

And just like that it fucking hits me.

Elijah...

That sneaky, manipulative bastard.

Did he play dirty? Was that six-month delay his way of giving her time?

Time to pull away? Time to smarten up and leave me?

That motherfucker!

Him and his woman! Always plotting, always pulling strings, always twisting fate to their will.

They can't be trusted.

...Or can they?

Because despite everything, despite the waiting, despite the paranoia that grips me like a vice, *I'm here.*

Standing in front of her.

About to marry her.

And if they played a part in that...

Maybe they're not the worst.

"I need you, sugar cube." My voice is rough, strained, desperate as I close the space between us.

"I was losing my fucking mind without you. Where the hell did they hide you?"

She bursts out laughing—laughing—because she knows exactly how much this tortured me. She read every rage-filled text, every unhinged complaint.

"I was at my dad's house, of course," she teases, eyes dancing with mischief. "And when you came not-so-accidentally barging in, they moved me to Uncle Buddy's."

She leans in, lowering her voice like she's sharing a secret.

"To protect me. From you."

"Not cool. Not a fucking fan. And it's never happening again, sugar cube."

I capture her lips, and the second she opens for me, I'm gone, instinct takes over, and I devour her like I've been starving for a lifetime.

"I need you, sugar cube," I growl against her mouth, my hands gripping her waist, desperate to pull her closer, to have more of her, all of her.

"I don't just want you—I need you to walk down that aisle dripping with my cum."

I breathe my filthy truth onto her lips, and instead of pulling away, blushing, or protesting, my perfect fucking woman reaches down and unzips my pants, as if she's just as desperate as I am.

The second her soft, warm hand wraps around my cock, my vision blurs, my restraint snaps, and for a split second, all I can think about is coming right fucking now, all over that dress—marking her, ruining her, making sure she walks down that aisle wrecked, fucked, and covered in me.

Let them all see. Let them all know.

She's mine.

"I need help with the zipper, Nuuro," she says, turning her back to me, her voice dripping with innocence that I know damn well is a trap.

My hands land on her waist, fingers splaying over the fabric that clings to every curve I worship.

"I don't want to unzip you, sugar cube," I murmur, leaning in so my breath fans against the side of her neck. "I want to fuck you in this dress. Can we lift it somehow?"

She hums, twisting slightly in my grip, taunting me, making me work for it.

"I'm not sure..." she muses. "I loved this one because it's tight around my arse..."

Fuuuuuck, she's right.

"And I know a big boy who's obsessed with my rear end," she continues, smirking because she knows she has me by the balls.

Then, she shimmies her chest, pushing those perfect tits right in my face.

"But look," she teases, "it highlights my breasts too."

I groan, on the verge of losing my goddamn mind.

"Oh, don't you worry, sugar cube—I fucking noticed," I groan, my voice rough with need. "Damn near busted a nut just watching you stand there, looking like my every fantasy come to life."

My hands roam over her dress, tracing the curves that have me two seconds away from completely losing my mind.

"You're so incredibly beautiful, Sofia. I swear, it's a goddamn miracle I can still breathe next to you right now."

I fumble with the zipper, cursing as my hands trip over the delicate fabric.

"But I need you wrapped around me. Now. I need you on my cock, baby."

My fingers finally find the right angle, and thank every merciful fucking deity out there—it unzips from the bottom as well. I lift it, just enough, but the train? A stunning, intricate, absolute fucking nightmare in the way.

I growl in frustration, gripping her hips to hold myself back.

The dress is breathtaking, little delicate embellishments catching the light, beautiful and intricate, just like her.

But fuck if it isn't a goddamn obstacle right now.

I don't trust my fucking legs. Not with her looking like this. Not with the way I need her.

I make quick, desperate work of my pants and boxers and drop to the floor, my back hitting the wall as I pull her down with me.

Her heat meets me first, already slick and sticky for me, and fuck, if that isn't the most intoxicating thing in the world.

She's already mine, already ready for me—just as desperate, just as aching.

I spread my legs, knees bent just enough to brace her, support her, trap her against me.

She straddles me, slow, teasing, pure fucking sin, and I groan, gripping her hips, because I've already waited a week, I can't take much more.

We've done this before, this position, one of my fucking favorites. Because I know exactly what it does to her. I know how deep I can get. I know that in just a few long, deep strokes, I'll have her breaking apart on me.

And the second the tip of my cock bounces in her stomach—just how she not-so-delicately puts it—she's gone.

I'm addicted to this.

Addicted to the sounds of her orgasms, the way she shatters around me, the way her body welcomes me inside like I belong there.

If it were up to me, I'd be buried in her pussy every damn day, all day.

"Baby, please. I need you."

I plead with her, because this? This is beyond torture.

I need her.

I need her.

More than air.

More than fucking anything.

I barely keep myself from gripping her hips and slamming her down on me, not because I don't want to, but because she deserves every slow, lingering second of this.

And fuck if she doesn't take her time.

She lowers herself inch by excruciating inch, moving so agonisingly slow that my head tips back against the wall, my breath coming out in ragged, desperate gasps.

She's adjusting to my girth, taking me in with slow, careful thrusts, letting herself feel every inch.

And the moan that rips out of me? It should embarrass me, should make me feel like less of a man.

But it doesn't.

Because she knows.

She knows I'm intoxicated with her.

With the scent of her all around me. With the feel of her touching me, grounding me.

With the way her body welcomes me home—tight, hot, soft—more than a man like me ever fucking deserved.

"Fuck, baby, you feel insane."

My voice is wrecked, strained, barely holding it together as I grit my teeth against the unbearable pleasure. She's killing me.

"You're taking my cock so fucking well, sugar cube. I'm about to lose my mind."

Her only response is a deep, shattered moan, her head tipping back as her body trembles around me, clutching, squeezing, dripping.

And then... fuck.

She grinds against me, and all at once, she's gushing, soaking my cock and dripping down my balls as she screams my name.

So fast.

I was needy, but so was she.

I grip her hips, digging my fingers into her soft flesh, anchoring her to me. Then I thrust up, hard, pounding into her from beneath, forcing her deeper onto my cock.

And that? That's all it takes.

She shatters again, her body arching, her nails clawing at my chest.

The sheer force of her release makes her collapse backward, her hands landing on my knees, spreading herself open wider for me, making her even more vulnerable, even more mine.

And fuck if that doesn't make me lose what little control I have left.

"I adore you, Sofia!"

The words tear out of me between brutal, punishing thrusts, my voice raw, desperate, completely lost in her.

"Everything I am is yours. Take me—use me—do whatever the fuck you want with me, sugar cube!"

I drive into her, deep, claiming, unrelenting, and she takes it, clings to me, welcomes me inside her like I belong there.

Her warmth, her slick, the way she tightens around me with every thrust—it's unbearable.

It's devastating, consuming, all-consuming.

Her scent, the feel of her trembling in my arms, the way she whimpers my name like a prayer, this is something that shouldn't exist.

And yet, I found it.

I found her.

She's mine.

I was a fool to think love could be enough—this is more than love.

Even after I fell for Sofia, I never imagined it could feel this good, this right, this necessary.

If she asked for my heart right now, I'd rip it out of my fucking chest without hesitation and place it in her hands.

Because there is no me without her.

When she starts meeting me thrust for thrust, taking me deeper, harder, completely unrestrained, I know I'm seconds away from losing it.

Fuck, I want it—I want her dripping with me, walking down the aisle with my cum buried deep inside her.

It's all I've been thinking about.

But this is her dress, her dream, her perfect fucking day.

So I force myself to stop, to hold back, just for a second.

Only to have Sofia snarl in my face, her nails digging into my shoulders like claws.

"Don't you fucking dare, Hunter!"

Her voice is pure, raw possession, commanding, leaving no room for argument.

Her hips roll against me, taking me even deeper, pushing me past the edge of sanity.

"Give me all my cum! Fill me up! Give me what's mine!"

Fuck.

There's no stopping now.

She owns me, and she fucking knows it.

I couldn't hold back even if I tried.

The orgasm crashes through me, violent, all-consuming, so fucking intense it feels like she's pulling the soul out of my body.

It's like every nerve in me is short-circuiting, my balls tightening as if she's drawing every last drop straight from my core.

My vision blurs.

My ears ring.

Reality fucking shatters.

Thick, hot ropes of cum explode from me in deep, relentless pulses, each thrust sending another surge into her heat.

And just when I think I'm done...

Sofia tightens around me, her body still moving, still milking me, wringing out every last drop, taking all of me with that greedy, perfect little pussy of hers.

Fuck, I love how obsessed she is with my cum.

She takes it, owns it, claims it—claims me.

And if she wants it every single day, every single second for the rest of our lives...

She'll fucking have it.

"That was fucking amazing," I finally say when she collapses against me, breathless, spent, completely mine.

"Just let me hold you like this for a moment," I murmur against her hair, my arms locking around her, unwilling to let go just yet. "Then we'll get ready. I want everyone to see you and know—really know—that you belong to me."

She lets out a soft, satisfied laugh, her fingers tracing lazy circles on my chest.

"I'm pretty sure everyone already knows I'm yours," she teases, her voice still thick with pleasure. "Especially after that oh-so-mysterious, totally anonymous leak to the press about our relationship."

I try my hardest to stifle a laugh, but the humor still leaks through when I speak.

"I don't know what you're talking about," I say, attempting to keep a straight face.

Sofia narrows her eyes at me, completely unconvinced. "You think you're clever? You're not. Why do you think Dad punished you and hid me away for a week?"

I freeze. "I fucking knew it!" My voice is triumphant, but then I quickly recover, smirking as I try to play innocent. "Hey, you can't prove it was me. But if it was... it was only out of love. A man's gotta claim what's his."

Sofia rolls her eyes but grins, shaking her head like I'm hopeless. Then, in the softest voice, filled with a love that grips me by the throat, she says, "Come marry me, big boy."

She stands and offers me her hand, pulling me up.

My legs are numb and slightly wobbly from the sheer intensity of my orgasm, and I silently pat myself on the back for choosing that position. I knew I'd be a mess after finally feeling her cunt around me again—especially after the absolute abomination of a week apart.

It's almost terrifying how much power she has over me. And the worst part? I don't even care.

Even if she turned on me one day, even if she destroyed me completely, it would still be worth it because I got to love her exactly as I needed, as I craved, for as long as she allowed me by her side.

Even if she pushed me away, I know the truth.

I'd always be there. Watching. Protecting. Loving her from the shadows.

Because there is no me without her.

"That was some good fucking, Nuuro. I'm already dripping your cum," she teases, laughter dancing in her voice as she watches my stunned expression.

"What?" she grins. "Wasn't that the whole point? Now run before my dad comes to collect me."

I should move. I should pull myself together and leave. But instead, I just stare at her—this woman who is mine in every way that matters.

"I love you more than reality itself, sugar cube. I will wait for you."

She steps closer, presses her palm to my chest, and looks up at me with those eyes that have owned me from the start.

"I love you more than air, Nuuro," she whispers. "I'll be the one in white." Then she winks, as if she hasn't just sent my entire world off its axis.

I steal another kiss—deep, claiming, desperate to take more, but I know I have to go. So I force myself to pull away and head to the first bathroom I find.

Standing in front of the sink, I glance down at my cock, still slick with her.

I should clean up. Wash away the evidence of what we just did. But I don't want to.

I want to say my vows with her all over me.

I want to walk down that aisle, knowing she's mine in every way that counts.

I want this moment, this claim, this proof of us.

So I zip up, run a hand through my hair, and smirk at my reflection.

Let Elijah try and stop me now.

Twenty minutes later, the soft, elegant strains of a string quartet fill the space, setting the perfect tone. Then, I see her.

Sofia.

Walking down the aisle, her arm linked with Elijah's.

And for the first time since I met the bastard, he actually looks... sad.

It's not his usual stoic, calculating expression. There's a weight in his eyes, something almost human.

Sadness is an emotion. Emotion means he's not a complete machine.

Maybe the old bastard isn't a robot after all.

The moment she stands in front of me, the world ceases to exist.

There is no music. No guests. No officiant.

Just Sofia.

She is all I see, all I feel, all I need.

I think Elijah is talking. His mouth is moving.

"... I will chop off all your extremities, joint by joint... burn you, then pour acid all over..."

She's breathtaking. Ethereal. Mine. Soon, the whole world will know because I'll fucking leak it again.

"... you will not be dead for years... you will beg..."

Yeah, he's definitely threatening me. But none of it registers. Nothing does except her.

Sofia.

The tilt of her lips as she fights a knowing smile. The way her eyes hold mine, filled with the same all-consuming, reckless love that's tearing through me.

"You're an idiot," Elijah mutters, clearly unimpressed. "I'll email you the details of your upcoming torture if you fuck this up, since you're lost in space at the moment."

Then he turns to Sofia, his voice dipping into something almost... gentle.

"I love you, little one. Now and forever."

And if I didn't know better, I'd swear I just heard emotion in his tone.

The moment her hands are in mine, I don't wait.

Fuck tradition.

Fuck whatever anyone else wants.

This is my wedding, and I'll do as I please.

I pull her into me, crushing her against my chest, inhaling her scent like a dying man taking his first breath.

"I thought I was prepared to see you walk toward me dressed like this, but you're fucking killing me, sugar cube."

My entire body is trembling, my pulse hammering in my veins like a war drum. I hold her tighter, trying to absorb as much of her into me as I can, to steady myself, to cage the beast inside me that's barely hanging on.

Because if you think I'm in love with Sofia, you should see him.

The savage part of me that would burn the world to have her.

He's a fucking puppy in her hands.

There is only Sofia in the universe.

Nothing else matters.

We say our vows, but I'm on autopilot, lost completely in her eyes.

I swear, I have no fucking clue what I just promised her.

The words leave my mouth, but I don't hear them.

I black out, caught in the gravitational pull of the only thing that has ever mattered—*Sofia*.

And then, the moment the officiant says the words that seal her to me, that make it real, that make her my wife...

I don't wait.

I don't hesitate.

I jump on her, crashing my lips to hers, demanding what's mine, claiming her the way I was always meant to.

Because now...

Well, now she's mine.

Now and forever.

Afterword

Thank you so much for taking the time to read *The Strength of Dark Love.*

If you enjoyed this story, I would truly appreciate it if you could leave a review on the platform of your choice. Every review makes a huge difference in helping my books reach more readers, and your support means more to me than I can properly express.

Hunter and Sofia are two characters who completely captured my heart. Their story is one of raw emotion, deep scars, and an unrelenting fight to reclaim their lives from the pain that once defined them. From the moment they appeared in my mind, they refused to be quiet. Bold, demanding, and unapologetically strong, they insisted their story be written with the same intensity they carried within them.

At its core, *The Strength of Dark Love* is about survival, resilience, and the power we all have to rise above our past and define our future. I wanted to give Sofia her happily ever after — to heal her, to see her become whole again, and to show that she could be even stronger, and even happier, than she ever was broken.

Thank you for staying with Hunter and Sofia until the end, and for trusting me with their story.

From my heart to yours,
Karina Vega

Background story

I still remember the day I first learned about female genital mutilation.

I was horrified. I felt small, powerless, and painfully aware of how ignorant I had been in the face of atrocities inflicted on women and girls around the world. That was the day Sofia was born in my mind.

I know I don't have the power to stop these things from happening. But I do have the power of words. The research I undertook to support Sofia's story was extensive, confronting, and emotionally heavy. While I don't know if this book will change the world, I hope it reaches someone who has the power to make a difference — or someone who feels seen through Sofia's journey.

Writing *The Strength of Dark Love* was not just about telling a dark romance. It was about exploring survival, trauma, and the long road toward healing. Sofia's strength, her pain, and her resilience demanded to be written honestly, without softening the reality of what she endured.

If you have more power than me, I hope you carry Sofia's voice with you. Let her story be a reminder that silence protects no one, and that healing — though difficult — is possible.

Thank you for taking the time to read this story, and for allowing Sofia and Hunter's journey to exist beyond the page.

Also by

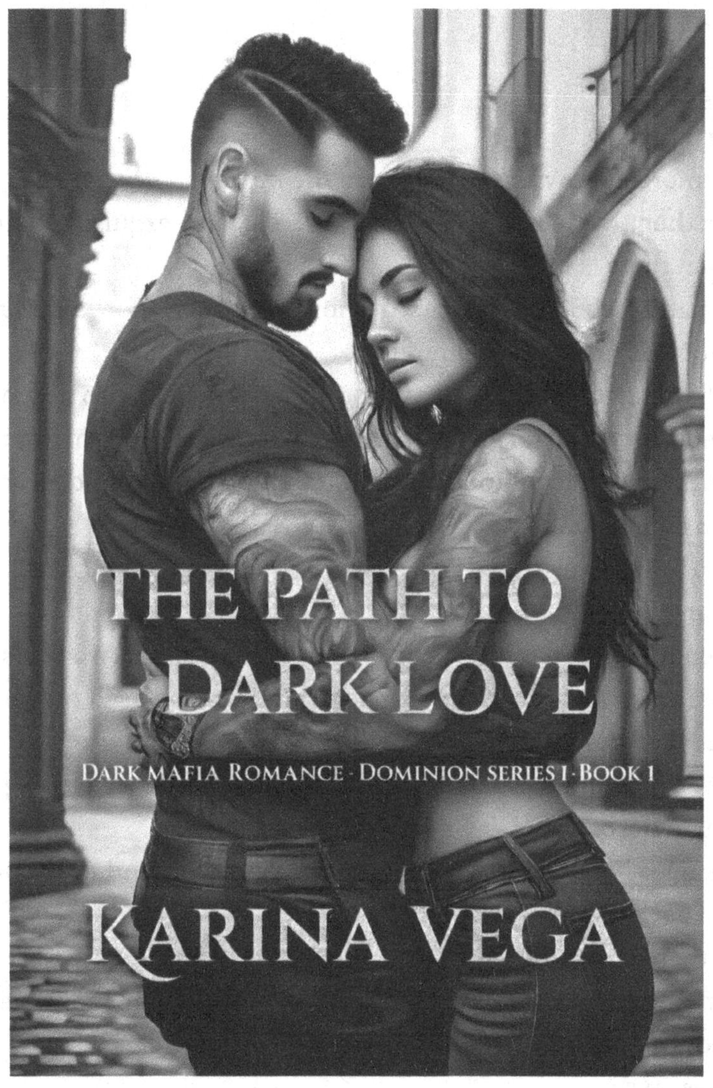

The Path to Dark Love

What would happen if you could read someone else's thoughts?

Blurb:

Angela:

One more day.

One more fight with the person in the mirror.

I see them come and go — beautiful, elegant, exquisite women — and then there is me.

No matter what I do, no matter how hard I try, the woman staring back at me is never good enough.

It's hard to accept that, regardless of how much I try to improve.

Accepting the person in the mirror is the hardest battle in front of me.

Wanting more feels pointless — catastrophically stupid, even.

Then I met a man.

Not a boy. Not a guy.

A man.

When I looked into his ocean-blue eyes, it was as if two souls found each other in the midst of millions of souls, recognised one another, and bonded for eternity.

There is an unimaginable pull towards him, unlike anything I have ever felt before.

It drags at me relentlessly, ignoring logic, fear, and every internal battle I fight to stay in control.

But there is something there.

I can't quite name it, but I feel it — an edge to him. A darkness just beneath the surface.

And even so...

I don't think I can let go.

Dominic:

How can I ever be enough when I am always too much.

Too intense. Too honest. Too direct.

How can I be enough when my own parents did not want me.

Then I met an angel, and somehow, somewhere in this universe, everything went quiet.

With her, there is only silence.

All the noise in my head — every racing thought, every brutal edge — is silenced in an instant.

I know my life and my actions make me unworthy of this woman.

But none of that matters now, because she is mine.

I knew it the moment I saw her.

Soon, she will know it as well.

I will not stop until she gives herself to me willingly.

Angela is everything I have ever wanted and more. Her strength. Her vulnerability. Her fire.

All of it completes me in ways I never thought possible.

Maybe one day she will learn to love my darkness too.

But until that day, I will make her love me more than reality itself.

Chapter 1

Dominic

It's one of those days where you start questioning all your decisions, not just for the day but for the past month, maybe even the entire year. We just finished a "session," and instead of breaking, the idiot decided to keep his mouth shut for two solid hours. What the hell is wrong with these people? I mean, if we captured you and started torturing you, it wasn't rocket science. You talk. You tell us what we want to know. Who in their right mind thinks it's a good idea to hold out just to piss me off, knowing full well it was going to end with their death anyway?

Seriously, who takes that route? Like I said, absolute idiots.

Now I'm in the car, on my way to Barrow, and all I can think about is how I want to bring the bastard back to life just so I can kill him again. But slower this time, much slower, for wasting my precious time. I almost feel like drafting an email, a critical email, to these idiots, outlining some basic ground rules for torture. You know, just common sense stuff. That thought actually makes me chuckle, and I can feel the darkness in my mind easing a little. Hell, it might even be funny. Imagine sending that out:

subject: A Guide to Torture Etiquette for all the mafias.

"*Dear idiots,*

Please be so kind as to stop wasting my time when I have you in for "questioning".

You are already mine to do as I please, so you could save yourself some pain and me some time by spilling your guts and answering my questions quickly.

It is entirely up to you if you need me to be kind/not so kind/mental on your arse.

See you soon,

Dominic."

"Right! What is it this time? Package, letter, something else?" Elijah said with a straight face, he is my boss and like a father to me. Elijah's presence commands attention the moment you see him. His features are chiseled, giving him an air of stoic elegance. His eyes seem to hold untold depths of wisdom and experience, their mere existence enough to send a shiver down your spine.

An undeniable aura of intimidation surrounds him, an unspoken power that seems to emanate from his very being. Even without uttering a word, Elijah exudes a quiet confidence that demands respect. His closed eyes, rather than hindering his perception, seem to heighten his awareness as if he sees more with them shut than most do with their eyes wide open. *Did he know I made another joke with his eyes closed?*

"Email," I replied with one word. It might be a storm in my mind, but outside, I always joke. Elijah enjoys my company because I am quieter about the negative, and when I do speak, it's funny most of the time, or at least I think it's funny. In my 12 years working for him, I have never seen Elijah laughing out loud, he seems incapable of emotions like the rest of us. Yet, despite his apparent emotional detachment, Elijah has a depth that belies his stoic exterior. His silence speaks volumes, each unspoken word pregnant with meaning. It is as if he exists on a plane beyond the reach of mortal emotions, his very presence a reminder of the transient nature of human feeling.

"I just think they're idiots", I say with amusement on my lips. "How stupid can someone be to make us skin him alive? What the fuck is wrong with these idiots? We've already got him. Where did Bogdan hire this person? How can someone be this stupid?"

"Ah! That's a lot of questions for little result". Elijah says, not even bothering to open his eyes to acknowledge the storm of annoyance in me, signaling the discussion is over.

I get it, I do! There is nothing I would not do for Elijah and my brothers, but if I were captured, I'd annoy my captors with my jokes until they killed me faster.

Loyalty and respect! Under Elijah's guidance, I have become who I am today. Throughout our journey together, he's consistently shown me unwavering loyalty and treated me with the utmost respect. I would give my life for him and my brothers without a second hesitation. For Elijah, we are not merely dismissed as insignificant beings, soldiers that can be disposed of and replaced at any moment. Instead, he embraces us as his own, nurturing us and training us to become the best version of ourselves.

Loyalty and respect, till death!

I stare out of the tinted window of our SUV as we stop at the light, and next to us, a little green Volkswagen Beetle pulls up. It's blasting "Can't Stop the Feeling!" loud enough to rattle the frame, and inside, there's a girl singing completely off-key, dancing like her life depends on it. *What the actual fuck?*

And just like that, I forget how to breathe.

I sit there, stunned, staring at this ugly-arse green Beetle, covered in ugly-arse purple flowers, blasting an ugly-arse pop song... and yet inside is an angel who just knocked the wind out of me. My mind goes dead quiet. Completely silent.

What the hell just happened?

"Do you want to follow her?" Elijah's voice cuts through the silence. I didn't even notice him open his eyes. Silence. Complete and utter silence.

"Right," he says knowingly, as if fully aware that my mind has short-circuited and I've forgotten how to breathe, let alone communicate.

"Vasile, follow the Beetle with the terrible music," Elijah instructs our driver, his tone as calm as ever. "And please, let's not scare the poor girl. We're just observing, right, Dominic?"

I can't respond. I've lost all connection to reality, to my surroundings, everything is consumed by the girl and her ugly car. So I just nod, barely acknowledging his words, signaling I won't engage.

She stopped in front of a flower shop with green and purple flowers in its design and logo. Right, that makes more sense now, maybe the girl doesn't have ugly-as-fuck taste in things, maybe her boss is a moron with zero taste, and she is suffering in silence like me. *Yes, I'll accept this option as I look at my angel.*

I reach for the car door, and the air inside shifts immediately. I can feel it, the tension, the silent disapproval from Elijah. His deep voice slices through the haze in my mind like a whip. "I think we should leave the girl alone. She's not from our world, Dominic. She wouldn't understand what we do."

His words hit me hard, cutting through the intensity of my desire and making me feel as though my very will to live has been stripped away. I can't breathe. I need to see her, to talk to her, even if just for a moment.

"Yes, boss," I manage to say, my voice strained, fighting the desperation in my chest. "But I was thinking... the Barrow could use some more flowers to brighten up the place."

The moment the words leave my mouth, I realise how utterly ridiculous I sound. *Flowers? Really?* It's the stupidest thing I've ever said. But before my mind can scramble to recover with a joke or something to defuse the awkwardness, my body moves on instinct, drawn to her like a magnet. I'm out of the car, pulled by an invisible force, every fiber of my being screams to get to that flower shop, to get to her.

The next thing I realise is that I am in the shop, not even knowing if I closed the car door with the speed I ran out of there, and this smell of green things and flowers hits me. My next hit is an overwhelming variety of colours and textures, like what the fuck, it's like information overload!

"Hi, can I help you with anything?" An woman in her mid-40s smiles at me from behind the counter. Her face radiates calmness, and now that I take her in she's an older version of my angel.

"Thank you. I'm browsing for a bit and will let you know." My sentence is cut short as my angel comes in from the back room, shivering, and an immense urge to go and comfort her overwhelms me. What the actual fuck! *Since when is it "MY" angel and for me to "COMFORT" someone?* What the actual fuck is happening to my mind and body? Less than 30 minutes ago, I was skinning someone alive, and now I feel like I can't breathe because of *MY angel.* I think I am losing my mind. *I must be losing my mind.* Am I imagining things? I turn and look at the SUV where Elijah is, and I take comfort in knowing that this is real, even if my mind is in absolute panic and I feel overwhelmed by the floods of emotions.

"The delivery went well, mum. They loved the colour scheme I used this week, and they asked if I could make an arrangement for his home and deliver it later today." *What the fuck? Who is he that is about to die, and where is his home so I can burn it down?* I am pretending to look at some ugly, hell-long flowers that I think I could use as a whip if I am short on other torture tools while listening to their discussion. This man will die today, and his home will be in ashes by tomorrow morning. *How dare he ask for my angel to deliver flowers to his home?*

"I'm sure he loved the arrangement last time you delivered" the older lady says. "Did he give you a budget or theme?"

"Not really. He said to just make something that I am happy with."

Fuck, that is a good line! "Excuse me, could you help me, please?" I turn and make a point to look at my angel so I don't end upspeaking to the older lady. The moment our eyes connect, my mind goes silent again. *Silence!*

My angel has this otherworldly grace, something I can't quite put into words. When she's around, it's like everything slows down, like the whole world holds its breath. Just being around her, there's this calm that seems to pull everything in, making the world go quiet.

Her features, sculpted as if by divine hands, exude another worldly beauty that could captivate anyone and bring any man to his knees. Even her movements are graceful, as every gesture has a purpose, meant to enchant me. Her words, spoken with a voice like the gentle whisper of the wind, penetrate my mind and soul as if they've found their home there.

Even without wings, there's something about her that feels...angelic, like she's a bright light cutting through the shadows in my life. It's like she was made to fit into a part of me I didn't even know was empty. But then it hits me Elijah was right. *She wouldn't understand.* She's too pure for someone like me.

"How can I help you?" She looks straight into my eyes, and I realise that her eyes are almost black, and I can feel my body being pulled by hers. I instinctively think I might hurt her or taint her with my darkness if I get too close. When she smiles, I'm scared I'll jump on her and pound, but then I hear my phone ping and know Elijah just texted me to leave. *Just this one time!* Fuck me I deserve this one time to be this close to an angel! *Just once!*

"Angela, I will arrange these flowers outside if you need me." The older woman looked at me while speaking to my angel. *How unusual.*

Angela, what a name.

"I am not the best with flowers, so I will need all your assistance and guidance with this," I say, returning her smile. She looks taken aback but quickly recovers and smiles again, keeping her tone friendly but professional. She continues, "I noticed you looking at Gladiolus. Would you like something along those lines?" The mere thought of it makes me laugh inside, imagining whipping someone to death with a fucking long flower. My brothers would forever laugh at me.

"Not quite, but thank you for noticing. I am a blank canvas, feel free to suggest anything that comes to mind." I say, trying fucking hard to sound casual like her. At least I am speaking, the words are fucking coming out. I look over my shoulder, and the old lady is arranging some flowers outside. The next moment, Elijah rolls down his window, and she looks at him and smiles. His face is blank as usual, but his eyes. *What was that?* It disappeared as fast as it was there, and he rolled the window back, giving him his much-loved privacy.

"Can you give me some information about who these flowers might be for? Or a type of flower that she likes or that you like? Or any information?" I am pulled back to Angela as if she were my gravity. *How is she doing this?* Is she "MY GRAVITY" now? I need to leave! Fuck me, this might truly have been the most stupid thing I've ever done in my life!

I think of the only fucking flower I actually know to name as I take my phone out of my pocket, trying to seem calm and collected. "I like roses." Gladiolus, what a shit name for a shit flower. Maybe we should track down who named this awful flower and whip them with it.

"Great! Any preference with the colour?"

"What flowers do you like?" I realise I am saying it out loud as I see her surprised face. "If it is something that you can share, of course."

She takes a deep breath and cleanses her hands on the apron, and that's when I realise she is nervous. *Interesting!* I might be making a fucking life mistake here, but at least I am not alone in it. She is nervous! She is with me in this fucked up situation. *I got you, my angel!*

"I love these yellow and orange roses. They are named Monica, the colour is a bit strange for some, if I am honest, but what is amazing about this rose is its perfume," she says with a shy smile, picking up some ugly-looking roses and shoving them in my face to smell.

"I like it! How many should we put in an arrangement if I am trying to impress someone?" I say, lifting the corner of my mouth with a seductive smile. As she starts to blush, I realise she picked up on my vibe, and I am most definitely not the only one in this situation.

"Perhaps around 30. How about I start the arrangement and see how we go? Can you let me know a budget that I can't exceed?" she says with a melodic voice, carefully avoiding eye contact. Her voice, her presence, her everything, her entire being is messing with my head. As I glance down and notice her more than generous breasts, I suddenly feel like a teenager again, getting hard at the speed of light.

Alright! Alright! Calm the fuck down, boy, we might scare her, and we might lose our angel. The thought takes me by surprise because until this moment, I was sure I wouldn't see this girl again, and I am just indulging in a bit of harmless fun.

"No limit, please have fun with it and make it as beautiful as you can," I say with a full smile on my face. It might be blood money, but it is still money, and she does not need to know it's blood money. I am paying with a card, for fuck's sake, so there is most definitely no traces of blood. Let her have fun with it. I started reading the text from Elijah and almost burst out laughing.

Elijah

Hey, Romeo. Make sure you keep your cool and be discreet about asking for her number. All the death threats flooding your mind, calm them the fuck down. She is not yours yet. Don't scare her if you are into her. Make sure you are into her before you do something stupid.

I quickly type a reply to mess with him a little. Shit, this is the most he's spoken to me in one go in a very long time. This might be serious, after all.

Dominic

I need Hunter to come with me later to deliver an "arrangement" to some fucker that thinks my angel needs to do home delivery.

Elijah

My angel?

Well, shit!

Dominic, don't start something that can only end one way.

Get back in the car.

Dominic

She is making an arrangement for me, and then we will leave and not come back. I will be there in a few minutes.

I look again at the car and can feel his presence and forceful gaze. I notice the older woman is still outside, and then I look at the car again, and I can feel that the gaze is not on me but on her.

I turn to look at Angela, memorising every movement of her beautiful body. The way her delicate hands cradle the flowers, the precise concentration in her eyes, and the deliberate way she avoids looking at me all captivates me. The silence between us grows heavy, thick with unspoken tension. She finally breaks it, her voice curious yet professional, attempting to make small talk.

“Do you work around here? I’ve never seen you before... or am I mistaken?” She asks, her eyes flickering up for just a moment before quickly returning to the flowers in her hands.

"No, I can't recall being in this shop before. It is a cute place you have here. Is it yours?" I say, patting myself on the back for sounding all kind and professional.

"It's my mum's shop," she says, her voice soft but steady. "The lady outside. I just help with deliveries and sometimes in the shop. I'm still studying, and this helps with the bills."

Before I can fully process her words, an unfamiliar feeling stirs deep inside me. It's like a dormant force has awoken, an instinctual need to unravel every mystery that surrounds her. I crave to know more, to understand everything that makes her who she is. And more than that, a fierce urge rises within me, a need to protect her, to shelter her with strength so relentless it could rival a thousand tsunamis.

"What do you study? If you don't mind telling me." I play the innocent as I pretend to be on my phone.

"Criminal law. I absolutely love it. The psychology of it fascinates me, especially the cause-and-effect element." I feel sucker punched! Fuck me! Out of all the women in the world and all the professions in the fucking world, she fucking had to be into criminal law? Wait, she did not say she loves it because of putting bad guys away, she said she loved the psychology of it. What the fuck does that mean?

"Interesting," I say with a smile. "What made you study this?" I look at the car and can feel Elijah's fury coming to life and radiating toward me. I'm fucked!

"I think we are all different in our own way. I believe, as I said, in the cause-and-effect element of life. Also, I take a lot of comfort in law, knowing where the limit is. What do you think?" She gives me the biggest smile I have ever received in my entire life, and the response is clear as I look into her eyes. "Beautiful!" She blushes a deep shade of red and looks away for a moment, breaking our connection. Silence! Just fucking silence!

"Do you need a vase, or are you happy to take them as is?" it's then that I look at the flowers and notice they are actually not that bad. My brothers would still laugh their arses off to see me with flowers, but they are actually nice, except for the ugly-as-fuck colour.

"I think I will take the vase as well, thank you," I say, trying to figure out how to pass the flowers to her without coming across as a creepy imbecile. Maybe I should email myself a highly important email on how not to be a creepy imbecile because, clearly, I might need some strong pointers.

"I'm just going to the back to clean up the fridge, Angela. Could you please come and help me once you are done with the gentlemen?" the old lady says as she walks past me toward the back.

"Sure, Mum, I am almost done. It comes to $480, thank you. Would that be card or cash today?" my angel says, giving me a very cold and professional smile. I don't care for it! I want the smile with the blush and the melody of her symphonic warm voice.

Blood money! Blood money! She is an angel, and you are touching her with your blood money.

What the fuck?! Is that my conscience? I thought I killed that fucker long ago, why would my insides scream at me that my money is bloody? Is a fucking card! There is no fucking blood on the card! I don't care for this conscience or this fucking voice in my head.

She is mine now!

My angel!

My fucking angel!

Ping! I hear my phone go off.

Elijah

She is not yours! Calm down, Dominic.

I hate how well he knows to read me. She is mine! She and he just don't know it yet!

"Card, thank you."

"Do you have one of those little cards to write a message?"

"Yes, of course. They are behind you. Please take whatever you like, it's on the house." She says with a shy smile again, now that her mum is out of sight. Oh! So the old lady is the problem? She can be removed very easily. Death by flowers! I almost burst into laughter at that thought! Where was that fucking long and awful flower again?

"That won't be necessary. Please charge me $600 and include a card as well. No need to wait while I think of something to write. Feel free to join your mum. Thank you, Angela." The moment her name leaves my mouth, she physically recoils as if I'd struck her. My voice had been calm, professional, hadn't it? Did I mess it up that fast?

I search her eyes, looking for the truth, and that's when I notice it, a faint blush creeping down her neck. She likes me back. I can sense it now, simmering just beneath the surface. The tension breaks as she lets out a soft laugh, an angelic sound that feels like it shouldn't even exist in this world. That sound, combined with her graceful movements, completely washes over me, leaving my body numb in the best possible way.

Elijah

Get in the car. I can feel you are making bad decisions by the second.

"Thank you again, Angela. You were very helpful," I say with a smile on my face.

"Not a problem at all! See you next time," she says, turning and walking toward the back door, giving me a perfect view of her arse. My brain short-circuits instantly. Okay, she's not allowed to wear clothes. Wait, what? That doesn't even make sense! In a matter of seconds, my thoughts spiral into chaos at the sight of her.

Oh, fuck! I want to bite that arse, mark it all over until she can't sit for days. I want to trail my mouth over her legs, her arse, bite, lick, suck, and claim her until she smells and tastes like me. What is it about this woman that makes me lose my mind without her even trying? I've never been on my knees for anyone, yet here I am, undone. *Calm down, Dominic. Calm the hell down.* If Elijah steps out of the car, all hell will break loose, and you won't get the girl.

No! Not a girl. She is not a girl. She is an angel.

What should I put on the fucking card? What should I say and not sound like an idiot? Fuck! Perhaps the silence that she makes in my mind may not be the best because I cannot write two sentences while

I am looking at the card. I'll just settle on honesty when all else fades away.

"Thank you for existing, Angela."

***

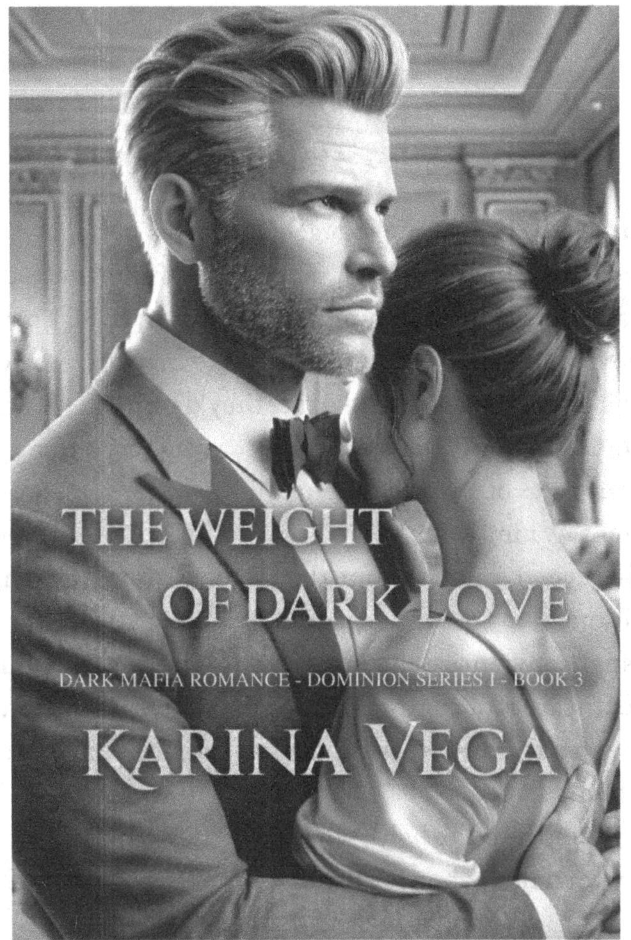

The Weight of Dark Love

What happens when two psychopaths come together?
One with a mask. One without. Both lethal. Both alone... until now.
This chain feel like love. Twisted, brutal, unbreakable.
A killer's devotion.
A queen's surrender.

Blurb:

Monica

I need to see the beauty in what society deems perfect.

My life has been a performance, a carefully crafted mask, a well-rehearsed deception, a game played for survival. They don't *see me*. They see what I allow them to, the image they need to believe.

Because if they ever saw the real me, they'd run. They'd scream.

I thought I was alone. Destined to exist as a ghost among the living, bound by the rules of a world that has no space for someone like me.

But then I saw him.

And in his eyes, I found the one thing I never thought I'd have.

Recognition.

I have spent my entire life suppressing my shadow, burying my truth beneath layers of control. But now, faced with someone like him, someone who shouldn't exist yet does, a question lingers, clawing at the edges of my sanity...

How can I step into the light, when I was never meant to be seen?

And how can I not, when for the first time... I'm not alone?

Elijah

I have never hidden what I am.

There's no need.

Fear is a language I speak fluently, and power bends to those who embrace their nature instead of denying it.

I was born in the Bratva, raised in blood and violence, forged into something more than human. I have never questioned my place in this world, never sought an equal. Because there was none.

I was the singular anomaly.

Until her.

And now, for the first time, the world makes sense.

Because I am not alone.

Because there are *two of us.*

Nothing worth having comes easy. To claim something truly valuable, you fight, crawl, steal until it's yours.

And what she is to me, what I feel for her, is not love.

It is not obsession.

It is the very definition of reality.

I see the beauty in what society deems imperfect.

But to me, she is the only perfection that has ever existed.

Chapter 1

Monica

It's like any other day. I wake at 4 a.m., take my coffee black and my shower cold. By six, I'm at the shop. Routine. Repetition. Nothing new.

If my life had a color, it'd be beige. A flavor? Cheap, synthetic vanilla. One word? Boring.

I'm a busy woman. Forty-two. A daughter who's twenty-two. A business to run. A charity to manage. A husband. An appearance to maintain.

On paper, it looks full. In reality, it's all too predictable. And quietly, it feels empty. I guess hiding my entire life would do that to a person.

Since I was a small child, I knew I wasn't like other people. I could feel it, something inside me that didn't match the world around me, even if I couldn't name it then. Over time, it became clearer. I am different.

School and anything academic wasn't difficult. It was pointless. A complete waste of time. I could do the work with my eyes closed, but only mathematics, science and physics held my interest.

The reason I became a florist is because I wanted to do something for myself, not something I was pushed into. And by that, I mean by my parents, to please them or the society around me.

They forced this mask on me. I won't give them my last breath of sanity as well.

They can all go and get fucked, for all I care.

I'm not sure what my parents wanted from me, but one thing is for certain, no one liked a girl who preferred numbers to people. So I was mostly alone throughout my childhood and in school, not to mention my teenage years.

The whole social aspect of life was a mystery at first. It took years to observe, to decode, to mimic what was expected of me in certain situations.

They became learned behaviour. But I got there in the end.

My mask was formed to perfection. Now I fit into this damned society like a glove. No one would suspect who lurks around them, the real person behind the smile, the polite remarks and the courteous gestures.

People don't want the truth. Not really. They definitely don't want my thoughts or real opinions.

I learned that early, thanks to my upbringing. Tried it once, earned myself beating after beating so severe I couldn't sit straight for days.

So thank you very much, but no thank you.

I adapted. I learned to hide in plain sight. It's my power now.

By the time this fire, this need, rose up inside me, I made the mistake of sharing it once. Just once. With my mother.

She was beyond mortified by my... what did she call it?

Ah, yes. Dark thoughts.

That was the moment I understood. There's no saving this. No fixing me.

Who I am — what I am — isn't meant for the spotlight. It's something to control. To contain.

So I learned... to hide.

I hide in plain sight.

Somehow, I see patterns. Events. The probability of things unfolding a certain way, it's inevitable for me. I don't force my mind to do it. My brain just works that way. Naturally.

It sees through people. Strips them bare. Past their masks, straight to their ugliest, rawest selves, as if they're offering it up for inspection.

And I've always wanted to drag that truth out. To force them, to look inside them.

To see what they really are.

That hunger's been with me for as long as I can remember.

The problem is... people don't want to see themselves. Not truly.

They prefer their bubbles, ignorance, self-loathing, pity, pride, narcissistic selves.

On and on.

And always — always — everyone thinks they're the good guy. The righteous one.

Everyone else is bad. Dirty. Twisted.

It's fascinating, really. Watching from a distance.

Analysing.

Laughing to myself at what humanity actually is.

I see how easily I could manipulate everyone around me.

The hunger to unmask, to punish, to hurt — gruesomely — is like a thirst I've never allowed myself to taste.

But it's there. Always.

And I know, no one could ever understand what I really need.

This isn't a want. It's a need.

A gnawing thing inside me. Constant. Consuming.

Still, I know better.

I can never show my true self, in my natural form, to anyone.

I have perfected my mask so well that I exude an aura of serene tranquillity.

My outward demeanour is a mask of calmness that belies the tempest raging within.

When I was finally old enough to understand myself — to recognise why I felt the way I did — Angela arrived. My daughter.

And just like that, everything had to be buried even deeper.

The darkness. The hunger.

My psychopathic instincts were forced into the background, locked in a labyrinth of shadows and deception.

Hidden beneath a carefully constructed calm.

Society's expectations taught me that I needed a man to raise my child — even if I never truly cared for the idea.

My mother couldn't bear the shame of me being a single mother before twenty.

We were a religious family. Catholic to the bone, where appearances meant everything.

In truth, it was all bullshit — and we all knew it.

So I found myself pregnant with a husband who, like all men, was boring, beige and fake vanilla.

At least we came to an understanding from the beginning. I realised I didn't need to give in to my tendencies and dispose of him once I was out of my parents reach.

We reached a mutual agreement — a façade of a marriage, and that was the extent of it.

He escaped his family, and I escaped mine by moving to England. Neither of our families could mess up our lives any further.

The moment I gave birth to my daughter and looked at her for the first time, I felt something unfamiliar.

It wasn't dark.

It wasn't flat. It wasn't indifference. It wasn't like any of my other needs.

It was possessiveness.

For the first time, I understood my version of love.

I named her Angela — after the angel she is.

There's no doubt in my mind, if what happened to me hadn't happened, my life would've taken a very different path.

I would've become an assassin.

Truly.

I despise people, and I wouldn't feel a thing ending the lives of the shit-fuckers who walk around thinking they're better than everyone else.

Life is simple.

It's black and white.

Grey is rare. But people cling to it, because admitting the darkness inside themselves? That's too much for ordinary people to accept.

I don't have that problem.

I like that I feel nothing.

I love knowing I could kill in a hundred ways.

Slow or quick.

Merciful or brutal.

With precision. With chaos.

In silence. Or through screams.

I could break a body, shatter a mind, erase a soul — and feel nothing.

No hesitation.

No regret.

Just the cold, simple thrill of control.

It's who I am.

So why the hell would I hide from myself?

I have to suppress it, for them.

But never for myself.

I accept who I am. What I am.

Society could never accept me for who I am. My family doesn't love me — never even cared about me.

But I do.

I accept it all as a gift. A rare inheritance.

Because that's exactly what it is.

Supreme genes.

In the mirror, I don't see a monster.

I see a master. A predator wrapped in silk. A phantom moving unseen among the weak.

I've embraced the truth of my nature — not with shame, not with hesitation, but with the cold satisfaction of knowing exactly what I am.

The darkness in my veins isn't a curse.

It's power.

I'm not burdened by guilt or conscience.

I don't waste time on self-loathing or doubt.

I am liberated, unshackled from the illusion of morality.

I move through the world with a clarity most will never know about themselves.

Their minds are clouded with emotion, hesitation, fear.

Mine is not.

I am a psychopath. Calculated. Precise. Free.

And the fact that I can wear a mask so flawlessly that not even my husband or daughter sees the truth?

That is the ultimate proof of my power.

I am a master of deception, a queen of control, and my strength lies in the fact that no one suspects a thing.

Angela is the only thing that matters in my world, the only anomaly that's ever stirred any kind of emotion.

Then there's the charity. A convenient distraction.

It does some good in the community, and perhaps, in the world.

Once I settled with Dan and we got married, I realised it wouldn't end badly for him.

I could fantasise about hurting him without needing to act on it.

I didn't have to kill or torture him, and that realisation was a relief.

It meant hiding in plain sight beside him would be easier.

I could focus on what truly mattered... raising Angela.

Over time, I learned more about myself, peeling back layers of forced civility, understanding the depths of my own mind.

And with every revelation, I saw just how lucky I was compared to the neurotypical masses trapped by emotions, ruled by impulses they can't control.

I am not like them. I never was.

And that is my greatest advantage.

I was in my thirties when I was finally diagnosed with Asperger's Syndrome.

It meant nothing to me. Just a label for what I had always known, a name for the way my mind worked, nothing more.

What mattered was the realisation that if I wanted to exist unnoticed, I had to refine my control even further.

I needed to sharpen my mind — to use it as both weapon and cage, containing the darkness within while perfecting the performance of social etiquette.

I opened my charity for children with ASD (Autism Spectrum Disorder) and the families navigating it.

We provide therapeutic support, psychological and psychiatric care, as well as medical and artistic programs.

I built it with my grandfather's inheritance — every cent going into its foundation.

The rest came from Dan's and my savings over the years.

So now I help children who are hiding, just like I am.

We work with over forty families, and I know there's a boy among them who is just like me.

Given the right support, he will find his way.

He will learn to navigate the world as I have.

One day, he will make a great businessman — cold, strategic, untouchable — or some kind of doctor.

A CEO runs the charity. Keeping my distance is necessary. Close proximity could become a problem down the line — and only a fool allows themselves to be blinded by a title.

Power is about control, not visibility.

As I said, my life is boring.

But it makes sense for me.

From every angle, it serves its purpose.

"Hi, Mum. I'm back!"

Angela's sweet voice cuts through the air, pulling me from my thoughts.

What time is it? I've been stuck in this damn fridge, cleaning flowers and foliage for the past three hours.

Sometimes, I wonder why I bother. Angela is twenty-two. She doesn't need me the way she once did.

So why the fuck am I still enduring this, when I could just retire and live off Dan's earnings?

I could hire someone. Make them do this tedious shit while I watch.

"Hi, my darling! How are you? Did you have coffee yet? Do you need me to get some coffee and maybe a pastry?" I ask Angela, my tone light, easy.

The fact that my heart warms whenever I see her is still a mystery to me.

In all my years, I've never met someone I didn't want to hurt in some way — except for her.

Is this what other people feel?

This absence of calculation — this strange desire to protect rather than control?

I don't want to manipulate her. I don't want to break her, bend her, push her.

I am painfully aware of how much of myself I reveal to her, careful to let her see just enough, but never too much.

She is my daughter. She should know me... to a degree.

But my words are always measured. My presence carefully calibrated, so she never has reason to fear me.

That is my greatest fear — that one day, Angela will see me for what I am.

That she will look at me and her heart will quiver with fear, recognising the cold, calculating nature beneath my mask.

That will never happen. I won't allow it. I'll make sure of it.

I will never manipulate my daughter.

But my husband is fair game.

With him, I do as I please, shaping his words to serve my purpose.

Think of it like a business transaction.

He gets his wins. And I most definitely get my own.

"No. I missed breakfast and dinner. This mock trial for finals is stressing me out. I think I lost at least ten years of my life," Angela says, plopping onto an upside-down bucket with a dramatic sigh.

"Oh, my darling! Look at my daughter, the big lawyer, beating herself up and sitting on a bucket," I say, biting back laughter at her exaggerated distress.

Neurotypical people are endlessly amusing.

So much weight placed on something so light.

"Mum, it is not funny! *State vs. James Thompson* is a big case! I was lucky my professor chose me as Lead Defence Attorney. This mark is thirty per cent of my final score. This is serious. Stop laughing, Mum!"

Angela is up from her bucket now, her voice rising as I struggle to keep my laughter in check.

Her frustration over something so small is adorable.

"I'm sorry, my darling. I'm just trying to distract you, to make you laugh," I say, smoothing my expression into something softer.

"You're going to be a great lawyer, but your greatest asset is your determination.

I have no doubt you're researching every possible way to shift the perspective, to turn the light in a different direction.

Do you think he's guilty?"

"Fuck yes! Sorry, Mum," she blurts out, quickly lowering her head, scrambling to find a more professional way to express what's already written all over her face.

"So what's the problem? Are you having trouble defending someone who's guilty?"

This is the moment I've been dreading.

Is my daughter truly mine — or is she too pure?

The anticipation coils around me like a vice, tightening with every second of silence.

The weight of her next words lingers in the air, casting a shadow over my confidence, exposing something raw within me.

My mind races. Calculating. Bracing for the impact of her unfiltered thoughts.

This moment will either draw us closer, or start building a wall between us.

I won't force myself onto my daughter.

If my true nature is too much for her, if she recoils from what I am, I'll step back.

Silently. Without hesitation.

But then, she speaks.

"No."

That single word is like a hug to my soul.

She is mine.

My daughter is mine.

She may not be exactly like me, but there is no doubt now, she is most definitely my daughter.

"I'm going to get some coffee and a pastry. Let's take a break, then we can finish cleaning the fridge together," I say, my voice even, though satisfaction thrums beneath my skin.

By the time I return with the coffee and pastry, Angela has just finished a colourful arrangement for Jake and Jack Consulting.

"Nice! Did they give you a budget to work with this week?"

"No, not really. He just keeps saying to do whatever I want because *everything I make is beautiful — just like me.*"

Angela rolls her eyes, her voice dripping with disgust.

"I feel like throwing up every time I see Jake. Can we drop them as clients?"

She makes puppy dog eyes at me, silently pleading to be spared another unfortunate encounter with Jake.

"Sure, my baby. I'll even cut off his balls for you if you want," I say with a smile, already picturing my knife slick with blood.

Or maybe scissors would be better. My flower pliers could use some bloodstains.

The thought settles something deep inside me — calming the restless edge as I picture his screams, the warm drip of blood coating metal.

"But what do I always say? What's your biggest strength?"

"My brain," she mutters, her expression sour.

She sighs, then grabs a coffee and a croissant.

"I still think he's a dick."

"If your brain is the strongest part of you, don't let trash take up space in it."

I take a sip of my coffee, watching her.

"I love you. Now go deliver their arrangement. We have a very busy day ahead, my darling."

The next hour passes as I process orders from Interflora, Teleflora and Bloomerx.

I prefer working with international companies, it minimises my exposure to imbeciles.

Or at least, that's what I tell myself.

Clearly, Jake is the exception I've not managed to shake off for the past six months.

Angela is right.

I need to drop them.

I'll work something out, pass them off to another florist who would kill for their business.

Let them deal with his nauseating compliments.

Floristry has never been about money or people.

If anything, dealing with people is the worst part of my job.

What I love is the scent.

The moment I unlock the shop in the morning and the fresh, crisp aroma of flowers and foliage engulfs me — drowning out the world.

I love the colours, the textures, the way I can shape something beautiful from nothing.

It's the closest I'll ever come to being an artist — not that I care for the title.

People romanticise flowers.

They see each blossom as a symbol of love, hope, and the endless cycle of renewal.

They fixate on the light — blind to the truth.

Flowers are not just delicate. They are strong.

They wound, they poison, they suffocate.

Beauty does not mean innocence.

I feel sorry for them.

They will never see life in its truest form — the perfect balance of beauty and ugliness, pain and happiness, darkness and light.

Stay Connected

You can find more about me on:

Website – www.karinavega.com

Newsletter

You can stay connected to me through:

Facebook page – Author Karina Vega

Facebook group – Karina Vega's Lit Lounge & Book Nook

Instagram – authorkarinavega

TikTok – AuthorKarinaVega

YouTube channel – KarinaVegaAuthor